Molly September

A NOVEL

Maggie Secara

Popinjay Press
Los Angeles

In Association with Literary Underground

MOLLY SEPTEMBER

ISBN 9780981840123
LCCN 2011905927

For author news and updates visit
maggiros.blogspot.com
www.facebook.com/maggieswriting
Literary Underground www.litunderground.com

Cover art © 2011 by Larissa Neto www.larissaneto.carbonmade.com

This is a work of fiction.
All of the characters, organizations, and events portrayed in this novel are either
products of the author's imagination or are used fictionally.
Don't learn history from novels. Don't make me explain this.

To the cinema memories of
Errol Flynn, Paul Henried, and Douglas Fairbanks, Jr.
Brenda Marshall, Olivia de Haviland, and Maureen O'Hara
this book is fondly dedicated

Maggie Secara

The Ensemble

At Port Royal

The Gentry

Sir Roger FitzRobert	King's Comptroller in Jamaica
Henrietta Lady FitzRobert	His wife
Molly September	Their difficult niece; an heiress
James Cridden MacBean	Sir Roger's clerk
Col. Jack Rhetford	Commandant of the King's garrison at Fort James, formerly a soldier under Cromwell
Sir Simon Benning, Royal Navy	Captain of the *Blackbird*
Ensign George Alcott	A very junior officer
Oscar Trout	A merchant of Port Royal
Celia Trout	His daughter
Drake Ffoulkes	One of several idle young gentlemen of no consequence
William Lord Vaughn	Governor of Jamaica Sir Henry Morgan, formerly Lt. Gov. of Jamaica, presently in London explaining himself to the King

The Commonality

Max	A knife sharpener
Nancy	A kitchen maid
Archie Half-hand	A beggar with no sense of timing
Harry Driscoll	Proprietor of the Saracen's Head, a tavern
Jesse	A weary tavern wench
Rosie and her sister	Professional girls of the town
Bert	A jailor given to drink
Father Titchfield	A Catholic priest

Random soldiers, sailors, citizens, servants, and loose women

Aboard the Jealous Mary

Dick Prentiss	An expert Pilot
Jimmy Fitts	His oldest friend
Davy York	Captain of the *Jealous Mary,* an English privateer
Will Keaton	Davy's lieutenant and quartermaster
Paul DeRoet	Another very good, if less colorful, Pilot; Prentiss's backup
Turk	A master gunner and general malcontent
Ned Courage }	Two of
Black Tom Dougherty }	Turk's cronies
Owen Jones	A fiddler
Matt Christy	Another, pleasanter master gunner

Muggs the Goat, German Jack, Rob Thomas, Derek May, Hughes the Carpenter, Toby Millikan, Gil Denham, Dan Rhys, Jeremy March, Billy Mariott and others who comprise the *Jealous Mary*'s crew:

On Tortuga

Jock McQuarry	A tapster and retired pirate
Lily	his French wife
Annette (Annie)	A mother of many children
Chrétien	Her oldest son
Jean, called *Jeannot*	Her youngest son

Other of her children whose names remain a jumble

On Martinique

Armand de la Valier de St. Juste	An admirer from Molly's

	schooldays, formerly a captain of musketeers
Eugénie	His step-sister
Jonathon Angel	A pirate in the background

Aboard the English Testament

Pieter "Preacher" Mendez	Captain of the *English Testament*, sailing against all flags
Long Kate Riley	The tallest and most extraordinary of Preacher's many wives
Lakshmi	One of the Preacher's more common wives
Williams	One of the Preacher's officers

A rough dozen other wives and numerous crewmen

Already departed

Rafe September	Molly's father; by consensus, the finest pilot ever to sail these seas.
Marjorie FitzRobert	His wife; Molly's mother

Log & Rutter

Credit where Credit is Due

Chapter headings are for the most part taken from music (Purcell and others), poems (Herrick, Marvell, and the naughty Earl of Rochester), dance tunes and dance manuals (Playford) of the middle and late 1600s.

Lyrics where quoted are from period songs and poems, including Pepys, Rochester, and the ever popular Anonymous.

The author wishes to express a special indebtedness to Karen Monahan and Kit Wiscaver who read so many drafts, asked so many pointed questions, contributed so much real enthusiasm, and who read draft after draft till their eyes bled.

Also fond even baroque thanks to James Newton Howard for the score for the film, *Restoration*; to John Tams for *The Music of Sharpe*; and to the numerous consorts, ancient and modern, who have contributed all unwitting to Molly's career.

Special thanks to Clan MacColin of Glenderry, the Guild of St George, and the Kriegshund Fähnlein under Lloyd Winter's command for the excursions into living history.

And above all, to my long suffering husband, the inimitable JimDear, for more patience than I'm sure I deserve, more thanks than I can say.

I

LADY'S CHOICE

UNDER THE DIAMOND glare of a Jamaican summer sky, the shops and markets of Port Royal had been open since dawn. Mind you, not all of those who came to trade here came to do it honestly. This was a buccaneer's town, still in its extreme youth, cheerful with potential. Most of the gaudy wealth that flowed through the markets and the warehouses close at hand came from the ships of the King's enemies by way of English privateers. And those fine lads, whom the Dutch and Spaniards petulantly called pirates, sailed in and out secure in their letters of marque, for which license King Charles—God save him—took only a modest share.

By midmorning, the great market that was the center of a certain kind of social life churned busily, if ironically, in the shadow of Saint Paul's church. Folk of all colors and ages filled the red brick plaza, chattering in half a dozen languages, swirling eddies into cramped corners, and surging paths somehow through the center. At the cinnamon and salt-fragrant edge of the press, a small boy and his grandfather hawked peppery fish and rice in the shade of a striped awning, their skin as dark and shining as the fish was white and crisp.

As the day grew hotter and even Englishmen abandoned mercantile enthusiasm, trade fell into decline, and the boy's voice grew more strident as he shouted the virtues of the old man's specialty. All about them, just as earnest, other hawkers cried their wares to a crowd beginning to dive for the shade of their own verandahs. Good herbs or buttons, ribbons or a clean shave! Embroidered silk from India or cherries from the Japans. If it were to be had in the whole world, it could be had in Port Royal, but not at the height of noon.

The great bells of St. Paul's banged out twelve brazen beats. Merchants large and small began to think about shutting up against the mid-day heat, and made a last bawl for attention.

Fine strawberries, picked this morning.
Last chance, ha'penny a pint! Ha'penny farthing for two!
Fresh fish for your dinner, none like 'em!
Two for one, milady! Two for one!

And in the midst of all this, a youngish fellow idled obscure in a tide pool of shade, an island of serenity. At first glance, one might easily take him for a gentleman by the lace at his collar and the cut of his doublet. A less casual look would discover that the lace was largely shredded or absent, and the somewhat dated slashes of the russet jacket were not all put there by his tailor.

The hair that curled over his shoulders was in this light an indifferent shade of brown and, unfashionably, his own, topped by a loose-brimmed felt hat. Still, he held himself with languid grace, rather like a gentleman of leisure, and the rich touches of his costume would serve to hide him in any company. Except for a decided sparkle in the hooded blue eyes, he seemed almost asleep, certainly indifferent to the busy passage of affairs about him.

St. Paul's clock ticked over another minute. Almost imperceptibly, the fellow straightened. On the horizon: a merchant of evident prosperity, given the volume of feathers on the crisp black hat, stalking behind a liveried African who elbowed a path through the thinning crowd, shouting to make way.

Coolly, Dick Prentiss judged his bearings, instinctively took wind and sun into account, and launched on an intersecting course.

"God save you, sir," he said as their paths collided. "Damme! Lord take me, sir, I do pray your pardon! So clumsy of me. Well no harm. A pleasant day to you. A very pleasant day!" Still chattering in the lightest, commonest way, he veered off and sailed back into the crowd.

The man snorted at the liberty, swore, and brought his walking stick whistling through the space Prentiss no longer occupied. Baffled, he wheezed, peering about myopically, then had to hurry to catch up with the servant who had pressed on without him. In fact, it would be at least twenty minutes before he would need his wallet, wonder whether he had remembered to bring it with him, and slap his servant for letting him leave it behind.

Long before that time, Prentiss was already crouched loose limbed in the lee of a mercer's silk-hung stall, counting his take. Luck, the faithless bitch, was with him this morning. Four gold sovereigns and a number of Spanish reals spilled silver into his hand. He turned over the shining pieces of eight, relishing the weight and feel of each against his palm; bit each one to test its metal; frowned when one of the silver pieces was mostly brass. That one he flung aside, largess for the feral children who infested the place. Shouts rose in treble delight out of the noise somewhere over his shoulder, briefly recalling his own peculiar childhood behind a crooked smile.

Cheered by the jingle of bright wealth and children's laughter, Prentiss slipped the gold and silver glittering into his purse. Then out of nowhere, or perhaps from somewhere quite nearby, another sweeter sound and a fragrance sharp as violets touched some chord in his mind so that he turned up that odd grin, squinting into the noon glare. The battered leather bag nearly dropped through his fingers.

The face that took his breath away belonged to an angel wreathed in golden red curls, and dressed all in rose-colored silk and cascades of lace. She had stopped, just inches away, with the sun shimmering haloes out of that astonishing hair. Too young and much too charming, she braved the midday glare hatless, the strings of some feathered confection sliding through small, neat hands.

He tried, briefly, to shake her off. It was embarrassing, for gods sake. Just a girl. A damned pretty, probably light-minded, certainly rich red-haired child who (*bloody hell!*) could be nothing but trouble.

Damn.

He looked away, or meant to, but somehow she still filled the sky above him. With an involuntary squawk, he lost his balance, collapsed over his heels, and sat down hard on a rock. The booth shuddered and so did Prentiss.

With real concern, the girl turned her attention from the bright folders of silk and camlet to the clumsy fellow at her feet. He shrugged without apology as if he had meant to do that all along, and met green eyes round with alarm. She moved as if to say something, but modestly looked away, only to return moments later. Cocked head, quizzical look, unspoken query. Was he all right? The ripple of well-made shoulders seemed to say yes, just in time to earn him a view of a superbly corseted back.

Entirely aware, he supposed, of the effect she already had on him, the girl added a decided toss to those curls as she returned to inspecting a clutch of velvets, while all he could do was shake his head and admire. Green eyes and red hair: a disastrous combination.

In a moment, though, he managed to find his feet, straighten his jacket, realize what a less than perfect picture he presented. He'd lost his less than perfect hat in the last engagement. He did need a shave and, honestly, a new suit of clothes. At his most practical, he should have been thinking how to turn this little sweetheart's interest to his advantage. Parts of his brain knew that. The others were not listening.

The girl looked his way again just slightly, peering under pale lashes to find him standing now, still watching, with the generous curve of his mouth crinkling up his eyes. This time she gasped and instantly turned away. But curiosity persisted, and eventually the sweet face creased into a reluctant grin.

Little by little he memorized her, front and back. The gown, the eyes, the shimmer of light across the translucent skin; the agreeable swell of her bosom where it blossomed pink above the smoothly corseted bodice. Now that he was standing, she seemed so small, hardly more than a child, but with a woman's slender hands that moved with sure grace as she examined the wares. What was it, he wondered, about a woman's hands that spoke to him so clearly?

Part of her hair was drawn away from her face, fancifully knotted at the crown of her head leaving a light fringe of ringlets to dance above the eyes (such eyes!) while the rest spiraled auburn over bare shoulders. A pale gold sash circled a tiny waist and dropped to a pair of frivolous tasseled ends. And those incredible eyes kept glancing up into his frankly merry stare.

He had to fight laughing out loud. Good God, who was this little cat? Who was she? And how in God's name had he missed her?

It couldn't last.

The fascination dissolved under an acid comment from the stout and stately woman at the girl's side. A governess? Some interfering in-law? Not (God forbid) her mother!

"Molly, my dear," the old party whined. "Pray attend, if you please. You must choose something or we shall go home empty handed! Now, look here! This color suits you well."

Molly! Hardly a name for a fine lady, he thought with delight. She'd have heard that before.

She had returned her attention to the counter. "Good lord, Aunt!" *Thank God*. "That makes me look jaundiced. It will never do."

Never? He knew better than to hang on every word, he thought as he raked his hair back from his face. Perhaps it did need a trim. Did she mean something else, something for him alone? Or was she just a child playing peek-a-boo? The laughing eyes that sought him again from under pale lashes gave no clue.

The old lady dragged on the girl's arm and sighed forcibly. "My dear, are you well? You seem distracted. It must be this perishing heat! We'll go."

"Not at all, Aunt Henrietta," Molly said tolerantly. "You forget, I was born in these islands. On Barbados, aye, but 'tis all one. I am quite comfortable."

But her relative was not to be gainsaid, and pressed on regardless. "And I shall be to blame when you faint from exhaustion, which is vulgar, or pop out in freckles, which is worse!"

The lady paused to shudder then rattled on, but Prentiss had already stopped listening and so, he thought, had Molly. True, red hair was not now well-thought of in the best society, as everyone certainly knew, and freckles might as well be the pox. Happily, Dick Prentiss was not the best society and so was free to choose his fashions, like his women, as he would, and Molly seemed, to his further delight, not to care.

"Just a moment longer, please, Aunt!" Her eyes flickered to his over a shameless grin.

"No, it is time to go home, child! Come along."

Prentiss shook himself, sensing an opportunity about to be missed. Watching them—well, her— was fascinating, but it had gone on long enough. With this much information he should certainly be able to compose an opening remark, make contact, at least get her last name! His lips parted to speak.

"Hello," she said with a gracious tilt of her head. Mischievous light gleamed out of a face as open as a rose.

Caught quite off guard, he acknowledged the gesture from the shards of his composure.

"Lady!" And started to reach like a gentleman for her hand, but the Aunt intervened with an imperious rap to the knuckles.

"None of that! Come away this instant, you wicked child."

Molly squeaked with alarm. A grim hulk in strained violet satin, smelling of camphor, the old lady pinched her impossible niece's elbow between two vexed fingers, and forced her across the High Street as quickly as she could move. As their voices vanished into the ambient noise, Prentiss could just make out the last despairing quarrel:

"Molly September, I vow, I have no hope of making a lady of you! I do not know why I try."

"Nor do I, Auntie dear," sighed the sweet voice, fading. "Nor I." Pale rose and deep violet vanished into the thinning crowd.

"*Molly*," Dick said aloud with the slightest trace of a sigh. She had a voice, he thought, like all the bells of London ringing on an Easter morning. No, better, the chiming bells of the Mass at the elevation of the Host, and just as precious. Was that too much? Very well, perhaps. Still—

September? An uncommon name but one he knew. Different bells sounded, but for the present he could ignore them. Right now he only knew that she surely had the face of a cathedral saint, round and sweet with a rosebud mouth that wanted kissing, and a figure his hands ached to hold.

Prentiss shivered suddenly, blew a couple of deep breaths in a row, and combed long fingers through his lightly curling hair, teased up in the first breeze of the day. In a moment he'd be reciting poetry.

... a rapture of charms
At the thought of those joys I should meet in her arms.

And something ta da dum di dum something. Where had that come from? Never mind. He'd better get his concentration back or lose the rest of the day, and that would never do. A single gull screamed overhead.

The market crowd abruptly refocused in front of him, this time with a friend in the middle of it, and just the one he needed.

"Jimmy!" He flung up a hand and shouted over the din. "Here!"

Jimmy Fitts crossed over, artfully dodging the rumbling carts and carriages of Market Street. "So?"

Prentiss's oldest friend was tall, though not so tall as Dick, and forever lanky where Dick was neatly muscled. Never handsome, still he had his own kind of decent looks, marred by the scars of a long ago small pox. Though he might never win the girls Prentiss went after, he seldom slept alone.

"So, indeed!" Dick pressed one of his fresh-caught shillings into his friend's hand, and threw a comradely arm about his shoulder.

"What's this for?" Fitts asked doubtfully.

Steering into the crowds where they would not be overheard, Prentiss said, "You look to me like a man what wants employment."

Jimmy, the less whimsical of the two, allowed a knowing chuckle and added, "All right, what's 'er name?"

"What's that?" Prentiss stopped in apparent dismay, suddenly confusing the flow of traffic behind him. Three men and a flower seller collapsed into each other, swearing. "I haven't so much as mentioned…"

"God's death, man, how long have I known you?"

Prentiss shook his head, sighed "Much too long," and walked on, choosing the most direct course to his point after all. "Tell me this, then. What d'ye know about a red-headed wench called Molly September? Sixteen, maybe. From Barbados."

Jimmy nodded thoughtfully. "Any kin to Rafe September, the pilot?"

Prentiss shrugged, teased again by the thought. Jimmy went on, "Old FitzRobert, the King's Comptroller? Y'know Rafe wedded his sister, but she died I think, a bit after he did. There was a lass, aye. You mind him talking of her? They sent her away somewhere. France, I think. Catholics."

They had known Rafe September as well as anyone, maybe better, but the man had kept his family to himself.

Dick smiled at the ready gossip. Of Jimmy's many talents, his most natural was gathering information. He knew everybody and everything of value in Port Royal, where to find them, and how to retrieve them. Did you wish to rob a certain house? In exchange for a share, he would examine it for you, determine the easiest entrance, draw the maps, and seduce the chambermaid if required. He knew by Christian name every household servant in town.

"Come on, man, think. Might Rafe's little lass be a woman grown by now, and home from school?"

It was Jimmy's turn to laugh, caught up in his comrade's eccentric enthusiasm. He scratched thoughtfully at his beard, thinking of hot water and a razor.

"Aye, that's as may be. Might be as much as sixteen, seventeen say. Educated, I expect. Refined. Rich, by all accounts, and much too good for the likes of you, my lad. If it's her."

"If it's her. Look you, I want to know for sure. Who she is, where she is, anything else of interest. You know I'll make it worth your while. It's been a lucky day."

Jimmy only shook his head and tossed the one silver coin. Ten shillings today, that made. It would do.

"For you, the special rates apply. But God's Blood, Prentiss! Rafe's little girl?"

They each looked away and shrugged the thought aside. "You'll be at the Saracen's Head tonight?" said Jimmy.

"Where else?"

"Where else indeed. I find you with Alice again, I'll break yer arm!" Jimmy Fitts punched him in the shoulder by way of punctuation then thrust both thumbs into his belt and strolled away whistling.

The warm scent of summer roses hung rich and still in the late sunshine, thickening the air over the garden where, in the shade of her uncle's big brick house, Molly September sat to receive the daily lecture in deportment. No matter how disordered her life might have been before, it had certainly become predictably tedious in the months since arriving in Jamaica. A carefree island childhood and three wild years in Paris must, she supposed, be paid for, and this was to be the coin. Not enough to lose both parents one after the other. She would be plagued by busy relatives until she joined them.

An hour or two of horizontal relief from contact with the vulgar masses had restored milady aunt, so that when came she down to the small but pleasant garden, Henrietta was quite prepared to deliver her unchanging message. And gently reared, no matter milady's view, Molly did just manage to struggle through the meal without argument. To be fair, she did it without speaking at all, which was half the trick.

The sermon came in two parts, more or less identical, one at the close of each course. The second began as soon as the dinner things had been cleared in favor of the chocolate pot and sweet biscuits, and the silent serving maids gone away. Even the opening words had not changed, as if repetition would stand in for sound reasoning.

"I simply cannot imagine what you thought you were about," said Lady FitzRobert. "My word! Speaking to ruffians in the public street!"

"You had rather I spoke to him in private?" Molly answered, barely suppressing a giggle while she avoided the basilisk glare. The perfect shoulders lifted in a graceful shrug as she raised her glass. "Honestly, *ma tante*. We spent the whole morning in the market and accomplished nothing except to exhaust your poor feet. And all you can remember is that I had two words with an attractive scoundrel."

"Attractive! A savage like that, attractive! You haven't enough young men fluttering about you already but you must pick them up in the street. I do not know where these shameless ideas of yours come from."

"Shameless? Good lord, Aunt, it's not as if I asked him home to supper."

"Faith, I think you would have done!"

Molly felt her anger rise and fought it back. This way lay madness and fruitless argument, and worse still, Henrietta was right. The rogue might very well be charming, but after that? Romance was for poetry. She could not permit herself to imagine anything after that.

"Peace, Aunt, please!" she said after a thoughtful, she hoped penitent, sort of pause. "It is a thing of naught. Pass the cakes, please."

There was to be no release. Everything she did was wrong.

"A large appetite is unbecoming in a lady of quality."

"Then I am a lady of no quality, I suppose." Molly dusted crumbs from the folds of her crisp afternoon gown, pale blue silk ribboned with daffodil. The gesture, done properly, showed off the rich wine-colored lining of the sleeves. "Simply hopeless. Perhaps you should turn me out into the streets with the likes of that 'savage', as you call him."

"Molly!" Henrietta spoke with a vigor she usually reserved for recalcitrant servants. Clearly this was not going quite as she had intended.

"No truly!" Molly brightened with reckless mischief. In for a penny. "Don't you think I would make a handsome gypsy?" She avoided a wistful sigh. "Or perhaps I should go to sea. Would your friend Captain Benning take on a cabin boy? I know, I shall buy a drum, and go for a soldier. Colonel Rhetford must need another drummer boy."

"Enough!" Already pale with displeasure, two sharp lines creased the aged brow between the eyes. "Molly September, I will not listen to such talk!"

"Oh Aunt!" Summoning up apology as sweet as she dared, Molly put a conciliatory hand to the old lady's satin-cased arm and hurriedly changed wicked smiles for something like contrition. Even an honest priest would have forgiven her. "Dearest, you know I am only teasing, surely."

Aunt Henrietta allowed herself to be placated somewhat.

"As we both know, it isn't a cabin boy Captain Benning is after. I suppose you have no interest in being the captain's lady—*Lady* Benning, if you please."

Molly tossed her much-admired curls, knowing how the afternoon light would flame in her gaudy hair. Knowing, too, how the hoydenish gesture would infuriate her Aunt, and how she would regret it, she did it twice.

"I don't much care for your Captain Benning," she said with a shudder. More sincere than she realized, she added, "He has been through two wives already. That should be enough for any man."

"Do not be vulgar."

"But it is true," Molly pouted, crumbling biscuits in her long fingers. "They say he beat them, and I'll never stand for that, no matter how rich he is, or how handsome." And he was handsome, in a dark, uncomfortable sort of way, which made it worse. "He makes my flesh crawl."

Then against her better judgment she grinned, catlike, as a new thought crossed her mind and came out of her mouth. "His Ensign, however…"

"You wicked girl! George Alcott is a puppy! A boy! And of no family at all! What sort of match is that?"

"Why, no match at all, my dear. And that is the point. My mother always said …"

"No more!" Henrietta rose with a dramatic clatter of silver and china, quite serious, not to be defied. "Your mother had so little care for her name as to bring up a child with pirates and Frenchmen. If you persist in this attitude, you shall never be a lady of any kind, and I shall never see you married at all. Never! And then, my girl, what then!" Poor old thing, tears stained the pleated folds around her eyes for frustration and social, even moral, outrage.

"But I do not want to be married!" Molly slapped the napkin angrily to the table, clattering the chocolate pot and forks and glasses.

Henrietta blanched under her talcum. Surely every girl wanted to be married! Indeed, a girl with a fortune must be married. The very thought made her dizzy. "Now you will tell me you wish to become a nun, I suppose."

"Hardly that." Something unfortunately like a sneer wrinkled the fine features. "Oh Aunt! I've just come home and all you can think of is getting rid of me!"

She had sworn in three languages to be good, but this was too much. It was always too much, and hopeless besides. "You must realize I've just finished mourning my mother! I'm not yet eighteen. You can't ask it of me."

Passion choked off the words. She wanted desperately not to cry, not to beg, but especially not to be married. At least not now, and certainly not to that monster Benning.

Lady FitzRobert was unmoved.

"You are a stupid, stupid girl," she said coldly. "No one asked me whether I wished to marry. Roger was no hero out of romance. But I relied on my family's good care for me, and I," she stressed, "have been grateful. You are quite finished with mourning and quite old enough to be wed. Your mother, God save her, was no older than you."

Now Molly's head snapped up, her whole body trembling.

"You may not speak to me of her," she snarled. "She had the life she wanted, in spite of all of you. And she was happy! We all were! Shall I be more afraid of you than she was?"

"Your mother chose to abandon a perfectly good match for a shameless liaison with that pirate."

"Rafe was no pirate!" Molly shrieked till the servants filled the windows. "Never say that!"

"A pirate," the older woman pronounced. "And in the end, it killed her."

"No!"

But Henrietta was far more offended than threatened by the fury of a slim young girl with clenched fists. In glacial dignity, she said, "In my house, my girl, I shall say what I please. But since you cannot speak sensibly, we shall say nothing more. Nothing, you understand?"

Knowing she had failed to keep her temper or the peace, Molly nodded, trying not to grind her teeth. Henrietta was not finished.

"You have completely ruined the day for both of us with your insolent humors. Your Uncle Roger will have more to say to you, I am quite sure. And when Sir Simon Benning offers for you, I expect you to be agreeable."

Fear nudged anger aside. "You mean he would force me?" Molly whispered.

"You will be expected to be agreeable," Henrietta said again and brushed crumbs from her gown. Rising, she made a stately way toward the house while servants rushed to wait on her. She had made her final statement.

Molly's despair drove her to the ground in a lake of blue and daffodil sighs. Tears at least had not betrayed her, but it hardly mattered. No one cared. No one in the world.

Streets away, the tavern called the Saracen's Head crouched in a perpetual murk, the air stale with layers of tobacco smoke and the bitter odors of sweat mixed with watered wine and ha'penny ale. The heavy sweet tang of rum swagged from the high roof beams and walked on its own across the spongy planks under foot, as present as truth.

As the day faded without cooling, the room grew almost foggy as twenty years of spilled punch breathed out of the floor. Its one virtue was that, being walled in grey stone and half buried in the sandy earth, it stayed almost cool compared with the sun-baked world outside.

So it was now, in the long dim space between sunset and summer night, when discreet business could be carried on away from the rattle of the city streets and before the inn filled up with the evening's custom. There would be noise in plenty later on: wheezing music from a concertina and bawdy singing, raucous and off-key but enthusiastic. Just now, it was nearly empty.

Dick Prentiss, having had such an interesting day, had decided to start his drinking early. Now he slouched comfortably on a wooden trestle, his long legs stretched out to prop his feet on a stool, his back to the wall. Sandy bits of stone and mortar bored patterns through his jacket and shirt, but his attention was principally taken up with watching dust motes swim through the lambent golden light slanting in from the doorway at the top of the steps, too bright to look at square on. One hand nestled the warm bowl of a clay pipe filled with good up-country tobacco: an indulgence, but what the hell. The other rested lightly around a jack of rum, his second and nearly empty.

The rich stink of tarred leather mixed pleasantly in his nose with the sharp sweetness of liquor and leaf. Equally pleasant thoughts twisted a good-natured smile across his face and into the cornflower eyes. Odd bits of poetry still staggered through his head, but he no longer cared. It had been a very good day.

Prentiss blew into the air to watch dust swirl through the light.

A very good day indeed. He had made enough to cover his room and his bar tab, and still have a good bit left over. Perhaps a new jacket. Crimson, maybe. At least a new shirt, with all the lace intact. Certainly a new hat. And aye, there was that red-haired lass to consider.

The smile deepened as she crossed his mind for the hundredth time. A fine-looking wench indeed. And well fixed. And ill content. Perfect for his usual habit. The smile wrinkled into a sudden frown.

On the other hand, this time could be different. What if she wasn't just some pretty pouting miss waiting for a husband? He turned the odd notion over a few times.

If she is Rafe's daughter, he thought, she might well be more than a match for you. What then, my lad? Going to fall in love, I suppose.

He snorted derisively, and slapped the rum down with a bang and swore aloud. "Ha! Not bloody likely."

He was shaking his head with disgust when a wiry, athletic silhouette appeared in the doorway. It paused, letting eyes adjust to the change in light, then noisily jogged the wooden planks down to the floor, and resolved into Jimmy Fitts.

Dick called lightly, without raising his voice. "Jimmy!" His friend's head snapped about, seeking the sound while still accommodating the dark. "Here."

"I suppose you're drinking?"

"I suppose you're breathing? Driscoll, y' poxy ape! Some rum over here for Goodman News! I was just thinking about you, my lad."

"There's a surprise." A second leathern jack hit the table with a slosh. Fitts took a long, slow pull at it, wiped his mouth on his sleeve, and gasped. "Christ! That's terrible stuff!"

"And the girl?" A silver shilling slid across the much-polished trestle. Even friends require to be paid for good service.

"All right. King's Lane. The prettiest piece you've looked at for a long time. Not like that last. The house, I mean, not the wench."

"Never mind the house. The girl, man. The girl!"

"Anxious, are we?" Jimmy took another swig, then leaned in on confidential elbows. "Red hair, right?"

Dick wanted to object, to define the color more particularly as red-gold, or golden red, and add something about the quality of her smile. He settled for a nod.

"The fat old party is Lady FitzRobert, and the uncle is Sir Roger, like I thought. King's Comptroller, whatever that is."

"He handles the money. (Who *taught* you?) Get on with it!"

Jimmy just shrugged. "So ye're not interested. Belike someone else may be. Aye, the girl is Rafe's Molly all right. Born and bred on Barbados. Not exactly the model of Colonial society, but a very pretty fortune from her mother, plus whatever Rafe left. You ever meet the mother?"

"Never."

"Nor I, but the servants all say the girl's a terror, just like her. So they're blithe t' marry her off." He stopped, sipping meditatively at his drink. His eyes seemed to wander off idly.

"Are you going to tell me what I need to know," Dick growled. "Or am I going to…"

"What? Do me damage? The sharp fella that's going to tell you how to get near her? You mean me?"

Prentiss glared, but made no further move, except to signal for another drink.

"That's better," Jimmy said. "King's Lane. House is called 'The Arbours'. Second floor. South corner. White curtains. Most of the servants are at the other end of the house."

"Can I get to her without going through the house?"

"I can. You're out of shape. Too much easy livin'."

"Oh, I'll manage. I've been landlocked for a year and more—God! Two years! Can it be two? But some things you don't forget."

"That long, aye." Jimmy nodded with secret understanding. "Try three years, if you please. Remind me, Prentiss. Is it my turn to rescue you, or t'other way round?" Dick only stared, owl-eyed. "Well, never mind. She's yours for the taking, though I'd have a care. They've got a ball on tonight. That means officers, even the Governor maybe. You'll want to wait, unless you've got something to wear while chatting with Lord Vaughn."

Fitts could only wonder at the extraordinary speed with which Prentiss departed the tavern, and shake his head. Then Alice came down the stairs to wait tables and ply her evening's trade. Swiftly, he moved to get in an early bid, all other thoughts aside.

Molly did love parties, she truly did. Especially when they were thrown in her honor. But not when her future was seen to depend on it and a betrothal was meant to be the outcome.

No matter how she complained, she could not escape being presented to the farce that was Colonial society, certainly not when it was in her uncle's house.

She had tried, long in advance, to persuade them out of it, but both Roger and Henrietta were adamant. Even as she was dressing, she rehearsed the conversations as if they were lines from a comedy. All it lacked were fancy dress and Morris dancers.

The Time: A fortnight ago
The Scene: A dining parlor
Aunt Henrietta (scolding):

I will not let you be so foolish. We have tolerated these

whims of yours for long enough. Your future must be seen to. Should Sir Simon fail to ask for you, you must be properly introduced elsewhere.

Molly (haughty):

Am I a prize mare to be auctioned to the highest bidder?"

Aunt Henrietta (adamant):

Not another vulgar word, my girl. Invitations have been delivered. Barring earthquake or hurricane, there will be a ball in your honor—and you will be honored."

Molly (contrite):

Very well, Aunt. (aside) But I shall plan my escape!

Finis

And though the melodrama made her smile now, the curtain had certainly rung down on that scene. Henrietta would not be swayed. Roger would not discuss it. That was that.

Molly strove for the days thereafter to behave, to throw neither a temper nor a hairbrush, to stay indoors and avoid the sun for the sake of her complexion. To submit to a few restorative lessons with a cadaverous Italian dancing master. (She tipped him an extra crown each visit, in the interests of his health.) To be, in short, all she was expected to be.

Her relatives were quietly pleased at their success, with the exception of the little business in the market this morning, and the disaster over lunch.

So now she stood before the looking glass one last time after dismissing the maid. The sounds of guests arriving, of carriages rattling to a stop, disgorging their occupants, then rattling on; of laughter and the tinkling of glasses and silver floated up from the house below.

Warmly predictable, two parlors and the dining room would be a vast collection of merchants, dealers, and officers and their wives and daughters and earnest young friends, each taking stock of the other and examining the gracious if slightly vulgar home for new acquisitions, and routinely assessing the investment. Already the cackle of someone's costly girlfriend shrilled above the growing murmur.

Molly's eyes narrowed critically as she skipped a few *spezzati* and a turn to watch the textures of the grass green damask (out of China, courtesy of Capt. Manley's *Dove*) flutter like starlings through the lamplight (beeswax from Venezuela by way of the *Bonaventure*).

The front edges of the mantua caught up at the sides with clusters of saffron ribbon (diverted from the Archbishop of Mexico) revealed a petticoat of rich crimson satin deeply embroidered (souvenir of the Manila treasure fleet).

Cream-colored Flemish lace spilled above pale elbows, exposing pearl bracelets which (thanks to Capt. York) matched the strand at her throat.

Her mother's clustered emeralds, part of the prize of Panama, gleamed darkly in her frizzed and ringletted hair.

Well, it would just do, she thought. A small smile slipped across her lips. She wondered what Armand would think, if he were here. Would Eugénie's darkly handsome brother approve of all her liberated finery, the spoils of war? She thought he might, even though Port Royal was not quite Paris. He would catch her and tease her in the hallway, caressing, and whispering of delight, and she would deny him yet again. But she would take his breath away. Yes, he would approve.

A prick of tears started into her eyes, but she fought it away. Armand was not here, nor likely to be. Paris was thousands of orphaned miles away, and the old life gone forever. No more innocence, no more games, no more secrets.

She squared her perfect shoulders and put all of them out of her mind. Eugénie and Armand were dead to her, and she to them. This dreadful business was now, and the best must be made of it, whatever that was.

Well then, she would put on her most sophisticated face and be charming as only she knew how. She would dazzle them all. Just over her shoulder, her mother's portrait, grave and lovely, seemed to agree.

A fan of tortoiseshell and fine Spanish lace—of course— fluttered into her hand as she took her place at the top of the staircase. Voices pattered into a modest hush, then, to a music of sighs and delighted murmurs, she stepped lightly down into the blaze of extravagant candlelight. The houses of Maracaibo must be a ruin of darkness.

2

A SET FOR AS MANY AS WILL

AS EXPECTED, MOLLY'S appearance collected considerable comment from both the gentlemen and their ladies, though the opinions registered by either gender varied somewhat.

"Simply lovely," sighed one sturdy matron whose husband, like Henrietta's, kept his money in various kinds of contraband. "Ain't she lovely, Oscar? And such nice manners."

Oscar Trout, a wealthy landowner of unruly complexion, agreed with a great deal of nodding and wheezing, which shook dust off the curls of his one good wig to rest like flotsam on his shoulders. His eyes blinked compulsively, squinting up as he talked.

"Quite, me dear. Yes indeed. Celia, darlin'." He addressed his wife's oldest girl, about Molly's age. "Trot over and chat her up, eh? Been to Paris, y'know. Aye, she's quite a, quite a...." He caught his wife's look of looming disapproval and wondered again what had ever possessed him to get married. "Quite a charmin' little thing, Ain't she?"

Celia's mother hustled Oscar along to speak to the Governor, Lord Vaughn, leaving Celia to pout daintily before mincing towards familial obligation. Though she reigned supreme among the circle of her acquaintance, she took no delight in welcoming a pretty, vivacious rival.

Who the devil did this creature think she was, anyway, with her easy French manners and her famous father. So Rafe September had sailed with Henry Morgan. Just another freebooting privateer, wasn't he? Was that any reason for all the young men and some of the older ones, including Celia's own admirers, to be circling her like hawks? This would never do.

The evening pattered on, garlanded with rich food, eye-watering perfumes, and an indifferent pack of musicians for the dancing. Maintaining against all odds her sense of humor, Molly was almost enjoying herself. For gossip, this place was nearly as lively as Paris, though it could not be expected to match the French court.

Not that she had ever been presented at Court, but one had friends, one heard of things. Even schoolgirls eventually heard everything about everyone. And here, in any case, the matter of gossip was so bourgeois that any scandal was quite out of proportion to its cause. The chatter at least flowed and the dancing kept to a decent standard.

Young men surrounded her, and a few curious young women as well, in pastel finery rimed in lace like sugared sweetmeats. Even some of the great merchants, her uncle's partners and associates, circulated into her company to pay their compliments and be charmed. So far, to her great satisfaction, there had been no sign of the odious Captain Benning.

Molly had been in Jamaica for almost six months, secluded in formal mourning, so her social appearance had been restricted. Still, here in the Islands, the straight seams of conduct so revered in Europe tended to relax under the humidity.

Uncle Roger's associates had, in the ordinary course of things, come to call and so, in an informal way, she had met quite a few, and made her own judgments. Thus she was already acquainted with both Colonel Rhetford, who delighted her, and Captain Benning, whom she loathed. Both were frequent callers at The Arbours.

Port Royal might be entirely supported by piracy and privateering, but its lively trade did require to be defended. The king's enemies did not all take well to being boarded and sunk by

Englishmen, and occasionally attempted despicable acts of their own.

Moreover, Jamaica, being more than just Port Royal, presented other, more immediate issues, from runaway slaves living in the hills to neighbors bickering over boundaries on the other side of the island. As commander of the garrison at Fort James, whose guns overlooked the most vulnerable points of Port Royal's harbor, this peculiar duty fell to Colonel Jack Rhetford. And now, liberated at last from some official crisis, he was here to wait on Mistress September's presentation ball.

He did not swagger into the room as another soldier might, but strode with simple assurance, having already weathered his bit of history. Twenty years earlier, he had come to Jamaica an ambitious young captain to help take the island for Cromwell, and survived to hold it for the King. With every change of religion and Parliament he had found promotion, while remaining too honest to make a fortune out of it.

Still, heads turned almost against their will, eyes made contact, civil nods exchanged. Some resumed their own affairs, aware he had no influence. Others knew he would join them, or not, as suited him in the course of the evening.

As for Rhetford himself, he did no more than enter in his usual manner, and make his way with some diffidence from cluster to cluster, accepting a drink, declining a bite to eat, bowing over a lady's hand.

The guest of honor, in spite of being attractively framed by half the eligible men of the city and their plainer sisters, almost permitted herself a pout when he first, and correctly, gave his courtesy to her Uncle Roger, locked in ponderous conversation with a gaggle of bankers. Though Molly hardly could be said to want for company, she liked him, and, oh don't be silly, he was old enough to be her father. She liked him, no more, and hoped to call him a friend, in time.

For the moment, she tried to attend to Celia's dithering with sly looks and unsubtle gestures about finding someone's earring in someone else's garden. Then the air changed somehow and Jack Rhetford was in the circle, inquiring for her hand. He was taller than she—everyone was—and looked down from eyes seamed with years of squinting across battlefields and open sky. At a lean, respectable forty, his hair was just tending towards grey, that only underlined his natural authority. Like many an old soldier, he had no patience with the long, curled periwigs now in fashion. The nearest he came to fashion was to part his own hair in the center and let it fall to his shoulders, to keep from looking like a fool in company, even if he sometimes felt like one.

"Mistress September," he said, and raised her fingers to his lips.

"Colonel Rhetford, here at last."

Smiling, she sat into a deeper curtsey than he probably required, and let him raise her up again, the whole sequence as smoothly governed as a minuet.

He seemed pleased that she had missed him.

"I hope you will forgive my tardiness, Mistress September. Duty called, I fear, as it often does."

"I shall forgive you on one condition, sir."

The emerald eyes glittered wickedly. Cecily finally stopped talking, though for the moment she forgot to quite close her mouth. No one spoke to the Colonel like that!

He nodded his query. "I am entirely at your disposal, madam."

"My friends call me Molly, and so, therefore, must you."

"Very well, then." A deep breath, recognizing the flirtation. "Molly. For clearly we must be friends."

"It's very odd," she drawled in her best drawing room voice, and forestalling any observations from the reactivated Celia. "Since leaving Paris, I've gotten quite used to Christian names. There is so little use for formalities here."

It was not the most sensitive thing she could have said.

"Here?" said Rhetford. "In your Uncle's house?"

"Nay nay, in Port Royal, sir. I mean, what use can there be in it? Oh, my uncle has a title 'tis true. The town is fairly drowning in titles! But a Baronetcy comes only at a fee, and his fortune is certainly no better founded than anyone else's. Not precisely the hallmark of honest trading is it, marketing the goods of privateers?"

Some of her companions seemed to squirm uneasily in their expensive clothes

"I say now, Molly," said young George Alcott, almost as red as his naval cassock. "That's not fair. My father is as honest as anyone's."

Other affronted voices agreed.

Celia took a preliminary breath but Molly said, "Exactly." The lithe hands sketched the patterns of her logic in the air. "And so was mine, with his Master's papers and his letters of marque, *la la la*, all neatly signed by the King. But when he married the daughter of one of his sponsors, everyone was shocked. Shocked, my dears! My faith! Not even the King has a bolt of cloth or a barrel of wine in these vast warehouses that wasn't gotten by marque and reprisal, no more than Celia's father has."

They were certainly shocked now, and Molly knew it but nervously persevered. "Good Lord, Colonel, look at their faces! You'd think I'd spoken treason."

"I expect they think you have, child."

"Celia, your dad is as willing to trade slaves as sugar. And George Alcott, as dear a lady as your mother is, the brocades and fine silk she sews for my Aunt and Lady Vaughn and the rest are all so much pirate swag, aren't they? Taken from Spaniards who doubtless deserved it, but stolen all the same. And where else in the world does fashionable society include the dressmaker's son?"

"Molly!" George Alcott had gone quite white under his island tan. "How can you? That is, well, look! Celia's nearly in tears."

Too late, Molly knew she had gone too far. Her fan flipped out like a live thing, fluttering at a furious rate.

"Mon Dieu, I didn't mean. That is … I never meant. *Jesu*! I only meant to say that among ourselves we need no such pretenses. I pray your pardon, all of you, if I have given offense!"

Rhetford placed a broad hand on Molly's arm and turned his sternest look on Alcott.

"That is quite enough, I believe, sir. Port Royal's prosperity rests on the buccaneering trade, as all know. Are you ashamed of that?"

"But, sir! 'Tain't fit to discuss such things, not with the ladies."

Rhetford's brows shot up over the long, patrician nose. The barest edge of a Scottish burr touched his words, as it might when setting down his own officers. "Ah well, as it's the ladies you're thinking of."

Alcott hammered again on the stark hypocrisy. "Well, I, that is, sir. I…"

"What's that, sirrah! I rather think you owe this lady an apology."

The boy swallowed and tried to stand to attention as he should.

"I'll express my regrets to Molly, and gladly, if she'll apologize to Celia and the rest."

"What!" Swift anger darkened the colonel's face; one hand curled toward the sword at his side, but he stopped short. "Does a gentleman bargain his courtesies?"

George drew himself up, pale and solemn, taking a breath to assemble his words, but Molly's nerves won out.

"Oh, but I *do* apologize. I have been trying to do so. I only meant... *Moi jamais vouloir dire tou tort!*" A babble of French spilled through the English in an idiomatic rattle none of them could follow, until Rhetford intervened.

"My dear," he said, before she could compound the error. From years of governance, inspiration came automatically. "Here now. Tell us something about Paris, won't you? Never been there myself. Too many Frenchmen. All puff and powder, I expect, eh?"

"Oh, rather!" Molly collected herself and laughed a little with relief. He reminded her of someone, another hearty fellow, quick to laugh. Well, for his sake, she would press on and hope for better. "Very stuffy betimes, but very, very elegant. Everyone is wearing ribbons simply everywhere now."

Celia, easily diverted, leapt in to an issue she understood.

"Oh yes! We've all been admiring your gown. Ribbons and bows simply everywhere, ain't there?" With a certain kind of simper, she managed to imply the ribbons were vulgar—which for Celia really was too much. "You must tell us everything, Molly. All those Froggie aristos and those beautiful clothes. Did you have all the latest things? Oh, I know you must have. I know I would if I lived in Paris. How did you ever decide what to wear?"

The few stalwart fellows who had not already faded away either chuckled or harrumphed and shuffled about, long familiar with Celia's habit of making them wait while she changed dresses three times between the fish and the meat. One or two excused themselves to get some air, but Molly gratefully moved through the garden doors with them. There would be no polite escape.

"Ah, *mes amis.*" Molly sighed, deliberately applying the foreign touch this time. "I had the best of friends. We did everything together, Eugénie and I. Well, perhaps not everything. Eugénie was more *reservé*, more shy. Except at a ball, and then she was simply dazzling. She is by far the prettiest of us. I envied her terribly, but her papa is a very wealthy man, very important, with a dress allowance in the quarter as much as mine for the year! Ah, Celia, such clothes! Never the same gown twice, I vow. But I did have a few nice things myself. And even ...." She had the grace to color shyly. "A pair of breeches, for fencing."

"Fencing!" Alcott, Ffoulkes, and Rhetford, politely bored just moments before, grew immediately animated.

The Colonel swore but no one flinched. "You don't mean to say someone actually taught you to use a rapier!"

A modest smile flickered across her face. "Aye indeed. And not too ill, I'm told, for a girl."

"Well, I don't hold with such things, m'self," said Drake Ffoulkes with an adolescent smirk. At seventeen, he should have been to sea long since, save for his mother's protective embrace. "Girls can't fight. Haven't the nerve for it."

Molly's clear face opened like a flower, filled with wide eyes. "A challenge, is it?"

"Eh?"

"Come Drake, cross swords with me tomorrow. In practice, of course."

"Oh Molly, no!" Celia cried.

Ffoulkes flipped a handkerchief out of his cuff and responded loftily, "I do not fight with girls."

"Afraid of losing?" said Rhetford through an infrequent grin. "All the same, Molly, I think it would not be wise. Bad form to embarrass a guest."

Molly sighed and nodded, content to withdraw while the lads chuckled.

"Very true, Colonel. Besides, I have nothing to wear."

She did of course, but for a change she saw her error before it grew out of hand. It might take less to cause a scandal in Port Royal than in Paris, but scandal there was and she simply hadn't the patience for it.

"Is that the end of it, then Molly?" said Alcott. "Is there no story, at least?"

She had led them easily onto the torchlit arcades of the verandah latticed in fluttering petals of bougainvillea, breathing with roses. A light breeze cooled the air and brought down, the lively color rising in her cheeks, while she waited for the servants to produce benches for everyone.

"Ah well," she said. "I shall be guided by your wisdom."

A chair appeared behind her into which she sank with utterly graceful thanks. One of the young men drew a pipe from his pocket and glanced, to Celia's annoyance, at Molly for permission, which she gave with a gracious tilt of the red-gold head. One or two others followed.

Rhetford declined the privilege behind his customary frown, but not before noticing with delight both strategy and troop movements in all this. Clever girl, he thought.

Small fine hands clasped lightly in her lap, she said, "My dearest friend, Eugénie de la Valier de St. Juste, has a brother called Armand. *Captain* Armand, mind you. He is a good deal older, of course. An officer in the musketeers! But he is—or was—fond enough of us both to spare some time, now and then. He is a master swordsman (and very dashing, Celia) and he taught me what little my poor woman's hand could learn. Firearms, naturally, are beyond me."

She turned huge, melting eyes on Ffoulkes, then on Alcott and the others in turn, and sighed again, piteously. "He was very patient." When her glance rested again on Rhetford, however, it was mocking. "Tell me, Colonel. Do you think ill of a woman who can use a sword, however poorly?"

He caught the playfulness in her eye, but answered squarely. "Never knew a girl who wanted one."

"Not a steel one, anyway!" Adam Eliot snorted.

The lads snickered at what was meant to be a coarse reference, and the girls flushed ferociously. Excepting Molly. She wanted to say that no honest girl wanted any other kind, but had the wit this time to hold her tongue. Harsher words than "whore" had been applied to her own mother. Instead, she raised a stenciled brow.

"Odd, isn't it, Colonel Rhetford?" she said.

"If we are to be friends, young Molly, it must be 'Jack'."

The fan flittered again, discouraging mosquitoes and blushes. "Isn't it odd then, *Jack*, how difficult it is to tell a plain story plainly. And you, sir, have not answered my question. Do you think me less womanly because a friend taught me to know the pointed end of a rapier from the dull end?"

A thoroughly delighted chortle bubbled from him without warning.

"Ha! A sword, a broom, or a creel of codfish, I take my oath! I cannot think of a thing that would make you aught but more enchanting. And that's my word on it."

"Colonel!" Celia squeaked. "God's Blood, Molly has made you into a poet!"

"Not bloody likely!"

"Aye, sir, 'tis quite true. I ain't never heard you speak so to anyone. Sure, you have never been so gallant to me."

As gallant as he could be while controlling the rare hilarity, he bowed. "My sword is even now at your service, should you require it, Mistress Celia. But if you ever showed such spirit, I am certain I would be prepared to respond to it in like manner. I only pity the man who takes up her challenge."

"Now there it is," said Molly with the lift of a conciliatory hand. "You see? Celia can't help being a lady any more than I can help being brought up with sailing men and stout ships and plain talk all around. Certainly she is better behaved in company than I shall ever be, much to my Aunt's despair. Besides," she laughed, "I am not at all sure we should look to the Army's well-known taste in women! Fear not, dear Celia. I am but a fleeting novelty. You are still the queen of Port Royal."

All those evenings sneaking into the playhouse had not been sinfully wasteful after all.

If her eyes twinkled merrily as Celia preened, only Rhetford had the wit to see it, although the persiflage was wearing him out. In fact, he had held out so long only for the sake of Molly's company. But as she seemed disinclined to part from her friends—or to let him skewer young Ffoulkes to liven up the evening—and he could find no excuse to draw her aside himself, it was time to make his excuses and retire. One day, he imagined, he would learn how to court a young woman. In the mean time, well, perhaps there would be other opportunities.

Molly used all her most charming tricks to make him stay, which he withstood until they exchanged courtesies once more. Thoughtful, her smile followed him as he abandoned her for other, more grown up company. In an odd way, she realized, she would have liked him less had he given in and stayed against his will.

That was it, she decided. Like her father, Jack Rhetford was a man who could not be bullied. Not for such a trivial thing as Society, at any rate. In fact, between the colonel and that charming rogue in the market, Port Royal might yet have something to offer. If only she could stay unwed long enough to find it.

Just as the contentment of that notion claimed her, however, she caught sight over Celia's shoulder of an elaborately curled black periwig that could only belong to Captain Benning, her uncle's favorite. Unnaturally pale and thin as he was, the full-bottomed wig quite overpowered his ratlike—nay, snakelike—even dissipated features.

Nay, that was unfair. His features were fine enough; only his character was verminous. The thick gold bullion encrusting the tailored uniform cassock only dressed up the truth without hiding it. A deep shudder raised the hair curling at the back of her neck. Perhaps he wouldn't see her in the shadows of the verandah.

No luck. He stopped with a hand to Rhetford's arm, who politely gestured in her direction. *Damn.*

"Fine. Let Uncle Roger marry him," she muttered, and leapt to her feet to grab George Alcott's arm.

"Listen! The musicians have started up again! Do you know Celia, a year's retirement from the world and I have quite forgotten how to dance." It was not entirely a lie. "I feel so clumsy amongst you all!"

"Nonsense, Molly. You danced quite nicely earlier. A mite rusty, I guess," the other girl simpered. "You haven't been to any parties since you came, being in mourning and all. I know you haven't because I go to all of them." Sweetly plump, restored to glory, she smirked like a tart, her mother's smile.

"Ah," Molly snapped impatiently, counting the seconds until too late. "It is a sarabande. George, you'll dance it with me, won't you?"

She grabbed his hand and all but dragged the hapless boy past Benning's perplexed, lightless smile.

"Mistress September," came a languid whine at her back. She paid no attention. "I say, Mistress September." Then: "Ensign!"

George skidded to a halt at the familiar ring of command. He turned, ashen-faced, still attached to Molly's desperately clinging hand. She had to let go before he twisted her arm, and then she was facing Benning at last.

"Going in to the dancing, Mister Alcott?" the captain lisped casually, as though he had not just called his junior officer to account.

Alcott nodded, controlling a slight tremor by tossing back his lank pale hair. "Aye sir."

"Pity ye do not dance well."

"Oh, but I do, sir." George caught the look as well as the tone of voice a fraction too late. "I mean, no sir. Not at all well. Not compared to yourself, sir."

"Then you will not mind if I lead Mistress Molly through this measure. Will you, sir?"

Alcott swallowed hard, but recovered manfully, out-gunned but not yet sunk. With a martial squaring of shoulders he said, "Ye'll have to ask the lady, sir. I am in her debt for this dance and another."

"Say you so? Well then, Mistress. Surely you'd rather have the arm of a bold seafaring man like meself?"

Inwardly, Molly scoffed at his slimy pretentiousness. But when she glanced at George, she saw he had already surrendered.

Damn twice! How could the colonel have left her! It was too unfair.

Rising from a rigidly correct curtsey, she forced up the corners of her mouth into something like a smile. "I would be honored, Captain. If Mister Alcott will accept my promise of the next dance instead."

George nodded, murmured something polite, and bowed over her hand, then presented that hand to his captain. Benning took it with never another glance toward the boy and led Molly onto the floor.

She tried to concentrate on the music and the steps, instead of the clammy touch of his hand. Investing the extra shillings with the Italian had paid off. Slippered feet seemed to find their own way, as long as she did not try to think too far ahead. And she was exceedingly thankful that Benning seemed to have no conversation to pursue, except for the occasional compliment, easily fielded.

When that dance ended, heedless of the promise to Alcott, Benning led her out again as sets formed up for *Newcastle*, a country dance jolly but dignified, lacking any flirtatious opportunity, for which grace Molly promised a candle to her patron saint. Still, the captain kept hold of her until Molly at last had to plead shortness of breath and the soggy heat of the evening.

In reply, he escorted her back to the verandah, now abandoned to the moths and leafy shadows. Till now the captain had held her hand in a cool grip, lightly dispassionate. Now that grip tightened, crushing the edges of his rings into her fingers.

She struggled to move away, but he pressed to her side. He spoke, his thin voice oddly husky.

"Molly."

But she had no intention of listening. "Forgive me, sir," she growled. "It is late and I must begin to say good night to my guests."

"Am I not a guest too, my dear? Pray, do not leave me yet. It is quite early yet. Look, the moon has not even begun to set."

"Moonrise was at ten o'clock, Captain Benning." She tried to be merry. "It is after midnight."

"No matter." His colorless eyes bore deeply into her, trying as it seemed to convince her of some passionate motive, but nothing reached her except nerveless cold. The thin, nasal voice continued. "We have many things to speak of, you and I."

Having no patience with his insinuating whispers, she spoke right out. "I think not, sir."

He seemed startled. "Surely your uncle has spoken to you on my behalf?"

"I cannot think what you mean, Captain."

"Oh surely, Molly, you must call me Simon," he said. While he interpreted her silence as maidenly docility, Molly fought the impulse to snatch her hand away and go for a knife. "Your father was a seaman, I know. Would it suit you so ill to have another seaman, a King's officer by God, for your husband?"

"Husband, Captain Benning!" He had managed to steer her into the deeper shadows of a trellised corner, out of sight of the salon. No easy retreat, to be sure. "As I have told my Aunt, sir, I am only seventeen and have just put aside mourning for my mother. I cannot even think of marriage!"

"Oh come, girl," he mewed. "My first wife was younger than you when I first took her to bed."

"Sir!" Her free hand laid a print across his powdered cheek, leaving a fiery imprint of her fingers emblazoned there. He only stretched the thin, humorless smile, and grabbed her wrist.

"'Sblood, me dear. Such a temper in so sweet a face. Don't underrate me, my girl. I am willing to overlook the—unconventional—nature of your mother's marriage. If you expect to make a better match, you had best think ..." He caught himself suddenly. The blaze went out of his eyes and he lapsed back into the stylish mode of unfocused idleness. "I have spoken too soon, I see. Well good, I admire a becoming modesty in a wife."

He cleared his throat self-consciously and shifted his grip, then bent to kiss both her hands. "Now, then. I fear I have kept you from your guests too long. We cannot endanger your reputation, can we? Perhaps you should run along to your Aunt."

Speechless with anger but managing not to snarl what she thought, she escaped in a rustle of grass green silk.

Lurking in the garden just out of sight in the darkness, Dick Prentiss scowled. The urge to simply knife the loathsome dandy for the girl's sake was nearly irresistible. She would only thank him. Hell, God would thank him! But the serpent slunk away, and the chance was gone. Another time.

The big window in the southern corner of Molly's room stood wide open as it did nearly all the year. Through the fine muslin draperies stirring softly in the night wind rode the scent of the sea and with it, the old free life she missed. Not simply Paris and the gay times there, but the wild days of her childhood: galloping ponies across the white sands of her own vast island, as it had seemed then. Or laughing with thinly disguised terror over the old gypsy woman who had threatened her out of the dark with many dangers and much sadness, on the night before she sailed from France.

Tonight's ball had not settled the restless longing in the least. If anything, the marriage conspiracy, all this grown-up conversation only made things worse. So many strangers, so many men presuming on her youth, insinuating themselves into her life. So many thrown at her in one night she hardly had time to learn their names. And all of them setting for her, totting up her fortune, appraising her like some prize mare they might buy on a whim. All but Colonel Rhetford. And one other, perhaps.

She rested a warm thought on that idea as she lay sleepless between the linen sheets. The nameless character in the marketplace, so handsome, promising excitement. Her thoughts paused lightly on the long, fine figure, strong and sturdy, the firm chin just slightly cleft; a straight but not quite perfect nose dividing the blue eyes that stared merrily out of a sun-browned face. What sort of man was that? A rogue, no doubt, though he had a shockingly aristocratic look about him. Even manners! Street thieves and Abram men shouldn't have manners, and surely he was no honest fellow.

She rolled to one side and blew out her candle. A grim smile etched itself across her lips as moonlight filled the room. Who knew what sort of man he really was: gentleman, thief, or a pirate lost ashore. Some rakehell friend of Drake Ffoulkes', for all that.

A tremor of guilty pleasure ran through her. I wonder, she thought, if a Jamaican scoundrel is at all like the Parisian ones Madame used to warn us about. Such men are dangerous. Such a man might promise anything and give nothing, take everything. And leave on the morning tide. And I, like a child, would let him.

Again, a memory of Armand intruded on her dreams. For all his charms, he was a known womanizer, some said worse, so she knew what men were, more or less. Ah, but it might be worth it! Her mother had not raised her to be a fine lady, had she?

God knows, she thought, I shall never be one, unless I marry as they want me to. And then what choice would I have? Would I dare to be anything else?

Even to imagine lying next to Simon Benning, a grey eel writhing in her bed, made her shudder. At least Marjorie had had a choice, and taken it, whatever it might have cost her.

Molly had been just a child when Rafe September, tall and handsome, last ruffled her hair with long scarred hands, and kissed goodbye, and sailed away, and not come back. Eighteen months later, she was fatherless in Paris, marring a sketchbook with her tears.

Marjorie had taken her to the Ursulines, lived among them in shadows and dreams, while Molly went to school and grew up almost by accident. And then one day, Marjorie slipped into the Seine, an accident she had made no attempt to avoid. But she had made her own choices.

And at least Molly had known her. Of laughing Rafe, she had almost nothing.

Now a scuffling of leaves outside the window, a muffled curse. Molly's reflections shattered in sudden alarm. She stiffened, listening to the balmy night air. A thief? A murderer? Or a cat in the ivy?

It seem particularly poignant to recall, just now, that all she had of her father was the memory of a merry laugh and a rumbling voice, and how above all things her mother idolized him. That, and a black-hilted knife lying useless in a drawer half a room away.

A random puff of breeze lifted the curtains, then a long-fingered hand slipped between them. A lithe, half-familiar shape eased lightly in at the casement and slipped to the floor. Quick, if a bit careless, and grinning a small, merry grin in the moonlight he was careful to disturb no further the night's even, easy quiet. She froze and squeezed shut her eyes, listening to her heart pound.

With a sure motion of that slender hand, he pushed aside the bed curtains and sat gently beside her. When she squirmed gratifyingly under the palm he placed over her mouth, and her dark eyes flew open, he knew she had not been asleep.

"Waiting for me, eh lass?" Prentiss whispered.

The jade green eyes gleamed wide more with anger than with panic. The muscles of her throat tensed to scream.

He did admire the flash of those eyes. "Nay, nay, my girl. None of that. You're quite safe." He felt her trying to relax the panic. "Quite safe indeed. You'll not scream?"

A tight shake of her head was all she could manage against the pressure of his hold. When he released her, his long fingers dropped to caress the slender curve of her throat.

"Is it you, then!" She was trembling, but with rage or something quite different?

"The very same. I would greet you as a gentleman should, but …" A futile flutter of his free hand. "I am as you see me. I'm called Prentiss, Sweet. Dick Prentiss to my friends, or Dickon, if ye like."

"I have had enough of gentlemen tonight! But whoever you are, you cannot be here."

"Can and am, Sweet. After watching you from the garden all evening, charming all those others, I think it's only fair to take my turn." When she said nothing, his handsome face fell into an expression of dismay. "Ah, have I mistaken you? You didn't want me to come? I was so sure this morning."

"What if you're caught!"

"Would you mind?"

"Hardly," she sniffed.

"Then cry out. I won't stop you. Let them take me. Or let them try."

"But if they put you in jail?"

"Anything, so Molly doth desire it." He'd seen a play once himself.

His self-conscious theatrics were too much to resist. Yes, she had hoped to see him again, and just this way, whether she knew it or not. The danger of it, the way it made her heart race, made her blood sing.

She sat up, huddling under covers drawn up to her chin to hide the silken nightdress beneath. Oh, his eyes were blue!

Her face lit with gaiety. "But who are you? What do you want here?"

"You."

A slender auburn brow flared. "Oh, aye?" He would have to stand in line. "To what end?"

"To no end at all, sweet Molly, but our own entertainment." His laughter stilled briefly. "Would you mind so much if they locked me up?"

"Lord, why should I?" Curls tossed, moonlight catching in her hair. "I mean, yes. I mean… Damn you, I don't even know you!"

A pleasant pause while he watched the light caught in that hair caress the porcelain shoulders, glisten in her eyes. "Then meet me in the morning," he said at last. "And know me better. Come to the flower seller's at daybreak, under the market bell. I have a day I want to give you."

"A what?"

"A day. The second best gift a lad can give to a lass. Say you'll come."

She tried to fight off the turmoil clouding her brain, but it was no good "You are quite mad, you know."

"Absolutely. Say you'll come."

"No!" But there was too much yes in her voice. In her heart. What else had she been wishing for but an adventure. She bit her lip, hesitating.

He said, "Say yes."

"No."

His hand still rested in the ivory curve of her throat, fingering the hair delicately curling under the exquisite ear. Now he pulled her face to him gently, inexorably. One small, delicate kiss, then another, just teasing her lips. Then when she responded, another, and stronger.

She kissed him, and the kisses grew deeper, until she could feel the fire in her body flare, and sense with wonder the response from him. She wanted to cast aside the sheets and tangle his arms and legs with hers, draw him down along the fiery length of her body. She wanted all those things Armand had promised would bring so much delight.

She wanted.

But then, reluctantly, she recalled who and where she was, and that what she wanted was impossible. And slowly she drew away, shivering as his fine dark hair dragged lightly across her breast.

The first indrawn breath quavered as he took it. "Meet me tomorrow. Say you will."

The pleading in his voice, such a change from the careless bravado, was at last too much. She tried to speak but her throat had gone dry. She had to moisten swollen lips, swallow, breathe.

"All right." She nodded, unsteadily. "I will. I swear. Now go away. Please. If you're found, they'll lock us both away and I shall never see anyone again, never mind who."

Instead of answering, he laid a finger against her anxious mouth. Then helplessly, exultantly, he kissed her again, and when he finally released her, brushed the wonderful tears starting from her eyes.

"If ye're not there by six, I'll call at the front door and fetch you myself." He grinned impishly. "And wouldn't that scandalize your Aunt."

Then he was up and away to the casement, leaving her flushed and dreamy-headed. "Prentiss," she called lowly just as he ducked out. He turned midnight eyes on her one final time. "Be safe."

The infuriating grin creased his face once more, and he was gone.

She tried again to settle into sleep, but her racing mind resisted. Rest came only fitfully and plagued with dreams. The moon was made of ivory and she had to catch it on a cord to give to her mother. The sea was made of glass and was the only road to some far place, and she had to walk the whole way with a string of beads in her hands, though she could not say where she was going or why it was so important to get there. Then the sea was a black, wild horse that leapt beneath her, or perhaps over her, hooves flashing blue in the morning light.

When the night greyed at last toward dawn, she woke surprised to find that she had slept at all. It seemed as if she had been awake the night though, yet there was no weariness in her. Happily, even gratefully, she leapt out of bed and threw open the much-traveled sea chest in search of her favorite clothes: an old red petticoat faded to muddy rose and a plain stuff gown that had once been blue; a soft linen shift, laundered to transparency and cut dangerously low, with sleeves that ruffled threadbare just below the elbow.

She laced the gown up tight and stood a moment, approving the pretty rounding of her bosom. Then she adjusted her shift again and tucked a scarf about her shoulders and into the corners of the generous neckline.

Don't she just look like Chloë the shepherdess! She laughed to herself in the looking glass, so changed from last night's elegant reflection, and wondered what Prentiss would think. Again she conjured his form before her: the long, sardonic face and the merry blue eyes, like sapphires in a gilded setting. She thought she would never tire of those eyes. How odd to be wondering about someone besides Armand!

Her hands trembled as she tied off the laces. Was this ridiculous? Almost certainly. Breath came rapidly in shallow gasps, until she realized just how tightly she had done up the old dress, and re-tied it with nerveless fingers.

She muttered while pulling on grey homespun stockings and sturdy brogues, the last of her Barbados legacy. What foolishness! Insanity! God punishes the stupid, not to speak of what Uncle Roger would do!

Another voice prevailed: Deal with that when it comes. Just go!

She took a final moment at the looking glass to pass a comb through her hair and catch it up in back with a green ribbon, red-golden curls escaping at her shoulder, then stopped. Her breath caught sharply at the reflection of Marjorie's portrait hanging behind her on the wall.

As though her mother had walked into the room, she started to speak, but choked on the words. Poor Marjorie, who ran away with a sailor. Surely she wouldn't mind if her daughter were a little foolish, just once.

No good talking to ghosts. She dropped her gaze from the reflection to smooth her skirt. But, well, maybe this isn't so foolish an idea after all, *eh Maman?*

Still trembling but paying it no heed, she put her hand to the door and was away.

3

ALL JOYNE HANDS

DICK PRENTISS SPENT what was left of the night and his single life in Huggins Street with one of the girls from the Saracen's Head. Jesse liked him, and he was pleasant enough to her, better than most. He had paid her for the whole night, and she was grateful, expecting the respite of a few easy turns and then a decent rest. But she hadn't guessed and maybe he hadn't either that he could spend the whole night drowning red hair and green eyes in the dark depths of another woman's body.

This quite decent lad, who was not bad to look at and always spoke her fair and paid in advance, and even bathed—this decent lad had always made her feel pretty, almost loved; enjoyed instead of taken. And if he had called her all night by some other girl's name, what matter? The pity was, he would never be back. That much she could tell. His wenching days were behind him, and the poor bastard didn't even know it yet.

When Molly reached the market, the bricks of St. Paul's broad square still glistened with the dawn rain as a pale, watery sky was just beginning to blue at the horizon. In an hour everything would be dry and stark and filled with people, but just now, only the most energetic dealers stumbled out from behind the stalls to raise blinds and tie back curtains and set out their wares.

The cook shops already steamed with the dark harsh smells of coffee roped with honey, and bitter chocolate brewed up with milk and cinnamon. Around those first fires, other of the bazaar's denizens clustered half-dressed before even thinking about opening up. They yawned, scratched, hacked up last night's rum, and shuffled through the dew to piss.

Molly found her new friend, her quest, her adventure at one of these, chatting with an old man, a knife-sharpener by trade, sun-darkened to the color of weathered teak who rattled even at this hour in the rapid mutter of Cork.

Prentiss looked tired, as if he had spent an ill night. Tired, and perhaps even vulnerable. The shadows around his eyes seemed to bespeak nightmares.

Nightmares? Not Prentiss, surely! Molly hesitated, suddenly doubtful. She had imagined, expected him to be immortal, impervious to pain or fatigue. What if he were no stronger than anyone else?

Her resolve, so firm a moment since, seemed now no better than childish rebellion. How could she dare? But the plump brown curls dragged behind his ears; the broad cut of that shoulder in a blue linen coat edged in rose; the trim line of his leg below the loose galligaskins; the plain dandiness of a fine new hat with a grey and crimson flash of feathers; even the subtle danger of a rapier slung from a baldric drew her even against her best judgment. By chance, at last, he looked up across the old man's shoulder, and saw her.

And smiled. The bright blue eyes drew up to echo the jaunty grin. She could not imagine how she had thought him weary or in pain. Not now, as he extended a hand to her, and it was all right.

She went to him then, and as she took the proffered hand, he folded her close under his arm like any country maid. The heat of him warmed her, like the sultry edge of sun lurking in the morning air, until she almost giggled at her own daring. Surely, in a moment, he would whisk her away into the promised day.

The chat with the knife sharpener, however, tuned to the whirling of a foot-powered wheel, fountaining sparks from each pass of a blade, seemed to have no end. Molly was not introduced, and she could find no entrance to the conversation. The hiss and whine of the sharpening wheel underscored a play of words she could not follow about people she had never heard of and times almost before she was born.

Nearby, the blacksmith's apprentices were firing up their forge, adding sulfur and hot metal smells to the growing day. A bookseller, just come from pastry and a boiled egg, wiped his hands on his coat before uncovering his stock with a connoisseur's delicacy. Testy because there had been no salt, he added a penny to the going price of any title in French. Just past him, the greengrocer coughed and laid out a basket of apples. He felt like hell, and snapped at his daughter who looked far too pleased with herself for so early an hour.

Prentiss nodded or laughed from time to time, and once or twice clutched her to him a little, but no more. Behind her, women from opposite ends of town with muffins to sell, or boot laces, or knitted garters in trays hung round their necks, greeted each other as old friends, crackling with gossip. The noise began to rise along with the sun.

A last puddle of rainwater was seeping into Molly's shoe. Unconsciously her foot began to tap out a soggy rhythm of irritation. Though she had never minded being decorative before (had she?) this was supposed to be different. For one thing, she wasn't feeling especially decorative in her old clothes and worn shoes. And for another, no one was looking at her.

"Dickon?" she said at last.

"Aye, lass?" said Prentiss, pleased that she had chosen the little used by-name.

"You did say just after dawn, and it is. Here I am."

"So you are, Sweet, and welcome. Tea?"

Taken somewhat aback, she managed to stammer, "Yes, please."

With no further word he handed her his own plain wooden cup. He brushed three fingers through her hair; and his attention was gone again.

He spoke very little himself, listening to the old man's tales of plague-time in London, long past, and how the fellow had seen the King once, the old King, mind, not the new one, but the one before, the first Charles, God bless 'im.

The tale droned on. Prentiss ignored her. She had a mind to tell him what he could do with his surprises, if this was one of them.

But then, she realized, he might let her go. Which could be worse.

She was not, however, accustomed to being disregarded. Her sense of daring was seeping away with the early chill, replaced by frustration at being treated like a child. All right then, she would give him a few more moments—just a few!—to remember his promise so lightly given.

"Prentiss."

She pouted prettily but, "A moment, Sweet," he said with a brief glance.

"But my boots are getting wet."

"They're good sturdy boots. They can stand it."

"Prentiss!"

"Your pardon, Max." The knife man's monologue skidded to a halt, his colorless old eyes finally taking in Molly's presence. Not entirely too old to care about a pretty girl, he granted Dick a moment's grace with a curt nod.

With no smile at all, Prentiss unwrapped his arm from Molly's shoulder, and took her a step away. A long, obviously patient sigh. "Aye, Lady?"

She blinked twice and stood her ground. "Are we going?"

"In a hurry? Other engagements? Meeting a lover?" He hadn't meant to be coarse, but there it was. The dimpled jaw tightened.

As if she imagined no menace and no insult in his posture or his voice, she shrugged and glanced aside. "It was your idea. If you've changed your mind, I can go."

"Have you changed yours?" So. A test. Did she know what she wanted? The delicate shoulders squared in her own kind of challenge.

"Yes," she said, crisply clipping the lie. Like a step in a country reel, she started to go round him, only to be brought up with a jerk when he snagged her hand. Her chin and the light in her eyes both rose defiantly as the first clear ray of sun struck a halo from her hair. Prentiss, watching it happen, knew he was doomed.

"And if I asked you to stay?" he said around a grin that would be the end of her.

The touch of his fingers sure but light on her wrist, and facing that look, she cocked a saucy eyebrow, trying not to melt. "Then perhaps I should stay."

The tension born of early hours and fractured nerves burst in a bubble of laughter first from Prentiss, then reluctantly but emphatically from Molly, and for no other reason than pure fun, he kissed her and she kissed him back, and all was well again, if somehow changed.

Old Max just shook his grizzled head, grumbling in disgust about young people these days and, head down, put his foot to the pedal and went back to work.

"Very well, Sweet," Prentiss said when he could speak normally again. "Very well. First round to you." Grinning, laughing, beside himself and trying to be sober but nearly drunken with her, he let her stand away a bit, then relented and drew her back into his arms.

He kissed her, lightly this time, and asked had she eaten. Took the tea from her hand and set it next to Max's uncaring foot. Ordered up a handful of cheese and mushroom pasties from a boy with a cart, piling them into her apron with glee.

"Come along now, girl, come along. Keep up, keep up!" he ordered, and marched them into the day.

Molly, dizzy with delight, stumbled along where she was bid, blinking at everything new, which was nearly everything altogether.

He started with the first flower monger they saw, where he spent a ha'penny on three tiny rosebuds, twisted into a nosegay. These he presented with a courtly bow, then without bothering to ask, arranged them in the lush springtime of her bosom. Like a milliner fussing with a hat, he fluffed and tweaked petals and leaves just so until, while she blushed, he put his hands about her middle and bent to fully appreciate the fragrance, flower and girl together.

Soft petals, prickly leaves tickled, teased up a delicate flush and a giggle which moved back in her throat as the storm of his breath met her skin. The wonderful tingling in her blood turned that flush to crimson, and flooded her long throat with color.

"Dickon, stop," she shuddered, the nerves showing. "Prentiss!" when he would not.

He finally emerged with a long sigh. "My rose of the Indies."

Playful, surprisingly relieved, she pushed him away. "Your blarney of the Indies, rather. Have you no shame at all?"

"Who me? Why, none at all, Sweet. None at all. Now come along and tell me the story of your life."

"I thought you were going to entertain me," she chided.

"Right again."

The kiss this time found only her hand, completing the gesture he owed her from the day before.

He kept his arm loosely slung about her shoulder, as careless and as constant as the smile that hung about his mouth. With the other hand he conducted his tour, punctuating with flourishes the sights of Port Royal unfamiliar to a convent-bred young girl.

Molly knew St. Paul's from weeks of dedicated Sundays; she had never seen Saint Dismas, the Catholic church, in little use since the English wrested the island from the Spaniards in Cromwell's time. Now that the King was securely restored and his Queen's Romish faith tolerated to a significant degree, it had reopened, but sat much neglected even by its still apprehensive congregation.

She knew the great market at St. Paul's where the new world came to trade; he showed her the fishery and the turtle pens down by the docks, and the incoming ships in the harbor, and the vast warehouses that stored the goods of half the world on their way to the other half. Everywhere they went someone shouted his name and a greeting and more often than not, a joke. Not a few shot a look her way, laughed, and ventured some lewd remark, which he answered in kind without stopping.

At the King's Wharf and Littleton's and Freeman's too where the great ships docked, privateers and merchantmen together, more voices called for him. Two or three asked when he'd be ready to sign on again, and to those he gave a bleak look and little more.

So he was a sailor, too, was he?

Once, he put up a hand to shade his eyes and stared into the glittery distance where an old friend was striking her sails and slowing into port. So far a carefree delight, Prentiss seemed suddenly thoughtful. The brigantine in the distance lay graceful into the wind, a fierce redheaded mermaid just visible at the figurehead.

"My father was a sailor, you know," Molly said. "A pilot."

He looked down at her as the sea breeze whipped the hair across his face, and shook off a shadow.

"Aye, Sweet" he said. "I know." And he hustled her up the boardwalk back toward the center of the town.

They rested from the heat of the day under the young trees of the park at the bottom of York Street, a green spot of clear air and sky in the midst of the muggy, unruly town. There they bought boiled sugar cane, brown and sticky as the storm-haunted air, and stood sucking it and each other's fingers to watch a company of players who shouted for attention from the platform of a rickety farm wagon. Before long, and not without apology, the troupe launched into a bawdy version of Pyramus and Thisbe lifted with spontaneous revisions from Shakespeare.

The players were all men, saving a slatternly Thisbe and a willowy pale girl with strawberry hair, a span taller than most of them and inclined to giggle, who spoke, when they could tease it out of her, for the Moon. By their manners, they might have been the rude mechanicals the eighty-year-old script called for, giving a performance slightly less manic than a tavern brawl. Moon and Lion and Wall stumbled and fought and swore at one another through their rash entrances and reluctant exits. Between speeches, those without lines sat on the edge of the makeshift stage encouraging the audience with catcalls and vulgar commentary.

Molly nearly doubled over, convulsed with giggles until she could hardly breathe. She had to hide her face in Prentiss's shoulder when at the death of Thisbe, Pyramus tormented his beloved's corpse with declamations of grief, and by twisting her nose when he forgot the line.

Lion pinched the Moon's behind; she swatted him soundly with her thorn bush. Pyramus did himself in with a painted wooden sword and fell with a crack across the edge of the stage to the grass, then got up and finished his dying speech through very believable yelps of pain, holding onto his side. The grief, at least, was sincere.

Molly gasped, "He'll have broken something, don't you think?"

Prentiss shook his head, still roaring.

"Nay, lass, naught but a bruised rib, to be sure," he said. "He'll have gotten that and worse any night in the ale house. Look again, I'll lay odds she pushed him. That one's his wife!" Better than a hanging, this stuff, and the words were good too.

And when it was done and the players all leapt up from their deaths to pass hats among the crowd, Molly added her own penny to the one Dick contributed, though against his argument. Players, after all!

They moved on, breathing in the salt and sea air, the tang of hot pavement, the rich green smell of the island rising in its mountains behind them, and Molly knew she had not been so happy since Paris. Borrowing Armand's cast off clothes and prowling the midnight streets with students from the University had been disgraceful and thrilling, but this was better.

Early in the day, a huge smile had settled itself all over her rosy face and would not move, though her cheeks ached. It sat there now, shining like a new sovereign, gilded and fine.

As the sun rolled well over the meridian, they strolled back towards St. Paul's courtyard, now busier than ever, being a market Friday and restored from the noontime drowse. This time Dick bought them steamed prawns snappy with nutmeg and fiery red pepper, wrapped in a twist of greasy paper.

Prentiss, whose head was spinning between infatuation and some other confusing, less familiar emotion, handed Molly her dinner with a quizzical smile. The wild humor that had claimed her intrigued and troubled him all at once. Burdened with cares he couldn't name, he steered her back to the park edge and an unoccupied bench under a pepper tree.

Dinner was better eaten sitting, so Molly sat. Dick stood over her, one foot on the bench nudging her skirts, arms loosely crossed over the cocked knee, mind whirling.

The laughter that had lit him so warmly seemed to sour in his mouth. The girl, this astonishing girl, was no less wonderful to look at, her hand no less sweet a burden than this morning. She had tolerated the odd, light-hearted kisses. She made him laugh, and laughed along with him.

What was wrong with him, he wondered, that he couldn't just take the gift of her company as he always did, with good cheer and an eye to the main chance? And what business had she being so damned pretty, and Rafe's daughter too?

Molly bit each fish and let it slide between her teeth, then tore into the shell to get the sweetest bit at the bottom, hot juice running down her chin and hands, and even that was beautiful. Almost at her feet, a gang of sparrows was hopping in among the gulls, pouncing on breadcrumbs and bits of crab shell. With cheerful malice she tossed out a shrimp tail and shrieked like a child at the brawl that ensued. Prentiss beside her made no sound.

"Finding the peasants amusing?" he said.

The emerald eyes raked up to meet his sardonic ones, wondering what that was supposed to mean. In case it were unpleasant, she chose to ignore it. "I can't help it. I'm happy. I have not been so completely happy since before my mother … I mean, since Paris."

"Paris?"

Paris, again. No, she had not mentioned it that much, but some contrary whim had put him in the temper to misconstrue.

She nodded, white teeth fully involved with shrimps. In a clear moment, she said "You can't understand! A day like this. You for company."

She licked her fingers deliciously one by one. He had to look away or grab her right there. He looked away.

What the devil was he doing!

Though her manner was undeniably gay and relaxed, Prentiss's discomfort grew. She liked him. She was adorable. This was impossible. Life ashore was supposed to be simple, damn it all. That's why he was here.

Still, she babbled on about her perfect life. Paris, in God's name!

"Dear Eugénie! She is surely married to that nasty draper by now. Very *aristo*, her family, but not quite as wealthy as everyone was supposed to think." Molly sighed with a fond mixture of regret and pleasure. "I have been wishing so to be back there. I have no other friends. Instead of … ah!"

She watched with dismay the expression that suddenly clouded his face, and wondered if she had been speaking French without realizing it. "But that was yesterday. Until yesterday I wanted to be anywhere but here."

"And now?"

"Now, for some reason," she said, "I have become quite fond of Jamaica."

She sparkled, he noticed, even drenched in cayenne and fish juice. It wasn't bloody fair.

"Have you then?" The comfortable voice lay quite cool on the heavy air, which Molly chose to interpret as wry humor, since she had done nothing wrong, not really very wrong. Had she? Nothing that couldn't be fixed.

"If I were at home… in Paris, I mean… Eugénie would be eaten up with jealousy to see me with you. And her brother! Oh, Armand would fume and call you out! Or convince you to join his regiment."

The flattery shocked her a little, but it seemed to work. His vanity had been touched, at least, and the cloudy expression passed.

Besides, it was all true. When, she wondered, would she ever learn to hold her tongue? Before or after offending everyone in Port Royal, high and low? Perhaps she *should* speak only in French. Then she could offend everyone at once and have it over with.

"Look at you, you're a mess," he said, and pulled out a handkerchief. With rough care, he put it to her glistening lips and chin. At the touch, he seemed to tremble, but that couldn't be true.

Then he was laughing with her again, or smiling at least.

"I knew a Frenchie once," he said smoothly. "Back when Jimmy and I were cruising, back in England. We sailed a bit of trade for a Cornishman called Penrhys and a Monsieur La Froige. Jimmy used to call him 'La Frog'."

Molly listened, fascinated. Through a day of chatter he had not once touched on his past. It *would* be smuggling, of course.

It hardly mattered. He was so good to look at, she had to drop her eyes to keep from staring at the strong-boned face, the startling blue eyes. She glanced briefly through the crowd just for the pleasure of returning to his face.

"Where were you born?" she asked impulsively.

Eyelids drooped, guarding his thoughts, but he shrugged. "England."

"Well, yes."

"London, then. Why?"

"It's just that, well…" Her head tilted winsomely. "I know nothing about you. How you live. What you do. What your favorite color is."

Too late she noticed the doors close on some secret, locked place. The fine shoulders lifted lightly as she examined her hands.

With a swift movement he flung a double handful of shrimp tails onto the grass for the sparrows, noisy with gratitude. Prentiss said nothing at all.

Fidgeting, crumpling the sticky greasy paper into a ball, she added, "I should not have asked. I'm sorry."

He had grown quite sober, but now one side of his mouth quirked a small grin.

"Green," he said, shaking off the mood. A strong, teasing hand reached out to stroke the sudden blush of her cheek. "Do you know how pretty you are?"

She flushed, as embarrassed by his frank appreciation as she was confused. Not knowing what to say next, she watched the birds take wing, shuddering into the sun.

"Look at me," he said. And when she hesitated, he dropped to her side, hunkering down in the dust of the street where he could look up into her darling face. "Please, lass." Very gently he brought her chin around with one irresistible finger. "You have the most extraordinary eyes."

"No!" she whispered hoarsely.

"But you do!"

"No, not that!" The extraordinary eyes had widened not with pleasure, but fear, staring past him.

She sucked back the bile that rose in her throat and just managed to stifle a whimper. What came out instead had all the harmonics of a good, full-grown feline snarl. "Bloody hell!"

On his feet at once, Dick whipped about, one hand already on the pistol at his belt.

The only thing Molly could mean was the pompous, nasty little Royal Navy bastard he'd last seen bothering her in the garden. Passing only a few yards away, Sir Simon Benning picked through the crowd as through a midden, a perfumed handkerchief to his mouth against foul airs.

Prentiss's expression twisted up in a superior sort of way. It was perfect. He had been longing for something to surprise her, and lead her away from the hell's mouth of his past.

The dark mood vanished. Professional scrutiny took only an instant: The captain was good at frightening young girls; Dick had seen the genteel mask slip last night. All right, yes, he might be more competent, more given to violence than his foppish manner indicated just now, but none of that should matter in a street Prentiss knew as he knew his own name.

Still marking his target, estimating as always wind, speed, and random chance, he lightly slipped the sword baldric over his head and handed off the rig, awkward in a crowd, to Molly. Then still without a backward glance, he tugged his new coat straight, resettled his hat, and left her with a grim smile and a word:

"Watch."

Molly snatched at his sleeve, but he was gone, leaving her sputtering and terrified and much too alone. So she hitched up her skirts, stepped onto the bench, trying to keep him in sight, trying to imagine what he might be planning, and knowing full well that whatever it was would certainly be applied to the unwary captain. And if Benning were to see her here and in this company, he could ruin her. The terror that had made her heart race now was real.

Prentiss could have been more careful, and would have been had he not been trying to impress a girl and, all right, himself besides. He threaded through the crowd on an intercepting course, trying to stay in Molly's view and still not lose his quarry. This, he knew, would be easy.

It would be done in an instant. The captain would never know a thing. The surging, polychrome, polyglot crowd would cover him, oh yes.

An easy touch, aye, from the small, professionally slender dagger; a bounce and a quick flurry of chatter, apology, time of day, God save you sir. Timing is everything. Over and done. Could Molly see?

Yes, and

Damn!

The last glance at her red hair cost him everything. The insignificant little knife snapped forward to nip purse strings; boots skidded on a trash-slicked stone. No matter. No, just enough to send him lurching into the captain's side, is all.

Benning swore and swung toward Prentiss even before the purse jerked from his belt, so there could be no mistaking the intention, no matter how bungled. A handful of sovereigns and a packet of fiddling small change spilled ringing to the street.

"Thief!" he cried.

For one long moment the two men stared right at each other, frozen in time until something, the flutter of a tumbling scrap of paper, a gull's cry, a woman's tinkling laugh shattered the moment. "Help ho! A thief!"

Faces turned.

Benning thrust a hand to Prentiss's sleeve but the younger man wrenched free, sacrificing the shoulder seam of his fine new coat, now printed with Benning's manicure. He'd be speaking to the draper about that shortly, Prentiss thought with curious detachment, then ducked and scuttled under two fishmongers and a poulterer.

Like an acrobat, he tumbled once, narrowly avoiding the captain's walking stick, a pear, an orange, and a disinterested tin box that appeared out of nowhere. On the ground, on the move, he managed to scrabble up some of the fallen gold and fling it at random into the crowd.

"Help!" Prentiss shouted, praying to misdirect the mob before it could bond. "Help! Murder! By Saint Paul! For godssake, help!"

And then he flat out ran. The crowd, hardly deterred by the lack of a particular object for its attention, took up whatever cry they heard, though a few were briefly distracted by the sudden largess tossed their way. But not all, and not Benning. Dick ran, pushing madly through the confusion, straight for Molly, small and horrified, who nevertheless stood her ground.

"Come on!"

He snatched her hand, dragging her from her perch though she was certain to slow him down. Behind them, the crowd had in moments become half the marketplace, and everyone knew his name. By calling for St Paul, he had signaled the others of his peculiar fraternity, true, and by that call the mob might yet be turned, or at least defused. Maybe. Benning's voice was louder and carried the force of law. And that, in Port Royal, might by itself be enough to confuse the issue.

There had been a laugh, Prentiss thought in a flash of mad hilarity. Laughter, and the tinkle of little bells, and, and... oh hell, let it go!

He heard his name as a confused echo in the shouting, and dared not think he was safe.

"There's a wench with him!" someone cried. Others took it up.

They might be voices to lead the hunt astray, out of professional courtesy if nothing else. They might be point men scouting the advance position. They might be headed towards Morgan's Line, or directly for him. Just run!

With Molly in hand, Prentiss took no breath for consultation, no moment for a backward glance. She had thrust the sword at him, then as if they had been partners forever, she hauled up her skirts and ran to match him.

Prentiss took them into a side street too narrow for this crowd to follow, and thence to an alley even less convenient. Then another side street opened up that led, almost instantly, to two or three new passages, each equally choked with filth and dripping with damp.

Without a word, they dove into one and out between the firetrap buildings of Huggins Street within sight of the Saracen's Head. Late afternoon, with the sun already westering, patrons would be mercifully few at this golden hour.

He was known here.

Everyone *knew* he was known here.

It was still the only choice. Dick pressed Molly into the niche of the tavern doorway and paused, listening.

Out there somewhere, the sounds of pursuit kept on echoing bouncing faint and confused. Whatever the password of *St Paul* had achieved, it had not diverted the chase entirely. No one's fault. Nothing works every time. Very well, the landlord here owed him a favor. Or the other way round. Whatever.

He pulled the girl down the stairs into the common room, slamming the thick-beamed door just as the crowd spilled into the street from east and west.

"Harry!" he shouted. "Quick!" Tossed the sword kit at the man, sailed his hat across the room, and dove over the bar. Molly flew behind him.

"Aw, Prentiss, not again."

Before Molly quite had time to breathe, Harry Driscoll pulled a lever next to a huge reclining wine cask then, with a great thump from a rawhide mallet, pushed in its head. The wooden disk pivoted on a hidden pin to reveal a closet rather smaller than the cask itself.

With an unceremonious arm, Dick shoved Molly inside as, with a quick, despairing sigh, he clambered in beside her. This escape plan had never been designed for two people, never mind skirts and petticoats, but what could he do.

"Good thing you're little," he said tightly, and tucked up his knees. "Harry, now!"

Driscoll leaned on the door till the latch caught. Mere seconds later, he was competently, and well within the law, at the other end of the bar tapping a keg of local rum when Sir Simon Benning and the mismatched arms, legs, voices, and opinions of fifty riotous idlers consumed with civic virtue and the promise of fun swarmed through the door and down the stairs, demanding the thieves.

In another dimension altogether, Molly and Prentiss lay cramped and twisted about each other like newlyweds, all elbows and knees, crimped into new and not yet natural positions, listening to the banging and shouting, the *charivari* amplified out of all recognition. The curve of the barrel forced one of his arms behind her shoulders, while the other bent curiously either around her waist or up into her bosom. He took the option you might expect.

While she considered dispassionately where his hands had gone, the overwhelming smell of old wine reached sour into Molly's sinuses, wrinkling her nose.

"I'm going to sneeze!"

He hissed, "You are not!"

She did not. Oddly, the stark smell of liquor, the thudding of her heart in her tight-laced chest, his strong hands at her breast, more than anything made her want to laugh. The tickle in her nose went away, but not the irony. She was quite ready under the stress and the scents of old wine, to faint, and could not seem to manage it. Aunt Henrietta would be so disappointed.

Nerves frayed, emotions tumbled like a crew full of raw recruits, Prentiss would have welcomed the easy recourse of a faint. As a man of the world, of course, no such retreat was available to him.

Nose to nose in the imperfect darkness, blue eyes and green eyes met in the hard-breathing silence, and forced what little light leaking in through the cracks to fill the bare spaces between them. Though her roses had long since been lost to the gutter, Prentiss thought, some of the fragrance hung about her, warmed with her own, sweet and intoxicating scent.

Even in the murk she could see his grin while the noisy, the cramped, the interminable minutes passed. Entirely unaware that she had herself been grinning like a fool for some long while now, she tried to smile back. The heat of the day, the temper of the chase, the warmth and the nearness and the frank maleness of this man, *God*, this older, much more experienced man who must be almost her father's age, for godssake, made her giddy; as giddy as when she had found him sitting at her bedside. What, in God's name, was she to do?

All too aware of the girl's sweet, fragrant body damp between his hands, under his knees, pressing into his chest, Prentiss poured what he had of trust and pure confidence without speaking into the diamonds of her eyes, the only points of light in the fume-filled dark. She was safe. She would be safe with him. He would keep her safe. Did she understand?

He would keep her safe, yes, from the world, but from himself? Ah, another question. With the uppermost hand, the tickling hand, he reached with slow, with utmost care to brush the tangled, sunbright hair from her naked shoulder, trace the amiable jaw line, brush back her fears; touch her lips.

Soft, soft, the lips parted under the callused fingertips, then found his questing mouth, and in the space of two startling heartbeats, he was kissing her, all doubts cast aside. Long fingers laced into her hair, both of them helpless, both lost.

Then just as suddenly, just as appallingly real, under a mechanical thump and a pair of swift blows from the outside, the barrelhead swung open at their feet, letting in a rush of sweet air.

They neither of them moved, nor wanted to, till at last, drinking in a last vision of her, Prentiss crowed for pure joy. He scrambled out, easing the cramp from his legs and letting her stretch as well, then drew her out.

"God's death, Sweet, but you can run! And where in Port Royal did they find that many honest citizens!"

"Folk like a good chase," she said, shaking her skirts and trying to pat out the tangle of her hair. "No matter it might be their turn next, eh? Oh Prentiss!" She threw her arms about him again artlessly. "I've not run like that since I was fifteen! No, since I was six! That time in Paris, I was on the other side part of the time."

He was pleased to see she was laughing along with him, rocking joyfully in his embrace, though underneath the pleasure he still wondered why. What sort of girl was she? She should be hysterical or angry, or something else... shouldn't she? His doubts had only been driven into a corner after all, and not gone away. Bothersome doubts, that niggled at his temper.

Over her shoulder, still reeling with her joy, the smell of her hair, the shape of her in his hands, Prentiss said, "All clear, then, Harry?"

Driscoll nodded sullenly, surveying the damage. "And none too soon for my liking, ye poxy bastard. Ah, God saving yer grace, miss, if ye'll pardon my language. I'll let ye make it up to me by cleaning it up. And we're even, as favors go, I guess."

"We are that," Prentiss said roundly, and slapped a silver angel on the bar. "So I'll thank ye t' put 10 shillings on my account and bring us two glasses of the good Madeira—the good stuff, mind you—to celebrate when we've done."

Harry grumbled, unimpressed by grand gestures, and stooped groaning with melodrama to right a tumbled trestle.

Molly stared for a long moment, taking the time to examine Prentiss's voice and manner as they adjusted to the moment and the company.

What sort of man was he, in sooth? A light-handed thief, that was plain, in spite of this brief folly. A sometime sailor who other men wanted in their company. A practiced seducer, very likely. But what else? He recognized Shakespeare and could tell the hour by the sun, confirmed by the church bells striking through the day. If these contradictory things, then what else?

Enough! She let the thought go under the plain delight of hard work, teamed with the best looking man she had ever seen. Humming some old dancing measure, she found candles for lanterns and re-dipped and lit the rush lights that had smoldered out. She even found a broom to sort out the mess of the floor.

He took the muscle work, righting the furniture that survived. Of the rest, he repaired what he could, hauled out what was hopeless. When she needed to reach something, he was there to bring it down for her. When he reached for the glue pot, she pushed it under his hand. Though engaged in different tasks, they moved in purposeful tandem, like the figures of a dance.

When they were done, and she finally had the expensive Madeira in hand which tasted rather like the cheap stuff laced with sugar, Molly asked, "Will there be any more trouble, Harry?"

The landlord shrugged as he wiped out a wooden mug with one corner of a greasy apron. "There's always more trouble. This one 'ere, this captain that was chasin' you two? He'll be more'n you like, I'll warrant."

"It *was* your Captain Benning, then, wasn't it? Bastard," said Dick, and marveled to see her grow so thoughtful so suddenly.

He half sat on edge of the table, staring down at Molly and wrapped again in a confusion of feelings. If only he could stop looking at her, he could get on with business. Today was his gift to her. By tomorrow, she should be spending her dress allowance on him. That was the way things worked, the shape his life had taken since, well, just since.

She shuddered and took a long draft of the dark sweet wine. "Sir Simon Benning is my uncle's friend. They want … They think I'm going to marry him. Of course, if he happened to recognize me in all this, I may be spared that." She breathed a small sigh. "Perhaps I should…"

The words trailed into silence. In that moment, the thought of the tedious life of a convent nun seemed preferable to marriage with that slimy villain. As an option it even seemed reasonable, and at least she would get to sing. Yes, perhaps she should take that way.

But Prentiss heard only the first part of her thought, and had to watch the rest of it play cryptically across the lovely, anxious face. Something almost settled in his mind; something unpleasant, but which had to be said.

"So then," said Prentiss.

Abruptly Molly came up out of reverie with a quick, trusting smile that tore through his heart but did not stop him. "You've had an exciting day, eh milady?"

She caught the hostility behind the crooked grin and easy words. "I have said that I did. The best. Just as you promised."

"You might have ended it in prison."

"I know that. Though I did not intend it when we started. Nor, I think, did you."

He shrugged amiably. "Every day begins with that possibility, for some of us. This was no different, except that I had your skin to think of as well as my own. Lovely soft skin though it may be." Again he drew a finger down her face, tracing the line of her hair, round an ear and down to her mouth. Ever so lightly, he bent and kissed her lips then asked, out of some hidden hoard of bitterness: "What would your father think?"

She cocked a curious eyebrow, for the thought was sentimental and nearly amusing. "If he were alive, he might have been with us." *He might have been you.* "My uncle will not be so tolerant."

"You knew that. But you still dared come out with me, a scoundrel, a nameless desperado."

His eyes sparked with incipient malice, though the rakish grin held. He felt stupid, baiting her, but surely she was as idle and brainless as the others he had used. Beneath her apparent fondness would be a securely held contempt, like all the others. There must be. Otherwise, this adventure was over. Had to be over.

"Aye, I did. That's the chance I took. What are you trying to say?"

"I might have kidnapped you. Or raped you. Or worse."

"You might have," she agreed curtly.

"I might still."

She lowered her eyes, took a deep breath to shut out his face, his maddening voice. "You might try," she said.

"And would you like that too? Would that be part of the adventure? Would you run home then to tell all your fine friends what a daring day you had while you plan your next fancy ball?"

He was wrong and he could feel it, but there was no stopping now. Something kept pushing him to test her, to make her afraid. What seemed to be tempered steel in her had to be flawed.

"Say what you mean," she snapped into the hard blue eyes. "If you are trying to frighten me, you should know you don't do it very well." Did he know how she lied?

Maybe he did. He sat back with a graceless sneer twisting his features.

"Hmm." He emptied the leathern jack and set it down with a satisfied bump. "Well then. I suppose you'll be going home, now your adventure is done."

"What else?"

What else could she do? Her brain whirled, seeking some anchor. This was worse than their conversation this morning.

Off the table and pacing about, he hardly waited for a reply. "Home to fine clothes and nice manners, your life planned and safe. Unless some beggar comes over the windowsill again, eh? And you? Your only fear is they'll marry you to some old pervert who won't keep your bed warm enough. Oh aye, then you'll want to know where I am, right enough, and be willing to pay for it."

"What?"

"Oh yes," he answered her sputtering. Of these points he was dead certain. "I know you well enough, Molly September. Never think I don't."

Furious, finally she found the words.

"You know nothing!" She spat each word with sharp definition. Her fists smacked the table in real fury and brought her to her feet. "If that's what you think I am, why did you bring me out at all? What game are you playing!"

Fist struck wood again. Tempers set and matched, they glared tight-lipped across half the room. The only difference was the barest beginning of hot tears just at the corners of Molly's eyes.

Finally, Prentiss broke the silence with a kind of sigh, as if all the air had gone out of him, and made another kind of decision. Sure, she was right. He leaned against the wall, and did not meet her eyes.

"Aye, Sweet. A game indeed. I had a notion to make a lady of quality—a lady of property, you see—to spend the day with me. And you came."

Slowly, the awful realization broke over her. The fire in her eyes icing over, she drew herself up like a queen.

"You've done this before," she said. "Haven't you? This is what you do instead of going to sea, or putting that clever brain to some honest living. And this time I am the prize, and a prize fool at that."

She waited, giving him time to deny something, anything, but he only sipped at his drink, remember with a start that it was empty, and set down again.

"I see," she said, seeing nothing at all. "Very well, then, if you've finished proving whatever you meant to prove, is time I went home."

She stepped with the shreds of her dignity shining across the wooden planks toward the door, but passed him too close. His hand lashed out to her wrist and jerked her around to face him. A dangerous half-smile twitched one side of his mouth into a smirk.

"Is that wise? Should you turn your back on me?"

"Shouldn't I?"

Armand had taught her how to break that hold. She would have done so and fled, but some other, more annoying feeling than anger worked against it. Stubborn pride, most likely, but maybe something else.

He said, "A lady needs an escort. Terrible things happen to fine ladies who walk out alone in Port Royal."

In a faded stuff gown and coarse, sturdy hose, she waited, coolly silent, a slight tilt of the perfect chin, gracious but haughty under the disheveled hair that fell across her cheek, as if waiting for her seneschal to make his report on the state of some rebellious province. No taller than his shoulder, she managed somehow to look down her nose at him.

"If you insist," she said icily.

"Oh, I do. Can't be too careful, y'know. Kidnappers and murderers and that. Rapists."

She slipped out of his hold just as he released her.

4

SET AND TURN SINGLE

LOCKED IN THE lambent glow of approaching evening, Littleton's Wharf reeked with the dark rich smells of pitch and tar and sea-salt, and of pepper, nutmegs, and rare woods liberated from the arrogant grip of Spain. Circling overhead, gulls cried, breaking the heavy air. Throughout the bustling, clattering daytime, slaves and porters unloaded stores of fabulous treasures from ships flying half a dozen flags, and from others whose only home port was the pirate stronghold of Tortuga.

Just now, as the hard blue leeched out of the western sky, only one trim brigantine, newly docked, still surged with life. At her figurehead, the laughing, red-headed mermaid named her for the ship Prentiss had spied while she was still entering the harbor: *Jealous Mary*. A privateer like so many others lying smugly at anchor, she flew English colors in honor of her sponsor, who happened to be the King.

Torches were just being lighted as the crew scrambled, securing lines, locking down, and establishing a watch. Prize shares would already have been sifted out and set aside, destined to be sacrificed on the diamond-chip altar of cheap women and even cheaper rum. Her buccaneers rolled ashore full of cash and trouble, confident that an inconvenient peace was unlikely to interfere with their recreation.

The last man ashore had to be carried, and those who bore him lacked the spirited cheer of their comrades. One of them was shouting for a surgeon as they came down the gangway and disappeared into the glare of the Customs House.

Watching them gravely, the *Jealous Mary's* captain was, in his middle years, a handsome man in the hearty way that captures even matronly hearts and disturbs every kind of father. Grey-eyed and Celtic, his hair a mass of rusty brown of which he was indecently proud, fell straight by nature's whim across the well-made shoulders of his good blue coat. The working girls of Port Royal would greet Davy York wildly and weep real tears when he left. And in between he would make love to them all, or as many as he might, before shipping out again, leaving a trail of golden gifts in his wake.

Tonight in Port Royal, however, he had to put business before pleasure. For this he was attired, impeccably as always when visiting the gentry, in his finest clothes, a little creased with storage. A long cassock flared over loose breeches, all in deep indigo pricked out with dozens of silver buttons. Under his left hand a silver-hilted sword of Spanish make swung from a gilt-embroidered baldric. Where his blouse peeked at waist and cuff, it was the finest Irish linen, almost transparent, and good Venice lace stood at his throat and wrists. In lieu of a servant, he took for dignity his first officer, stout Will Keaton, who carried with him the official version of *Jealous Mary's* log and manifest. The true version, of course, Davy carried in his head.

Molly hardly spoke all the dreary way back to King's Lane, nor Prentiss neither. He led her around a stinking puddle. She thanked him. He held her back when they crossed a street because a rumbling carriage was unlikely to stop and besides, it held people she knew looking prim and disapproving. She gasped as he touched her, but said nothing even then, and walked on, rolling her arm out of his hand when the vehicle had passed. Numb, she paced through the slanting amber light, ascending block by yellow brick block from the midden to bourgeois magnificence, pretending she could ignore the long-striding devil beside her, but she was weary and sad, and there could be no such ignorance.

She hated him He ought to be hanged. He was still twice the man Sir Simon bloody Benning tried to imitate, though he clearly thought her a light-minded idiot, good only to be used however pleasantly and cast aside. Not even that good, since he was casting her aside unused. She had, apparently, failed to meet his standards.

She almost smiled, grimly imagining Benning's reaction to the name of his thief's doxy. Oh, what a scene that would create when the Captain and her uncle next met! And God, what would Jack Rhetford say when the word went around, as it surely would, that she had elected to trade the ballroom for the gutter? Would he volunteer his sword for her then? What would he say, and why on earth did she care what anyone thought when the only thing she wanted was for Dick Prentiss not to despise her?

It was disgusting. She had flung herself at him, loved his company, stood there and waited for him to collect her after his bollixed attempt at cutting a purse. She had kissed him and oh, yes, longed for more, and so what? She had wasted the day, and possibly her life, if her uncle found out. Surely it was better to spend a day with such a man than a life with any number of posturing gallants who fancied themselves his match, but she had not intended to force the choice all at once.

Somehow she had fallen two or three paces behind him. She skipped up to close the gap again. He seemed not to notice.

Easily as alone in his thoughts as Molly, Prentiss was trying without success to avoid thinking at all. Twice in two days this paltry wench had turned his head around till he couldn't tell for sure what he thought or felt. No woman should be able to do that! No, not even Rafe's little girl. And yes, he saw the flaws in his accusations.

She was no giddy, twittering wench like those friends of hers, but clever, and funny, and bold as a lad. Red hair, he supposed, gave her the temper. He had other things to think about, certainly, and forced himself to do so. Then as he thrust her out of harm's way, or steered her round an obstacle, and sensed her running up next to him, the scent of her hair, the silken invitation of her skin only made him dizzy all over again. He walked on a little faster.

It wouldn't do anyhow. If he had made a mistake, no matter. The girl had her own plans, and what did he care what she thought of him. Let her marry that damned toad if she liked, and grow fat and shrewish and old before her time. She'd see if it mattered to him. Let her live with her *"perhaps I should ..."* and bother him no more.

They reached King's Lane and the side gate of the house where pepper trees and vine-grown walls stood anchored in shadow, backlit against the long shafts of sun that filled the lowering twilight and caught the weathercock in a noose of light. The gate, Molly saw, stood slightly ajar as she had left it, hours *was it only hours?* before.

She turned slightly and managed a tight good night without meeting the glacier of his face, almost afraid to speak at all. She might cry and that would be too awful. If she started to cry she would never stop.

From the house a sudden storm of shouting exploded, filling up the garden and half the street. A step back in alarm, then a deep breath and she pushed at the gate, preparing to trade spite and contempt for argument and accusation with no further hindrance.

Without warning, Dick caught at her arm again and pulled her round to face him. It was getting to be a habit, annoying at best.

"Let me go."

"Your last chance, Molly."

"Chance for what?" she snapped, and all her anger showed. "To play the next round? To be your fool twice? Why? Are you doing this for a wager, or is it just idle malice? *'Once more and none can mend it?'* Christ, how clever do you have to be before you can call the trick a success?"

His grip on her wrist tightened, pulled her closer till her breath was warm in his face. "Prove me wrong. Come with me. You don't belong here and you know it."

"Because you say so?"

"What? No! No, look..."

"I don't have to prove anything to you, Dick Prentiss. Ten minutes ago you knew with a certainty approaching perfect faith that I belonged nowhere else but here, with an endless round of parties and lovers to make up for my endless, empty existence. Now I'm... what am I now?"

At the edge of hysteria, she was nearly laughing, and the whole street must surely be listening. *"Ma foix"* she laughed. "It must be a terrible burden, being God?"

A long, tight pause, then he swallowed and said, harsh with restraint, "Damn it, Molly September, I do know one thing. If I'd known that bastard was your bridegroom, I'd have cut his throat instead of his purse."

He released her with a shove, whirled away, and was gone before she could retort. He was damned if he'd let her see the pain storming through him.

He needn't have worried. Stay or go, she had closed her eyes and her mind against him as she leaned an exhausted shoulder into the half-open gate and rolled with it into the garden. Prentiss's quick, light footsteps echoed, then pattered, then vanished, and she was left alone with a pewter sky, the scent of summer roses, and silence.

Not quite silence, no. Angry voices spilled from the house. No words stood out, not even her name, which was curious. Only the harsh snarl that was Roger bit the air, and the brief stillness that must be filled by mumbling servants. Surely the household was in an uproar, the town Watch called for, Aunt Henrietta threatening to faint, or worse, if anything was worse

The cat green eyes snapped open, bright and wet. *Damn*, she thought. *God damn you, Dick Prentiss.* And dear God, what had she done to earn this, to be fired from one hell to another in the space of an hour? Damn it, didn't he realize, in his Olympian wisdom, that his frivolous, trivial lady who was certainly too good for him, his giggling idiot, was about to be told she was a whore.

At least, she thought, as she kicked aside leathery leaves and fallen blossoms. At least she could have faced them with the whole day pleasant in her mouth, savoring it while they berated her. Her mouth and her mind filled at once with the taste of his kisses, as intoxicating as cheap Madeira, as sweet as boiled sugar cane. And, too, the sweet urgency, the passion lurking under his playfulness. *Set that aside!* So she brushed the leaves out of her hair, squared her perfect shoulders, and hoped vainly that she did not altogether smell of sour wine.

The kitchen door was nearest with its screened servants' passages to everywhere. She would go up and change for supper and reappear sweetly compliant. There might be questions over supper, but if Uncle Roger's roaring business did not concern her, perhaps her little adventure would simply disappear, as if it had never happened. Certainly, that would be best for everyone.

The door opened noiseless against the argument. Pausing just within, she stopped to slip out of her battered shoes and gather up her skirts in controlling hands. Then cautious steps took her past the one place where light shone clearly from the parlour, and from which she could be seen if any happened to look.

Furtively, she peered around the doorway. A hard male face, handsome but smooth with controlled anger, met hers and slid blandly away. A stranger, and clearly not interested in her whereabouts. Good.

A grim smirk twisted her lips as she darted across the danger zone and into the pantry staircase. She must seem no more than some kitchen maid sneaking in from stolen pleasures. And so, she thought, pursuing irony. So she was.

Nancy, who *was* their kitchen maid, nearly collided with her on the stair and started to cry out in apology. Molly shushed her with a hiss.

"You do not see me, do you understand?"

Nancy quivered, wide-eyed, and shook her kerchiefed head. "We called and called, Miss. Her ladyship said ye could starve yerself, if ye wished but it's been all day Miss, so I was just after settin' a tray by yer room."

"Just be quiet," Molly cut her off. "Say a word to anyone, and I'll slap thy silly face."

The girl's eyes widened and a gasp escaped her as the young mistress pushed past her in the narrow corridor and ran the last little way up the stairs. Molly had shocked herself too many times today to notice that she had spoken so harshly to a perfectly good servant, which she never did, or offered one violence, which she could not have dreamed of.

But when she hit the top of the stair she turned again.

"Wait!" she dared to call. Nancy had disappeared into the darkness below, but in a moment her freckled face peered up out of the gloom. "Nan, I'm sorry. Can you come help me dress?"

She jiggled the door and lifted the handle, bearing to the left with a fraction of counter shove to lift the latch she had secured the night before.

Yes, indeed. Prentiss was right. She had done this before; the trick was an old one.

The door opened with ease if you knew the trick, but she very nearly tripped over a tray just at her feet. Another inch and she would have spilled a brown jug of ale into a plate of bread and pale cheese. She left it for Nan to clear away, still untouched. Anger, frustration, apprehension would have driven off any appetite, even if she hadn't been eating all day.

Swearing heedlessly in two languages with words her relations had no idea she knew, she set to her laces, damning fashion that made it impossible for a girl of breeding to get in and out of her own clothes. As it was, she had to hope the kitchen wench would be silent and nimble-fingered.

"In the wardrobe," she said softly as Nancy popped the bedroom door closed with a muffled snick. "Lilac silk. The Flemish band. That's the collar, for pity's sake. And hurry, girl. I can be out of these clothes before you can cross the room, but 'twill take twenty minutes to look like a lady again."

Not twenty minutes but half an hour later she emerged, prinked and pearled, curled and powdered, and smelling delicately of lavender water instead of cheap wine. The dress was simply cut as befitted a modest girl of her age dining at home: a lilac silk of most delicate tint, a broad square collar edged in lace ringing her pretty shoulders, bare of jewelry. Because the evening was sickly warm, she looped a fan of Italian design around her wrist and shuddered it open.

One slim hand to the banister, she descended to the parlour, her face clenched into sculpted pleasantness. If they had not missed her, and apparently they had not, they should have no cause for questions. True, it pricked her pride to be so lightly marked, but then, it was her day to be disregarded, wasn't it. If only Dick Prentiss could see her now, the picture of what he most detested, how he would laugh.

In the parlour, Molly's name had not once surfaced, that much was true. Other miscreants instead occupied Sir Roger FitzRobert's passionate attention. He paced—stalked rather—from the spinet to Henrietta's tapestry frame to the hearth to the spinet again. The always florid complexion, blotching unattractively, warned of oncoming apoplexies as he listened with undisguised scorn and disbelief to the sonorous reading of the *Jealous Mary's* log by his clerk, MacBean. A spidery Scotsman malformed by too many years arched over a customs house desk, MacBean's voice cracked with the reading and screeched his own disbelief in the contents as he went.

"Sir Roger," he creaked before he had half finished. "This cannot be the whole list. The *Marquesa de Alva* surely carried more cargo than this."

Davy York's answering glare would have withered a more sensitive worm. He did not offer to strike the little secretary, though his fist curled to do so. Tight-jawed he protested, as he had from the start, of pre-existing damage and his too-efficient gun crew. It was difficult to properly sack a rapidly sinking galleon.

"I have told ye 'twas not our fault," he said. "Not with the *Marquesa* nor any of the rest, as few as they were. 'Tis the green season, as they say, with a storm round every corner. Ye may also have noticed we're at war, and their most high and mighty Spanish majesties are convoying their treasure ships with men o'war, or keeping them till Christmas."

Again he recounted the history of *Jealous Mary's* travails at sea, the superior numbers and newer guns of the Spaniards, the wiliness of the Portuguese, the tendency of the Dutch to run in guarded convoys. Not to mention the damage inflicted on his ship and the tragic loss of his pilot, Sym Daniel. And since the last point was the truest, Davy was quite sincere.

"Enough!" FitzRobert bellowed at last. "And more than enough, Captain, of your excuses and your lies. We are indeed at war, which is the only reason your trade is not classed as piracy. Wars put great holes in the King's purse. I am the King's officer, and the King's warehouses are standing half empty, while you do little either to fill them or, so it seems, to harry His Majesty's enemies in the compass of your voyage. I cannot send him a quarter share of nothing and I will not send him your lies!"

Davy's fist thumped on the bound ledgers on MacBean's desk, rattling the papers and upsetting both inkwell and secretary. "You've no call... "

"I've call enough, you scoundrel, to know this log for a false one. Am I expected to believe this? Look here: cloth of gold of tissue, ten bolts; of Chinese silk, the same; gold plate, 120 pieces; two small chests of silver money in pieces-of-eight. The rest of the list just as slender. Knife blades, thimbles, thread, and cooking pots! 'Sblood, fellow, am I simple? Next ye'll tell me it was stolen by the fairies! I should dearly like to see the real record of thy voyages. Or else I should like to see thee hanged for a pirate!"

But Davy York was not to be cowed by threats and epithets, no matter how angrily delivered. Even FitzRobert's contemptuous thou-ing to put him in his place would have been amusing, had not Sym's loss been so real.

Nothing in the world would incline him to tell up the full tale of his privateering. It was not done. It was not expected. It ought not to be asked. York would not fly in the face of honorable tradition to suit some absurd left-handed Calvinist semi-literate little plantation Irishman with delusions of nobility. No, not even for the King himself, God save 'im!

On the other hand, that little serving wench whose guilty glance had caught his eye some minutes back might not be a bad repayment for her master's ill humors. He should have to find the scullery door after this little scene was played out.

"A pirate, am I?" York said quickly. "Naught but an honest merchant such as yourself, and on the King's business, too. My letters are in order, as you have reason to know. If it's all the same, I'd as soon report directly to the Governor as to you if I'm to be treated in this fashion. Either way, a quarter share of the prize, no matter the value, goes to the duke of York for his Majesty's share." He paused to let a sly smile slip lightly into the corners of his mouth. "Doesn't it?"

The odds were better than even that Sir Roger shaved the figures some when reporting to England, and Davy York was a cheerful gambler.

FitzRobert hesitated only a moment, but a telling one. "Of course it does. The governor appointed me to that task, and carry it out I shall. And to the full measure, damn you!"

"Uncle, such language!"

MacBean still cringed, but four male heads turned, FitzRobert snapping around in a fury at being interrupted. Molly stood framed in the entry, lamplight wreathing her curls in an auburn nimbus and shimmering off the rippling silk. She looked to each: her uncle's imminent explosion damped for the moment by grudging courtesy; the ship's lieutenant Keaton, a stranger in grey; the captain, mature but handsome, glimpsed from the scullery, and in whose eyes recognition seemed to light, masked swiftly by amused comprehension.

And finally, in a yellow coat and too many ribbons, Captain Sir Simon Benning. His usually vapid face wrinkled into a frown, as though seeing her for the first time. Her glance swept smoothly away from him. Had he seen her well enough? Would he remember?

"This is no business for ladies, Molly. Especially not rebellious girls who spend the day pouting. Now go along in to your Aunt, I say."

"Not pouting, Uncle dear," she said earnestly. "Only ill from the excitement of last night, and praying to know how to be a more obedient ..."

"None of your guile! Go find your Aunt and tell her how reformed you are, if you must."

"Come, come, Roger," Benning interrupted with nasal disdain. A frothy handkerchief flicked from his wrist. "You've wasted enough time on this fellow. I suspect you will never know more than he chooses to tell you. As the Governor, I venture to say, will never know more than you choose to tell him. And he the Duke. And so on to the Angel Gabriel and the Almighty Himself, I suppose. We understand these things. Why waste the evening and spoil our supper?"

He uncrossed his gilt-fringed and beribboned knees and rose to attend Molly. "Besides," he continued, without looking at her. "We have other matters to discuss which do not concern the, hm, lower orders."

Then with proprietary certainty, Benning took the girl's fingers and raised them to his lips. After the first shock of his clammy hand on hers, she successfully suppressed a shiver at his touch, which York noticed but Benning evidently did not.

Expensively schooled to be charming even against her will, she gamely held her pose. Sir Simon accepted her composing sigh for one of fondness and bared his teeth in a near approximation of a smile.

Sir Roger was not content to let the business go. "This is insupportable, and I will not accept it."

York stepped in with his rough grace.

"With your permission, sir, his honor has the right of it. I have submitted my records. The goods will be unloaded, as usual, at your warehouse on Freeman's Wharf in the morning. If you like, you may review the cargo yourself against the manifest shortly after sunup, or you may send your, *ah*, man."

Roger turned on him with a snarl; his hand balled for a fist though Davy over-measured him by a foot and could have stopped the blow without a thought.

"Get out, then, Captain York," he blustered. "But take fair warning. This cannot, and will not continue. Thou'rt reputed to be the best captain in these islands, after Captain Morgan, of course."

Aye, Davy thought, and he's in the Tower.

"See thou maintain that reputation and thy rewards will be rich enough. But do less and not a gentleman in Jamaica will back thee!"

Leaving FitzRobert with the last word, since he would have it, Davy nodded his courtesy, bowed generously to Molly who received it with grace. Then he recovered his hat and turned to the door. With a brief, careful nod to Sir Roger, Will Keaton followed.

They had to listen to Davy's sudden laughter echo from the street as the front door closed behind them. Sir Roger's basilisk glare turned at once on MacBean.

"You, too. Get out," he snapped, and then he turned on Molly. "And as for you, my girl."

"Manners, Uncle. Very poor ones not to have introduced me."

"What?" Taken aback a step. "To a scoundrel like that? The fellow's a privateer and a pirate and no business of yours. The question of manners lies rather with you, I think, than me. Sullen and shut up in your room all day, refusing to come down, even to speak when called for. You abuse the privilege of my house, young woman. I will not have it."

Before she could protest, Sir Simon came timely to her rescue. Timely, for she was unsure how long her pose of repentant innocence would hold.

"You shall not be required to have it much longer, eh Roger? Trust me to tame a spirited wench with a house and babes of her own, eh?"

"Hmph. A wench like this one should be made a mother and soon, I'll warrant. But forgive me, Simon, two marriages and you've yet to show any brats."

Benning waved aside the objection.

"Frail girls both," he said with an air of dismissal. "Alice should never have made the journey from England and, well," he sighed. "No matter. Poor Philly."

Molly shuddered again, this time with something like real fear. Philadelphia Townsend, the second Lady Benning had, rumor said, been beaten to her death, though the incident had been passed off as a carriage accident. Or a series of accidents: a tumble downstairs, a fall from horseback, a reaction to oysters out of season. A singularly unlucky woman, Lady Benning.

"I admit that I overslept, Uncle," said Molly in her smallest voice. "The ball was so very tiring. 'Twas well past midnight when I retired, as you know, and I fear I am too young for so much wine."

She paused to marshal her thoughts, write the next lines, and consider very carefully the next move. "I did speak to Captain Benning last night, as I am sure you know, and I have spent the day in thought. That is, I have turned my mind."

"I should bloody well think so!"

"Roger! The lady!"

"Hmph. Lady indeed," he grumbled, confiding secrets to his friend. "Twice now since she came home we've caught her wandering about the town without so much as a servant. Nasty old clothes, hair blown about, dirty face, looking like a damned gypsy! Went to watch the ships sail in and out, she said. All day, watching the ships sail in and out! Imagine! Oh, but!"

Mid-bluster, he recalled with a shock to whom he confided the scandal. "But you will keep a tight rein on her, my dear Simon, I am sure."

It would not be so easy as all that, not at all. Benning had slowly withdrawn his hand and taken a step away, eyeing her critically. "Oh yes?" A single eyebrow arched with suspicion. "Is that so?"

Molly dropped her eyes demurely and murmured, "I fear me so, Sir Simon." Her hands clenched like a penitent's and she turned upwards a face stricken with humility, on the verge of tears. "I have prayed to be more obedient."

"Perhaps what you need is a proper master," the captain said, his voice subtly transformed. "Or perhaps a turn in the jail."

"What is that, sir!" *Damn.*

"I had not mentioned it, Roger, but my purse was cut today in the high street. There was the common blackguard who took it—and bungled the job, I assure you—and a red-haired wench, his doxy. They ran off together and disappeared somewhere near Huggins Street. There's no way to be certain, of course, but I thought it was the wench who led the way."

"Strike me, sir, you can't mean my niece!"

"Captain!" Molly protested, pouting with disappointment that he should think such a thing of her, even as the blood left her face. "You cannot mean me." It was unjust, indeed. Assuredly she had not led the way!

"Aye, Mistress," came the weedy sneer. "I do indeed mean you. I did not know you then in your filthy lightskirt guise, but I can see that dirty face in yours. As plainly as I see your harlot's hair!"

Something snapped and the words "You bloody liar!" were out of her mouth before she heard what she was saying. She had been prepared to give in, with compromises, to what was clearly the only course, and now even that was closing to her! Was it beyond salvage?

"Forgive my language, please, Uncle. It appears I spent too much time last night in vulgar company! But, upon my honor, this is the most terrible lie."

"And I think me you have no honor to swear on, Mistress."

"Benning! This is outrageous! In my own house!"

"Yes, Roger, in your own house." The colorless eyes narrowed like a viper's. "Tell me, sir, are you certain this is your sister's child, not some gypsy in borrowed manners and stolen finery?"

"Uncle!" One slippered foot stamped in fury. This was totally out of hand! "This is nonsense. Neither of you can believe this! You must not! Whatever you saw, sir, it was not I!"

"How long you will continue to harbor this bawd in your house, Sir Roger? A common street thief, the consort of every low sort of cutpurse and coney-catcher!"

"Uncle, please." Her voice went low and desperate. "Sir, this is madness!"

She had been prepared, even eager for discovery, but not for this. What had Prentiss brought her to?

FitzRobert glared at her with revulsion.

"Aye, she is my sister's child, indeed. In nothing more certain than in this. We have tried every way to break her, but the pernicious influence is too strong. There is the taint, as well, of her father. But this is a family matter, my friend. I must tell you to leave this to me, and ask that you speak of it to no one."

But Benning would not be so easily quieted. Scorn wrote itself in every line of his narrow frame, overriding the foppery of his clothes.

"Whom should I tell, in sooth! To whom should I admit this outrage, this exquisite shame, that I should have contracted myself and the honor of my name to a practiced whore. How can I? How?"

Thin lips rimmed with white, he gripped his expensive walking stick as if to bring it up for a blow. He managed instead to say, "Oh leave I shall, have no fear. I shall not return. Perhaps when this disease has been cut away from the body of your house we may speak again. Sir Roger."

The folly of it all felled her. Overwhelmed, her knees gave way and she sank to the paisleys of the carpet in billows of lavender silk, tears spilling at last against her will. This was not what she had planned. Not what she meant. She was ruined—actually ruined!—and for something that was not even her fault!

It was Prentiss's fault, Prentiss's foolishness that had wrecked her, and he'd not so much as share the blame. This time there would be no rescue, no timely doorway, nor friendly tavern keeper. No clever plan. Every avenue was blocked, every window boarded up. Her anxious foreboding increased as it became clear that the only sound in the room was her own friendless weeping.

But Roger FitzRobert was not a man moved to pity by a young girl's tears. Not, especially, this young girl. Glaring over her, his face a blotched mask of loathing, he growled, "Are you finished?"

It was too much, all this; simply too much. Since a thick, pale, and uncomfortable dawn—when no one she knew could have warned her, no more than she would have listened—the day had filled with contradictions had sizzled like wild beeves on the buccan fire. And now tedious, mundane as dishwater, all this. The horror was not, in the end, at all what she expected.

Perhaps she was indeed no more than a silly little girl, out of her depth in the dark. She was only seventeen, for the love of Christ! How at seventeen could she presume to know the world, to out-plan, out-think, out-face those charged with her good order?

"I said, have you finished with your vulgar play-acting?"

Unmanaged, ungoverned, and not quite sober, somehow control asserted itself and the tears subsided. Breathing steadied, she brushed tears aside with the back of a slender hand and raised her head, prepared to flinch.

"Get up, you slut!" Roger snapped. "Get up, I say, damn you." His own beringed fingers wrapped vise-like around her upraised arm and he dragged her up.

Her feet caught clumsily in the folds of her skirts, and she fell back, tripping. Sensing rebellion, the back of his other hand laid flat across her face, spinning her against the wall as he loosed his hold. She cried out with shock and sudden, overpowering anger, and at least she was standing.

"I have warned thee, wench. I have given thee every advantage, every honor, been more than tolerant of thy wickedness for thy poor mother's sake and forgiven thee God knows a hundred times. But this is how I am repaid! I have taken a serpent to my bosom, loved it as a father, tried to teach it to unlearn the evil."

"No!" No hope, no reprieve, and no further need to submit. Enough dissembling. She lashed out: "No! Not evil!"

"Aye, the evil of her parents lives on. My own sister, that sad, sinful girl, debauched by that brute September. And now look at you, as much a whore as she. And I would have given thee to my friend, a decent husband, thou ungrateful baggage. To my own friend."

"I would never have married him," she hissed, her back still to the wall. "I will never marry him. I'd rather die."

"If you like." The implication was ominous. "You may have time to consider that choice, my girl. Or to wish you had. Because by God, I have a contract with Sir Simon Benning, and I will increase the dowry, have you beaten, or whatever I must do to hold him to it. But I will have you married and out of my house before the week is done!"

"Never! The law says you cannot force me!"

"Oh now she pleads the law, does she? Have no fear my girl," FitzRobert said ominously. "The law will break thee if I cannot. Or I'll see you dead before I'll let you spoil my plans. And until then, I'll have y' locked away till y'learn to obey! And y'may cry down the house with your complaints, my girl, I'll have none of it!"

He came toward her again, clearly intending to haul her away. She screamed, and raised clenched fists, prepared by her misery. She would fight him if he touched her. She would make him pay. And as she turned, her near hand fell on the alabaster box of pins Henrietta kept with her embroidery.

She snatched it up and would have thrown it, pins and all, but he was too close. His hand fell across hers like iron.

"Nay, none of that, you witch. You've spit needles enough at me today. I'll have no more." He struck her face again, this time with the flat of his palm. She screamed again, so he hit her again, less gently. "Quiet, I say. Ruthven! Geoffrey!"

Two huge footmen scuttled in from wherever such thugs lurked, waiting for orders.

"Here!" FitzRobert said, and flung the girl into their hands. "Take this wild cat up to her room. I want her locked in—and bring me the key! And as for you, girl, when you've had time to examine your memory, we'll discuss what you really did today. And how much you charged for it!"

But Molly found her voice stopped along with her tears, choking on fury and unalloyed hatred. There was no hope and no outlet, but she would not accept the defeat. She would speak no more, think no more, save how to claw a way out of this fix. The rage smoldering in her jade eyes said all she would for now. Color high, red curls all awry like no lady she had ever seen, she allowed herself to be led away.

5

LET NEVER WEATHERBEAT'N SAIL

DICK PRENTISS WANTED no part of the company that reveled at the Saracen's Head, but he wanted the oblivion that came with them, and Harry wouldn't throw them all out in any case, so there was nothing to be done. He didn't want a woman either, though his dark brooding created more offers than ever. If he wanted anything at all, it was to hit something, or somebody. To feel something shatter under his hand—bone, wood, or glass, it made no matter. So far no one had obliged him with an idle remark that he could take amiss.

He sat instead in the same old place in the smoky gloom with Jesse leaning over him pouring yet another tot of rum. Her warm dusky scent lingered even after she had moved on, though it had to be said she had been holding her breath while she poured. Bathing had not been high on his list these few days.

He sighed for the hundredth time, or was it more, and made himself stop in mid-breath. Archie Half-hand, the beggar, was rattling in one ear about his own exploits with women, which were, at the least, imaginative. Prentiss tried more or less to pay attention though for three nights running now, he had found the subject of women increasingly irritating. What was so irresistible about women anyhow, he wondered.

"An' belike it's boys yer fond of then, eh Prentiss?" Archie chuckled out of a long-ago broken jaw, throwing in a mighty elbow to the ribs for punctuation. "Eh? Eh?"

But Dick's really quite nice face wrinkled in confusion. Just a moment ago the conversation had involved a bearded lady and a dwarf. "What?"

Archie thought that an even better joke than the first. "What's so great about women, sez Prentiss! Ye sick, lad? French disease, eh lad?" The invading elbow again.

"That's enough, man. Lay off."

"I thought that's what you was doin', Prentiss. Layin' off! Hark now, my lads, I think me our Prentiss is in love!"

That did it. On his feet, rum spilt, temper alight, this would do. "Right!" he said over the low laughter and a double handful of the old man's shirt. "I said, that's enough, Half-wit!"

The room came to an abrupt silence, set off by the scuffle of benches pushed back and the intimations of a fight. He took a breath, then another, and the urge to bash this particular face passed. He put the peddler down more easily than he had picked him up.

"Sick, aye." He nodded, distracted, as though seeing the room for the first time in days. "Aye, that's it."

He disengaged the filthy shirt from his clenched fingers and by force of will relaxed the raised fist before he could do further harm to the poor bastard, who was still cringing and grinning like a dog. "Sorry."

"All's well, Prentiss lad. All's well, aye. Ye've been poorly, like, a couple days. But it don't mean nothin'. All's well." The rattling went on, as meaningless as before.

And all Dick could see was red hair and green eyes dimly aglow in twilight, and a haunting smile. Then as suddenly as he had risen, he threw a coin to the table and pushed away. Jesse, two tables down, looked up in silent dread, trying to smile as he marched toward her. Three nights now. Four, and all the same.

He hardly looked at her as he snatched her wrist and, with only a moment spared to let her put down her tray, dragged her away. He flung another coin in the direction of the bar. Harry Driscoll snagged it out of the air and nodded. Then the tavern noises closed again around them.

"Aw Prentiss, not now," Jesse said piteously. "It's so busy down here, and all the lads in from the ..."

"I won't keep you long, love, I promise. It's just—" He stopped, not quite knowing what he wanted "just".

The obvious thing, of course, but something else. Or someone else. But he pulled her upstairs anyway, saying no more.

In her own little room, Jesse marked with passing pride the silver comb and the looking glass he had given her, and the lacy petticoat too good to wear, from one of the *Jealous Mary's* lads just arrived. In fact, since coming home, all Capt. York's lads had been pleasantly generous and almost sweet-tempered, but for that scowling foreigner they called the Turk and one or two of his pals. She shuddered at the thought and shut the door.

"So then, love. Here we are."

Aside from the first intimations of rain at the window, a rumble of thunder, and Prentiss's harsh breathing, up here above the crowds all was silent. He leaned her against the door, and his arms closed around her, the hands urgently caressing. He kissed her lips lightly, and the hollow of her throat, and buried his face between her tired breasts. In a moment, of habit, the nipples were hard and the coarsened skin already gooseflesh under his touch.

And then, as for the last three nights, he stopped. Just stopped, as if waking from a dream remembering who and where he was, and worse: who she was not.

With a ragged sigh he pressed his head to her shoulder, and said yet again, "Damn."

In the long silence, she put her arms around him for sympathy, but even that was too much. He shivered slightly.

"No," he said and pushed himself away. "Look, Jess, I'm sorry."

The voice, cracking, betrayed him and he could hardly meet her eyes, tarnished brown instead of emerald. He pressed a silver sixpence into her hand anyway, wrenched open the door, and flung himself out in some mood that was not panic, not that, of course not.

He had a room of his own to go to at the top of the house, so he went to it feeling impossibly alone, which was stupid. The whole business was stupid. Shut away by himself, no one would know just how stupid, and useless and stupid and impossible... and... and stupid... *Bloody hell!*

He closed his own stout door behind him, shaking as if with a fever. The little place was small but sufficient: a narrow bed and a chair, a bottle of brandy; a book; a candle to read it by; even a window with a narrow view of the sea. Lonely, yes, but it would do. God damn, it would do, wouldn't it?

Throwing off his coat and boots, he flung himself to the bed with the brandy and a book his eyes wouldn't track, especially after he threw it across the room. And then there was nothing for company but the brandy and the cloudy image of Molly September, and the sound of her winsome laughter tickling his mind. The last line of a song someone had been bleating earlier kept running round his head:

...I break the hearts of half the world,
And she breaks mine.

Stupid song.

Maybe, he thought with something like despair. Maybe that old bugger in the common room was right. Maybe he was in love. If love were a loathsome disease, he had all the symptoms. But that was ridiculous. No woman had ever made a fool of Dick Prentiss, and none was likely to now.

Of course, he'd never failed with one before either, without being blind drunk. This incapacity, if that's what it was, was a temporary inconvenience, no more. It wasn't as if he was ever going to see the green-eyed bitch again. Was he?

The edge of a storm just skirting the island broke over the sandy spit of land that supported Port Royal. It rained all night and all the day after.

He lay alone in the tangle of his thoughts until the drenching heat, unrelieved by tropical rains, turned his room to a lime kiln rendering nothing but evil dreams, and sleep was no more than a sweat-soaked longing. Exhausted but oddly settled, he indulged in a shave and changed his shirt, and finally trotted downstairs, clear and focused for the first time in days.

Congratulating himself on his recovery, he took care to look about him first, charting the waters as you might say before committing to the voyage. From the second landing he had altitude enough to survey the room, hazy with tobacco smoke and other fumes, and when all seemed well, he jogged down the last steps, his senses all in tune.

The regulars were there of course, one or two already dizzy with Driscoll's watered rum and cheap wine. A few of the *Jealous Mary*'s crew, as well: that was a good sign. Likely they'd been here all along, he thought with mild irony. And he just hadn't noticed. In any case, he'd come to certain conclusions during the night, but the one face he wished for in particular seemed absent. Soon enough remedied.

A huge laugh roared out of a murky corner and bellowed his name.

"Prentiss, there you are, ye light-fingered bastard! And not before time!"

"Captain!"

And there was Davy York, beaming and vulgar and grinning like unrepentant sin, snugged up tight between two under-dressed street girls, one of them not a day above thirteen.

Prentiss pushed through the smoky press to clip his captain in a massive embrace.

"God's death, man," said Prentiss with real pleasure. "I have longed to see your face!"

"And I yours, my lad. And I yours, let me tell you! Jesse, lass, bring that bottle here! And you, my lad, you owe me a drink."

Dick swore and straddled a chair, his whole face lit up with eagerness. "Strike me, but it's good to see you!"

"And you lad. Where's that friend of yours, that Jimmy Fitts, eh?"

"Does he tell me? Working, I guess."

Davy nodded sagely, and winked. "That's the Presbyterian in him. He'll get rich."

Jesse arrived, red-eyed, the strain of the long day already showing.

"Good girl!" Prentiss grinned as she poured. And when she turned away, gave her backside a hearty whack.

She twitched because it was part of her job, rolled her eyes, and kept walking.

"And look at you, clean shaved, bathed and smelling of sandalwood. And just as I was gettin' easy with that beard!"

Davy took it all in almost soberly, nodding blithely.

"New sweetheart, eh? Last time you were so hot over a lass was, ah, let me see…"

Prentiss winced. "Madam Serena's, some while past, as you well know. Christ, Davy, you should be buying the drinks!"

The captain's eyes narrowed, crinkling just at the edges with humor. "What I owe you for that little game won't be paid in rum, my lad."

Prentiss scoffed easily. "A joke, and you know it. There never was as much danger as Jimmy and I *tried* to get you into, and only fair, considering how you left us in Aruba. Not to mention the profit you took."

Davy brightened instantly.

"Aye, that I did. And ye'll buy your old captain another drink in memory of the times, and to pay for leaving me in the cellar while you burnt down the best shugging house in the Leeward Islands!"

Prentiss chuckled, shook his head with recollected mirth, and flipped a couple of bright doubloons on the table.

"At least it was a wine cellar."

Davy carried on.

"And at least it wasn't raining. I can't sail till this cursed weather lifts and while I'm at it, tell me where the name o' the risen Christ have you been? It's a twelve-month since I've seen you, here or anywhere."

"Then we've missed each other," Dick shrugged. "Here, mostly, working the ladies, and the odd bit sleight of hand."

"Y'mean an odd hand on a slight bit?"

Davy had been drunk for a long time. In fact in the four days since the confrontation with old Fitz, he had spent mostly winding from grog shop to grog shop—a slender challenge in a town built on little else but taverns, brothels and gaming houses—and his humor was at its height.

Prentiss had little appreciation for its finer points just now. He laughed anyway. "It comes easy enough, and it makes them happy enough."

"Not their husbands, I warrant, eh?"

"Ah no, and there's the pity. They should appreciate me more for the service I do 'em. But that catch has gotten old: sweet-talking matrons for the charge of a new hat. You start feeling sorry for the plain ones and caring for the pretty ones." All the more so when they had red hair. That thought he shook aside.

Davy winked and took another pull at his rum, drained it and called for more. "Landlocked too long, that's your problem, my old lad. You belong at sea. It's your natural element. Ah now, no argument. You know it's true."

"Exactly!" Prentiss pounced on the idea with an excitement that startled even himself. His brilliant idea, so promising in the sleepless shadows before dawn, could only take real shape in his captain's hands. "Just so. Man, it's been more than a year, but I swear…"

Davy winced. "Lots more than a year, my son. Two years, no, three Since we got back from Panama."

For a moment a shadow stumbled into their good humor, but he waved it off. "But 'tis a shame! Shame on ye! And you the best pilot I ever sailed with."

It wasn't entirely true, as they both knew, but it would do for flattery. Thoughtful, Davy scratched over the stubble of this morning's shave. "But aye, being as you're so nice with the ladies and all, maybe you've lost your touch for the wind?"

"I could lose *you*, ye bastard," said Prentiss, no longer so willing to be offended. "Try and catch me!"

"And the ladies?"

"Lost already. Captain mine, the only lady I fancy is called *Mary*, and a damned jealous bitch she is, as you well know."

"She is that, aye."

Expansively, the captain called for more rum, flinging one of Dick's doubloons towards Jesse, and fingering the other one lightly. Then he licked the greasy coin, and turning to the older of his girls, pressed it to her cleavage where it stuck like a Carnival jewel.

"Here, darlin'," the captain said, and kissed her off his lap. "Betake your two selves to dinner whilst we talk business. There's a good lass." He kissed the younger one too, and sent them away cheerful, then leaned in toward his pilot, as quiet as a thought. "Now look you, there is some other wench, isn't there? Eh, lad? I've been hearing things."

Prentiss met the boozy question with his own dead sober restraint. "Do you need a pilot or not?"

"Oh aye, no question. I've just lost Sym Daniel to a Spanish bullet."

"That is a sore loss. He was good!"

"Aye, and Denny Valmont's staying behind. Going to grow sugar cane, he says! So I do need you, true enough. But I need the whole man, lad. Not half a heart left behind in some wench's pocket."

"There's no wench has me in her pocket," Dick snapped. "Not now, not ever."

"Nay," said Davy, sitting back easily. "I can see that, right enough."

What did York know about it anyway, and what business was it of his?

"Ye'll see what ye like, but 'tis as I say, damn it. Besides," Dick grinned, suddenly sunny. "Have you looked at Jesse? A pleasant, bouncy lass but, Davy! After Madame Serena?"

From the roar of laughter that followed, Dick knew he had successfully misdirected his captain's probing, as he might mislead a Spaniard across a foggy reef. And as surely as the Spaniard's imminent demise, he had a victory over Davy York. Now, if only he were sure what he'd won. This called for another drink.

Davy only continued to laugh and recalled his girls who'd not, after all, gone very far, though the coin had disappeared. He offered the younger one to Dick, who gracefully declined explaining that his taste ran to ladies whose charms were fully-grown. The child actually pouted, then swore at him and flounced away.

"To the ladies all!" Davy called, raising his glass and his quarterdeck voice. "A bad lot, the lot of 'em, bless their tiny hearts."

"And to *Jealous Mary*," Prentiss added. "God save all tarts." Half the room rose with a roar in his echo. Aye, the company of good fellows without a ribbon amongst 'em, and his proper work to do again! That should get the bitch out of his head for good and all. "Christ, I have been ashore too long!"

"Damn me for a ducat if that's not truth!"

That settled, they got down to serious drinking.

The squally afternoon passed into drippy evening and thence to muggy night. At some point, plates of stew appeared in front of them which they fell on with a will. Prentiss recalled but failed to mention that he had eaten almost nothing for three or four days. Davy was, in fact, aware.

They talked some and laughed a good deal, entertaining each other and half the room with tales of their exploits, suitably embroidered, as Prentiss rediscovered old friends whose numbers grew as the night reclaimed Port Royal.

Then someone started the concertina going round, it's wheezing growing better or worse by turns. They were oiled enough to sing eventually, and did so, prompting each other for the words at need.

Most of the girls drifted in and out more than once. And in between the japes, Dick and Davy sat head to head, repairing the state of the universe and plotting its overthrow. Jesse came back once looking tired and wanly cheerful, but Prentiss never saw her.

The night proceeded to disintegrate, until some soggy lad from the crew of the *English Testament* stumbled in from the street and failed to negotiate the steps hidden in the blue murk, and fell into the concertina. Someone cheered. The box being in the hands of Black Tom Dougherty, one of York's men, this was not taken at all well. There came a bawl of filthy names and a scraping back of tables and a garbled shout. Curses began to fly, then furniture, and the brawl was on.

Dull-witted, Prentiss had begun to wonder what had, indeed, become of Jimmy. "Bloody damned fusty-, fustyilarian, never a-around when you need him," he muttered, turning one veteran combatant idly over a table. He and Davy moved instinctively into battle mode, though neither could actually stand without the support of the other. "Damned ir-, iresp-, damned rude not to be here for a fight."

Archie went down hollering, dragged from the staircase by a pair of hairy hands. One of Davy's girls shrieked and dived under the table that half collapsed on her when some drunken sailor fell through it from above.

At Dick's back, York said not a word, but grinned exultantly through clenched teeth as each blow found its target. The luck may have been in the others being as drunk as he was, but no matter. It was a satisfying end to a troublesome shore leave.

Then a space cleared around them, and a moment to breathe. Prentiss began to feel dangerously sober, and his knuckles were bleeding.

"Ho Prentiss! Hey!" someone called, but too late. Just as his head was clearing, two men launched at him from opposite angles. He took one out with a well-placed fist, but the other completed the tackle.

"Jimmy?" he shouted. "Here!"

A joint stool crashed over his head, and Dick Prentiss's days ashore were over.

It turned into a riot, of course. The city watch should have broken it up, but some of its members were already involved, and the rest seemed to be away at their own party in some other part of the town.

In the end, uniforms arrived from Fort James. Muskets were fired, flames put out, and the entire room rounded up and shuffled off through muddy streets to the moist, tubercular jail hard by the turtle pens.

The causes of the business were of small interest to the soldiers or their officers, and in fact, to the participants. It was only clear that the crews of rival privateers had spent their drinking money in the wrong public house, for most of them ended the night behind bars, instead of leaning on them.

6

TO THE VIRGINS, TO MAKE MUCH OF TIME

PRENTISS SURFACED FROM a nightmare of fuzzy lightning and muffled thunder to a curiosity. The tender head with the tender lump round as a fresh goose egg turned out to be his own, and that made no sense, no sense at all. Twigs of filthy straw poking through the linen of his new shirt helped convince him otherwise. With a shivering moan, he rolled upright to peer blearily about him.

A low exclamation burst like wheezing cannon fire over his ears. "You!"

He moaned again, covering his head, and tried to roll away from the sound.

"Here, Jailer! Turn this one over. Let me see the villain's face again."

More booming, no sympathy.

Turning away only made it worse. He seemed to be bruised nearly everywhere a man could be both bruised and living. Nothing broken though, he mused with a certain analytical detachment. No pain sharp enough. All dull.

Interesting.

"Here, you. On yer feet!"

A different thunder, more bear-like, if bears were ever drunken and stupid and left in charge of prisoners, interrupted his analysis. A steel-toed boot by chance connected sturdily with the one spot on his body not already offended.

Pain! Yes, that was sharp enough to be pain. A hand seemed to hold him partly suspended but braced, apparently, against a wall. Then a narrow, powdered face swam into his hazy range of vision. Its smirk would not have been a pleasant sight even had it not been framed in the glossy black curls of a fashionable wig.

"Well, well, Master Cutpurse. We meet again."

Prentiss's brain took the face and the words at equal value with the fact that it was daytime and the jailer's breath stank of cheese. He stared, owlish and uncomprehending, at his accuser.

"Hmm?"

"You are a sorry excuse for a thief, are you not? I suppose you've spent all my money by now? Whatever you did not fling all over the square."

Still nonsense. Prentiss blinked. "What?"

"Come, come, man. Surely you remember our merry chase through the town the other day. Who's the coney now, my fine coney-catcher?"

He tried to shake away the cobwebs, but they were the only thing that held him at anchor. His brain, belike, had come loose in his head; shaking only batted it about inside his skull, which hurt like the devil. Had the fellow said money? Merry? Molly?

"Molly, eh?" The feral grin thinned mercilessly. "I knew it. The little slut thought to make a fool of me."

No wait! That was wrong. Dick tried to pull the warping edges in, and make the face resolve. Oh yes. Molly's bloody bridegroom. Definitely not a friend. Sweet Molly. A low groan of comprehension and utter gloom escaped him.

"Ah," said Benning, straightening. "Recognition, at last. That's enough, jailer. Keep the others out of trouble until Sunday morning. Their captains may ransom them after morning prayers."

"And this 'un, sir?"

"You can drop him, now. He'll swing soon enough, never fear."

Released, Prentiss hit the straw like a new kitten, disturbing a rat and several million fleas.

It was Saturday night again before Prentiss woke from anything like normal sleep. His body was one painful, bruised ache and he felt he ought to apologize to somebody, maybe Davy, or some girl, until he recognized the nagging remorse for the hangover it was. His memory when it came was in grand shape, though. The fighting, the soldiers, the jail were all in place, ornately framed for emphasis. Even that slimy toad, Benning. Christ, what foul luck.

Hanging, eh?

He turned the thought over thoroughly. No. His head still banged like an old anvil, but he definitely did not want to die. Not that he was afraid of death. That was a terror long dispensed with. But not hanging, no. Too undignified.

So where was Jimmy, damn it? Or slippery Davy, who had somehow managed to stay out of this pesthole. Where was the damned rescue party? God, he was thirsty.

He found the energy at last to look about him, sizing up the situation. A cell to himself. Condemned for sure. Iron bars in a tiny window at just about eye level inside was just above gutter level outside. Jimmy Fitts would practically have to lie in the mud to talk to him. He hoped it had stopped raining.

The straw on the floor was rancid and old, home to fleas and better not to think what else. The walls were scratched and scrawled over, drawn upon in the lampblack that stained the upper corners. The whole place had not been on the right side of healthy in some years, by the smell, and *Christ!* The stink!

Fully awake now, the physical pressures began to gnaw at his consciousness: hunger, a raging thirst, and a desperate need to piss. The slop bucket in the corner was mercifully empty. That pressure relieved, he could concentrate on suppressing the others. Well, he'd been hungry before. And hung over. Probably not this badly hurt at the same time, though the damage did seem superficial. What would Molly think to see him now?

A thin smile pressed across his face at the thought of her. He tried to ease into a more comfortable position on the floor. Would she laugh, tell him it was only his due. Might she weep over his poor battered body? That would be nice, but not likely. Especially if she understood the battering had come after three days—no, four—of trying without success to forget her in debauchery.

A man could do worse, he considered, than to have a pretty wench as his last thoughts. The honey smell of her hair, the bright spark of her eyes, the nearness of her body there in the dark, hiding from that puking pox-ridden worm Sir Simon bloody Benning. And her spitfire nerve. He sighed. Christ, he was thirsty!

Then, a scuffling sound outside and a face hunkering down to the barred window: "Prentiss?"

"Jimmy!" Better than last thoughts of a red-haired wench would be a friend with the jailer's key.

"Hey-ho! Still alive, then?" Fitts's whisper held a touch of wry amusement.

"Aye, and small thanks to you. Where've you been?"

"Right here, mostly. You've been half-dead. You ever try to rescue half a corpse?"

"I got you out of Folkstone, didn't I?"

"Aye, and not let me forget it since. But at least I was awake for most of it."

"Then it's your turn, lad, to set things right, and I'll never mention that other time again."

"It won't be easy. I need help."

"Then get Davy. We'll put to sea when the tide turns tomorrow night. It is Saturday, isn't it?"

"It is. But you're not to count on Davy."

Dick's face, giddily cheerful, blanched. Why was everything so stupid? "What do you mean?"

Jimmy was shaking his head. "On our own, captain said, or he can't use us. Well, you. I still haven't decided if I need to go back to sea. Life is fine and dry ashore, and the food's better. More girls."

"Damn it, Jimmy, you're blathering. I've got to get out of here. They're going to hang me."

"Not for brawling," Fitts protested.

"Of course not! No, I fumbled a toff's pocket the other day. Showing off for that bloody redhead. But not just any toff, oh no. One of the girl's famous suitors. And the bastard's been in and named me. The rest will be let go tomorrow morning when Davy and the Preacher come to claim 'em, but I'm to be hanged in the interest of English bloody justice!"

Jimmy's expression did not seem to alter. "I see. It's that girl's fault either way, then. That's the trouble."

"You're still not making sense."

"You heard me. Davy says it's her fault yer here. Says she's thrown yer timing off. Ye were slow an' stupid, he says, and he's not sure he can use you unless you do something about her first."

"But I never said anything about her. He didn't … You faithless bastard, you told him!"

Jimmy never flinched. "Start shouting and I'll have to leave thee here, mate."

Bewildered yet again—it had been an awful day—Prentiss sank to the moldy straw in plain despair. Though every movement ached, he ran agitated hands through his long hair, disconnectedly wishing he could bathe. The silence grew until he thought Jimmy must have gone away after all. "Jim?"

"Aye?"

"Maybe she'd help."

"D'ye think?"

"Not a chance. She isn't like the others, man. So I had to drop her. Pretty hard."

Realization dawned. "Sweet Jesus, man, ye're in love with her!"

In the gloom, Prentiss shrugged. "Don't be an idiot. She's a little girl."

"Rafe's little girl," said his friend. Then there was all that silence again, and this time Fitts had gone.

While Prentiss abused his freedom till he lost it, Molly chafed at her captivity. Three days later she was still pacing. By Saturday evening she had measured the length of her room uncounted times, trying not to wring her hands or any other such insipid, girlish thing. The pacing continued, furious and useless.

With a rustle of polished linen and Flemish lace, she flung herself into a chair and picked up a leather bound book from the night stand. When Mr. Herrick's lines only swam before her, she threw it down again. Drummed fingers on the chair arm. Went to the dressing table and jerked open the drawer.

Her father's dirk gleamed again in its oiled wrapping as she drew it out. It balanced cool and neat in her hand, though the blade was as long as her forearm. That was it! She could kill him! With a little flip, it turned in her fingers and stabbed into the walnut veneer brought all the way from England.

"Now pull it straight back out or you'll snap the point," said a smooth Cockney voice behind her.

Swift as thought, she snatched up the dagger—pulled straight out, aye—and whirled to face the window. Against the candlelight, the windowed corner was all in shadows. A man, but not Prentiss.

"There are people in the house. I can scream."

Lazily, Fitts threw his long shanks in over the window seat. "If ye'll put down the knife, I'll be telling why I've come."

"Stand where you are. I know how to use this."

"Aye, Miss, I expect you do."

"I suppose you're Uncle Roger's twisted idea of a joke?"

He sighed heavily, automatically sizing up the furnishings for resale. "And I suppose th'art going to talk all night when I have news for thee."

"I said stand where you are! No. Move into the light. I can't see your face. Now. Who are you?" she said again when he had slipped into the circle of lamplight, unknown.

"I hate talking to drawn steel myself," he said softly. What was the distance between them? Close enough to talk, but far enough for safety. "I'll tell Prentiss his message went unspoke because of that."

"Prentiss!" His name clanged in her blood, but she snapped back angrily. "What's Prentiss to do with anything?"

"Put the knife down, eh?"

"Oh, all right!" she fairly shrieked, then jammed the knife back into its sheath and slapped it down flat, within reach.

"Better, lass, better. Now listen. D'ye happen to know where the lockup is, down by the dockside. 'Cause that's where ye'll find him tonight."

"What?"

"Poor bastard's got himself arrested for brawlin', and some officer tagged him as cutting purses in market. And leading him a fine chase besides. There's talk of hanging, see, and he's a mite nervous."

"No!" She had no intention of caring, she didn't care, how should she care. "I mean, what is that to me? What's a common street thief to me except the ruin of a night's sleep and my reputation?"

"He had some notion," Fitts went on. "That you might help to get him out."

Good God! And wasn't that the maddest thing she'd ever heard! "Ha! Help him? If I had any mind to help him, how could I? I'm as much a prisoner as he is."

"Ye might have some pity on the lad, then, since the officer that pinched him had some hard words for you besides."

"Sir Simon, I'll warrant, that swine," she spat. Her fine nose wrinkled in distaste. "If it was him you wanted help with, I'd gladly ... "

"Aye, well, they mean to hang our Prentiss, see, on this fella's say-so."

Her eyes went wide as her skin went cold. "Hang?"

She startled a look up at his drawn, pox-scarred face. Somewhere in that hard exterior was loyalty, devotion to his friend, as well as impatience with a recalcitrant female. That loyalty spoke to her of an affection she understood and longed for.

"He is your friend," she asked softly. "Isn't he?"

He shrugged. "We're mates. We've sailed together. I've pulled him out of the fire before. So what?"

"We're not even friends. I don't even like him. But still…" Still, as she spoke, she began to see the bits of a plan swarm into shape. "I might just owe him something. And maybe…"

The thought trailed into silence. Finally she tugged at the satin ribbons that laced across her dressing gown. When Jimmy did not turn his eyes away, she snapped, "If you please, Master …"

"Fitts. Jimmy."

"Well, Master Fitts, I can't very well go running about Port Royal in this, can I? If you want my help, you'll have to let me change. In private, if you please."

A lopsided grin seamed his ravaged face. "I'll wait below. By the gate. Look you hurry, though," he said, and disappeared as he had come.

Finally, her energy had useful purpose, sent her flying around the room gathering up supplies. An old shift whose pleated sleeves ruffled at her elbows. The rest of her street costume from days before, freshly laundered to her Aunt's dismay. A dark hood to mask her traitorous hair; and a battered straw hat. Too warm for a cloak, she settled on a scarf for her throat, against the damp.

In a pocket of the gown she tucked the little bag of coins cached in the back of the dressing table, and a comb, just in case. And her father's dirk, of course, hiding in the folds of the skirt.

She threw a last glance back at poor Marjorie's wistful portrait, then tricked open the door. Somewhere on the far side of the house, Uncle Roger was engaged in his customary late-night debate with his dinner companions, but their sounds were faint. She slipped down the pantry stairs noiseless in soft shoes.

"Nancy?" she hissed.

No answer from the kitchen wench's alcove under the stairs. Out on the town, eh? Molly smiled bleakly and passed on by. Then she was herself out in the velvet night of Port Royal and Jimmy Fitts, waiting at the door. took the lead.

Anonymous in the evening crowds, they made a way through the torchlit streets and alleyways. Behind even the greatest houses, shapes crept through the shadows, writhing like vipers. Barely seen in the corner of her eye, they disappeared if Molly tried to look directly at them.

The courage she had somehow found in the amber glow of her own room was rapidly sinking into mere foolhardiness as they raced out of some murky alley into brilliant, jangling Huggins Street. It scarcely looked like the same place.

Music and shrill laughter, shouting, and somewhere the crack of pistol shot spilled from the brick and plaster taverns and bawdy houses that lined this end of the muddy avenue. Here was Littleton's, the Blew Bell, the Bull, the Saracen's Head.

The Saracen's Head? "What is this?" Molly demanded, and dragged Jimmy to a halt in a darkened doorway. "I asked you a question, damn you!"

To Fitts, holding her wrist, the sudden stop nearly cost him his footing on the greasy cobbles. "What's the matter with you? Come on."

"What are we doing here? Where is Prentiss really?" she cried over the din. A pair of drunken girls caromed off the wall and into her, then launched back into the street, singing merrily.

"*We three drunken maidens, came from the Isle of Wight!* Nay that is wrong for i'faith, we are but two, Sister! Ho ho, then again, Sister! *We two drunken maidens...*"

"Where is he," she said again.

"In the lock up, like I said. Look here."

Painted signs swung crazily over the doors of the grog shops, stirred by a night breeze that carried green mangrove smells down to the dockside. As Jimmy urged her further on, she swore her objections until she finally understood his purpose. "See?" he said.

The scowling Mussulman of the Saracen's Head swung over darkened windows in its narrow close, though his portrait could hardly be seen for the years of smoke and filth that had disfigured it.

"Proof enough? Like I said. Closed till the Constables get their fee."

Molly edged cautiously past the black hole that gaped where the door had been. The dark within was deep and absolute. She took a deep breath as if to speak, then changed her mind. Nodded.

"Take me to him."

Jimmy had gone this way many times and knew it blindfolded. Down Lime Street, along Curry Lane, through Thames Street and its vast treasure houses, and down to the sea. The late wind here could do little to sweeten an atmosphere redolent of salt sea and tar and rotting rope. Everywhere was the little sound of lapping wavelets and straining hawsers where the great ships rode at anchor.

Then there was Fort James on the near arm of the bay, lowering over the entrance to the harbor like an ogre guarding its hoard, and winking at its brothers Charles and Carlisle at the other two points of the town. The shortest route from here to the lock-up was under the very walls of Fort James's garrison.

They paused at every corner, whispering plans and watching for soldiery before changing streets. But while people passed them from time to time, there came no challenge.

Then all at once their goal was in sight: a squat, ugly building in the tawny local stone half sunk in the ground between the turtle pens and the fish markets, and reeking of both. Only a sullen red glow pretended to light even one of the gutter-level windows, though plenty of light leaked through the venerable seams of the wooden front door.

"There," Jimmy hissed. "Under the red light."

"Dear God, it's a dungeon!"

"Hush! I've seen worse."

"I want to talk to him." Heart in her throat, she started forward, but Jimmy snatched her back.

"Are ye daft? We'll go to the door, like we said."

"What if they've moved him!" she snapped. "What if he's dead? You said you didn't want to rescue a corpse. This has to be worth it."

"But …"

She turned on him, glaring. "It's my plan, we do it my way. Now let go of my arm."

"Right. All right. But you must stay quiet, and let me go first."

She nodded, jade eyes bright with nerves and determination. Then taking a deep breath, Jimmy faded across the unprotected dark, around the puddle of light thrown from the only bright window. His lightly shod feet might never have touched the ground for all the noise he made. Pressed up against the jailhouse, he motioned Molly to follow.

She followed, wondering yet again what she was doing, and cursing her foolishness. Then she was there, standing in a sullen stain of red that oozed from the narrow window at her feet. She waiting, catching her breath, willing her heart to stop pounding.

Below, the sounds of something, or someone, stirring. Jimmy's hand covered hers a moment, a reassuring touch in the chaos, then she was on her knees in the gutter where her uncle said she belonged, peering in at the grate.

"So there you are," she whispered at the familiar silhouette, though the face was shrouded in darkness. A muffled oath, and long fingers, still bruised from fighting, wrapped through the bars. In the shadows and half-light she could barely make out the cobalt glint of his eye.

"Molly, lass! What kept you?"

"What kept me!" all her anger melted away at the sound of his voice. "You ask a girl of nice character to leave her home in the dead of night. On a moment's notice? For you? I'm still in trouble for the last time. Good Lord, Dick Prentiss," she chuckled. "Who do you think you are?"

He reached out for her through the bars and caught her hand where it lay just on the ledge.

"Just a scoundrel in trouble, as always, Sweet," he answered with a confident grin. "And you the very lass to get me out of it again."

"And what makes you think I'm going to help you? After the way you've treated me?"

"Because I'm a great handsome devil and you can't help yourself, that's why. Besides, I'm the man who's going to take you away from all this."

"Oh are you?"

He nodded wisely. "I am that. Just as soon as you and Jimmy help me out of all this. It's half your fault, y'know."

"My fault."

"If you hadn't been so much in my mind I'd have been lighter on my feet. Now go on. Do you two know what you're doing?"

"We do."

"To it, then lass, and we'll laugh about it all in the morning."

"Try not to think ahead more than an hour at a time, all right?"

Before he could say more, she had moved away with a gritty crunch of gravel under foot. The scent of her left him giddy.

"You ready?" Jimmy hissed from a shadow while she positioned herself at the door.

"Aye aye, sir," she said.

Her hair was already tossed and wild from running. She pinched her cheeks and bit at her lips to bring up the color, then drew her shawl over her head to appear the more pathetic. Timidly, she knocked.

"Eh?" A thick voice grumbled within. "Eh, wazzat? You hear something, Bert?"

Oh no, not two of them! She knocked again, more firmly. "Sir? Please, sir, can't you let me in?"

Squat and thick-limbed and going to fat, the jailer who opened the door reeked of ale and sweat and other things less identifiable and far less savory. Molly tried not to breathe.

"Why, what's this?" he said, adding a fruity belch as punctuation. "It's nowt but a lass." As he threw the door wide, she could see that he was alone after all. Drunk then, and talking to himself. Maybe this wouldn't be so hard.

"Aye, sir," she mewed in a very small voice quite unlike her own. "Please, sir, ye've got me poor foolish brother locked up in 'ere, and I've got to see 'im."

Hidden in the shadows beyond the yellow light spilling from the doorway, Jimmy Fitts smiled a thin, uneven smile. Clever girl, and a natural actress.

"Yer brother, is it? There's a lot o' nasty lads locked up here, all right. Ask me, none of 'em 'as got a father, never mind a family."

The rummy guffaw said he thought that quite the cleverest thing he'd hear all night, which it likely was. "Which nasty one might be your nasty brother, then?"

She blinked twice owlishly, and tried to place the accent, while stepping aside as he belched again. Never mind, it didn't have to be perfect. She took a chance and dared to match him, thanking God for a musical ear.

"Oh, he's very tall, sir. And most 'andsome, and his name is Dickon, and he's not at all dangerous. He was just there the littlest while and the Watch came and locked 'im up. And our poor mother only just this hour told what happened. We've been all night worryin' about 'im."

Jimmy's smile broadened against his will, hearing the change. A very clever girl indeed. It might even work.

"Hmph." Bert snuffled, feeling closer to the little girl already. He wiped a filthy sleeve across a dripping nose in fellow feeling and said, "Well, let's see now. Don't recollect no cove called Dickon."

With a terrible cry, she flung herself at his aromatic chest, sobbing horribly. "Oh no! That ain't true. Can't be true! What am I to tell our old mam!"

The black brows knit in confusion. was it a question he should know the answer to? He thought not, but he'd been wrong afore. Still, there was this pretty weeping child practically in his arms. He tried patting her head clumsily to comfort her. "Well, well, well, lass, come in then, come in. We'll let ye look 'em over once."

He motioned her further inside while, with the door still wide open to the night, he grabbed once, no twice, for a ring of iron keys.

A cool touch on her shoulder signaled Molly still as Jimmy stepped in lightly past her. A joint stool scraped slightly as he lifted it overhead. Playing fair, he shouted first:

"Oy, Bert!"

Bert turned in time to watch the stool break across his eyes. A second blow smashed into his shoulder, and he went down with a sigh.

She should perhaps have checked to see if the man was killed, but Molly had already scooped up the keys and a lamp and was running down the narrow stairs to the cells. Most were crowded with buccaneers and other ruffians too cramped and flea-plagued to sleep, and most of those called out to her, whistling and snatching at her skirt as it swept by. Dick stood waiting for her in the very last cell, beaming.

Molly snapped, "If you ask me what kept me, I swear I'll leave you here."

"Just open the door, love, and I swear I'll never say such a stupid thing again."

"Hold the light for me. If I can't turn this key, you may not get the chance." She fought with the rusty lock, pausing only to push the hair back out of her eyes.

"Lean on it, girl. Lean on it."

"*You* lean on it!"

His hand snaked through the bars to cover hers.

"All right, one more time. Push!" With a crunching great noise, the lock gave way to its key and the bars swung open, and Prentiss pulled Molly hungrily into his arms. For a long moment they remained oblivious to the snickers and lewd suggestions of their audience.

A mad longing flamed up in the center of her being as he held her, fiercely still and quiet amid the clamor. With a ragged sigh, too soon, he drew away a little until she was aware and a little frightened of a matching passion in him. Delicately, oh so carefully, he placed one last, small kiss on her mouth, and she was devastated.

Then "Come on," he rasped, and grabbed her hand.

"Hey!" cried all the rest. "You gonna leave us here?"

Prentiss looked back dizzily from the foot of the stairs. "Eh? What for? York'll be here in an hour or so, and the Preacher too."

Jimmy called down from above. "Make haste, down there! No time for chat. The Watch'll be by in a minute."

Prentiss grinned. "See there, lads? No time. Or we'll none of us make it out. Ye'll thank me later."

They had nearly gained the landing when one surly voice rose above the mutter. "Ye'll owe us for this, Prentiss."

"You especially, Turk?" Dick called back gaily.

"Aye, thou whoreson bastard," the Turk snarled in reply, adding something vile in Turkish. "Me 'specially."

Prentiss just laughed and tossed the key ring into the nearest cell.

"If ye scramble, ye can get yerselves out. We're in a hurry." And he vanished with Molly into the light.

Hastily, Jimmy slapped a knife into Dick's hand, which promptly found a home in his boot even as he surveyed the trussed and battered jailer.

"Still alive, eh? Oh that'll hurt proper for a while. Nicely done, Jimmy. Trust me, Molly, he deserved it. Now look, we'd best split up. I'll find us a place to doss for a few hours, then I'll meet you at the *Jealous Mary*."

But Fitts looked doubtful. "What about the wench?"

She blinked, but said nothing.

"I'll worry about Molly. Let's just get out of here." They dove for the streets and the covering dark, but Dick paused one last time to put a hand on his friend's shoulder. "And Jim? Thanks."

"Aye. Again. Now be off." He took the alley to their left and disappeared.

Somehow hours had sped by since Jimmy first appeared in her window casement. Now carelessly, Prentiss took Molly away from the dockside and into the warrens of the inner town. The streets, damp from the cleansing rain, had for a brief time a fresh- washed look in the fugitive light of a late rising moon. The sea chill wrapped Molly's shawl more tightly around her as they walked, till he unlaced his fingers from hers to put his arm about her shoulders. The precious warmth of his body flowed generously into hers, comforting without words.

"Surely we'll be hunted," Molly said at last.

Prentiss smiled easily, though the blue eyes were dull with fatigue.

"We'll not be found. If we run, someone will chase us. As it is, we might be any couple of lovers. Ah, Molly!" he sighed.

He stopped suddenly, pulling her once again into an embrace. Speechless, he clung to her, wishing for words. Eyes squeezed shut against the world, against the pain still throbbing in his head, ribs, and almost everywhere else; against red-gold hair and temptation.

Buried sweetly under his arms, Molly's mind was racing. How she loved the feel of him, the good man smell of him. How hopelessly, in spite of everything, she even loved him! And what then? Lovers, said he? And what was she to do while he sailed away, as her father had done. Have his children and keep his little house, like poor Marjorie? Hardly!

Trying not to think, she could not avoid the thoughts. Finally, she took a deep breath and pushed away just a bit. She thought with frustration how impractical men are. But she said, "We must get off the street, my dear. You've had no sleep, nor have I. You're still hurt. And we have to make some decisions, you and I. 'Twere better done rested."

He met her eyes, lifted a hand to her hair. Then something seemed to rustle behind him, soft. With a low oath, he thrust her aside and kicked out. A knife flew silver from the hand of a man not three paces behind them in the steamy alley. He tumbled on instinct, coming up with his own knife clenched in his fist. Molly too, he marked, had her own dirk drawn and her stance showed her ready, with no girlish squeaks or questions.

In the gutter under the opposite wall, a lump of ragged clothing stirred, raised a bleeding face to the moonlight. Prentiss lowered his guard.

"Aw, Jock," he clucked in disgust as all his bruises sang out in pointless pain. "Don't you ever sleep? It's me, damn it."

A sniveling whine emerged from the grimy party. "Och, Prentiss. 'Tis mortal sorry I am. But how was old Jock t'know, eh? How?"

"Christ Jock, go home! All's well, Sweet," Prentiss said, without another look at their assailant. Knife vanished effortlessly into boot, though a pain sliced down his side with a gasp as he straightened. "You can put that toy of yours away, if you like. And nice work it was too, love. Remind me to ask you, sometime, where you ... Ah! Damn!" Pain crested, then withdrew.

"Prentiss!" O God, don't let him swoon! He leaned heavily against her, his skin clammy and pallid, breath ragged and short.

"Ah, Moll?" he rasped. "We should get inside."

"All right. Where?"

"Here's fine. No one will expect."

"Here?" She looked about in distress, trying not to panic. Between the ordeal in the jail and this latest crisis, he was nearly unconscious, and she was lost. Then she realized, for the second time tonight, that she did know where she was after all. Huggins Street, or an alley way opening into it. It was quieter, less of a riot than it had been earlier, and so hardly looked itself.

The other grog shops were busy with their late night trade, but ten paces away was the dark and boarded up door of the Saracen's Head.

"All right. Prentiss, please, I can't carry you. You'll have to walk." He murmured his agreement, but his body was reluctant. "Dickon! You can't stop now." He was fine just a moment ago! "Come one. Just a little further."

Somehow her cajoling reached him. "Aye aye, stop pushing. I can make it." He dragged in a deep, shattering breath and found from somewhere a surge of energy, though he was mortally tired. With it, he stumbled but did not fall down the stairs to the taproom floor with Molly close behind.

"Did anyone see us?" He propped himself on an overturned bench.

"No one. No, you can't fall asleep yet. Where now?"

Somehow they managed to maneuver through the debris and into a ground floor room with a bed. The place was certainly empty, of humans at least. What other sort of beasts lurked in the walls she hated to think, but there was no better place to go. The room was mostly clean and surprisingly airy, though its one window gave only onto another stone wall across the alley.

It would do for some security. Driscoll's own room, maybe. The sheets seemed almost fresh. Well, that was a blessing and a surprise.

"Dick" she said softly, unwrapping him from her shoulder. God knew she was ruinously tired herself. "Here, sit you down. Now boots off. And your shirt, love, aye. That's better. Ah!"

She gasped at the bruises already yellowing on his shoulders and across his ribs.

"It's nothing, lass, nothing. Nothing broken. Just need to sleep." And with that he rolled onto the flat, sour pillow and lost consciousness.

Molly smiled ruefully, lifting his feet onto the mattress and drawing up the sheet. She loosened her stays and pulled the worn blue dress over her head and kicked out of the petticoats, and collapsed beside him. There was hardly room for two in the narrow frame, so she cradled his head in the hollow of her shoulder and drew closer. She was weary but exhilarated, and sleep would not after all come easily. Then too, she had never shared a bed with a man before.

How wonderful, she thought, wide-eyed in the darkness, that his body should fit so well with hers. Impulsively she brushed back the hair from his cheek and traced a delicate fingertip just across his mouth. His lips twitched in a kiss.

As if burnt, she snatched her hand away. Oh, how stupid, she thought. I've been kissed before. And Armand was always touching me, when he could. And I liked it, too. But…

But she had never lain down beside Armand, never given in to his urgent temptation. This was different. Quite, quite different. Again, her fingers traced the line of his face, combed through the tangle of his long, damp hair. In sleep, he shifted a little, burrowing more comfortably into the warm swelling of her breast. One hand unconsciously reached out to curve around her waist, drawing her closer.

A line of delicious fire danced along her spine. The touch of his hand, the planes and angles of his body on hers were enough to drive her mad, yet she dared not let him wake. Sleep, for now, was more important than any kind of lovemaking.

He moved slightly again. There again! The hard contours of his body against her thigh.

Gingerly, having nowhere else to put her hand, she allowed her free arm to drape across his middle, though she thought at any moment to explode. *There. Not so bad.* She willed her self to shaky control. Shut her eyes and blinked away desperate tears on a shuddering sigh.

I'm still a virgin. Eugénie said it would hurt. I can wait. Armand promised it would be very, very sweet. How can I wait? I shall go mad with waiting. But he is hurt, so hurt. It will wait.

She held him to her until she finally slept as well.

7

A CREATURE OF THE NEW AGE

ONCE UPON A TIME a pretty young widow came from the efficient staff of a country estate in Hampshire to be a nurse in a fine house in the city of London. The house, like the estate, belonged to the Earl of something, Prentiss had long forgotten what, and Jennet Prentiss settled down comfortably to tend to the Earl and his Countess's children. It was a good household, though as many noble houses in those days before Cromwell, inclined to a certain carefree manner.

The earl's younger brother had an eye for a pretty woman and no head at all for strong drink. He courted the nurse shamelessly with flowers, fine ribbons and laces, and the trinkets a young gentleman uses to delight a girl beneath his station but not beneath his notice. He tried to give her money, but that she refused. He wanted to meet her alone, but she tried to avoid him. He even hinted marriage, though his family would as soon have let him marry an actress as the children's nurse.

But Lord Richard was not only persistent, he was very attractive: tall and slim, stylish because it suited him, athletic because it came naturally to him. He had a knack for numbers and a way with words that might have made him a scholar, if a gentleman were interested in such things. His hair, when he left off his fashionable wigs was dark, almost black, and his eyes were unreasonably blue. He did everything with an air of perfect grace, even get drunk. And Jennet Prentiss was, at 20, a widow of two years and a little more, missing the company of a husband. She was not only very pretty, with her pale hair and eyes, but she had been pleasantly married to a man of healthy appetites to match her own. Two years, she felt, was a very long time to be without a man. Finally Lord Richard's face and form, as well as his charming petitions, became irresistible.

Their romance was furtive and nerve-wracking, once it had got underway. A large household affords almost no privacy, and her duties with the children left little time for adult occupations. Too often they met and coupled, then hurried away, she to her work and he to his clubs. When he talked drunkenly of marriage again, she wept for shame. She loved him and even indulged the fancy that he loved her, but there was no hope for them. And then her monthly courses stopped, and the world skidded to a halt.

The Puritan mood was in the air. A pregnant nursemaid could not be tolerated in the nursery, or for that matter anywhere in the household. The Countess was furious, though the Earl seemed no more than amused. In his father's day, he said, they would have married her off to the blacksmith and thought no more about it. But her ladyship would have none of that. Then Lord Richard went away as an officer in the King's doomed fight against Cromwell; Jennet was given a little money and turned out of the house.

She brought up her boy in two rooms by the Thames in Greenwich where the great ships docked, and tried her best to earn a living as a laundress and seamstress. The men she knew sometimes gave her a few coins for the boy, and kissed her merrily. She taught Dick to write and read with some success, and tried to teach him the fine manners she remembered, but he spent most of his time on the dockside talking to the sailors and living by his wits.

When he was 12, he disappeared for a week; he returned with foreign coins in his pocket and sharp new ideas about the stars and the balance of international trade. With his father's agility, he began to learn the pilot's craft, just as his father's light touch had got him pennies to take home to his mother—when he thought to go home. He had his father's charm as well, and eventually found ways of making that pay too.

At 20 or so, he met Jimmy Fitts at the port of Hull in the north, two displaced Londoners in a dockside grogshop where they fought over a girl. By the time Dick had beaten him soundly, the girl was gone with a local chandler. The young men, bruised and staggering, laughed and got drunk together. Almost ten years later, they were still comrades.

None of this occurred to Prentiss as he slipped easily through the morning crowds of Port Royal. He had been living in the streets or at sea all his life, which was why he had no trouble now liberating a purse here and there in the market day throng. He actually paid for the ale, fruit, half a capon and biscuit as well as the featureless breeches and deerskin buff coat in the rag shop for Molly. Just in case. There was a chance, maybe, that he would think of a way to take her with him. And a slimmer chance, he thought, that she would come. Either way, she might need to move about in disguise, however thin.

The day had stayed grey with morning fog, an unpleasant indication of bad weather. Well, that would give them a good wind for Tortuga, even if the clouds passed. The breeze now was damp and warm with a clean sea smell that caught at his senses with an almost sentimental tug, but with a practical one as well. Soldiers seemed to be everywhere, poking into shops and doorways with an urgency far beyond their normal daily rounds, and the grey light cast no shadows in which to hide.

All this trouble just for me? He marveled with a quiet smile. There must be more to Molly's poxy bridegroom than I thought. Or he wants us to think there is.

Carefully, he chose a circuitous route back to Huggins Street.

Either it had been earlier than she thought when they finally found their bed, or she was less tired than she imagined, for Molly awakened before noon. A moment's confusion as her eyes flickered open. The room in which they had sheltered was still mostly grey, little more cheering in the foggy light that filtered in from the alley than it had been by moonlight. But she was certainly not at home, alone, in her own lace-draped bed.

Not alone, no. The warm shape that fitted so comfortably along her body was no girlish dream, no fancy. With a wan twist of her lips that might have been a smile, she turned to look. Curled in the curve of her back lay a large striped cat, purring contentedly.

"No!" she moaned, and bolted upright. Instantly, the cat hopped away. "No, Prentiss. Oh, no!"

Stunned into action, she threw back the blanket and ran on bare feet to the door. "Prentiss!" she cried, though her voice cracked in the echoing vault of the deserted common room. "Prentiss, you lying bastard!"

The Saracen's Head had not changed: tables and benches thrown about; a broken concertina dangling from a cold candle sconce; some blood stains browning in the cracks of the grey stone floor. And no Prentiss. The shock of his absence dragged her awake, twisted her stomach with anger and despair.

Not abandoned. Not again!

Hopeless tears began to well in her eyes, not green now but grey as a stormy sea. The aching muscles and weariness of the night's adventures surged back to underscore the pain of his leaving. Numb with hurt and shame, she stumbled back to the little room and slammed the door behind her with a shuddering bang.

Soldiers in the street heard it but, unable to place a location, paid no mind. Molly fell into the tossed bedclothes and wrapped up in them like a frightened child. Her mind refused to work; only the tears came on without orders. Bit by bit she thought about getting dressed, going home. Or trying to go home. Her uncle would kill her, of course, but that was all right. Yes, certainly, that was all right.

No, wait. Not all right.

After a while she reached for her father's dirk where she had left it by the bedside and drew it out. A beautiful blade, a bright line of fine steel set in a carved round hilt of black briar, capped with silver. She clutched it to her, curled around the pillows. There was some comfort, some courage in Rafe's legacy, but her thoughts still whirled.

If he comes back, I will kill him.

He won't be back. He's gone.

Stupid. You knew he would be.

They cannot disown me. I have my own money, my inheritance. I will claim it. I will marry George Alcott … no! Jack Rhetford. I shall claim my fortune, and I will have my own house, and they will not be able to stop me.

Her chin set with determination under eyes lighted with passion. Her hair spilled wild red even in the foggy morning light like a flame across the pale satin of her shoulders. She took a deep breath and thought she had made a decision.

Still her body would not uncurl from its tight, reassuring ball. Daring, the cat returned to settle calmly at her feet. It preened a little, washing its face, then tucked its nose under a paw to sleep. This time, Molly let it be.

When she woke again, she had been dreaming about France. Only half asleep, she had almost heard Armand's voice, deep and sensuous even when whispering across her ear. Eugénie's tinkling laugh, brittle and nervous, came from somewhere behind. Oh, the music room, of course, where Honoré had just finished playing the spinet. Pink warmth flushed across Molly's cheeks, though she lay alone and frozen with indecision, one hand stroking the cat.

Then too, she thought of Armand shouting, stamping to distract her even as she faced him over crossed rapiers. She wore pantaloons of violet satin and a short Dutch doublet pinked and swagged with ribbons. He had tried his best that afternoon to flick away the bows, one by one, that held the doublet to the pantaloons, but all save the first one eluded him. When she actually forced the steel from his hand, his sword shimmered away in a singing arc of silver and clattered to the polished floor. He was not amused, and he dismissed her trick as an accident. Then she did it again.

She had grinned with broad satisfaction. Madame did not approve of such sports for her young ladies. Picnics, parlor games, the spinet, sketching and discreet flirtation were acceptable; riding and fencing with wild young men were not.

She would not have approved of Prentiss at all.

The door clicked but did not open at once, and Molly froze. Carefully, she refreshed her grip on the black hilted knife and rolled to look. Well, certainly she knew that Driscoll would be back eventually; she had forgotten that.

Cautiously, the door swung wide to display Dick Prentiss's slim, oddly patrician figure lounging carelessly in the doorway. Somewhere he had bathed and washed his long hair so that it hung in damp ringlets around his shoulders, and his clothes were fresh if not entirely new. A careful twist of a smile hung tentatively about his face, one flaring eyebrow for a question mark.

"Awake, I see," he said.

Molly was silent, still eyeing him warily. She wondered if he saw the knife, and whether he thought she would use it. She took a short breath and decided what to say.

"Once again, eh?"

Puzzled. "What?"

"I thought you'd given up this game."

Then he thought he knew what she meant and moved further into the room. Yes, that was indeed a knife, but would she use it?

"You know I have. I *thought* you knew. Did you think I would leave you?"

"You're a dangerous man to a young and virtuous maid."

He laughed a little and put down the bundle he had carried in. "And who said you were a maid last?"

She smiled wickedly, in turn. "Armand de la Valier de St. Juste, who should know."

"He took it?"

"My virtue? He tried."

"What else did he fail at, I wonder."

"Well," she said, stirring against the bedclothes so that the dirk showed plainly in her hand. "Once upon a time he could have taken this from me. Not any more."

The easy expression froze on his face, the eyes cold. "I suppose that is meant to be a challenge."

"If you like."

Her eyes never left his, though an almost tangible wall had risen up between them. Her hand, the knife, never slipped from the position she had taken, though she wished for a moment that she had not stayed on the bed. The mattress would give when she wanted to push away from it, and that was a disadvantage Prentiss would doubtless exploit.

Seconds passed.

Outside, wagons rumbled through the streets, people cried their wares and haggled prices; a bridle jingled, dull in the heavy air, on a courier's horse taking a short cut through a side street.

She knew Prentiss mocked her, standing there with that unreadable smile frozen in his tanned and weathered face. He must think her a child with a dangerous toy who ought to be disarmed. The glint in his eye was diamond hard.

He decided not to outwait her. With a lazy shrug, he turned his back on her to lay out the contents of his bundle.

Suspicious, her eyes followed him while she slipped her feet off the bed. A bottle of ale, some apples, the remains of a capon. A pistol and powder came out as well, which he examined in Molly's view then put down, and a handful of gold and silver coins. Everything unpacked, there remained only the breeches and shirt he had bought for her. These he picked up and shook out, considering them for size while she tried to read his mind, still on guard.

Then careless, he dropped a coin. Her eye followed it. The shirt flew at her face. Astonished, she shouted and tore it away from her eyes, lashing out with the knife but not catching him at all. The blade, caught up in folds of canvas, jerked round and round and twisted finally from her hand, and he flung it away, shirt and all. When she could see again, he was standing over her, the pistol leveled at her breast.

"A knife's a lovely thing, my girl, but it lacks a little advantage. If you take my meaning."

Speechless with anger edged with fear, heart pounding, the movement she caught in the corner of her eye was her own hands trembling. In part of her mind she was certain she had been right in wanting to kill him. Trust was a terrible thing.

Then he turned the slender iron muzzle away to point it over her shoulder toward the open window. And pulled the trigger. The flint struck steel and sparked black powder; the powder flashed in the pan with a surprising dull hiss and a ribbon of white smoke, but there was no shot, and he let the pistol drop. With a howl, the cat bounded away, but Molly sat very still. She stared up at him in horror.

"You must not let yourself stiffen up like that, Molly lass," he said lightly. He sat beside her, not mentioning that she was still almost naked. Gently he opened her nerveless fingers and wrapped them around the pistol's inlaid grip, then took her into his arms. Overwhelmed at last, she collapsed with a sob as he gathered her up.

"You've a good eye," he whispered. "But I surprised you. You were looking right at me!"

On several shaky breaths she finally said, "Perhaps I was distracted."

"Always watch the eyes."

"But that was what distracted me, you see," she said with a sad, whimsical laugh. "But it wasn't your eyes I wanted."

She stopped. "You bastard, Dick Prentiss. I wanted to kill you! I thought you weren't coming back. And then I thought … Oh, I don't know what! I believe you are going to drive me quite mad."

Hungrily he folded his arms about her, drawing her into him as if he thought she might disappear. Last night he had been exhausted, overcome with pain and ill use. And now—God's eyes, the child was a virgin!

"What am I going to do with you?" he said at last, shaking his head. Even seated on the hard bed, she came no higher than his chin. He kissed her hair and tangled his fingers in it. He kissed her forehead, then tilted up her face to stare, searching, into the stormy eyes, damp with unwilling tears. "Whatever shall I do with you."

"Make love to me?"

"You're just a little girl."

"I'm seventeen. Make love to me."

"Then what? What do you want to do?"

Anything. Be with you. Wait for you. Keep your house and have your children. "I don't know," she said.

"Then let us make love. We can talk anytime."

She had been kissed before and well, and liked it. She had even, now, lain next to a man and knew something of the surprising shapes of his body. But when he stood before her and stripped off his clothes, she caught her breath.

His skin was marked with the hurts of the past days, and scars from forgotten wounds. A knife had grazed his ribs once, maybe twice, and a sword had caught him across the upper part of his left arm, the habitual fencer's wound. His legs, slim and strong, seemed unmarked, though one pale thread might have been the trail of a passing pistol ball.

She hardly moved, watching him.

Then he drew her shift over her head and, taking her face in his hands, he kissed her eyes and her mouth and her throat. Wildly, she felt the blood rise into her cheeks. Her breasts rounded taut and the nipples hardened into tight brown points under his questing fingers. Oh, she had been touched before, and liked it too. But now his hand found the hot damp place between her thighs, as with his other arm he pulled her down beside him.

A low moan escaped her, murmuring against his mouth. Lightly, lightly he tickled and nipped at her lips while his fingers played her body. Wonderfully, her face blossomed into an ecstatic grin, a laugh of joy. Her own hands explored the male hardness of his body burning with expectation.

Tearing her mind away just slightly from her own pleasure, she dared the thing she had never dreamed of, and smoothed her hand down the firm line of his chest. A shiver of delight answered her touch on his own brown nipples.

Then dancing lightly across the taut muscles of his belly, she followed the heat to its source rising hard between his thighs. She almost snatched her fingers back again in amazement, but returned them again with delight. So hard a thing, already swollen then growing greater against her hand, but soft to the touch as a child's face, as a silken gown. A niggling fear that such a thing could not possibly fit inside her touched the ragged edges of her mind, but was driven off by every maddening sensation.

His mouth on her breast, sucking and nibbling daggers of pleasure, his manhood pulling away from her hand, then offering again. The bonfire in her body leapt ever higher till she thought it would burn her soul away.

All this she had had hints of, teasing, playful, laughing in a hidden alcove or wrestling like puppies on Madame's grassy lawn where it met the river. But nothing had prepared her for the next moments. Gently, slowly he opened her thighs and slid his hard wonderful body between them. His long hair fell across his shoulders into her face.

Her hands clasped across his slender back, while her knees lifted instinctively, compulsively. Now his hands were wound in her hair, his eyes blue as midnight above her.

She cried out as he entered her, hard and strong and hot. "Wait!" she gasped. "Stop!"

Quickly he retreated. She lay still for a moment, gasping, her face twisted in a grimace of exquisite pain knotted up with desire. Her hands rested lightly against his chest. "Wait," she whispered.

"Have I hurt you?" His eyes filled with concern. Molly bit her lip and nodded tightly.

"But I want you," she added, and tried to smile again. "Eugénie said it would hurt. I– I just didn't know."

Tenderly he touched her face now wet with passion and maidenly hurt.

"You are so beautiful," he whispered huskily. "So little. I could go more slowly, but 'twill not make the pain less, in the end. But I hate to hurt thee."

Her fingers tightened in the fleshy curve of his buttocks till he shivered with delight.

"I have thy body, Master Prentiss. Methinks I owe thee mine."

Lids stained purple with fatigue ad stress closed over the eyes like smoky jade. She hooked her ankles around his thighs. "I shall not be less afraid of thee for waiting, nor want thee more."

Bending again, he kissed her, deep and long, fingers tightening again in the dark red satin of her hair. Teasing her once, again, finally he entered, a long swift stroke. She cried out again, and blood came, but he pressed forward again, farther and deeper, pounding with the pounding of her heart.

It hurt, oh God, it hurt, and seemed never to get better. But she held to him, hopeful and tearful, begging him not to stop. Then he seemed to shudder, and a low groan escape his throat, and his back was suddenly a wash with sweat, and he rode forward one last time with a muffled cry, then settled lightly over her body, and stopped. Balanced on one arm, he reached to push his hair back behind his ears, then brushed her own auburn curls away from her eyes.

The look she saw in his face was tender, quizzical, expectant. She wanted to tell him something pleasing, but she could not lie to him. Not now.

"I did hurt you," he said. She nodded, her breathing still ragged.

He sighed and rolled aside but left one leg flung lightly across her. One arm propped him up to look at her, the other hand traced delicate patterns idly around her breasts and down her stomach along the silken line of her hipbone. Her eyes flickered closed again, and she shuddered happily. He watched her body, not her face this time.

Molly sank back into the pleasant dreaminess that had come before the hurt. She smiled when his hair brushed her belly again, and his mouth close over one satin breast while his free hand fondled the other. Her own fingers reached for him again, running lightly along the back of his neck, combing through the long, damp hair.

Lightening burst in the palms of her hands as she felt his lips and tongue work across her body, and she rolled toward him again to lie against the whole long hard line of his form.

Grinning, Dick pulled her around and over him, bearing up all her little weight to set her astride him.

"Maybe this time, Sweet," he said. And gently he lowered her body over the renewed uprightness of his manhood.

She winced at first, for the pain had not changed. Then something sparked deep within and she burst suddenly into smiles that fought with the drying tears. Pleased and surprised, she fell forward onto her hands, her breasts like flowers against his chest, sliding against him. With her hands braced on his shoulders, she moved to the rhythm he set, till little by little the spark began to flare and grow, and she cried out with surprised joy.

She rode him on waves of ecstasy till he cried out again and exploded into her deep and deeper, clutching her to him and thrusting up while the bed creaked and bent beneath them. She gasped and whimpered against the ring of pain that still remained, till even that was overridden in the flood of pleasure that rose from her loins and crested in her mind.

Later, much later, Molly slept sated in his arms. A small smile played about her mouth, bruised and swollen with kissing, as though she had never doubted either him or her decision. Her body was sore and aching but with a sweet ache that only comforted her. She slept, thoroughly content at last.

Prentiss only wished he were as serene. Davy and *Jealous Mary* would sail on the evening tide, with or without him. It seemed less than fair that leaving Jamaica should be so needful just when he had found such a good reason to stay. But what could he do with her?

"Molly," he said, and caressed her shoulder, throat, flawless cheek. She stirred slightly. "Wake up, Sweet. We have to talk."

She murmured something lewd and reached for him again, but he stopped her hand. "I said, we have to talk. Wake up, lass."

The long almost invisible lashes swept open, and Dick nearly fell into the moist jade of her eyes again, but he caught himself.

"Kiss me first," she said.

"Stop that, you bawd," said Prentiss, grinning. He turned her hand palm upward to place a kiss in it. "I thought you were content."

"For now," she answered with a soft smile, and put a kiss on his chest.

"Women," he sighed.

"I suppose you really do mean to leave this time, now that you've got what you came back for."

"Come now, you wanton. Leave off!"

Withdrawing his arm from under her head, he vaulted out of the narrow bed to grab up his clothes. She sighed heavily to see his whole body again, firm and beautifully muscled as she remembered. "You'd best dress and eat something. Look, here's wine."

Without a word she found her shift and pulled it over her head, then rummaged through her things until she found a comb. In Driscoll's cupboard, she turned up a looking glass, and between the two tried to bring some order to the wild tangle of her curls.

"At least you've had a bath."

"I smelled like the Pit," he said, pouring the wine. "And felt like the Devil's own football."

"You could have let me know you were going."

"I'd have had to wake you, and I thought you'd rather not. I expected to find you still asleep."

"I see."

"So," he said heavily when she finally joined him at the little table.

Molly suddenly realized when she had last taken a meal, and fell to the bread and chicken with single-minded enthusiasm.

Prentiss laughed. "I thought ladies of quality all ate like little birds."

"And when did you last mistake me for a lady, sir?"

He laughed again. "Hours ago. But truly, Sweet, we must talk."

All the smiles dissolved, and she dropped her gaze. "I know," she said. "You are going to leave, aren't you?"

Prentiss nodded. "Yes. But what are you going to do?"

"I cannot stay here."

"No. Where shall I take you, then?"

Her shadowed face snapped up to meet his again. "Take me?"

"How can I leave you here? How can I take you home?"

Inside, Molly's emotions warred with her understanding. Part of her had stopped listening at *how can I leave you* while the other part knew that was a different idea from *leave you here*. Then, angry at wanting to be in love, she took refuge in misunderstanding. She snapped, "There's the door."

He responded with a hard glare. "You've rescued me. That whoreson suitor of yours really was going to hang me, you know. I reckon 'tis only fair to rescue you from him as well."

"You mean, you're the man who's going to take me away from all this."

He nodded.

"I want to go to sea," she said all at once, just as the thought was forming, and was shocked to hear herself say it, even as she realized it was just what she wanted. "Yes, that's it exactly! You can take me with you. I can be a privateer, like my father."

In despair Prentiss shook his head, then laid it down on his arms. She could not quite tell whether he was laughing.

"Molly," he said finally. "Girls do not go to sea and become privateers like their fathers. Nay stop, they do not! What would you do aboard ship? Besides fight off all the other men." He paused under a lifted brow. "I assume you would fight them off?"

She touched a hand gently to his cheek. "Do you doubt me?"

"I have no idea." He kissed the hand and sighed "I think I shall never know you." Then he sat up, sighing and took her hands in his. "Lass, your dad was the finest pilot in these waters. Everyone knows it. D'ye know, I knew him, and liked him too. He was patient with the bad-tempered, ill-educated brat I was. Even taught me a thing or two."

It wasn't quite true. Or rather it was true, but less than accurate, and for now a half-truth was better than a whole one. "But your father's good reputation is not enough for my captain to make exceptions. Besides, it's main bad luck having a woman aboard. Everyone knows that."

"You could hold me for ransom, then be enthralled by my charms."

He made a face. "You listen to too many ballad singers."

"You are not much like the lovers in the ballads, but I still like you."

"I should think you did, you randy wench. Nay, don't touch me, woman! It's getting late. Driscoll will be back any time now. We have to decide something for you."

Her jaw set with a stubbornness that would have made her Aunt Henrietta shriek.

"I think I will go to sea, Master Prentiss. I want to be with you, and unless you can swear that you never want to see me again, so I will be. I wonder," she said with her chin in her hand, "whether Marjorie had this conversation with Rafe."

"I'll wager she lost."

Molly nodded. "But he did take her away. They went to Barbados and he built her a house. But then," she grinned evilly. "My father wasn't also a street thief and a cutpurse, was he?"

His bright eyes danced, remembering the old days. He said only, "Depends on who you ask."

That made her frown, but she waved it away in a moment.

"Talk to your captain."

Prentiss shook his head again, still grimly set against it, while he tied back his hair with a string. "Davy York will never have it. Never." He sank into reverie even as she watched.

York? The fellow her uncle was so angry with, before his temper had turned on her.

Thoughtful, Molly returned her attention to breakfast and another draught of the sweet red wine. She imagined, quite by the way, what her uncle's steward would have to say of eating fowl with red wine, but the stuff was far too cheap—cloudy, with a float of litter to the surface—to worry about the color of the meat that went with it.

Right now she was so hungry she hardly cared, but the image was entertaining. Entertaining too, Prentiss's reaction to her demands. She had not expected to meet such soft objection.

I really must be mad, she thought. Because he's perfectly right, of course. What am I going to do at sea. Play the spinet? Embroider? I should let him take me somewhere. Barbados would do. Perhaps find our old house—Marjorie's house. But then what?

She wished she could wash her hair.

"We might," Prentiss said, as if he had read her thought. "We might do that, what Rafe did. You must have friends on Barbados, or somewhere. We could ..."

But Molly was shaking her head emphatically. "If I had, I would never have met you. Except in Paris, my only friends are here, in this room."

"Hmm."

"Please Dickon. Talk to your captain. My father's name should carry some weight. I'll put on boy's clothes and I'll ..."

He snorted with laughter. "And will everyone believe Davy's signed on a lad with these." He bent to take both her breasts together between his hands, and placed a soft kiss in the deep valley between them. He stopped as she gasped with delight. "Quite a cabin boy. Sweet, you are too slighting of your charms."

She blushed furiously and tried to pretend his touch was of no matter to her, at least for now. "Then why did you bring that suit of clothes, Master Prentiss, unless you'd already thought of it."

He grinned a little ruefully. "I guess I thought it might come to this. And no matter what, 'tis easier for you to move about as a lad while they're looking for a lass. I did not mind to tell you there's a garrison full of His Majesty's finest combing the island for you."

"Me?"

"Ha! I've surprised you at last, Mistress Know-All."

"But that means Colonel Rhetford ..."

"Aye it does. Your uncle's doing, I imagine. You didn't suppose they'd let the niece of the King's Comptroller run away as easy as that."

She surprised him again with the excitement that came over her. Her creamy cheeks blossomed into roses almost as bright as when she had first learned to enjoy him. She threw back her head in that infuriating, vulgar way her aunt despised, and fairly hooted with laughter.

"Then we have no choice, my dear. Have we?

8

CHEERILY AND MERRILY

FROM THE AFT quarter to the forecastle deck, *Jealous Mary* swarmed with activity throughout the long, hazy afternoon. Hastily repaired rigging for the sleek brigantine was still being replaced, fresh water and provisions brought in, crew secured to replace those lost to the sea or to idleness. And Davy York, her master, supervised it all with an agreeable tyranny, his finer manners left aside with his finer clothes.

The crew numbered, in a good season like this one, something above sixty rowdy buccaneers. Privateers, licensed to harry enemy shipping in the King's perpetual wars with the Spanish and Dutch, they were not entirely the righteous merchant seamen Davy represented to his sponsors. Honest enough, as their calling went, their Sunday prayers tended to be sketchy and restricted, in the main, to the Lord's name and titles taken in vain.

Even allowing for the loose democracy of the sea, their captain governed them with a firm hand. If his ordinary manner was indulgent and jolly, his temper was swift, and they jumped when he told them to. There were those who had sailed with him for years out of plain love, though they would never have said so, because he was a good captain and a lucky one: a rare, fair feature in a man whose crew lived on his skill in a sea fight, and fought for no pay but their rigorously apportioned shares of the booty. He had been a success in his profession for fifteen years and more. They would follow him anywhere.

Under his good-natured gaze, it was an unhappy buccaneer who had to herd goats aboard late in the afternoon. The ugly, malodorous beasts nagged and bleated and butted at his thighs as bandy-legged Muggs drove them up the gangplank. Davy leaned into the larboard rail of the quarterdeck and laughed till his eyes ran with tears.

"Ye'd not find it so funny did you do this yerself, Cap'n!" Muggs bleated.

"I'd look a damned sight sillier than you, me lad. And you laughing just as hard. But 'tis not so high a price for fresh meat, now, is it? Go get 'em below, the sweet-tempered darlings."

"Evil-tempered devils, more like," spat one-eyed Muggs. "Damn their beards." He continued swearing to match anything the goats might have to say. "My old woman has a better temper!"

"And belike she's just as sweet between the sheets. Master Keaton!" Davy shouted to the noisy dock.

The able Keaton, a broad felt hat slapped on his bald head, sat on a trunk behind a rickety table signing on new hands from the rowdies and malcontents that hung about the docks. Most of the regulars were already returned, slipping aboard in ones and twos to take up their duties, hiding themselves in work, chastened and hung over.

"Master Keaton!" Davy called again.

The older man squinted up a sun-reddened face into the white glare that framed the *Jealous Mary*'s master.

"Aye, Captain?"

"Any sign of our roving pilot?"

Keaton shook his head with a dissatisfied twist to his mouth. "Paul DeRoet's been 'round, though. I told him to come back."

"Sign him on, then. If Prentiss can't get himself here, well…" He shrugged eloquently. "Good to have them both, if we can. Keeps me from having to do it all meself." He turned away then spun back to the rail. "Find me a fiddle as well, Master Keaton. Or a drum, at least. We're sore in need of music."

"Ye'll be dancing all the way to Tortuga, Captain!"

Davy turned again to oversee the new rigging. Prentiss was the best, and a good friend besides. But a man with a wench ever on his mind was unreliable. If Prentiss tried to bring the girl aboard, as Jimmy Fitts seemed to think he might, there'd be something to say about it, no matter who's daughter she was. Last thing Davy wanted was some doxy making trouble among the men. She'd be pretty, of course, which would only make it worse. Then, "Fitts!" he snapped as Jimmy rushed past him.

"Aye, Cap'n?"

"Where's that mate of yours?"

Jimmy grinned and barked a laugh. "With his ginger lass, I guess. Giving her something to remember him by."

"You're sure?"

"Nah. What's ever sure about that one?" Jimmy scoffed. "But 'tis a fair guess. They'll have gone to ground somewhere. He'll have her and get it over with. He's ready to sail," he finished with a knowing wink. "That much I do know."

"I can't wait all day. The tide will come whether he will or no."

"Oh he'll come, Captain," said Jimmy Fitts, nodding with a certainty born of long friendship. "He'll come."

"Aye," Davy answered doubtfully. "Well, so long as he gets here." And he waved Jimmy back to work.

But a moment later, Fitts was back with a worried frown. "Davy, that lad Gib just came aboard. Says Black Tom and old Ned Courage are back in the lockup again, for drunk and resisting the guard. Again. And Gib says someone's been following him. Some bloke called MacBean, he says, from …"

"Aye, I know where from." Davy's plain, sturdy face split in a broad smile, easing the intense anxiety so lately riding there. "The nervous Scotchman from FitzRobert's."

"Aye. Gib says he's still trying to shake him off."

York chuckled unpleasantly. "Persistence deserves a reward. Just put Gib to work and never mind about MacBean. In fact, let everyone never mind MacBean, understood? Let him slip aboard, even, if he likes."

A loud guffaw exploded from him suddenly. "He's so fond of seagoing men, perhaps we should indulge him in our company, eh Fitts? And I'll see to Ned and Tom myself. Keaton, you mind things here. Don't sail without me!" he called, and trotted down the gangplank, now goat-free. "And when Prentiss gets here, tie him down!"

Jimmy could only stand and fold his arms, watching his captain disappear into the dockside swarm. He sighed, rubbed at the new gold ring itching in his right ear, and wished to hell he were away from Jamaica already, and Prentiss with him.

By dinnertime, affairs in King's Lane were rather more emotional. It seemed to Lady FitzRobert that there never had been silence in her house. The shouting had been going on now for days, all the more since this morning. Would it never end? First privateers in the parlor, then Molly screaming down the house like a fishwife, and now the girl vanished and soldiers everywhere in every room, trampling the garden, molesting the servants.

She would tolerate Colonel Rhetford because he was a gentleman, and Captain Benning because Roger did, but the rest! And Roger was no better. Seized at last by a fitful distemper, he had taken to his bed where even now he was submitting under duress to being bled.

Henrietta winced as she always did when the apothecary salted the last of his leeches and let it drop into a blue glazed jar. Everyone knew a sharp steel knife was less painful and more efficacious.

No matter how she worked to be a good wife, bustling between his friends, fluffing pillows, trying so awfully to straighten the rucked linens, her husband only bellowed.

"Let be, woman!"

"Roger!"

No one else in the world spoke to her like that. It was confusing and irritating. Not that he cared. She left the room sniffing at her lavender scented handkerchief and when she slammed the door, she was right: no one noticed.

"Find her, Rhetford! You must find her! This town is not so large it can hide a gently bred, inexperienced, seventeen year old girl."

"I thought we had agreed," drawled Benning from the other side of the room. "That she is not altogether inexperienced."

"She is a child, sir. She has been misled, nothing more."

"And you have no idea, Sir Roger," Rhetford went on. "How easy it is for *anyone* to disappear among 5,000 people. She could be strolling through the market square even now, and we might never know it."

"The King's Peace is so lightly regarded."

Rhetford felt silence the best answer to that, the King's Peace being a matter of concern to men like FitzRobert only when it was convenient. Well, it was the nature of colonial society, he supposed, and could be worse. Perhaps.

He avoided the inevitable sigh that came with such conversations, and said, "The King's Peace is what we try to maintain for ourselves against the Spanish, the Dutch and the Portuguese. And what we hope keeps our own buccaneers from burning the city to the ground on a whim. As you know yourself."

"I know my own business," Roger snapped. "I expect you to know yours. Do you really mean to tell me that soldiers—your soldiers or any others—cannot find locate a pretty wench!"

"In a town famed for pretty wenches?" The colonel's lips twitched into an unwilling smile. Molly was uncommon pretty, but an army's taste was broad. "Not if, as we fear, she does not wish to be found."

Benning smiled again. "There you see? And she does not wish to be found because she has allied herself with this thief."

"Simon, please!"

"He named her."

"'Tis a common name. There must be a hundred Mollys in Port Royal. Her mother never would call her Mary like a Christian. There's a Molly in our bakehouse, for godsake. Any gypsy might be called Molly."

"Yes," Benning sneered. "Any gypsy. The Colonel will assure us, I am certain, that everything is being done to find her?"

Rhetford sighed. "Everything, aye." He was growing impatient with this prinking, perfumed dandy. No wonder the girl had run away, if this sorry villain was what they meant to marry her to. "But we have missed your effort, Captain."

"Mine?" The flare of a delicate black eyebrow indicated Benning's utter mystification. "How should my command be of any service, pray?"

Rhetford gestured toward the wide window that looked out over the pleasant circle of the bay. A dozen ships of varying sizes were even now standing out to sea, stealing away on the rising tide and the evening's freshening breeze. Storm clouds still hung ominously at the horizon, blackening the deep purples and golds of the late sky.

"I hesitate to point out to a man of the sea such as yourself, sir, that Jamaica is an island, and the sea is a wide place. There are more places to hide a wayward girl out there," Jack Rhetford nodded to the horizon and its burden of ships, "than here in the town, would you not agree? Sir Roger may not wish to remember how his sister left home," he added with meaning.

Furious, Roger's bloodshot eyes swiveled, popping red from their sockets. "I would not."

"But the case may be the same, however distasteful."

Benning's bland expression froze, but he only sniffed his annoyance. "My dear Colonel," said the captain. "And with all due respect to my good friend, Sir Roger, I am as happy to see the girl go to the Devil, if that's her mind."

"God's death, Simon, what are you saying!"

"Forgive me, my dear, but you are well rid of the baggage, and you know it. Whether she returns or is found, we should only have to go through all this again. She wants a good beating, if you ask me." A small light informed his eyes. "If she's run away, well …"

"Well?"

Sir Simon shrugged in the most refined manner. "Well, I think Sir Roger can take some comfort in the inheritance she has abandoned."

"Captain Benning!" Jack Rhetford had contained the small explosion as closely as he could but, but he could dissemble no longer. "If she has run away, as I am convinced she has, it was surely as much from the prospect of life with you as from any wickedness you or her uncle may ascribe to her or her parents. I for one applaud her judgment! If she is not discovered by nightfall, I shall presume she has escaped this island by sea, and I shall order the search ended. That is my final word. Good day, gentlemen."

With a perfunctory flourish of his plumed hat, he turned on his heel and stalked from the room.

Suppertime in Huggins Street passed as all the other hours of the day had done, in grey irritable impatience. Molly paced—and she hated pacing, even though part of her thrilled to the wanton sensation of legs thrust into a man's wide breeches, and the unconfined freedom of shirt and jacket. All the parts were patched and dull, and made for some broader body, but clean enough and serviceable.

Still Prentiss would not let her leave the room, and waiting for evening was only boring. What good was a disguise if all she could do in it was wait? If he had brought her a needle, she might at least have occupied the time making it all fit better.

Harry Driscoll had indeed come home, not altogether happy to find Prentiss and his doxy there before him. But he grudgingly allowed that for two silver pieces of eight, the Watch would find no one here. So Prentiss paid him and locked her in to wait the day while he went out. The parting had been sweet but muggy afternoon passed with impossible slowness.

Outside the splintered door, Molly could hear the place beginning to draw some business, and the tavern girls returning one by one. But there was nothing to do but sit and drink cheap wine and dream, lingering fondly on the best parts of the morning. The pain and quick terrors she chose to ignore, and were already fading. As for doubts, she refused to entertain them. Often.

When Prentiss finally came in, the breeze outside had turned to a light wind, and the room was growing almost chill with the damp.

"Are you ready?" he asked sharply.

"Ready." She tried to sound sure. "Where have you been?"

"Out. Making a wee living. Thinking. Getting my sea chest aboard and all. Come on. Get your things. The tide will be changing within the hour and we have to get aboard. Both of us." He tossed a light grey mantle around her shoulders, then caught her waist. His eyes flashed diamond blue into hers. "Tell me again. Is this what you want?"

God, if I only knew! "Yes."

"Do you know what this means?"

"I shall find out if I don't."

"Y'know there's no chance in a thousand you'll be taken for a lad."

"I do not mean to be. I rather hope to be invisible for a while, that's all."

He still seemed doubtful. "Am I going to have to hold off three-and-sixty buccaneers to defend your virtue?"

"You know them better than I do. But I'll tell you this, Dick Prentiss. You get me on that ship, and I'll show you who needs defending."

He breathed a deep and uncertain sigh. "I surely hope so, lass. Now let me kiss you, Sweet, and we'll go."

He meant it to be quick, but she came into his arms warm and eager, and he was loath to let her go. Then good sense finally got the best of him; he set a hat on her knotted hair, bundled the cloak round her, picked her up and put her out into the alley through the window.

Together they picked their way through Port Royal's back streets, staying to the alleys. Only once did they nearly encounter Rhetford's soldiers, but they ducked aside in time. The rest of the journey was less eventful than their easy walk away from the lockup only the night before.

When they reached the *Jealous Mary*, the brigantine was filled with lively anticipation, the final preparations to sail completed, as swarming as an anthill. They slipped aboard almost unnoticed just before Keaton would have had the gangplank up and the anchor away.

"Davy's lookin' for ye, Prentiss," said the lieutenant. "Says he missed you this afternoon." Molly pulled her cloak more tightly about her and grabbed her stomach as if about to be sick, and Dick hustled her past his Lieutenant.

"Aye, well, I'd enough to do without looking up and down Thames Street for him. Here, I'll just put young Robin to bed, then I'll be at Davy's entire service."

"Eh?" Will Keaton passed a thoughtful hand around his shiny head.

"I say I'll be right back," Dick called over his shoulder. He pushed Molly smartly before him, then snapped. "Let's have that plank up and ready to sail, shall we Master Keaton!"

"Aye-aye, Pilot!" Keaton answered automatically and began shouting orders to get under way.

A few steps under the poop, a short ladder climbed down to the sailing master's cabin that would belong to Prentiss and Keaton by right of duty, shared on this voyage with the second pilot, DeRoet.

Low ceilinged below the Captain's cabin, but decently appointed, the bulkheads were paneled with teak, and at the back a long mullioned window leaded with beveled glass gave a broad view of Fort James and the grey sea beyond. Within, oaken shutters could be bolted across the glass against a storm.

Molly gasped with surprise as Prentiss ushered her within.

"D'ye like it, then?" he grinned. "Good," he went on before she could answer. "I expect you to stay here a while."

"What!" Her face, brightened with pleasure, fell again. "Oh no, Prentiss, not again!"

"I said, you're to stay here," he said with a very firm set to his chin. "We're getting under way and I've no time to make introductions. Davy can wait to meet you till we're well out to sea, if you take my meaning."

She frowned, trying to consider this rationally, and finally nodded over pursed lips. "How long?" was all she said.

"Tide's turning. Wind's up. Not long at all. Be patient, Sweet, that's all." Lightly, he reached slender fingers to caress her face. "Trust me a little, for the novelty of it?"

She smiled, a little mocking, and caught his hand, holding it to her cheek as she tried to fathom his secrets from his eyes.

"Of course."

His face burst into a wide grin and he hugged her once fiercely, then went away. The cabin door shut with a click, then a grating clunk as he turned a key to lock her in.

Left alone, Molly threw off the smothering cloak that held the muggy air closer around her, and smelled of rum and raisins. Wrinkling her nose, she leaned against the door to survey her newest prison. At least it was change of scene. If she'd stayed at home, she'd still be locked into the same boring old room.

The cabin was graceful and uncommonly tidy, she noticed with a smile, for a room that had never seen a woman's hand. But it seemed crowded, cramped under the deck as it was. The ceiling had barely cleared Dick's head, and he'd had to duck under the doorway. In fact, everything seemed just about three-quarter sized, as if made for children and their dolls.

Even the bunks looked small. Built into an inner bulkhead, they flanked a tall wardrobe elaborately carved of oak, carved with acorns and oak leaves. Lion-headed latches of ivory and brass braced a pair of long mirrors, scratched and spotted, in the doors. The thin mattress of each bunk lay railed like an infant's bed above a double set of drawers with handles of ivory and brass. No, she realized on inspection. Ivory and gold.

Under the curve of the great window a massive table was bolted to the deck on brass plates, and above the table swung two brass lanterns trimmed and newly filled with oil. Nearby hulked a dark sea chest sweet smelling of cedar and fitted with iron bands and leather wrought with silver tracery, tarnishing slightly towards pewter. The domed lid displayed some coat of arms: Spanish, Molly decided by the motto painted beneath.

She smirked, wondering if the wily Don missed his treasure chest. Wondering, too, if some of this was what made up Dick's mysterious afternoon errand. How much of all this was his, what Keaton's, and what belonged to anyone else?

Stacks of rolled charts and a few well-bound books lay behind leaded glass in locked compartments, and a huge, worn old book lay open on the table. Every flat surface—table, cabinet, or bedstead— was beveled with ivory bars secured with brass pegs to keep steady whatever might be set there in rocky weather.

Nothing was new, but everything seemed well-used as well as well-cared for, as though the men who lived here took some pleasure in their possessions, as well as pride. Pride and caution, since everything was locked.

Molly sighed with resignation and threw her little bundles into a corner. Then she sat in the leather-bottomed chair behind the chart table and opened the book. She found to her delight it was a rutter, a log of sorts containing notes on tides and winds and the shapes of the coasts, and the reefs and shoals of the islands, and the positions of the stars.

Surely, she thought, it must be the captain's. Initials appeared here and there: DY—that would be Davy—along with others. Older pages were written in older hands and browner ink. One slippery fellow had only marked his entries with an elaborate S. A later correcting hand seemed to say RP—perhaps that was Dick, if he was also Richard—then more DY. A fresh correction was unsigned. She shrugged and made a note to ask later who all the initials were. There were figures in the margins, sketches, calculations and corrections she could see no use for, and it seemed to have a language all its own, but at least it was not locked away and would do to pass the time since there was obviously to be no exploring.

An hour later, maybe more, and Prentiss had still not come to let her out. Feet slapped overhead, men urgent at their tasks heedless of her presence. Unidentifiable voices drifted down with the clank of anchor chain; an Irish fiddle sawing out a lament that turned inexorably into the steady rhythm of a work song; the thunderous crack of the sails loosed from their bonds and set into the wind; the raucous sea gull cries of the quartermaster and the sailors echoing to each other in the rigging.

And all about, the anguished creak and sigh of the great ship itself as Prentiss at the helm turned her out past Fort Charles and Sandy Key and into the wind.

The watch changed, and the smells of cooking began to drift down to her. Getting hungry and losing patience, she wandered restlessly staring into every locked, glass-fronted cupboard, then sat again, puzzled over the rutter, or stared out of the great window. By what she could guess from the charts, they must head first to the west away from the spit of sand that cradled the town, then south and clear the last arm of the island at Salt Hill. She watched, wondering if she would be able to tell the changes as they happened.

Captured by the colors of the sea and bounce of the sun, she stood in the window to watch Port Royal's long sandy profile recede to a line on the horizon. Then coming about on the larboard tack, even that disappeared and left nothing in the distorted view but rusty sea and the indigo verge of the eastern sky, and the gleam of the first star.

Growing all the while more discontent, she sat again, only to throw herself out of the chair once more to pace off the dimensions of the cabin. Uselessly she rattled at the door, but the lock held firm. She found the wine, a small onion bottle in blue glass, like any other, stashed under a mattress, but quite a decent canary, if one liked that sort of thing.

"I am so tired," she muttered as she gripped the cork. "Of being shut into little rooms like so much useless baggage. I could have stayed home and been treated like this."

Aye, her inner voice agreed, and she took a hearty swig of the sweet wine, enough to make her cough. Aye, and married that vile corruption of a captain, too. Now *there* would be a little room with no way out!

Well she'd been locked in better rooms than this, and with less wine. A slow grin crept across her face as she drew the slim black-handled dirk from her pack. A terrible thing it might be to put such a fine blade to carpentry, but there was hardly a choice.

Carefully she began working at the edges of the brass lock.

It was awkward, working on her knees, and more than once the point slipped and nicked the edge of a finger. She swore and kept going. A little blood seasoned the wood, yes, that's right. Prentiss would be angry, of course, but well, there it was. She had to get out of here, and though she worked for a good long while, no one came.

Very well. If Prentiss was afraid to face his captain with her, with Rafe September's daughter for godssake, she would simply have to take matters into her own hands.

At last the wood, splintered and ravaged, seemed ready. The bolt drawn behind it would simply pull itself free at a firm tug. Well, maybe two. At last, Molly paused and stood up, pressed an ear to the door. She heard no movement in the passage.

All around her, there was only the creaking of timbers and the shuffle of feet overhead. She held her breath, tightened her grip on the smooth ivory ball that was the handle, and gave it one sharp jerk. Nothing. All right.

She rubbed sweaty palms on the light serge of her breeches, then took another grip. Tugged again. Yes! The last bits exploded and the door flew inward, pitching her into the room over her own feet. She thought she could step back with it, but stumbled as the door came with her, then *Mary* came about again and the roll of the starboard tack threw her forward to balance once again.

Neatly done. More or less. She still held the iron handle fast in her grip, which must count for something.

With renewed determination, she dared to poke her face, rosy with exertion, into the dim light of the passageway. The whine of the fiddle above now sang louder and sadder than before.

Then, just where the passage disappeared into utter shadow, a pinched, frightened and unreasonably green face disappeared in a blur that seemed to include steel framed spectacles. With it, the sound of a muffled oath.

Almost as quickly, Molly flung herself back inside, shutting herself in again with her back to the ravaged door.

Caught!

But wait. No, that swiftly vanished face had been both grossly out of place and oddly familiar.

Delicate auburn brows knitted together as green eyes narrowed. *Too* familiar.

She dove for her packing until she found the other weapon. Gently she drew the pistol from its oiled wrapping, checked its primings, then returned to the door. Cocked and ready, she pulled open the door, less dramatically this time. There again was the ghastly face, hovering now at the level of her own, blazing eyes rimmed with red.

"You!" she gasped, and with a small but capable hand grabbed James Cridden MacBean by the collar and dragged him within, slamming the door behind him.

"Mistress Molly!" the little Scotsman squawked. "Lord above, the bastard has kidnapped ye!"

"Good God, sir, I might have killed you! What is this!"

No taller than she and consumptively thin, irresponsibly-dressed for a sea voyage, he spoke with haste, his voice ragged.

"*Och*, I've that devil York dead to rights at last, so I have," MacBean went on, oblivious. "Kidnapping, on top of all else. I knew Sir Roger was right about the villain all along, and now he's kidnapped yer precious wee self as well. Never fear, Mistress. I shall have ye outta here."

"Fear, Master MacBean?" Molly scoffed, impatient. "My only fear is that Captain York will think I am responsible for you and put us both over the side."

"No fear of that, Mistress," he hissed. "I've a safe hiding place. We've but to stay clear of the filthy beggars until ..."

Furiously, she shook him, her bright lips twisted with disgust.

"Be quiet, you idiot. We've been away from the dock for an hour and more. How do you... Never mind, just answer me."

He gulped painfully, realizing her pistol adjusted the grimy spectacles on his pointed nose and stared; his stomach gurgled noisily.

"Did my uncle send you?" she snapped. "Or did you follow me?" The pistol never wavered from where she held it poised and unwavering at his chest.

"I followed one of these naughty fellows myself." A glimmer of avarice entered the strained expression, as if he expected great reward for his boldness. "D'ye ken, the whole garrison of Port Royal is out lookin' for ye, mistress. I myself was following one of these here pirates just to see what they might know. Sir Roger dinna trust 'em, the godless heathens."

The whole garrison? Oh my.

"Well!" she breathed over a reluctant smile. "That won't last long, if I know Colonel Rhetford. Though I'm flattered all the same."

She took a deep breath to settle her courage. The man was an idiot, sure enough, but now she had a plan, and a tool to work it with. "All right, then. Come on." She gestured sharply with the gun.

When he seemed unwilling to comprehend, she grabbed his arm and pushed him firmly through the door, hustling him along the passage to the ladder. "Up you go, sir," she said.

"Nay, Mistress, nay! That way goes to the main deck!"

"Aye, so it does. Now move while there's still no one to stop us. Move, I say!"

Molly jammed the pistol under his rib as endorsement. She might be little but she was certainly determined, and the timid secretary with no plans or weapons of his own had no choice but to obey. Quaking in very sensible fear of his life, he went where he was pushed.

On deck, the sky was lighter than Molly expected, watching from her confinement. An early moon lay low and huge on a pale horizon, and only a few stars glimmered yet in a still, blue twilight. Sails set to an angle with the wind that tossed her hair, the *Jealous Mary* ploughed an easy wake through the darkening sea.

There were men about in plenty as Molly emerged, but for a few moments it seemed as though she and her prisoner must be invisible in the shadows. Voices came down from overhead, the end of an argument lazily pursued.

"I keep telling you, she's not just some wench. She's Rafe September's daughter, and that should mean something. She has the old man's temper as well, as I'll be finding out soon enough if I don't get back to her."

Well, at least he hadn't actually forgotten about her. And he *was* defending her.

"But a wench still, Prentiss. And a pretty one too, I fancy."

"More or less," Prentiss said carefully. "Look, she can handle herself. I've seen her."

Then with a whoop and a thump a thick, unshaven shadow tumbled out of the rigging almost at her feet.

"Captain!" The Turk slapped to the deck in Molly's face, snatching the pistol from her hand and spinning her about all at once. "Eh, Davy!" he called. "It's that ginger *rahim* from the lock up. Look you, lads, at what I've caught!"

Stunned, her nerve nearly shattered.

Another voice said, "Aye, Captain." And then a hand came from behind and swung her about, this time into the squinty face of Muggs, stinking of goats. The crowd that formed ignored MacBean altogether, though he was close to collapsing in a pile broad Scots nerves.

"Look!" cried a black-haired man with one eye and no improving patch for the other. "We've caught us a wench. And a bonny one at that!"

When Molly shrank from his touch and reached for the knife at her belt, Turk growled. "Couldn't stay away from us, eh? Well my dainty, which of us do you fancy first?"

Molly screamed "Prentiss!" which made them laugh. So she called out his name again.

"Must be Prentiss she's after," someone sang out. "D'ye think?"

"He'll take his turn like anybody else!" growled Turk, and other voices nameless and nearly faceless out of the twilight joined the chorus as recognition swept over them.

Some remembered her face, others did not, but they were obscenely delighted with it all the same. At the far edge of the enclosing ring, Jimmy Fitts stood, impassive.

Then sharp as penance, Davy's voice rang out above the hubbub.

"You get away from her, Turk, damn yer eyes! Muggs, Taffy! All of ye swine, back off! Prentiss, I warned you. Mr. Keaton, break this up."

"But 'tis our wench, Davy," Black Tom whined. "She's the one got us out of the lock up. Now she's run away to sea, I guess."

"An' I guess we know what it is she wants to see, eh lads!" Ned Courage roared. Then howled, as he reached to snatch at her and she put the first four inches of Rafe's dirk through his hand. The circle widened dramatically.

"She's brought a pet with her as well, Davy." Jimmy spoke up at last. "Some kind of toad."

"Can we toss him overboard and let her stay," Turk said slyly, now eyeing Molly from a safer distance.

"I said back off, damn it. Prentiss, get down there. I thought you said she could mind herself."

"I am minding myself I think, Captain," Molly shouted, as she swept the knife out again and further widened the space between herself and the unruly crew. "Though I'd not mind a hand. Prentiss, where are you!"

"All of ye, stand off!" Prentiss snapped. They moved aside for him grudgingly, but they moved. "Lotta help you are," Prentiss said to Jimmy.

Fitts only shrugged, limpidly meeting the iron gaze. "Your lass, Pilot, not mine. Sir."

Taffy the Welshman spat and muttered, "That's the way of it then, is it? Captain's doxy?"

"Not mine!" Davy called. "She belongs to Prentiss."

Molly sneered at her tormentors. "Ha! *Pilot's* doxy, if you please."

"There it is, then," Davy added. "But she is under my protection."

She cocked an eye up to the broad, familiar face grinning at her over the rail, and blinked.

"And what valuable protection that is, sir! You won't mind if I make my own defense, I hope. All on your orders, of course."

A laugh erupted from Davy as terrible as it was delighted. He seemed to be trying to say something further, but no, he waved off any idea of it and stepped back out of sight.

Truth to tell, he recognized her father, younger and lighter, but nevertheless Rafe's voice and, dear God, his attitude in every syllable, even in the set of her jaw, but prettier. Oh much prettier! There was no way to explain it without getting stupidly sentimental, so turning away for the moment was best.

Davy looked over again and barked a laugh.

"Of course, lass. Ned, see to that hand. I'll not have you claiming invalid pay all the way to Tortuga. Clear away, you idle dogs!

Then he disappeared again with laughter but no further word. Grudgingly the rest backed off, some even finding employment while others hovered.

"God's teeth, girl," Dick hissed. "Couldn't you wait?"

"Wait! I'll be an old woman waiting for you. You left me there long enough to be 'rescued' by *this*." Nose wrinkled with distaste. "This toad, as your friend here says."

She had always despised MacBean, and Jimmy Fitts was rapidly entering the same category. He might have come to her aid, but no.

"What toad's that?"

Prentiss's eye followed her gesture down to where MacBean lay slumped on the deck, his senses and himself finally parting company. That is, he had fainted. "I see. Davy! You'll want to have a look at this."

Prentiss dragged the little secretary into the open air and called for a bucket of water.

"God's blood!" said the *Mary's* master, reappearing like a spinning top, turning and returning, over the quarterdeck rail. "If it isn't Customs House MacBean. Haul him up here, and this famous wench of yours as well. I've hardly seen her face yet, and I do hate to be ordered about by strange children, no matter how bright-eyed."

"Aye, Davy," Turk snarled, still at a safe distance. "Some of us don't care much for a tart aboard that won't be shared. It is against the articles, is it not?"

"Belay that, you dog. And the rest of you be about your business. Do you tell me you signed the articles without knowing what's in 'em? Ask me again when you're sure!"

In a moment, when Molly stood defiant before him, he was only a little gentler. "All right, my lass. It's too late to take you home. So what am I to do with you?"

She shrugged defiantly. "I'll work my own way." Her pistol and dirk restored to their places, her eyes blazed with green fire, which made every man of them catch a breath.

"So eager to get started, you couldn't wait for our Prentiss, here?"

"We have been at sea for some time, captain. I haven't eaten in hours. And if our Prentiss here was still arguing with you, then it was time I spoke for myself."

York could hardly keep himself from grinning. Such bold talk from a girl! Then an angle of light or shadow or something caught the angles of her face in some way and he suddenly twigged. "Strike me, you're that lass from FitzRobert's house! Christ Almighty, he's sent you to spy on me! Damn me!" He shook his head sadly. "What a world it is. The old bastard don't trust me."

"No, Captain," she answered. "Or rather, yes, I am the girl you saw there, though truly not to my best advantage." And now a grin of her own invaded the creamy oval of her face. "But Uncle Roger don't—doesn't—trust me either, you see, so you're perfectly safe. I am no spy."

York nearly wept. "*Uncle* Roger? Sweet Christ, Prentiss, is this how you repay me for offering you an honest living?"

"It's all my own doing, Davy," Molly said, beating Prentiss to the answer. "I know it isn't the usual thing for a woman, but it's what I want. And Dick seems to think well enough of me."

"I think well of my mother, but I don't take her to sea!" York muttered. "Well …"

The steel-grey gaze came fully to bear on her then, appraising. "Not as a passenger, then, but a working sailor, eh?"

She nodded. "If you'll teach me."

The hard look turned now on her lover, unsmiling and unforgiving. "Is that what you taught her to say?"

Prentiss's shrug was eloquent.

"He's taught me a few things, I guess," Molly said, with a toss of her head. "But I speak for myself. I'm not a child."

"Sure and you are, my girl." York met her defiant eyes and held them, and held them a long time until she perhaps grew bored and took to examining the sky, as if that was why she'd come. "Hmph" he snorted at last. "Rafe September's child, that's sure. I still ain't pleased, though. That knife your dad's?"

"Aye, it is."

And the questions began. "Well taught with it, I see."

"Well enough."

"I don't suppose you've ever killed a man?"

"I've never had the need."

"Could you, at need?"

Her hesitation was brief. "I'd have killed your man Courage if he'd been closer. I will if he tries again."

Davy nodded, approving, and went on. What languages did she know? He allowed as how good French might be useful betimes. Where had she been? He was content that she was not a quiet kept girl with no knowledge of the world. She neglected to mention the convent.

She was not afraid of heights. She was never seasick. Yes, she had been at sea before, many times. She had handled a sword. That was odd for a woman, but odd was beginning to look normal for Rafe's little girl, and Davy began to wonder why he had imagined otherwise.

Molly stood up solidly under the catechizing, slightly smug that she had so many answers pat, without stammering. She tried hard

---

to keep from looking at Prentiss at all, lest she should seem to need prompting. When she was aware of him, she felt only peculiar warmth, something like pride, which pleased her.

Finally as the moon inched up from the horizon, Davy seemed to be running down, though he still declared no decision. From time to time, while Keaton governed and DeRoet steered, the crew sent out scouts, passing and repassing in search of clues.

Black Tom had just taken his turn, smooching up his mouth at Molly in a lewd parody of a kiss. She glared. He did it again, grabbed his crotch, then strolled away whistling.

A whimper at their feet drew attention to MacBean, who squirmed under the captain's sudden, direct glare, hard as sunshine in the darkening air.

As he rose to his knees, the waspish Scot opted for what he hoped would be his most forceful opening.

"Captain York, I demand you put about for Port Royal and set me and Mistress September ashore at once."

Molly coughed her surprise, but Davy chose a thin smile, stormy eyes narrowed.

"I must apologize, MacBean. Oh, I do pray your pardon … *Master* MacBean. But unless you'd care to race with the sharks, you are with us for Tortuga. Stand up, damn you! I'll not carry on a conversation with a wharf rat whining in the scuppers. Get up, I say."

The little man could not leave off sputtering. "I cannot be a party to piracy! Sir Roger would never—"

"Ah ha! So FitzRobert did send a spy! Thinks an honest privateer such as I would cheat an honest merchant such as he." Davy shook his head sadly. "I am shocked, Mister MacBean. Truly shocked. Such terrible mistrust between partners. What has the world come to? Taffy!" he shouted.

"Aye, Captain!" The sturdy Welshman popped up beside him.

"Take this ugly lubber below and keep him close confined." When MacBean squirmed to object again, York went on. "Nay, nay, that's enough from you. Much as I'd like to give ye to the sharks this minute, I'm afraid ye're a guest of the *Jealous Mary* — at your honored employer's expense, of course—until we find transportation for you back to him."

Taffy's horny hands closed about the scrawny secretary and hauled him away, spitting and by now actually swearing.

"Close confined, I said," Davy added. "I don't want him wandering about! And as for you two."

His attention swung abruptly back to the Pilot and his roaring girl, as they said in London. His wild, dressed like a boy, problematical girl. Molly thrust out her chin in stubborn pride, while Prentiss only grinned.

"You, mistress, are here on Prentiss's assurance and my sufferance till ye've earned a place." He paused, but neither of them replied. "Agh!" he spat at last, and nodded toward DeRoet at the tiller. "Paul will manage a few more minutes, but I won't tolerate him standing your watches, is that understood! Now. Go and get the lass some supper. I suppose she'll bunk with you, more's the pity," he added with a wink.

"Davy!" Keaton objected, whose quarters contained the bunk in question.

"Enough! One more person whines at me today, he (or she!) will be shark's food, and that's flat. Work something out."

And that was the end of that.

9

CELIA LEARNING ON THE SPINET TO PLAY

"JUST LIKE A RAPIER, only the balance is out there." Prentiss gestured out across the leaf-shaped guard to the pitted grey steel of the cutlass. "It's blade heavy, see? And it favors the edge, instead of the point."

Molly nodded, her jaw set in grim concentration. "Aye, just like a rapier, only nothing like it at all."

"Now then, come at me!"

She swung, clumsy at first. Then feeling the balance, she flipped a clean curve out across her body to come in at his left hand. Steel rang against steel as he blocked the blow, and the weight of the sword took too long to recover for the riposte. Dick tapped her shoulder then danced back out of the way.

"That's it, lass. That's it. Find the balance, and use it. Bring it back clean. Try again," he urged.

But the classical training of the *salle* betrayed her. She swung right and missed, exposing herself. Dick leaped into the space and tagged the inside of her wrist.

Molly yelped. The cutlass dropped with a dull clang to the heaving deck and rolled a little away.

"Nay, lass, nay. That won't do at all," Prentiss warned. "Come now, it's hardly a fatal blow."

"September, you tell me?" laughed Davy, who was marshaling "More like December from the looks of you. I thought you said you could fight! You're not crying? Is she crying?"

Molly only glared, sucking at the sting in her wrist. She shook off the two angry tears that started in her eyes, then re-tied the scarf that caught back her auburn curls, and bent for the sword without taking her eyes from Prentiss's charming, jeering face.

This time she took a better stance, lower and more square. Refined sport was one thing. This was more like the street fighting she had once or twice run into—and away from.

So here was blue-eyed, lithe Dick Prentiss laughing and taunting, encouraging her, daring her to best him. Run in, slash, keep moving. Duck, aim low, and roll if you have to. Come up running. And never, *never* let up.

For herself, Molly said nothing, thinking only of Paris and Armand, and *Damn, this thing is heavy.* Perhaps fewer thoughts of Armand than before.

Port Royal lay far behind them now, its noise, its stinks, its glittering dangers not even a bleached bone on the horizon. Two days out, the *Jealous Mary* beat a lazy path through the Mona Passage through the islands. The line of deep green slightly to the north was Hispaniola; somewhere to the south hulked the massive body of the Spanish Main and the jeweled cities of Cartagena, Maracaibo, Portobello, Veracruz. Overhead the sky curved white to dazzle the eye, deepening to pale blue green where it met the gleam of the cresting sea.

At the bottom of her fighting concentration, Molly's mind rested, nearly content. She had wished to go to sea, and here she was. She had wished not to be sold into marriage, and now it was certain she could not be. Even if they put about now and returned her direct to Port Royal, her value as a bride would be nil. Naturally, a gentleman of birth and fashion such as Captain Benning would never tie himself to her tarnished reputation, no matter what fortune she brought him.

Right now, her fortune lay at the edge of Prentiss's cutlass, flinging sunlight into her eyes. She laughed aloud, and moved in.

They fought for nearly an hour, slashing and dodging, chasing across coiled rope and stacked stores, the ring of steel a constant descant on the air.

Dick teased and made jokes while he fought, tumbling under her blows like an acrobat to swing up, sword poised at her breast. She swept it away just in time to keep from being impaled.

Grimly serious, she answered him in kind. Her training had encouraged small flurries of attack, separated by moments of study and reflection. Now instead, whenever she had an advantage, she pressed it, fighting on, hardly stopping to breathe. Grim and intent, she paused only when he disarmed her, or stopped to show her a trick or call for water. Or, as now, when he yelped and Davy cried "Hold!" And with a roar beat up her sword.

"I said hold, you bitch! Ye've cut his wrist."

Molly skidded to a halt, breathing hard, and lifted an eyebrow. "Hardly a fatal blow," she observed.

"Aye, as may be," said Prentiss. "But if I cannot hold the sword, I can't kill you, now can I?"

She draped her agreement around a charming shrug. "Does that mean I win?"

"In a manner of speaking, I suppose you do," Davy warned with an answering smirk. "But it's not over." He shouted, "Ha!" and leapt at her, his own broad cutlass in his fist. A madly cheerful light of mayhem danced in his eyes. Her arm sprang up to stop it just in time.

Prentiss shouted, "You draw blood on that girl, and I'll murder ye!"

York only crowed up into the sun and called back. "Mind yer manners, Pilot."

Instinctively, she beat the blade away, ducked and stepped aside. He struck again, his sword glancing along her own. Thus they engaged, but York was fresh and his pride was engaged as well.

He was Captain here not because his master's papers said so, but by the rough democracy of the Brethren of the Coast, which gave command to whomever could win and keep it. If there was one thing David York could do, it was out fight every man of his crew. This one little chit of a girl was not likely to change that, and everyone should know that.

Prentiss shouted encouragement and advice she could barely hear, but the ferocious intensity was all Davy's, though he had stopped laughing. Again and again Molly thought she had covered herself only to find him patiently waiting for her to notice the blow pulled just short of her throat, or hanging over her head, that might have killed her.

The flat of his blade found her elbows, wrists, and calves no matter how well she fought. Till finally, time and exhaustion took their toll, and Davy's blade came pounding in on the edge of her own one last time, beat her to one knee, and struck her weapon aside with a blow that numbed her hand to the elbow.

Her point hit the deck. His hung in the air over her eyes, suspended but inexorable as Time.

She froze, staring up at the honed edge scant inches from her nose.

"Ye'll hate me," said Davy smugly, hardly breathing hard at all. "Ye'll hate me if I tell ye how stupid ye look, cross-eyed like that."

Weary beyond imagining, Molly ducked under the blade and pushed it aside as she flung her own away. It thudded against the gunwales and rolled to a stop.

"Aye," she breathed. "I will." And sat down hard on the grey planks of the deck, sheeted with sweat. "Not bad for an old man".

Her ears still rang with the sounds of combat, so it took a moment to realize a patter of applause and a low cheer had exploded from the gathered watchers. Taffy, Nick Trelawney, German Jack and some of the others burst into rowdy jeers when her face registered dismay. Clearly, they had been watching for some time. They must have been there all along.

Her first thoughts were angry, but those dissolved almost against her will as one reluctant corner of her mouth tilted up. "Well, Captain?" she said, panting still.

"Well, I think you'll do." A boisterous cheer raised again, never mind the mutterings of Turk, Ned Courage and Black Tom. "If this old man's opinion is worth anything."

Still, Trelawney the Cornishman wanted to know: "Aye, Davy, but say there's a full deck of Spaniards fighting like all bloody hell, and the cannon and all, eh? No bloody practice time then, is it?"

Molly glanced from him to York again and accepted with hard-breathing thanks a jack of watered rum. "Aye, Davy. That's fair. Will I live to tell about it?"

"Lass," he said. "There's no telling what a man will do under fire till he's fired on." He handed his sword off to Keaton in trade for a rag to wipe his brow. Someone else passed him a drink. "But I think you'll do. We'll see, won't we? And we'll practice you some more, later on, as well. Prentiss, you villain, who's minding the tiller?"

Dick shrugged. "DeRoet. The watch changed before we started. And I was thinking a meal might be in order."

"God, I hope so!" Molly croaked earnestly. Another round of laughter, a sweaty hug from Prentiss, and Molly was glowing. This, she thought in exultation, was exactly what she had in mind!

And so the days passed, alternately exciting or lazy and slow. At first, contrary winds drove them back out of their course for a day or so. Rather than fight it, Davy elected to wait, still in a hunting mode. By the time they rounded Cape Tiburon, though, he'd had enough and bade Prentiss take them north again. Then slipping up the Windward Passage and around the eastern tip of Cuba, they fell out of the wind for half a day while the current carried them again out of their way. Inevitably the sameness of the days began to weigh heavy on the crew, and the heat and idleness led to hard pranks and drunken gambling. Tempers shortened. This should have been one of the busiest routes on the passage to Spain, crowded with treasure ships, but they had been lucky before. They were not now. The occasional ship skidding within their view seemed too far to chase or too well armed.

The delays gave Molly time to settle in, or make a start at least. She stood Dick's watches with him, dressed in loose breeches, buff coat, and shirtsleeves like all the rest, with her father's dirk and a brace of pistols thrust through her sash, like the bravest of them. She tried to avoid touching him, no matter how innocently, where they might be seen, but it was no good. If the others flirted or flattered in their rough ways, she threatened some and charmed others as their manners indicated, until her courage and her manner won a grudging approval from a few. Among those who did not fall to her charm, Turk and Jimmy Fitts figured most bitterly, though for rather different reasons.

Finally, as the rocky point of Cap Haitien just nicked the sky off the starboard bow, Dick announced *Jealous Mary* to be a day out of Tortuga, the little island's turtleback still a slip of shadow on the horizon. They might expect to round into the protected channel sometime the next morning, if the winds held fair.

From early in the day, the men off duty all lay about the deck in the shadow of their bellying sails, drinking through the last kegs of rum and strong wine, and smoking what they could to make the time pass in pleasant fog.

At mid-day, they rigged canvas and blankets for shade and slept. As the sun fell toward a pale blue late afternoon, a few tossed dice, alternately cursing and cheering their luck and each other. The wind quickened. Muggs slaughtered a goat for supper while Millikan fired up the galley. They ate. They drank some more and fell into sentimentality, of one kind or another

The fiddler, a quiet Welshman called Owen Jones, sat in the rigging sawing out a weird, wild melody from the mountains of his home while, in appropriate counterpoint, Will Keaton and some others traded tales of ships and phantom crews that sailed to the horizon or into the fogs of the Bermudas, never to be seen again.

From this cheery company, Turk drunkenly lurched to his feet with a curse and a great belch.

"Goddamn it, Quartermaster," he snarled. "You make my skin crawl. All this talk of haunted islands, and ships that disappear in a calm sea. Between you and that bally whore yonder, I am sick all the time." He spat noisily to one side.

"Pour out some rum and shut up, damn you," Ned Courage muttered. His hand was still enflamed and throbbing from Molly's spirited defense days before. Others rumbled general, boozy agreement, but Turk was drunk enough not to be stopped, and still sober enough to stand.

"You know what we do to women like that where I come from?"

"(Where did he come from?)"

"(He was pissed up on a wall and hatched.)"

"*Inshallah!* We stone her!"

"Eh?" said one. "A rum little dell like that one? Seems a waste."

"Stone her, aye. Her brothers, her father would cast the first stones. Her own mother would spit on her."

Lacking a stone, he could throw only a poisonous glance forward where Prentiss and Molly stood elbow to elbow, leaning on the larboard rail and talking quietly.

"Izzat all?" said Courage through a hiccup.

"What?"

"Just stone the silly bint? No boiling oil? No cutting off her little fingers? No hot irons, nothin'?"

"Oh leave off, Ned," grumbled Black Thomas. "Ye sound like my old captain, time I was in King's Navy."

"Sounds like my wife!" said another.

("Christ, it's too hot for this.")

The tawny, cruel face contorted with fury, his fists curling as if ready to strike. But the grim look on Keaton warned him off. Instead, he spat again and moved away, swaying with more than the ocean's rocking.

But there was no escape from the liquorish good cheer and melancholy, short of diving below to the cramped and airless spaces between the decks with no better company than the grey rats. And the close heat of the forecastle was unbearable. Still, he could retreat only so far before encountering someone else, so now it was Jimmy's turn.

Turk came on him suddenly, clapping a grimy hand to the Englishman's shoulder. Jimmy had a pistol leveled at Turk's navel in the time it took him to turn around. He too had been preoccupied with the lovers cooing at the rail.

"Put that away," Turk snapped. "You crazy? You want to kill someone?"

Willfully misunderstanding, Jimmy agreed. "Maybe I do. And maybe you'll do." The other man fell back a step against his will, so intense was the hatred in that look. "You touch me again, mate, I'll blow your bloody balls off."

Turk widened the space between them by another step, and smiled. The oily, glassy-eyed expression proved almost as disgusting as his scowl.

"Not me, boy! Not your old comrade, eh? It is not me you are angry at, is it." He gestured towards the lovers. "It's that bitch of Prentiss's, eh?"

"Just get away from me. I ain't interested in your outraged morals, so clear off!"

Holding his ground, Turk nodded knowingly. Parts of what seemed like an idea were swirling through his befogged brain and would not be put aside.

"He ain't the same, is he, as last time we all sailed together. Got that dear sweet lass with him all the time. No way for a man to behave and we know it. Don't we?"

Jimmy shrugged and tucked the pistol absently back into his belt. "He likes her. And she's got no one else."

"Girl like that don't need nobody, does she? Girls like that in every town."

Jimmy's indifference began to flare into anger again. Turk changed his tack. "Girl like that, she makes a man a baby. Settle him down, sew his buttons, make him go to church and pray. Pretty soon, maybe start a little farm, eh?" He chuckled venomously. "A pretty sight, that. Prentiss raising sugar cane."

"Not Prentiss. Not him. No woman's ever had a hold on him. Not even his ma."

Jimmy turned away to gaze out over the eastern seas and sky, emerald green under an early rising moon. But Turk refused to be put off.

"What will happen, you think. He worry about her all the time, afraid she'll get hurt. Next thing he'll be taking chances, being stupid, eh. Get us all killed trying to save her skinny neck."

"Look, mate," Fitts said finally with a sigh. "What's between her and Prentiss is between her and Prentiss, if you take my meaning, so lay off. 'Tis sure as hell nothing to do with you. If she wants to be pirate queen of the Indies, that's her affair, too. So you just go bugger a cannon, or a goat, or whatever it is you do for fun, see, and leave me some peace."

"Piece?" The Turk grinned like a split melon, all his black and broken teeth filling his mouth like an apothecary's cupboard. "Maybe that's as may be. My advice to you, boy, is if you want her, take her. Just leave some for the rest of us. If she means to be a whore—"

"Right. That's it." Jimmy's fist came around, connected with Turk's ugly jaw with a solid crack that rocked the man back on his heels. "Now just shut it."

Without further conversation, Fitts himself went forward to stir the confrontation he had been avoiding.

"You'll be sorry you did not listen to me, Fitts you bastard!"

The moon hung low in the sky, milk-pale and nearly full, its radiance against the rippling sea still no more than the suggestion of a faint green road into the horizon that would glow with daylight for hours.

The music of wavelets slapping against the *Mary's* hull beat sweetly to the song of the Welshman's fiddle, and Molly was dreamily content. Beside her on the burnished rail, Prentiss stared not out to sea but into the astonishing halo of her hair, limned with sunset, and her face, a shadowed silhouette against the jade sea that matched her eyes. Almost carelessly, she reached to cover his slim brown hand with her own smaller one.

"You know," she said at last. "Do you know, we've been all this time together and I still know almost nothing about you?" Then she laughed her low, musical laugh and shook her head in almost melancholy humor. "I must be a terrible fool."

Her face turned up to his, a shock of green eyes and auburn hair that went straight to his heart.

Carefully he said, "I suppose I could say the same."

She nodded, suspicion confirmed. "And you're not going to tell me anything now, I can see. Well, I am a fool then. I don't mind."

"No, truly!" he said. "What do I know about you, you naughty wench? That your father was the finest pilot that ever sailed these seas, but everyone knows that. That you went to school in Paris. That you prefer life with me over marriage to an aging pervert, and showing very good sense in doing so." Then he smiled gently. "And that's enough."

"Ah?" she returned. "But who was your father? And where did you go to school? And what marriages have you run away from, eh?"

At that he rolled his back to the rail to stare out over the russet and blue sky through the rigging.

"My mother, who was a laundress, said my father was a great lord, but she might have said anything to please me, and herself. I went to school in the English Channel and the Bay of Biscay. And all the marriages I have left behind have been other men's. I think you'd not like to hear more about that."

But Molly, frowning now, was not so sure. "Not," she said, "if you don't want to tell me, I guess. But I don't understand."

"No, nor likely to either. So let's leave it be, shall we, Sweet." He slipped his hand from hers to wrap around her shoulder. "It's you I want now, and that's enough knowing, it seems to me."

She said nothing, the question so clearly closed. When she started to shake herself away, he spoke again, this time in a strained, husky whisper.

"I'm near thirty years old, or thereabouts. I can speak bad French and worse Spanish. I can read and write, thanks to my ma, and do sums thanks to Dan Rafferty who taught me the stars as well. I can sail a trim ship and lift a gentleman's wallet and charm a lady out of a new hat. I can sing a fair tune badly, and I worked three days in a shop once. No, really. I've no discipline at all, save at the tiller, and too much pride by half. And," he concluded while Molly tingled with wonder. "I reckon Molly September is the liveliest wench I've ever come across, save one. What d'ye think of that?"

She spoke up from the delicious curve of his arm, pouting amiably. "Save one?" she demanded, and he grinned.

"Our *Jealous Mary* of course. I'd never stand safe on this deck again if I admitted there was a more winsome lass than *Mary*, and in her hearing."

"Ah. And I thought I was about to hear some deep revelation."

"Revelation! Revelation, by God, come below with me and I'll reveal something to ye." He grabbed her hair in handfuls and pulled her to him, not at all against her will. "You know more about me than any woman has since I was a boy, Molly." His words rasped hot in her face. "But there's a price."

She too felt the blood rising, the center of flame light up her heart and body till every part of her tingled with fierce joy. "Oh yes?" she breathed.

"Oh, yes." His kiss came down hard over her mouth with a wild and passionate need.

With the wind in the starboard quarter carrying away the sounds of Keaton's stories and the eerie fiddle, and their own preoccupation, they never heard Jimmy approach. It was long minutes before they became aware of him standing, watching their kisses, hardly an arm's length away.

Prentiss parted from Molly reluctantly, but with a pleased, besotted look that Fitts found only more infuriating.

"It's not bad enough you bring your doxy aboard, is it?"

"Hm?" Prentiss said, a trifle dreamily. "What?"

"You think there's any man here who don't need a woman, but for you?"

"Come on, Jim."

"I want to know where you get so free to flaunt your wench like the admiral taking his lady for a cruise round the harbor."

"Dick, let me go," said Molly softly.

"No, you stay here," Dick said, a little harder. "What is it really, Jimmy? Molly's crew now, like you and me. Davy says so."

Fitts did not trouble to hide his sneer. "Oh, aye, that's well said. Friend Davy needs a baby pilot so he's willing you should bring along your poppet."

"Jimmy."

"But it ain't fair, is it? It mayn't even be legal, by the Articles of the Brotherhood."

This time, Prentiss shoved Molly behind him, his face lit up with anger. "Just what do you want."

"What I want is …" Jimmy's chest heaved with inarticulate passion, trying for freedom, until it burst from him in staccato patter. "I want … I mean, there's some here as feel it should be share and share alike, or none for any. A wench aboard ought to be free for all, or left alone. I mean you should have bloody left her in Port Royal with the rest of your toys."

"You faithless bastard."

"Give me no faithless," Fitts snarled. "I've stood by ye, aye, and saved your neck too often, too, to take that off of you, *Master* Prentiss. And it's your best I'm thinking of, after all, ain't it."

"My best, aye, I can tell."

"Wait!" Molly suddenly cut through Prentiss's cold and waiting fury. "Stop it, both of you."

Startled, they turned together as if both had forgotten she was there.

"This is a new tack, Jimmy," she said softly. "What's sharing alike got to with Dick's best interests, not to say anything of mine. Or is your trouble something else again?"

"I don't say it is."

"But?"

With difficulty, he pulled his eyes away from her, small and pale with the twilight dancing off her hair and gleaming in her eyes. Tonight, his argument was with Prentiss and with Prentiss alone.

Sure it was.

"I should have left you in jail rather than go to her. She's changin' you, makin' you chancy. Or she will yet."

"Oh?" Prentiss's voice went low and deadly in its unutterable calm. "Meaning?"

They had been friends so long, Jimmy should have known better, but he plunged on, reckless.

"Meaning she's a bloody little whore that's going to get you hanged, and maybe the rest of us too. Meaning ..."

But he had no chance to recite his catalog. In his passion, Jimmy had carelessly stepped inside Prentiss's range. When the fist caught him under the jaw, the breath to say more puffed out of him with a grunt. He spun half around, into the side rail, but Dick grabbed his shirt and laid on a second blow, and dropped him to the deck

Molly gave a small cry of sympathy and started to go to him, but Dick stopped her by an elbow.

"Leave him. He's not dead. When he rouses, you'd best be out of the way." He sighed massively. "My best friend," he said, shaking his head as he bent to one knee himself beside the other man, and shook him. "God damn it. My best friend. Come on now, lad. 'Twas naught but a tap. Come round, Jimmy darlin'. All the girls are asking for you."

If the steady breeze had succeeded in misdirecting the sounds from the deck, it just as effectively carried the noises of their scuffle to those downwind of it. Jimmy Fitts was just beginning to shake his brain back into place when Davy appeared, lowering over both men like an avenging angel. With Turk and Keaton to his left and right, he might have been St. Peter flanked by the seneschals of Heaven and Hell.

"So help me, Prentiss," Davy said behind a deadly calm. "This is what I tried to tell you. I let you bring one wench aboard, and I've got to find a dozen more."

"Bugger off, Davy." Dick stood, his full height an inch over York's though slightly less imposing. "I thought this was settled."

His captain shrugged. "Well, I'm not going to put her overboard, if that's what's ruffling your tiny mind. But there's some here just don't see it our way, my lad. And right now I'm hard pressed to disagree with 'em."

"He called her ..."

Davy put out a hand. "And what kind of girl do *you* think runs away to sea, Prentiss? Tell me. No matter whose daughter she is. I will not have some randy wench causing trouble."

"You bloody ..."

But Davy gave Prentiss's fist no chance to land. He blocked the incoming blow with one sturdy arm and delivered a powerful one of his own with the other, which sent Dick sprawling. Jimmy, who had just begun to groan awake now lay pinned to the deck by the wilted body of his friend. When Molly rushed to him, York only laughed.

"I wouldn't do that, lass. But it's your funeral."

Dick came up shaking her off, dizzy with anger and wiping blood from his mouth with the back of his hand. He came roaring toward Davy but other hands caught and held him back while York's laughter doubled.

"By God, Prentiss, I've wanted to do that since Martinique! Christ, but ye've a stout jaw, too," he said, shaking the sting out of his hand. "Now, I have said that the lass is welcome for her father's sake, and I meant it. Any man that says contrary, I will deck him myself. If there's aught else to be done, I'll decide it when we reach Tortuga. In the meantime…"

But his conclusion was interrupted by the raucous blat of the watch horn, and a wild shout from the fighting top. "Sail ho! Captain, a sail!"

All eyes turned up to where young Owen Jones swung in the shrouds. Davy called "Where away?"

"On the quarter, three points to starboard. A Spaniard by her colors and riding low."

Instantly the mood of the ship turned festive. "By God's own balls, a man's work at last! All right, this bear baiting's over, lads. Tumble aloft! There's work to be done. Prentiss, you relieve DeRoet; I want you taking us in."

He threw a hand down to Jimmy to lift him to his feet. "Fitts, you look out for Molly here. Aye, you. She says she can fight. See she's armed and placed, since it's her first time. Owen, come down from there! Let's have some music!"

"Davy, I'll need more sail if we're to catch her."

"Mr. Keaton, see to it. Well, Fitts? I gave an order."

A curl of distaste warped his mouth. "To wet-nurse a girl?"

"You want to spend this fight below? I gave an order, damn you." Then he grinned at Molly. "Now we'll see what you're made of. Adventure you want? Adventure I provide."

He smacked her shoulder to send her off, muttering afterwards "Pirate Queen of the Indies, eh? Your old man is rollin' over in his grave."

Whisked away, Molly had no more time than to touch hands with Prentiss, then the chase was on.

They pursued the *San Pedro de Ayala* eastward above Hispaniola through the best part of an hour, overtaking her finally out of the bronze glare of the western sky. Prentiss's steady skill at the helm drew *Jealous Mary* within gunnery range almost before the Spaniard knew she was under siege.

Cannoneers ready, the first shot boomed out across the narrowing seas between them, falling short of the *San Pedro* by no more than fifty yards. Catching the wind, Prentiss moved the *Mary* in to close the gap further as the crew of the ponderous galleon leapt to lay on enough canvas to escape. But at 600 tons, she rode too heavy in the water to gather speed quickly. The single shot was the only warning she would get.

"Here!" Jimmy Fitts thrust a cutlass into Molly's hands. "You think you can use this? Now's the time to prove it. Those pistols primed?"

She nodded, still silent, heart racing faster as the *Mary* beat swiftly toward the prey.

"Good. Make 'em count. Pistol first. Then the sword. Best keep that knife handy as well. Can you use both at once? Good. I can't look out for my left hand and yours besides."

He took her arm, scrambling them into position along the starboard rail, out of the way of the five 9-pounder guns that waited only on Dick's skillful maneuvering and Davy's command to fire. There would be little wait.

"Never fear!" she shouted over the growing clamor. "I won't shame you."

"Stow it."

The galleon hulked low and unsteady in the water. Even with all her canvas spread to the winds. *San Pedro* was far slower, even were she empty, than the light and speedy brigantine with the laughing redhead at her bow. As if her sponsors trusted in God to protect their treasure unaided, the owners had scrimped on armaments to make more space for gold.

She was also dangerously and inexpertly loaded and woefully under-defended. Fully half her weight must be in treasure off the Spanish Main, freshly plundered and homeward bound. There would be gold in coins and plate, and silver; ropes of pearls, rough emeralds from Peru, and diamonds maybe; coffee and bitter chocolate besides, all rattling around in haphazard splendor between decks.

So they had a few deck guns, but precious little powder or shot, and a hundred men to defend her, if they would. She was outgunned almost by definition, and her crew knew it. They could not scramble fast enough to get off an answering round of fire. Her only answer was to run.

Molly fairly sparkled at the prospect of danger. For the first time in many months, even years, she knew why it was good to be alive. Delicate nostrils flared at the sharp smells of gunpowder and quick match, hot lead and iron. Experimentally she hefted the cutlass again and again, reminding herself of everything Davy had taught her so far, certain it would be enough.

Her tongue flicked redly across lips dry with tension, recalling Armand's lessons, as well as his casual handsomeness, his hidden, subtle cruelties, and his arrogance. She wished he were here to see her.

A smirk at once innocent and deadly crossed her face, touching it with something like madness. Standing up straight and proud, even contemptuous, she became marginally aware of hostile eyes on her: the crew, almost to a man, watching the rise and fall of her breasts, hardly disguised by the golden deerskin buff coat, adding to her excitement and theirs.

They swore idly and viciously back and forth across the deck in half a dozen languages, to themselves and to each other. Ned Courage, at her right now, his hand still lightly bandaged, ignored Molly altogether. He only stood his position, body rigid with concentration, intent on the approaching prize and muttering a string of random obscenities under his breath like some arcane litany.

When she dared, Molly stole a glance up to the quarterdeck, where Dick stood almost hidden from her view by the great mast. His face a grim mask, he surely had no time to look for her. In a small part of her mind, she had the space to wonder at how much she loved him and to despair of his ever loving her at all. A man like that was faithless, surely. She thought she could handle herself well enough now among this rowdy pirate crew, but what if he grew tired of her, abandoned her when some new fancy came along?

"Ye're thinking, girl." Jimmy spoke, breaking her reverie. "That's dangerous. Stop it."

She glanced up at him fiercely. "And how would you know, sirrah? When did you last have a thought?"

The bellow of astonished laughter that followed from up down the line was just as suddenly stilled by a cry from the bridge, Davy's challenge to the Spaniard to heave to and give o'er.

The reply came as a Spanish oath and a cannon ball at last, booming loud but still short of the *Jealous Mary*. Davy's final word on the matter was the almost instantaneous roar of Turk's culverin, one deafening blast following hard on the echo of the Spaniard's.

By Davy's trademark contract with Fortune, round shot cracked the *San Pedro's* main mast, spilling timber and canvas and lines in an awkward tangle, fouling other rigging and delivering death or worse to crewmen below. Then, Taffy's fire blew out one of the swivel guns and the men behind it.

With the rest, Molly stood on the railing, one hand wrapped into the ratlines, the other testing and re-testing the balance of her blade as the *Mary* hove still closer to her target.

The Spaniard tried futilely to answer, boldly attempting to maneuver into a decent firing position, but *Jealous Mary's* gunners were quick and deadly, and San Pedro's guns were few. A few wild shots came back from hand weapons—one of Davy's lads screamed and fell, but little else.

The galleon rode so low, her fore and after castles sat almost level with the *Mary's* own, and her main deck was little more than a quick step across in the gently swelling seas. Grappling hooks shot out from eager hands, then reined up taut to bind the two ships together in their mating dance.

A pause. A caught breath. A moment suspended in time. A look. Some shouting between the captains, then Davy's sharp command:

"To it, lads! Don't let 'em get to close quarters!"

And they were across, screaming and cursing in the madness of pitched battle, and above it all, the wild singing of Owen Jones's fiddle, calling down the sky.

The noise was unbearable, a terrible, impossible surprise that had no end. No heroic tale of battle Molly had ever heard had mentioned the noise: the deafening blast of the great guns and the pagan roar of men screwing up their courage. Worse was the bitter smoke of cannon and musket fire that stung her eyes and clogged her throat.

All about them a brilliant sun-glazed day careened off blue water on all sides, and still she was half-blinded by smoke, terrified, and furious, all at once, with the motherless bastards who made her so afraid. Then the order came to board, and she knew she was shouting, but could not make out her own voice, lost in the ragged chord of conquest.

As she stumbled over the enemy's railing, she knew only that the livery of Spain came at her with a raised sword and for a precious moment hesitated. Well what Christian man would expect to find a woman—no, a girl, *por Dios*—brazen among the heretic pirates of England?

She caught him in the midst of his stall. Felt the halt just before her own sword found his throat. The blade bit and held fast.

Held fast. Confused, she edged towards panic. No one had told her the blade would catch on bone. Why had no one told her! What was she to do? It would not come away.

Slumping into death, the body nearly wrenched the cutlass from her hand. Then as it turned, pivoting on air, the grip of bone and tendon gave way to let the steel twist out of the awful wound by itself. Blood flew. She flinched away from blood and shattered bone and white, white shards of tendon, and would have sobbed for fear. But another man with twice her age and service came at her, his own face alight with the same fear and rage.

All right, now she knew. *Move!*

Slipping in blood and disordered ropes and broken gear, she stumbled back. This time the incoming blade poised over her gilded head just as Davy's had done how many minutes, hours, days ago. Again the look of wonder on the swarthy face, too much like the Turk's who hated her. Again, the pause that gave an instant's advantage.

The grip of a pistol butt filled her hand. Flame gouted from the barrel. Another monster fell. She hated it. She reveled in it.

This is not women's business.

This is what I was made for.

If I stop, I will die.

Vaguely aware of her friends at either hand, she pressed with them toward the main mast, herding the enemy and snarling like a she-wolf. Coherent thought vanished.

The trick worked again and again, her sweetly beguiling figure making up for her lack of stature or strength. Each man who ran on her, sword held high, took in the flare of red-gold curls and seductive curves, and paused. They came on just the same, but their hesitation held them back just enough that the blow fell less surely. Then her wrist twisted and her cutlass flashed, and the dirk beat aside the attacker with a life of its own, giving her time to strike home.

For a while she stood back to back with Jimmy Fitts. As some grizzled, one-eyed Spaniard leaped out of the rigging with a yodeling cry, his foot caught Jimmy's shoulder, almost spinning Fitts onto a third man's sword.

Molly jumped in to take that blade on her own, striking forward with her father's dirk. That was parried and a cutlass swirled above her, but Fitts recovered and cut in under her arm. Then Molly turned to see another bastard aiming a pistol straight for Jimmy's head. Her sword darted out again and came back bloodied. The pistol discharged into empty sky, falling with the hand no longer attached to its arm.

Jimmy swung about at the sound so close to his ear to find Molly leaning over her sword, face streaked with blood, angry tears, and sweat, and gasping painfully in the sulfurous air.

"You!"

"Aye." The syllable stuck dry in her throat. She coughed, swallowed, and tried again. "Aye. So tell me, do I qualify, Master Fitts? I," she croaked, straightening. "I seem to have saved your life. 'Tis well you took that other one from me, though, or we'd both be …"

"Save it," he snarled. "I don't want to answer to Prentiss for you is all. No more'n that." He stepped over fallen bodies and tangled gear to get where the fighting was still thick, leaving Molly frowning after him.

Someone swore in sibilant Spanish. She could feel the pause as once again flinty enemy eyes took in her soft, female shape, long enough to retrieve the firm grasp on the hilt of her sword, then whip it up in time. In a single swing from the shoulder, a smooth arc as lovely as any of Davy's crashed first on the edge of the incoming sword.

Then her knife beat his aside, and on the third beat balanced the parry with a slash to the middle. He fell, screaming—the first scream she had honestly heard since the action began.

The fighting seemed to go on forever. But when Molly finally beat the last man down and ran him through and looked up, and wiped the sweat and blood from her eyes with a dirty sleeve, the sun seemed hardly nearer the horizon than when they had started. There was blood slick on her hands, smeared on her face, lurid and nearly black in the glare of fires and hazy red twilight. The sword weighed even heavier now. Her slender wrist cried out to be relieved of duty.

Gasping, she shifted the weight of it, cocking the blade back to her shoulder. With bleary eyes she surveyed the rocking shambles of the deck that seemed to have gone silent around her.

She shook her head to clear it, blinking, trying to recall some detail of the past quarter hour. One pistol had disappeared, she remembered., tossed aside with no time to reload. The other remained disguised in blood, in her sash, unused.

Davy's men had the Capitano at bay. A ring of swords leveled at their bellies kept the remnant of the *San Pedro*'s men carefully back. Davy himself stood unarmed, legs wide apart and hands on hips, grinning and pleased with himself.

Molly could barely hear him over the ringing in her ears, but she knew the fight was over and that they had won. The *San Pedro* was theirs, or, properly, the King's. The groaning bodies at her feet no longer posed a threat to herself, her friends, or oh yes, her country.

Her lip curled with scornful laughter as she surveyed the tally of her victories. So much for respectability, Uncle Roger! Or for making me into the lady you all wanted Marjorie to be. Victory. Yes. While other voices charged, negotiated, lowered colors, the deck and its awful burden snapped at last into focus. Drained of rage, she gasped a racked and broken sigh, and bit back weary tears. So many dead, how many at her hands?

On a scuffling sound, she whirled, knife raised, choking back a sob.

"Nay, Moll. Moll! It's me," said Prentiss softly.

Sword and knife clashed as one to the deck, and she flung herself into his arms to bury her face in his shoulder.

Protective, he folded her into his embrace like a weary child while her sobs ran down. A little longer, exulting in the shape of her body in his arms, then he held her away lightly. "Enough of this, now, lass. Tears? From you?"

"Dick, I was ..." She stammered, then coughed again on the bitter air. "It was ..." Exultantly, she tilted her face up to his, shining with tears and streaked with filth. "I'm still alive!"

And that made him laugh the low, chuckling laugh that burst at last into a shout.

"Aye, that you are, Sweet! And Jimmy too, thanks to you. I saw that, and well done it was, too."

"It was indeed!" York's own roar came as he strode carelessly across the deck towards them, kicking aside whatever tried to impede him.

Dick draped an arm about Molly's shoulders like a proud parent. "She's as good as the best of 'em," he said with quiet challenge.

"Shut up, Prentiss, you mad bastard. She's no such thing." Davy pulled Molly away from her lover and planted a kiss squarely on her brow. "Not quite as good as the best, for that's myself and no woman will ever be that. Nor no man neither, damn yer eyes. But I must correct my last word on the subject."

This time a great kiss landed fair in the middle of her soft, giving mouth with something more than brotherly affection, which she received and even returned with astonishment. Then he turned to the others, leaving Molly dizzy and looking to Prentiss with an apologetic shrug.

"What I say is this!" said Davy, raising his voice to its quarterdeck bark. "I am right glad to have you here, Molly September, and no niggling whoreson stall whimper is going to say otherwise. I want that understood! Rafe's girl is welcome aboard my ship for her own sake any time we sail, and she's not to be trifled with or you'll deal with me. Even though," he said more closely, so that only Molly could hear. "I could wish yer old man might have had some mercy and sent me a lad, eh?"

10

WORLD ENOUGH AND TIME

"SO THIS IS PIRACY," Molly breathed as a shower of golden Spanish coins spilled through her fingers to ring merrily on the stone floor at McQuarry's place on Tortuga.

Prentiss chuckled lightly, admiring the glow on her face.

Davy nodded almost soberly, however, and added "Aye, lass. After I've reckoned out our noble sponsor's shares, of course, what's left is all ours. And now you might pick up the pretty darlings so I can finish counting them."

She scrambled to do so, while Davy scratched another entry in his book. The *San Pedro* had proved to be richly weighted down with gold coins struck in Peru from the melted plunder of Inca treasuries. There was jewelry, too, in plenty: gold and silver glittering with unset emeralds, rubies, and ropes of pearls; sacks of cacao beans worth as much as the jewelry. All this the merchants of Port Royal would turn into cash, eventually, but the money could be shared out immediately.

Five shares went to the captain and two each to the pilots and the lieutenant, with an extra share voted to Prentiss by the crew for sailing them in and out of a victory so neatly. To each of the crew would go a single share, still substantial.

Money had never meant much to Molly, since she had never been without it. But now, with cold currency shimmering in her hands as it never had before, she came suddenly aware that by all outward signs she had left Port Royal a pauper. The brief wave of dismay was immediately replaced by a warming sensation of wealth, and all her own. This somehow made leaving her legacy and her unlovable family seem a much smaller thing.

"Privateering, if you please," Prentiss said as Molly carefully piled the fallen coins in neat stacks on the table.

"Oh, aye." She shrugged, her graceful shoulders as expressive as her eyes. "Rafe used to say that *pirate* was a Spanish word. But it was exciting, wasn't it? Whatever we call it."

"And that's what you came for, is it?" asked Keaton. "The excitement?"

"I suppose it must be," she sighed wistfully. "This handsome rogue aside, of course. Mind you, I'd not give the money back just for the privilege. Especially since I've left Uncle Roger with my inheritance. But even that money was all from buccaneering, wasn't it, one way and another? So now." She glanced at Prentiss with mischief all about her. "What is so exciting about Tortuga? What can we do here that we couldn't do in Jamaica?"

"For one thing, we can't get arrested!" said Prentiss.

And Davy said, "Better still, we don't have to talk to your Uncle Roger, by God!"

But Keaton added cautionary tones. "You just watch it don't get more exciting than you bargain for, my lass. There've only been women of any kind on this island for maybe a dozen years or so. And most of 'em, well, they're a rough lot."

"Will, I am not a child."

"What he means, Sweet, is that some years back, when the Frenchies still ran the place, the old commander thought the lads needed some civilizing. So he sailed into Paris, France, and rounded up all the cleanest whores, and brought them back to sell by the pound at the settlement above the harbor, what they call Basse-Terre. But there's still a lot more lads than lasses, eh, Mr. Keaton?" Prentiss winked knowingly at the cherubic lieutenant.

"The commander?" said Molly. She looked confused, but charmingly so. "You don't mean Davy?"

"Hardly," Dick answered while Davy swore. "See, once upon a time, a long time ago, the king of France thought he could make a profit off these islands, and chartered a West Indies company. He let Jean Le Vasseur build that old fort up on the rock to hold Tortuga from the Spaniards. He got the docks and warehouses built as well, so's we'd always have some place for stores. Then King Louie got the idea maybe the lads needed more organization, so as to pay him a tax or such like, so he sent a bloke called D'Ogeron—that's the commander—to take charge of the buccaneers living here and over on Hispaniola, just across the straight there. Mind you, there were as many English as French on this island by then, so that made it more of a challenge."

"As colonies go, a farmer or two pretending to plant tobacco wasn't entirely profitable, see."

"Especially with the Brotherhood outnumbering the farmers ten to one. But, being a man of wit and inspiration, he figured out just what sort of chains hold a man best."

"And a few months later," Davy picked up the thread as Prentiss paused to lift his drink. "What should come sailing into the bay but a flash royal galleon and two hundred of the pickings of Paris. Old D'Ogeron was sold out by dinnertime."

"And why do you keep looking sideways at Mr. Keaton like that?"

"Why, because his Annie was one of those lasses, of course!" Davy roared. "And five or six of the ferocious brats you'll see running loose hereabouts are his. Well, *hers* at any rate."

"Now, look here Davy…" Keaton blushed and tried to object, but it was no good. His friends, convulsed with unmanly giggles, were hard pressed to keep from rolling to the floor.

"Why, William!" said Molly, picking up the merry mood. "I had no idea. You're married?"

Keaton's face went almost shy, a new rosy glow swarming across his bald crown. "Can't say what she'll think of me sailing' off with wenches, though."

"Just keep drinking," Davy said through his laughter. "You'll be explaining it all to her soon enough. In fact …"

"In fact, " said Prentiss, thoughtfully. "Y'know, I'm used to dossing wherever I happen to land here or there. But—" With a knowing hand he turned Molly's chin up so as to show her off with artistic flare. "I cannot dock this face just anywhere, nor leave her sleeping under McQuarry's trestles, now can I?"

"I should think not!" She snapped white teeth at his fingers, and laughed. "So you've no house of your own, then. Here in your buccaneers' paradise?"

"Ah," he said. "As a matter of strictest fact, no."

"Oh aye," Keaton grumbled, shuffling hastily to his feet. "Talking of home. I'll take my share and be off home now, if y'don't mind, Davy."

But Dick laid a hand on the older man's arm before he could move. "Not so hasty, now. It happens that Mr. Keaton, our lieutenant and esteemed quartermaster here, has a fine stone house just up the hill, and betimes he lets me stay there."

"Prentiss, for godssake! Annie takes one look at Molly and I'm a dead man!"

"Catches the breeze. Gorgeous view of the sea." He lingered lovingly on the adjective, "From almost any window."

"Gorgeous?" said Molly, intrigued. There was something else going on among the men. Some old joke, she could tell. But Keaton wasn't playing along.

"Davy!" said the quartermaster. "Say something!"

"Gorgeous," said Prentiss.

"Hot and cold running children in every door," Davy added.

Dick shrugged, "Aye, now and again."

"Night and day, more like."

"Oh, I like children. Molly likes—eh?" He checked. She nodded, barely controlling hilarity. "Aye, Molly likes children."

"There's no room."

"We don't need much."

"A bed," Molly prompted.

"A bed, surely. Maybe a pillow, naught else."

"And a mirror?"

"Oh aye, a mirror. No more, though."

"Mayhap a wash stand."

"Davy!" Keaton cried again, helpless under the onslaught.

The captain had been gazing cheerfully in some other, any other, direction. The rusty grey head swiveled round, eyes wide and glittering. "Hmm?"

"We'll be staying up at Keaton's," said Dick, with a wink. "If anyone's asking."

"Oh, good then. That box looks to be yours, Pilot. Lieutenant, the one next to his." He hummed a dance tune to himself for eight bars and shuffled papers on the table, then went on. "Oh, and your pick from the chest, each of you, for party favors. You'll be wanting something expensive now for Annie, I expect."

Will Keaton's expression held at *resignation*, with a touch of *hopeful* as if waiting for some countermanding orders, but the issue seemed to be settled.

"Aye Davy, that's so," he sighed finally. He snatched up the first thing in the treasure chest that met his hand—a triple strand of pearls a yard long—and turned for the door.

Molly jumped up gleefully and kissed him on the cheek. "Thank you, Will."

"All right. Well. Aye, I'll be telling Annie." Still shaking his head and biting his teeth, he was away.

Dick and Davy raised their glasses in companionable good cheer, but Molly turned with a playful pout. "Shares for all and naught for me, Captain?"

Davy raised the back of his hand to her in playful admonition. "Do you think so? When ye've signed the Articles like everyone else, then you'll have a share. Might help if you could run the rigging and all, tell a marling spike from a sounding lead, do a sailor's duty as well. We already have a difficult wench on the figurehead, so that job's taken."

She sat again and sighed, leaning her pretty chin in her pretty hands. "Curs't and sad, but at least not sleeping on the beach. All right, if you'll teach me, I'll learn. I did grow up among sailing men, remember. As for you," she said, turning to her accomplice. "I suppose with your fresh restored fortune, Master Prentiss, the delights of Tortuga will be irresistible to you. While I am being entertained by Will's numerous boys and girls?"

"What, jealous already?" Prentiss answered with a look of wounded pride.

Davy cocked a crooked smile. "And she hasn't even met Lily yet."

"Lily?" She straightened.

"Shut up, Davy."

"Dickon?"

"Oh now, Molly," he drawled. Gingerly Prentiss got to his feet, righting the stool just before it could fall, and took her hand. "Didn't I say I'd take care of you, Sweet heart?"

"I think you said something about taking me away from all this, but you never mentioned where."

"Well then, let me show you. Come with me, my dear!" He gestured expansively out to McQuarry's shaded courtyard. "Tortuga lies before you!"

"Keaton's first, I think." She shrugged her little pack of belongings onto her shoulder, and said, "Don't you?"

Deflated just slightly, he agreed, snatched up his prize box, and headed out the door. Then stopped, searched swiftly through the common chest, and lifted out a bright gold necklace. It spilled like fire over his fingers, sparkling with diamonds set into blue enameled flowers.

"Party favor, " he said, and tossed it at Molly.

She gasped and snatched it out of the air, giggling with delight. While she settled it around her neck, he reached in again to lift out a pearl and diamond ring on the end of one little finger.

"Something for Annie, eh, to keep the peace?"

Davy nodded, knowing. "Well thought of, aye. And aye, very pretty, lass. Prettier when you get women's clothes on again, though, eh?"

She stuck out her tongue, then picked up her own bundle again. Hand in hand, they headed out.

Only the Basse Terre itself was almost flat. The rest of the nameless settlement rose steeply away from the harbor along a serpentine path that wound up the face of the hillside. Now and then the track split off to clearings hidden in the trees, screened by tall grasses and low shrubbery. Stone cottages and wicker huts, workshops and animal pens, storehouses and something that might once have tried to be a church, all spaced out between to discourage any thought this might be a town.

Each flat-roofed house no matter how poor had some kind of garden, with turnips, cabbages and yams, and a gate to keep out the goats. As they walked among them, a babble of languages merged into an indecipherable patois of French and English, Spanish and Dutch that rattled the air in any sentence shouted by strident women at their transient mates and each other. The children and dogs had evolved some dialect entirely their own.

The air grew dustier and hotter as they climbed away from the harbor. From everywhere busy noises shook the air. Although women shrieked, and dogs and half-naked children of every age spilled out of every door place, like any country town in Europe, the resemblance to a proper village was purely superficial. Rather, it was more like an army's baggage train in winter quarters. Life was anchored by the women whose men went off for days or weeks at a time, and might return with fabulous gifts, or to have their wounds bound up, or not at all.

Now, where the first bracing foundation stones of the road from the fort began, a creek bubbled up over flat washing stones and into a trough where women white and brown came to draw cooking water and gossip over the laundry. Lawless or civilized, they might be free of society's burdens here, but women's work never changed.

Other women's work, Molly thought as she passed them. Not her own.

A few paces past the communal well, Dick had turned and was waiting for her in front of one of the tawny stone houses. Out of the dancing shade of a pair of fat date palms, she saw a fond smile slip over his face, as if he were happy just to watch her. She smiled too; stopped where she was for a moment to look back, admiring.

No matter the light, whether the colorless glare of midday, or the black shade of a broad-brimmed hat, he was without doubt the best looking man she had ever seen. Revealed in the sifting light, the middling brown hair seemed to have stolen a touch of gold, whether lifting away from his ear in the offshore breeze or plastered to his neck in straggling curls, dark with sweat. Straight nose, strong chin, dazzling blue eyes and oh yes, those shoulders. Yes, quite the handsomest man she had ever known.

He quirked an eyebrow at her, and held out a hand. "Coming?" he said.

She knew a stupid smile betrayed her, so she kept her words simply functional. "Are we there yet?"

The low stone house just above them rang with argument.

"*Mais ma chère*," said a voice that sounded something like Keaton's, but uniquely changed. "*Mon ange*. I mean, dammit, angel. Annie!"

"Annette!" A woman's voice shrilled in correction. "*Pas* Annie. How many times *a j'ai dit*? Annette!"

"Sweeting!"

"And how long have you been here. How long since you docked, and you drinking all day already!"

In the brief noon shade of date palm, "Ah," said Molly.

Dick nodded and agreed, "Ah."

"Stay here often?"

"My home from home."

Now stomping on floorboards and a smartish clap of maternal hands. "*Allez! Tout le monde, allez vous-en.* All of you. Out the bath and out of the house!"

A short, neat path edged with smooth stones marked the way to Keaton's shaded house. As Molly walked into Prentiss's easy embrace, already warm with exertion and pleasant thoughts, a shoeless, shirtless 3-year-old in bright red stockings and wet hair, shot out of the doorway and bounced off their knees.

Behind him, another slightly older, then another older again and a pair of twin girls getting tall and almost too old for this sort of play, tumbled out into the path clad only in their shifts and golden braids. The girls looked up at Prentiss, then at Molly, traded sly glances, then screamed and dashed away, giggling.

The oldest boy sprinted a few paces up the path, looking back as he ran. Caught off-guard, he stumbled on a tree root, rolled and recovered, then shouted "Hey, Prentiss!"

"Hey, Chrétien!" Dick called back with a wave.

"Ye won't let *ma mère* kill 'im, eh?

"Not a chance, lad, never fear."

"It's all right then!"

"*Absolument, mon brave.*" The accent was terrible, but the meaning was clear.

"Eh, *qui est* la pretty lady, *mon oncle? Si belle, eh?* Too *belle por toi,* old man."

With a startled laugh more like a cough, Prentiss shouted back, "And too old for you, my lad."

"I'm rising 12. How old are you?"

Prentiss looked at Molly then back at Keaton's oldest son. "Ha! *Much* too old, brat."

The boy put out his tongue and made to leave when Molly laughed, "Next year, then, *mon héros.*" And followed with a stream of gutter French that left Prentiss staring and the boy gagging on his own laughter, before raging off to find his friends.

Dick dragged her into a quick hug and teased, "Am I going to have to protect you from my godson too?"

"You heard me, not until next year!" When he started to growl protectively, she laughed into the eyes that never failed to set her on fire and added, "Besides, his eyes are brown."

"Ah."

"And his voice hasn't changed."

"Ah hah."

"And he isn't you."

Prentiss pressed on her a swift but thorough kiss, then turned her to the door in the yellow stone wall. "Remember, you've had warning." He stepped them into cool sudden dark. "Hello the house!"

The door that swung behind them was no more than a wicker gate, close woven, draped with brocades once destined for the Grand Turk's harem; the room within, a volume of shadows unlighted against the heat of the day.

And when their eyes had adjusted to the light, Molly found, against all expectations, their sturdy yeoman lieutenant had locked a fine looking woman near his own age in a fierce embrace, ending all arguments.

Politely, Molly looked elsewhere. She marked the furnishings. Had she expected something less? A table, a few chairs, benches—all well made and inlaid with fine work, and more in another room just beyond. Simple but rich, draped with exotic fabrics, the odd gold thread glimmering in the dusty sunlight filtering through narrow windows.

A carved and inlaid sideboard showed off the dull glow of pewter plate, delicate Dutch porcelain, and Spanish candlesticks, silver and gold, all lovingly maintained. On each wall, lugubrious pictures of saints flanked racks of muskets and swords of all kinds. At least the family was well defended, in this world and the next.

Taking off his hat with a flourish, "*Bonjour, ma belle, ma dame, ma petite* Annette?" Dick said carefully.

The woman was not petite at all, but handsome certainly, and sturdy enough to have survived first the streets of Paris and now these other, more rustic trials. The dark hair knotted at her crown was greying at the edges and her figure told the tale of many children. She was trim, though, and hard and tough as nails, and the pearls that were her prize looped haphazardly over sun-roughened arms and throat and hair. When she looked over

Keaton's shoulder in some annoyance at the interruption, her face flooded with recognition, not entirely displeased.

"*C'est toi*," she said. "You. Again." Her heavy lidded gaze took in the roaring girl at Prentiss's side, then returned to him. "You've been away long enough. I suppose you have brought me something, too."

Dick nodded, pressed the propitiating jewelry into her upraised palm.

"And this one?"

"My Molly," he said. "You'll like her."

"Madame," Molly said in her most conciliatory voice. "Please, if it's a bother, I'm sure we can—" But the woman of the house cut her off with an idle gesture, admiring instead the rich jewel.

"*Eh bien*, Richard. You know the way." She glanced at Molly again. "And find her some clothes, *par le bon Dieu!* Oh, if Isabelle bothers you, slap her and send her out."

"Little Izzy?? She's nine years old!"

"She has *treize ans*. Thirteen! Et *si précose!* Do as I tell you, *mon frère*. And as for you." She returned her attention to the big man still silent in her arms, who through all this had not once let her go.

Prentiss took Molly's hand and slipped passed them, muttering, "Christ, what is everyone's obsession with age today!"

Molly giggled and followed him into the kitchen, with its painted iron stove and copper bathing tub abandoned by children liberated by their papa's arrival. The table was littered with scraps of melon, banana, and bread crumbs: the end of an afternoon meal.

She smiled at the scene of interrupted domesticity, and was suddenly conscious of her boy's breeches, buff coat, and sailor's shoes. The feeling persisted as they passed through the kitchen, a pantry, and around the outer rim of the house. One stone room led into another until he paused at a stout wooden door and produced a key.

Keys? "So you do come here often," she said wryly. "I thought you said you just slept anywhere you happened to be!"

The door, warped with damp and disuse, resisted. Shoulder and hip expertly applied, it swung stiffly into a small room crowded with dark.

"Well, Sweet, I do have to put my things down somewhere."

He dragged thick carpets from the two narrow windows and winched open an outer door to flood the room with a golden-green light, hazy with dust motes.

Surprise upon surprise, Molly thought in wonder. For one wall was stacked with a dusty pile of fine wooden boxes, with folders of silks stashed in the corner, wrapped in canvas against the damp. Gold trinkets from Peru tumbled over silver Mexican saints, and gaudy regimental banners draped like sails across the ceiling beams.

The dark, deeply-carved bed that took up half the little room was also Spanish, and neatly made up, though its rope supports sagged and the velvet counterpane had been nibbled by something. Next to it, a little table inlaid with ivory, and a good oil lamp.

Then more wonderful still, within hand's reach above the bed, a rack of books ranged briefly but carefully through a world of subjects: from the astronomy and navigation that were his trade, to some poetry and a well-thumbed copy of Mandeville's *Travels*. If Prentiss, like so many of his fellows, had spent most of his plunder on drink and women and other vices, he had still managed to keep a few treasures of the eye and mind here in a place of his own. She could hardly breathe for the understanding laid before her.

Outside, a huge tree's rambling branches leaned over a stone wall. Its broad leaves filtered out the sun and heat, gave shade to exotic, nameless flowers and green twining things, now overgrown and mostly wild. And that was the second shock: that hidden above the hurley-burley anarchy of Tortuga, in a house filled with children and noise, was a private, tiny, quiet garden, a world all Dick's own, boxed in with a low barrier of stones and woven wicker. And just beyond, she could spy a clear view of the wide and perfect blue of the sea.

Gorgeous, she thought.

Molly moved as if enchanted through the room and out into a magical space where old leaves crunched underfoot and hummingbirds flickered overhead, and she tried not to stare.

"Where did this come from?" she breathed as she turned back to him, trembling as if she had stepped into fairyland. "How did it get here?"

"Oh, some dry winters, slow times. Jimmy an' me, we helped Keaton build Annie a proper kitchen one year; helped her put in that garden. Keaton likes to keep her happy, being he's away so long betimes. In between, this just happened, I guess." He shrugged lightly, watching with almost guilty pleasure the delight playing over her face. "I'm not entirely idle, you know."

Her eyes had been so busy with the books, the garden, the treasures in every corner, but now they returned to him. "So I see," she said. "But the rest of this. Banners? Books?"

For a moment it seemed as if he might actually blush. "Just the odd trifle, here an' there. Those Spanish grandees have more than they need, some of it worth keeping. Don't be too impressed. That red volume next to Montaigne there is the naughty Earl of Rochester."

She laughed, still curious. "But you've stayed away the last two years?"

"Longer. I was... sick once. Stuck in Port Royal, then just stayed." But now he looked uncomfortable, as if two people made the room unbearably small and intolerably warm. "Look, it's a long story. Point is, this place is mine alone, see. I— I don't bring the lasses here. Least, not till now."

There were things she would never need to know.

Three and a half years ago, almost four, Prentiss—with Davy, Jimmy Fitts, everyone he knew—they had all sailed out with Henry Morgan and though some felt ill-used most of them had come home rich and mainly alive from Portobello, then again from Maracaibo, and finally the greatest prize of all, hardest won, the golden city of Panama.

The horrors of that last fight did not bear thinking of: traveling disease-riddled jungle rivers by canoe and flat boat just to take the Spanish bastards from behind; forty miles that seemed a thousand, a week that seemed like months; near to starvation half the time; sick or watching friends rave with swift, nameless fevers the rest. Then the battlefield itself, and the insanity of a looted city that burned for days.

Despite the wealth they had come away with—some of them—well, she'd be happier not knowing. It was bad enough that he did. Rafe September had died there, and Dick knew it was his fault, his and Davy's.

Afterwards it had seemed best to live ashore, fight ordinary fights with ordinary bastards like himself. Breathe ordinary air. An idle life filled with rich, idle women, easy money, and cheap rum looked a far better fortune, so it did. Well enough that his pastoral retreat above the free-for-all of Tortuga's Basse-Terre should sit closed and locked five hundred miles away while he played the harlot in Port Royal. Until now.

Until now.

An odd line of the earl of Rochester's drifted across his thoughts: *All my past life is mine no more.*

He shook the thought away angrily. His past was his own, it need not be shared. Not to tell her was not the same as lying, not at all.

Still entranced, Molly had dropped to the floor to explore among the closed cases and anonymous piles of stuff. Murmured as she forced up the lid of a small rosewood box, intricately carved. Curious. One gold English angel, 10 shillings, strung on a twisted thread. A rosary of onyx beads with a battered brass crucifix, well-thumbed and smoothed anonymous with use. Her fine brow furrowed, trying to remember something.

"You know, I had a dream once…" But she let it go, and closed the box, and put it back where she'd found it, then looked up at Prentiss sitting cross legged beside her, clearly lost in thought.

He knew, or thought he knew, he might distract her with affection. She was romanced, enchanted, by secrets revealed and there was a perfectly good bed right here. All right, the ropes needed tightening, but neither of them would mind that for long. Women, he knew, were easy targets for romance.

Except

Except

She was not like any other woman.

She could not look at him; she could hardly take her eyes away from him. From the moment that door opened her world, already changeable as three-tiered velvet, had changed again. For as daring, enticing, as dangerous a rogue as she knew him to be, now she had proof that he was also a heart and a brain.

He had said he could read; he had not said what he read. She knew he was a fine navigator, everyone said so; now she saw the study behind it, the discipline he denied. And history and poetry! He had made himself out of whole cloth, and no one was to know of it.

There on the floor, knee to knee, their minds met, then their eyes, perplexed and qualified. Almost without thinking, he put one strong hand to her cheek and drew her soft to his kiss.

A kiss that at this moment seemed all she wanted in life. But instead she pushed him away and leaned back on her hands. "Oh no, Dick Prentiss," she said sternly. "I am not distracted so easily."

He blinked. "Wh– What?"

She could not put a name to the terrible sadness lurking behind his eyes, but she knew it had to be stalled and turned. So she smirked instead and tossed her head in that way she had. "I'm such a light wench, am I, that you can give me any wild promise and fail to keep it?"

"Molly!" His confusion was utterly real, and perhaps an acceptable exchange for other, more perilous emotions.

"Look about! Piles of gold and jewels in every corner—and no mirror?"

The laughter burst from him suddenly, sent him reeling over backwards until, lying almost flat on the floor, he reached long arms under the bed and dragged out a double armful of canvas and dust. Coughing, he untangled his legs and stood up so he could muscle the thing out of doors.

"Stay back," he warned from the shade of his own private garden. "This could get ugly."

Which made her giggle in anticipation and, taking orders for a change, hold her breath.

He gently laid the heavy bundle flat on the shady grass, turned it over, then untucked and unfolded and cut away the stiffly pleated canvas as trimly as he could. The dust flew up like a cloud of pigeons anyway. As he choked and gasped a bit, batting the dust away with flying hands, the stiff, dirty grey sailcloth slipped away to reveal a perfect and unspotted mirror in a vast gilded frame carved with roses and crosses and ecclesiastical arms and angelic hosts. Her promised mirror, on demand.

"Milady?" said Prentiss with a deep flourish of a bow, entirely too pleased with himself. "With the compliments of His Grace, the Archbishop of Mexico." He sneezed, very hard.

In quite real and childish glee, she actually clapped her hands and shouted.

"Oh Dickon!" she cried. "You're a magician! And," she added thoughtfully under a lifted brow. "And 'pon my soul, sir, that is the ugliest thing I have ever seen."

He bowed once more, giving grace to her unerring taste in accessories.

"Then I have done the nuns of the Convento de Santa Natividad a great favor in diverting it from their use. What do nuns want with mirrors anyway?"

They were still laughing and sneezing and *Now if I only had a comb* as she ran into his arms, when they became aware of a treble hiccupping and the intimation of infant tears. They turned toward the sound.

Crouching in the unguarded inner door: a boy-child of three or maybe four, red-eyed and naked as Cupid on holiday, its hands damply involved with its mouth. Without letting his woman loose just yet, Prentiss glanced over her shoulder to what he presumed was his youngest godson. Or nephew. He shook the problem away. Or something. Its gender, at least, was beyond question.

"Is that our Jean?" he asked pleasantly.

"*Nooooo!*" mourned the child. "*C'est Jeannot*, me."

Prentiss smiled, recognizing the baby name. "Very well, Jeannot then." It came out of his English mouth more like "Johnny" than "jan-oh" but the child seemed not to mind and the difference, after all, was slight.

Molly, on the other hand, wasted no time but broke from the embrace and crossed the little room to fall to her knees beside him. Gingerly, not wanting to impose, "Jeannot?" she said, automatically adjusting her accent and tone, like a minstrel, to the company. "*Ah mon pauvr' infant!!* Poor thing!"

She took its pudgy, rather sticky fingers in her hands and kissed them. "What, all alone?" The child nodded, hot and miserable. His red stockings, not surprisingly, had vanished. His whole body was smeared with Tortuga's unrelenting dust and he seemed somewhere to have found the only mud for miles around. The nose, too, was a sticky business.

"Well, *mon cher*," she said at last, when she had ascertained the child's name and age, and that Jeannot was a very good boy indeed. "Your *Maman* is busy just now, saying hello to your papa! But that's all right. *Voici*, here is your uncle Prentiss. (His name is really Dick but no one calls him that but me.) And I—" She glanced in Dick's direction. He shrugged lightly and bent his head in playful acceptance. "I am," she said, "your Auntie Molly. Can you say, *Ma tante?*"

Keaton's youngest child stared, wavering between misery and relief. He lisped "*Ma tante,*" and flung wide his pudgy arms. She bundled him into a hug, then stood up, with him still firmly packaged up. "Well, ain't you a mess now, my lad," she said in a whole new voice, straight off the London docks.

Dick started and stared at her as if she had suddenly become Chinese, but she paid him no mind. He was not the only one with secrets.

"Now tell yer Auntie Molly the trouble."

The child babbled. Molly kept smiling and listening, and wiped the child's nose and kissed its hands and the pale matted floss of its hair.

Dick just watched, silent, following her as she rocked in place, until he realized the odd ache in his cheeks was a huge helpless smile, the sheer broad joy of watching her. So young, yes, and bold as a lad absolutely, but a woman still: kind, sensible, patient even with someone else's infant. So—

He would not take it farther. Enough to appreciate and enjoy the moment life chose to give him. They came few enough.

"Ah ha," she said at last. "*J'ai compris.* Well you know, *mon enfant,* I saw melons in the kitchen when I went through. An' a great bath smack in the midst o' that kitchen too, eh *petit?* That's it, *n'est-ce pas?* You missed out on your bath? And your dinner too, *par foix.*"

Settling him on her hip, still prattling in two languages, she walked back through one stout stone room after another to the kitchen with its fine German stove and red tile floor, and the copper bath cooling in the middle. She set the boy down, making sure he was firmly planted on his chubby feet, and tested the water. Warm as the day, but no more.

"Well you are very wise," she said. "A foolish boy would still be sitting here, expecting to be courted with vassals and serfs at his side, and like as not drown himself just playing with his toy."

Dick coughed, but said nothing more when her cautioning frown turned his way at last. The smile breaking his face just would not go away.

"Dust," he said, waving the air. "Just the dust. Naught else, love. Truly!"

"But you, *mon brave*," said Auntie Molly, pirate queen of the western isles. "You instead adventured out into the wide world."

She flung off her sash and shrugged out of the wide-sleeved coat with all the cording and the silver buttons, and rolled her shirt sleeves to the elbow, then picked up and plopped Jeannot in the green and gold bath water—the captain of his ship and master of his soul. Jeannot giggled.

"And finding the wide world much too cold, when wet and with no clothes on—" She hunkered down beside him. "You wisely have come home."

With an odd twinge, she found she missed wearing skirts that would double so nicely as apron and towel. Then she shrugged the thought aside, picked up the ball of greyish soap Annette had left next to the bath, and put it to use.

"Oh goodness, just *voici les pieds*! Look at your little feet, all scuffed and dirty. These aren't feet, these are hooves! Are you a goat? A little goat?"

She tickled and Jeannot shrieked with laughter. "Dickon, find me a bowl or something so I can rinse his hair. Is that hot water? Excellent. Spill some cold water into it first, silly. *La la!* If men remembered being children… Ah no, that's right. They never stop."

She glanced up once at the unadulterated light in his face, and looked away, terrified with delight.

By the time the little boy was pink and clean from his hair to his tiny toes, Molly was soaked to the skin. And Prentiss could hardly breath for the unfamiliar, unwelcome emotion clutching at his heart. Unwelcome, but irresistible as the tide.

He knew he should run from it. He thought of escaping the room, the house, the island, but could not. He could hardly breathe. He had become a planet circling her star, and could no more escape than the tide escapes the moon. He had fallen in love with a girl he had no business loving at all. Embarrassed. devastated, overwhelmed with love, he couldn't stop grinning.

They found a stack of towels, small but thick woven linen, brisk, and gilt-edged, and between them rubbed the child dry, then found a framed box full of velvet cushions in the parlor to put him to bed. The little mouth yawned like a blossoming flower, and he fell asleep protesting that he wasn't sleepy at all.

Together they hauled the tub together stuttering on the tiles to the garden door and tipped it out. The splash flung up snakes and ladders of fragrant mud, spattering them both like marjoram and thyme in the rain.

"You're all wet," Prentiss said.

"Good lord, so I am," said Molly. Curls darkened and stuck to her cheeks, she stared up into his shining face.

"Might want to change yer clothes."

"Might."

"That would mean taking those wet things off."

"Aye, sir, it would."

The emerald eyes had become his world. He could not leave off grinning, and his face hurt, but he couldn't make it stop. "I know a place—"

"Would there be a bed in it?"

"Could be. Let's find out."

The gilded afternoon wore into blue evening. Children came home, or wandered in and out. When no meal was forthcoming, they went fishing or found their supper elsewhere amongst their mates.

Jimmy Fitts came and banged at the door, but no one answered him so he went down to McQuarry's feeling left out. Two girls who had been waiting for Prentiss were happy to settle for Jimmy instead, and he felt a good deal better at once.

II

IF LOVE'S A SWEET PASSION

TORTUGA'S BAY PROVIDED deep water anchor all the way to the beach. Jetties, docks, and careening area built out into the harbor provided services as thorough as Port Royal itself. Better, since no questions would be asked about odd things found in odd corners.

The *Jealous Mary* herself lay hauled up out of the water, her broad bottom careened for service. Rigging had been repaired and replaced in Port Royal, yes, but her bottom was fouled and required serious work if she was to keep her reputation for speed. Given the casual attitude of the island toward serious work, it would take a while, but of all places to wait, Davy preferred to be here in the congenial company of his own kind.

And that kind, in any weather, was most likely to congregate at McQuarry's. The tavern, like everything else on the buccaneer's isle, was a rough and ready establishment. No more than half built still, it was mostly an open yard in front of a ring of rooms that didn't yet completely surround another courtyard, both open to the sky, now spattered with starlight.

In the outer yard, the tables and rough-hewn benches lighted by a few tin lanterns and a yellow moon were barricaded from the common path by a low wall of stones and a few date palms. For extra shade under the day's glare, a patched topsail and jib stretched from the arms of a spreading tree over an improvised framework anchored on the opposite side of the pounded earth yard. Behind thick stone and adobe walls built out from the sloping hillside, the inner yard and common room breathed cool under palm leaf thatching.

It wasn't fancy but it was a damned sight better than in the old days, when the drinking was as likely to be done on the beach or around a hunter's fire deep in the tangled forest. Old Jock McQuarry's opening a public house in his retirement had brought a touch of civilization to Tortuga that even an influx of females had been unable to inspire.

Now, as night drew on, the place was loud with roaring laughter and the whine of fiddles, crowded with pirates and privateers drunk on success and as much rum as new-paid gold could buy. Here and there, new widows like Mary Daniel held court as other men sought to sign up as their protectors, by virtue of simply being alive. Some wept, but not many.

But as he sauntered into the yard with Molly bright and glowing on his arm, Prentiss shouted in mock dismay.

"Bleeding Christ! We *know* all these people! And I'm sick to death of their sorry faces. C'mon, love, let us adventure into the wide world!"

So they ran cackling while their friends threw things at them and jeered.

Tortuga by night was far stranger than urbane Port Royal. The green world of the steep, cavern-laced jungle hulked near and threatening, even though no panther's scream nor parrot's cry penetrated to the noisy settlement. The green smell of the island, though, redolently alive with the intimation of rain, overbore even the stench of sea wrack and smoking cook fires, and the spicy tang of rum.

There seemed to Molly a kind of magic in the air, as dark and uncontrollable as the ancient chaos, untouched by God. But in Prentiss's company she put such foreboding out of her mind as they plunged into the brilliant, torchlit throng of the Basse-Terre. Eight other ships beside the *Jealous Mary* lay at anchor in the harbor, and that meant people, hundreds of them, everywhere; clustered about cook shops and stews, and lounging in lighted doorways in the blue coils of tobacco smoke and other, more exotic fumes. Even the moonlit night was fiery with torches and carnival colors—not a red serge uniform anywhere—on folk of all colors and accents, wilder even than Port Royal. The babble of conversation was everywhere, loud and laughing and occasionally intelligent in a dozen garbled tongues.

Dick introduced her to half a hundred people, and a few names actually stayed with her. In nearly every dwelling large or small there was eventually a scream of female delight, followed by a cry of *Prentiss!* and a generously rounded body cannonading into Dick. Molly stood by grinning indulgently as her lover kissed whichever female lightly, then peeled her away with apologies and introductions.

Dazed with new, extraordinary feelings, he forgot most of them as soon as he said hello.

By the time they had made the rounds back to McQuarry's, though, things changed. The girl was the problematical Lily, who happened to be Jock McQuarry's wife, and the squeal of recognition was uncharacteristically low and seductive. She did not, like the others, throw herself at him. Rather, she simply appeared from behind and, with her hands about his trim waist, twisted up and under his arms into a slow, lingering kiss.

Molly had thought herself hardened to all this by now, but even her most tolerant smile began to crack as the kiss went on and on. She considered clearing her throat for attention, but changed her mind. A lady should not be so obvious. Vaguely aware that it might be a peculiar time to decide she was a lady after all, she sat down instead to wait and fume with ladylike decorum.

Lily, from what Molly was willing to observe, was a beauty all right, which made her much harder to bear. Fine featured, the pale cocoa of her skin and the high cheekbones betrayed an exotic heritage. Surely this was not one of D'Ogeron's Parisian wenches but some gentleman's by-blow on an African or even an Arawak girl. Perhaps her father was a Spaniard. No wonder Davy had tried to warn her.

Molly's own fine aristocratic mouth twisted askew. She wondered, idly, if Armand had married yet.

Someone put wine in front of her and she drank it, not even looking above the beringed and chubby hand that had set it down.

"So ye're Prentiss's lass, I hear."

The rumble was distinctly Liverpool. Cautiously, she raised her eyes. Looming over her like a beaming vision of Good Fellowship stood the notorious Jock McQuarry, who introduced himself and sat down rather delicately beside her. Her concentration elsewhere, she nodded without seeing him.

"Now you mustn't mind all that, him and my Lily," he went on with a shrug. "It's just her way. There's naught but a few of the lads she even fancies, and your Prentiss it just so happens is one of 'em, is all."

Molly answered with what she hoped was equal nonchalance to indicate an indifference she did not feel. "Why should I mind? I think I've spent the day and half the night watching him being fondled by other women, but aye, he keeps coming back to me."

She shrugged the charming shoulders. "The wine helps. I could wish he were not quite so enthusiastic about your wife, though. You understand of course, that I've been chatted up by a few of the lads myself. Some of them quite nice looking, to tell the truth. I don't suppose Prentiss noticed though."

Jock nodded, tight-lipped and knowing. "It's true what they say, then. You *are* a lady. I mean to say, you don't talk like the crib girls or the transport wives, do ye?"

An auburn eyebrow lifted curiously. "I could. I can. I've kept low company before this." She gulped at the wine without tasting it. "Tell me, Master McQuarry, don't you mind? I mean, she is your wife."

"Ha!" he shouted. "Christ about us, woman, and a fat lot of good minding would do me, wouldn't it. No, darlin', like you say of himself, she keeps coming back to me. Must be something about my ugly face she likes." And he chuckled with a rubicund and childlike glee.

Embarrassed, she looked up into his face at last, realizing that she had been talking to her hands, her glass, the table, anywhere but to his person. And *ugly* was not nearly accurate.

Jock McQuarry was easily the fattest, sweetest tempered, and certainly the ugliest tapster in the Indies. In the King's service he had lost an eye to a Spanish sword that went on to open up the side of his face to the opposite ear. He should not have survived the infection, but somehow he had. The wound had healed, leaving in its place a hideously glossy, puckered scar of which he was indecently proud.

She should have been revolted had she seen him properly at first, but somehow, seduced by the easy manner and pleasant lilt of his voice, his looks hardly mattered.

"'Tis a face of great character," she said with hard won sobriety. "Like the man behind it, I've no doubt." *Am I drunk?* she wondered, but the answer was easy. *Christ, I hope so, given how we've spent the day.*

With a barely tolerant sigh, she swung a slightly owlish look up to Prentiss. "Forgive me my dear, but I must ask. Don't she ever have to breathe? Or is this one a mermaid?"

It must have reached him, for he suddenly broke off, nearly choking, dragged back to simple reality by a few tart words from a cherished voice. He let go of Lily as if she were on fire.

"Ah," he said, and essayed a chuckle. "That's right, you two haven't met."

Wide-eyed, Molly shook her head slowly and mouthed a silent *No*, and blinked.

"Well then." He gulped and caught his breath along with part of his good sense. "Molly this is Lily, McQuarry's, ah, wife." His charming grin had not been sober for some time, so she was not surprised to find it a little askew just now.

"*Enchanté*," she said with deliberate irony. "I have met so few of Prentiss's female friends."

"Such a pity." The other woman's purr was velvet edged with ice. "You have had to make do with all the men."

"A hardship, in a way, but I've managed."

"Hardship, ha! Get it? Ha!" cried Dick, much too drunk for this exchange. "You see? Is this the best girl in the Indies or not." And in a moment he had returned to Molly's side, all thoughts of other women burned again from his sodden brain. "Isn't she grand, Jock, eh?"

The big man shrugged, declining to argue. "She didn't scream when she got a good look at this face of mine," he said. "That's something."

With a flourish, Dick pushed Lily into her husband's arms and sat down decisively at Molly's side. "Anybody seen Jimmy? God's death, I'm parched. Here, Jock, what sort of place are you running? A man's like to die of thirst in here. I haven't had a drink in half an hour."

"More like half a minute," Molly laughed, relieved. "But it's Hungary water you smell of, my lad, not wine."

He had the grace to grin sheepishly. "You're a good lass, Molly. And I love you. No truly, I do!"

The words made her heart race, but ah, he was drunk. Lightly, she joined her kiss to the others collected on his lips this night, and doing so wiped all the rest away.

"Ah," Prentiss sighed. The sweet golden mood of the afternoon returned to him like the richest sherry. "A good lass, indeed. The best."

"Master Prentiss, I believe you've been drinking. And no one's seen our Jimmy in hours. He's not here. I've asked."

"Oh, well then." He shrugged complacently. "His loss, not to while the time and get drunk with you, *ma cushla*." For a moment he caressed her hand in his. Raising it to his lips, kissed the fingers and the inside of her wrist with an impossible delicacy, and the palm of her hand. "*Ma cushla mo cri*, they say in Ireland. I think it's Ireland. The pulse of my heart, it is."

Her wrist downy against his cheek, his blue unfocused stare sought her eyes. Suddenly, "McQuarry!" he shouted, and stood up. "More rum here, I say! More ..." And quietly slipped under the table.

The next days passed in like manner, in a haze of wine and play. They slept through long mornings and made love in balmy afternoons that seemed to have no end. They sat on his bed (having tightened the rope lashings) and read lewd poetry.

As she expected, he did not mention love again. Happy that it had crossed his mind at all, she tried to pretend it didn't matter, and lost herself instead in the moment.

They found little projects to do. For two days together they even cleared away the leaves and straightened the little garden, and discovered flowers he hadn't known were there. Children sometimes screamed past them, but even that had its charm, being other people's children. When Annie and Keaton finally emerged from their seclusion, they all exchanged long glances and settled into the easy anarchy of the house.

The Frenchwoman scoffed again at Molly in her boy's clothes, so Molly picked over the heaps of plunder in McQuarry's back room and improved her wardrobe by a lacy chemise and a blue silk mantua, a shaped French gown that showed off her lush bosom, and two striped petticoats of Indian gauze.

Prentiss whistled his admiration, when he found her, and demanded a kiss.

"A kiss?" Molly wondered with a flirtatious toss of her red gold curls. "Why sir, I am surprised."

"Surprised are you," he growled in return, and grabbed for her hand and gathered her into his arms. "I've got a surprise for you, my lass! How is it we've had so little time together."

After the first shock of his lips had faded a little, she said, "Little time, sir? There is hardly an hour in the day when we are apart."

"So much time apart, aye."

"I must get a bath and wash my hair sometimes, you know."

"For all the good it does. Look." He was whispering now, his voice a hush against the hollow of her throat. When he had explored the sensitive region behind her ear until she shivered with delight, he looked at her and said, "Your hair is in your face all the time."

"I thought you liked it like this."

"Mm-hm. This is how you look in bed."

When he let her mouth free again, she asked dreamily, "I wonder if that door is locked."

"With your hair in such a state, I should think so, Madam. But as a rule, no one ever comes here in the middle of the day."

Molly brushed an errant lock from her eyes. "Trust me to do something no one else ever does."

Then, grinning, she put a hand to the buttons of her new bodice, but even before it was off her shoulders, his hands were on her, brushing aside the shift to tease her out into the humid air.

"Yes," she whispered as his hands moved over her breasts, cupping and gentling them. "It is very warm in here, isn't it."

With a sigh, he bent to bury his face in the scented valley between them, breathing her in like flowers.

"You are so beautiful," he murmured.

Smiling softly, she stroked his head, drawing the long sun bronzed hair over his shoulders and against her skin. She tickled the back of his neck while his hands slipped over her breasts, lips closed over one nut brown aureole, and a playful tongue made her gasp. Her shuddering sigh urged him on, even as her own arms wrapped over his shoulders. On his knees then before her, he loosened her pretty new skirt and drew it down to her ankles.

He took only a moment longer to slough off his own clothes, then as she stood watching him, his hands caressed her slender waist, the inner line of her hip bones, the slender roundness of shuddering flanks. Then they found the hot fastness of her thighs and probed lightly within, questing.

As if to see how his dalliance progressed, he looked up to her face with smoldering eyes the color of cloudy sapphires. She gasped suddenly as he shifted slightly and brought his tongue, just once, to where his fingers moved, and broke away at once. Both their shallow breaths raced faster.

Finally, he urged her down on a pile of heavy silk velvet embroidered with golden flowers, and she lay down happily with his lean brown body worshipping between her knees. His face sought the comfort of the round softness of her belly, his kisses gently tracing the curving pelvic line and brushing finally the gilded patch of curling golden hair.

Again, she gasped in surprise, as his darting tongue found the place fingers had already explored. Both palms in the soft inner curves of her thighs, his long fingers delicately unfolded her, and his tongue probed lightly within, curling about the one bright spot of darkness he sought. And in deep impossible silence, she was on fire.

At first, there was only the most slender line of delight, as delicate as the edge of a rose petal. She felt suspended in space, the softness of his lips and tongue the most exquisite pleasure, the warmth of a winter fire, the gentleness of a summer breeze. Little by little and ever so slowly, there was more, and still more.

With knowing hands and tongue, he found every sweet place within and without her body, till she thought she could bear the wonder of it no longer. Tears of joy filling her eyes, she sparked, hips leaping beneath him and drawing away only to thrust forward again, rising to his perfect mouth. Her hands worked convulsively in his hair, caressed his cheek and the line of his jaw where she could feel with her hands what the rest of her body knew.

When he stopped suddenly, she cried out in despair, but in a moment he was astride, entered her with fiery hardness and thrust forward with a cry of his own. Again, and faster he pressed her, brought her to the edge. Overwhelmed, she was laughing wildly into the tangles of his hair that brushed her taut breasts and her face even as her body seemed to disappear into the universe itself. She wept his name and God's and begged for more, which he gave and in plenty. Then just when she thought she could take no more, when fountains of flowers were blossoming inside and all about her, "Yes!" she cried. "Yes!"

Only then, at last, he lifted his head, rode forward with a long stroke, and another, and called on God as if from his very soul. "Ah, Molly!"

A few moments later Molly could not have found words to describe how she had felt, just then. The moment was so perfect, so exquisitely perfect, that she wept for happiness. Even when he stopped moving within her, he kissed and caressed her face and her eyes, petting her and whispering her name. Once he said something she did not quite hear, and when she asked, he said what seemed to be something else. But she smiled, almost sure he had said he loved her. No. He must have. But he might have said anything to please her.

The sun had passed its zenith before they had finished, and McQuarry's would be rousing soon. For now, while everyone else indulged in siesta, Molly drifted into sleep, rapt in contented smiles and love and his arms.

In the slow and generous weeks that followed, Prentiss found to his amazement that he was indeed rarely anywhere without her. Whatever his occupation or company, whatever the conversation, when she was at his side he was nearly if not entirely oblivious to other women. Those amazing moments when he first took her to the house kept repeating, those instants of delight that warmed him like golden sherry.

For the first time that he could recall, Prentiss's attention, drunk or sober, was all on this one girl. This exceptional girl. He must never have been happy before, he guessed, since this feeling was like nothing he had ever known. And if he hadn't risked telling her so, well, surely she knew. By his every look and touch and word he showed her, didn't he?

He loved her. That much was clear to everyone. Eventually even the smoldering Lily had to understand that. She did not, however, have to accept it, and in this she and Jimmy Fitts were agreed.

A long extravagant twilight, violet and tawny with the edge of a passing storm, was just sliding into a scented balmy evening charged with energy. Lily, in unlikely search of her thoughts, walked down the western arm of the harbor where white sand beach gave way to tide pools and rock. Far from McQuarry's, engorged with self-pity and anger, she hoped for peace and was yet again faced with that bastard Prentiss and his arrogant bitch.

Ten paces above her on the sand, Prentiss and Molly strolled past her, shoes dangling from their hands, on the way back towards light and company. Heads close in conversation punctuated by laughter, hands entwined, they trudged by without a glance in her direction. Molly shrieked as Dick's hand slid round and grabbed her flank in jest. While Lily watched, the younger girl screamed with laughter and ran a few steps along the sand, taunting him, and Prentiss chased her like a satyr at his sport.

Fuming, Lily clenched her teeth and cursed them both mightily.

"Ugly cow," she growled. "She won't have a red hair left on her ugly head when I have done with her." There was a good deal more in vulgar French that Molly would have recognized and matched, given the chance, but for now was blithely unaware.

Lily would have started after them, but a hand on her arm stopped her in mid-storm.

"I'm not sure what all that meant," said Jimmy Fitts. "But I expect I agree."

"What do you mean?"

Fitts's expression was smooth with certainty, sober and cool under its pale scars. "What do you think? Come on. Let's go somewhere to talk. I want your help."

"What for?"

"Shut up and come on. You want the wench out of the way, don't you? Get Prentiss back to his old self, the way it was, *don't you?* Well, I've got an idea."

He also had a blanket and a bottle of something strong in one hand. With the other he took her arm and directed her through the fading light to the end of the strand, to the beehive-domed shelter of a freebooter's empty shack. Finally in its shade, he let her spread the blanket and sit down, knees up, digging her heels in the sand.

"So?" she gasped, grabbing at the bottle when he let her.

"Like this. How do you really feel about Prentiss's Molly."

The black eyes sparkled with malice. "I hate her. I spit on her. I would kill her if I could."

Fitts nodded in happy agreement. "Just what I've been thinking. But what if we just got rid of her, eh? I've been 'round to see old Jeremiah Peace over on Hispaniola."

"So that's where! Everyone has been asking what happened to you. But *nom de Dieu*, why? What business could you have with a slaver?" She shuddered in apprehension. "That one makes me feel dirty all over, like a bath in fish oil."

"Aye," he agreed. "But he has his uses. And if we get Molly to him, he says, he has a buyer if she's fair enough. (God knows, she's fair enough!) She'll be a hundred miles away before Dick even knows she's gone."

Lily did not seem shocked at anything, except that Jimmy should betray such passion so plainly, and betray the man everyone knew was his friend. She might have pointed out that he was at least a little in love, or something like it, with the girl himself.

Instead she said, "She's too pretty by half. But how are we to get her away from Prentiss? They are never apart, not even for a minute."

Jimmy's grin bore some trace of strain. "Oh, I expect you can think of something. You're such old friends, aren't you, him and you? And we have other help. Turk, for one, and his pals. Then we'll need some distraction for the others. I've got a use for that MacBean bloke as well. We can blast her clear of him, and make ourselves a little profit into the bargain."

"Bah, you talk like a shopkeeper. Like my husband, all profit and plans."

Then her cool stare took him in as if for the first time. His face she knew well, but the long, hard lines of his body had somehow escaped her notice. Now she took the time to consider him.

Fitts felt his face growing warm under the frank appraisal, as if he had been drinking good wine. The golden roundness of her body had certainly not escaped his notice in all this time. It had taken a common cause to bring them together. She was vicious, certainly, but even that had its perilous charm. It was a long dry time since he had last had a woman, and this one was dusky dark and seemed to invite him, where the other troubling his mind was russet fair and untouchable.

"All profit and plans," she said again, hugging her knees. "And I am tired of thinking about that little whore. Doesn't anyone just want to make love anymore?"

Then she launched herself into his arms, pressing him back to the sandy blanket and the palm woven wall of the hut. Swept away, he let himself savor the surprise till her hands and her mouth assured him he had not lost his mind. For with a slow, deliberate urgency her lips and tongue moved from his mouth to his throat, making him whimper with unexpected pleasure. Her hands moved under his canvas shirt, pinking and stroking his skin. Sometimes a firm touch, then so light it was there only on the edge of feeling, delicious and unbearable. Then her hands were moving from chest to waist, and dancing over his hardening sex.

When he could force himself, he grabbed her wrists to make her stop. "This isn't why I wanted to see you," he gasped.

"Isn't it?" Her body moved against his, her musky scent rising from the lush gift of her breasts. "Did you want to seduce me instead?"

She smiled slowly, seduction now a moot point, letting her fingers tighten over the straining gabardine just enough to make him cry out in the shock of frustrated desire. Then she drew away, more immediately shocking than her advance, and leaned back into the shadows. "Perhaps we should leave the girl alone. Perhaps I can find a better man, eh? Impress me, Jimmy. Convince me I should help you."

He wasted no more time in protest. And if a tiny voice at the back of his mind warned of any dangers, he was deaf to the alarm.

Molly and Prentiss had run and played themselves away from the Basse-Terre again in the opposite direction until they stood on the beach, hands clasped in friendly communion, staring out to sea. After a while, he kissed her almost lazily, and when he stopped for air at last, simply held her folded under his arm, protective and artless.

"So now what?" she asked suddenly.

"What do you mean?" he snapped, without quite meaning to.

So Molly said, "Nothing."

Their silence had been companionable and loving, and she had not meant the question as a challenge.

Prentiss, sober and focused, was just confused. They walked on a bit, then stopped while she dug a pretty shell out of the sand while he stared out across the bay.

"You're not unhappy?" he said at last.

She sat down cross-legged, blowing the sand off the glowing pink shard of a cowry. "Of course not."

"Then what do you mean, *what now?*"

She shrugged, but her look was guarded. "Only that. Do we go back to sea, soon? Do we simply spend our lives forever playing games on Tortuga? Not that it isn't pleasant, of course, but still."

"Maybe. But I doubt it." He tried to guess her mind, but gave it up. Women were unfathomable, he knew it too well. This one more than others.

He dropped into a crouch beside her, to watch the colors shift in her eyes from sea green to jade to emerald in the changing light. "What would you like to do?"

She sighed delicately. The conversation was not going quite as she'd hoped. She felt jumpy, nervous, and her heart unaccountably was racing.

"I don't know," she said slowly. "This is pleasant, and the rewards are fine. I've no responsibilities. I'm free of apoplectic uncles and stupid aunts and ugly suitors. I've escaped a fate truly worse than death."

"You can't be bored."

She thought about this for a moment and nodded with a mischievous smile. "I believe I am. Look, we sailed away with all that noise and excitement, you and Davy teaching me to fight. You teaching me about ..." Love? That was dangerous waters, and she steered away. "Everything else."

That brightened the color in her eyes, he noted with delight. And one corner of her precious mouth curled with bewitching wantonness.

"But we've been days ashore!" she went on. "Weeks, even. There's nothing to *do*, Dickon! It may be all one jolly never-ending revel to you men, but ... I can't even get into trouble when no one cares what I do."

"Ha! Trouble is it? Sweet, the trouble you'd find here you don't want. Why do you suppose I'm never anywhere but with you? Aside from the plain pleasure I take in your company?"

Why couldn't he just say it, he wondered. What was wrong with him?

The frown that snapped into place came perilously close to a pout. "I can take care of myself."

"Of course you can, darlin'. And I know better than to say another word about that, don't I?"

She looked up from the rainbow shell directly into the rich lapis of his eyes, catching their sparkle into her own, and broke into a lopsided grin. The warmth that filled her just looking at him swept through her like a tidal wave, made her wish desperately to tell him how she felt. But that was trouble she would not dare, and could not ask for.

Instead she said, "Do you remember the first time you came to me, sneaking through the window, perched on my bed like a dream. I thought I must never have seen blue eyes before, yours were so bright. You, my dear, were trouble."

"Aye, and see how you've handled it."

"It seems so long ago."

He caught up her hand and placed a kiss in the palm of it.

"Be patient, Sweet," he said. "Repairs are done. We'll sail out in a few days time, you'll see. We have to put *Jealous Mary* back in the water, first, and tidy her up. That will keep us all busy. Even you, with your soft hands."

"You mean I should be bored while I can?"

"I mean you should kiss me."

She had been watching his face so intently, the sudden warmth of his hand on the firm roundness of her breast surprised her with delight. His kiss was deep and rich with promise, and anything but boring, and her nipples ripened and hardened under his touch.

"Never doubt me," he said at last, one hand tracing lightly through her hair as he fell into her eyes. "Never."

He could feel those three dangerous words lurking again in his mouth and swallowed them back, still uneasy. He could tell her anything else, from his childish nightmares to his dreams of glory, but not that he loved her. For that was nonsense, wasn't it, he thought as he kissed her again even more thoroughly. Or else unbelievable. He had told other women he loved them, but it had always been a lie.

And what might she say? Would she laugh? Tell him not to be stupid? That her love was saved for some romantic memory of

"Armand", whoever that was, if he existed? And wasn't it more sensible for her to love a fine gentleman—even a Frog—than a thief and a pirate.

But in his doubts he held her that much dearer, kissing her mouth and throat, caressing the rich curves of her body so soft and pliant under his touch. Inhaling the rich scent of her hair. Then her hands, too, explored his face, his chest, the curve of waist and thigh. Her hands and body worked their magic, loving him, till he was drunken with her.

Warm breezes stirred the palm trees swaying above the tide line. Until the rising tide began to send the sea sweeping up the strand to where they lay happily in each other's arms, they stayed content for now with dalliance and each other and the crash of surf on white sand. For half an hour they did no more than kiss and touch and laugh, the lightning of his lips alternately teasing and devouring hers, until an edge of water kissed around their toes, etching the single silhouette they made in the sand, and forcing them away.

Somewhere on an Atlantic horizon, air moving out from Africa began to circle into cloud.

12

DOWN TO THE VERY CENTER OF THE EARTH

NIGHT LED THEM back to McQuarry's in search of wine and noise and light. Molly had pulled bright red blossoms like little bells from some nameless bush and set them in her hair, and changed her petticoat for one with more lace and less sand around the edges. Feeling clear minded and cheerful once more, the roar of the tavern was music to her ears.

"There's only so much soft breeze and moonlight I can stand," she shouted at Dick across the din. He bellowed a huge laugh, ripe with Madeira, and she grinned back only slightly more sober.

"Well then, Davy!" Prentiss said to the Captain at his other side. "What say you? Isn't it time we sailed?"

"In this weather?" York looked thoughtful, but Will Keaton settled comfortably across from him was nodding his bald head with enthusiasm.

"Any weather or none at all, if y'ask me. Blinding snow, middle of a hurricane, I don't mind."

"What, Will, ready to leave your woman so soon?"

"God, Davy, there's no end to it. Keaton do this and Keaton do that, and Keaton get out o' my way I'm tryin' to dress the girl or

smack the boy and cook your supper and you never do nothin'
around here, do you? All with a babble of French I can't make out
more than half of, and that half words you don't want to hear in a
woman's mouth."

Molly giggled at the fortunes of the unwarily married.

"Is a fortnight of marriage so long then, Will?"

"Too long, my honey duck. And it's fair stunned I am that
Prentiss here still bides wi' yerself, God saving your pretty face.
What a man wants with a woman round him all the time I do not
know. God commands us to be fruitful. He never said we was to
live together!"

And with that he drained his own cup and called out for more.

"Belike we set a watch for passing ships and send a pinnace out
instead," Davy mused. "Those as want to could spend their time at
that, and I could please myself here. Would that do, d'ye think?"

"I think ye're addicted to women, Captain mine," said Prentiss,
and Davy roared back.

"*I'm* addicted? Prentiss, you whey-faced whoreson dog! At least
when I set to sea I can leave mine at home, where they belong!"

Molly's giggles turned abruptly to mild annoyance. "Lord, Davy,
not this again."

"Aye, lass, again and still. And ever after till you find something
else to amuse you."

"But you promised …"

"And I'll keep my word, my dear. Though you're worth your
own weight in trouble. But you earn your keep as well or better
than some. Like some pilots I could name!"

"So let's get to sea and watch me earn it, then. She's bored
already, Davy, and that's a fact."

"Bored!"

Furious, roaring, the girl rounded on Prentiss. "You bastard!"
she cried, then dissolved again in a flutter of winey giggles with her
head on her arms.

"And who's fault is it, then," Keaton added. "If you can't keep
her happy, lad, I can think of a few who're ready to volunteer."

Prentiss just grinned in cheerful disregard and threw an arm
around his lady, and pulled her in to the protective expanse of his
chest.

"T-Trouble is," he hiccupped. "She ain't inners—, inter— Shite!
She don't want anyone else, and that's the truth." She laughed,

sparkling with love. Drunk or sober, even to hear him boasting was a joy, especially since he was boasting of her.

"Even when you leave her alone?"

"I do not leave her alone," he said, so solemnly that all the men around him howled again, adding further to the general hubbub.

"Oh aye, that's faith," said Davy. Outside, just below consciousness and common room noise, thunder rolled. "She's not tired of us, I think, nor Tortuga neither. I'll tell you, speaking from my great age and wisdom, what it is. 'Tis you she's tired of, my lad, and that's the truth of it."

Thunder, and now a pale flash of lightening whited the sky. Out in the yard, the first light drops of tropical rain began to spatter on the canvas and rattle in the thatch.

Molly jumped as one touched her cheek, then laughed, all the while protesting. "No! God's death, no! I wouldn't trade him for any of you," she said. "One at a time or all of you together."

"Oh aye, she says that now! (*Bloody hell, it's raining.*)"

("*In the rainy season, fancy that.*")

"While he's in arm's reach," Davy said, and they fell to an intense dissection of the unreliable nature of women.

All talk of sailing passed into history and old stories of other times and other islands and better weather, though none, Molly noticed, of Rafe September. That was odd, wasn't it? Everyone said he was the best pilot who ever lived, yet they avoided talking of him. They said she was like him, but nothing else.

It was a foggy, peculiar thought that slipped away as swiftly as it had come in the next sip of wine. After a while, Molly drew out from under Dick's arm, and out of the conversation. Her smiles faded gradually as the odd sense of discontent surfaced with the earthy ozone smell of summer storm. But her brain was too distracted with wine and tropic heat and noisy company to hold that little thought for long. Perhaps, then, drink was the answer, as it seemed to be for the men. Wine could improve the whole world, did one give it time. Time she certainly had in plenty. But it required a good deal of wine.

The air was smoky with bhang and hashish, and tobacco haze roiling blue streaks over the heavier fumes. The heady reek of rum dragged at her senses, and the wheeze of the obligatory concertina was boring a fine, thin hole in her consciousness. Without preamble, she was on her feet Dick squeezed her hand as she got up and looked toward her, then turned back. Even a girl has to answer nature's call once in a while, and she was heading unsteadily for the door.

She leaned briefly in the doorway to let the night breeze play across her face, and listen to the patter of rain on the canvas sunshade. Then idly she stepped away, across the crowded courtyard and into the path. The rain was slight, it should pass swiftly. Perhaps it would wash away her mood as well.

Yes, she would take a walk, clear her head. That's right. So she did. And when the path split into two or three, she was sure to pick the one she knew.

Had she been thinking, she would have known better. The glow of torchlight faded too soon, still she was sure she knew the way. Unsteady feet found a path, or maybe a deer track, that led her along McQuarry's outer lane, and down and around and away from the lights until it somehow disappeared in a tangled stand of mangrove.

Frowning, she looked to either side, turned unsteadily to look back the way she'd come. There was no swarm of people, no friends here to warn or distract. Just a growing, containing silence and the crowded sky. No thoughts, no thinking, no worries. Good.

Leaning against a canting palm tree, she closed her eyes and breathed in the green dark air weighted with the warm breath of the storm and the pulse of the jungle behind her. The slightest breeze brushed her face and just lifted the edges of her hair, crimped with damp. There, in the darkness behind her eyes, already out of reach of the voices of her shipmates, she was alone at last. For the first time in weeks, entirely alone. The thought, tenuous as it was, produced a long sigh.

And then out in the distance somewhere, it seemed that music sang—the plaintive cry, barely discernible, of Owen Jones's fiddle weeping into the night. The sobbing aire matched her mind, the tune a lament for deeds undone and roads not taken; for maids betrayed and men's dreams lost at sea. She wanted to find the fiddler and sit by him, lose herself in the center of the music, letting it tear the heart out of her and show it to her in the wild and eerie strain.

On the impulse, she stepped out into the unfamiliar path in search of the music's source. Echoes fought her. Raindrops, heavier now, patted into the dust at her feet. Behind one shadow, the fiddle seemed to be just around the next corner. Around that corner, it was now behind her, teasing and tormenting.

Out there somewhere in the trees the sound was clearer and straight ahead, drawing her like a siren's call. The music sighed to a whisper, swelled to a wail, joined by another fiddle and an Irish bodhran drum. The chords tore at her heart for the sadness that could make such sounds.

Abruptly she halted, fingers wiping rain from her eyes. If she went on, she'd only be lost. Lost and wet. Lost and wet and sad. Lost and wet and sad and stupid. Lost and wet and...

A footstep crunched in the track behind her, and a pistol flint snapped back and locked into place.

"Well, well, well," said an ugly growl. "What's this then, lads, eh?"

Furious, Molly whirled, outraged at the intrusion. Turk, knife drawn. And Black Thomas and Ned Courage, Turk's right and left hand familiars, pistols drawn and ready.

Molly's lip curled with scorn, suddenly sober and unafraid. She brushed damp hair back from her face.

"Well indeed," she spat, with no attempt to hide her contempt. "If it isn't Old Nick and his two favorite serpents. How odd to find you sliding in the mire. What do you want?"

A viciously cheerful smile broke across Turk's face. "What do you think, girl, eh? You think Prentiss is the only man on Tortuga?" He glanced briefly at his lieutenants. "Take her."

Her father's knife appeared in her hand as if by itself, but they were faster and more accustomed to assault than she. Thomas had her by the hair and Ned, wiser than before, ducked under the silvery blade and swept her feet out from under her. Molly dropped to the dirt with a shriek, and the dirk rattled against the stones and bounced into tall grass. Between them they pinned her arms to the ground against her thrashing.

"If you touch me I'll kill you, I swear it!"

"Maybe if you are quiet and behave, I will let you live long enough to try. Tom!"

Black Tom had his whole weight on her arm, but his free hand found his pistol, primed and ready.

Against her rising anger Molly had to add the smooth cold circle of the muzzle under her ear. When she tried to shrink away from it, Ned's grip tightened in her hair and on her other wrist, twisted to the shoulder. She gasped through clenched teeth, refusing to give more than she must.

Standing over her, Turk's rank and sweating figure, hardly more than a thickness of shadow, tilted at a crazy angle in her vision. Rain tapped at her face and arms, streaking muddy channels across her skin. Her ears roared, the music vanished, everything gone from her mind but anger. Mesmerized, she watched in numb silence while he gleefully dropped to the ground, shoving her legs apart.

When she struggled, he aimed a fist at her face, then changed his mind. "He said no damage," he muttered. "Damn him for a weak-livered Englishman. What is a woman more or less."

The blow fell open handed but with full force, and she screamed in anger and despair. He hit her again.

Eyes blazing, only animal fury driving her, she spat full into his face, then turned away from the blow she knew would follow as his fist raised again.

He swore and muttered, "It is worth the price."

Explosions, pistol fire, and a huge, angry shout ripped the night.

The awful pressure on her head and arms suddenly vanished while furious shouting and a scuffle roared all out of sight. Blind in the rain, she lay exhausted and sobbing with relief, still frightened but safe.

Finally her anger gave her strength, and she rolled upright and felt about in the grass for Rafe's knife. When she found it, she was on her feet at once, but the fight was done. Turk lay in the dust unconscious with the side of his face mangled by a hard leather boot, Ned Courage dead beside him.

The tiniest unworthy beat of disappointment registered in her heart that it was not Prentiss who had routed her enemy.

"Jimmy!" she cried, and flung herself into his arms. His pistols had killed one and sent the other running.

"Enough, girl. That's enough," he said roughly, but let her hold him for reassurance while she sobbed out her fear. "Are you all right?"

She caught her breath before she answered. "Yes. Yes, he hit me is all. God, Jimmy, thank God you were here, or it, he…" The fear hiccupped away, till she could stood away from him, collecting composure.

"I heard the screams," he said in a peculiar voice. "But what the devil were you doing out here alone. Meeting someone, eh?"

She frowned and stepped back. "It was the music."

"What music, love?" This time the sarcasm was unmistakable.

"Owen Jones, or someone. I heard fiddles playing, and I wanted to find…"

Her voice trailed off into the midnight silence broken by the pattering of freshening rain and another crack of thunder. The music, like the flowers in her hair, had gone.

"Well, there was music, damn you. Owen!" she called. But whatever siren had drawn her out along the path into the trees made no answer.

"Owen Jones," Jimmy sighed. "Well that may be, and it may not. I wonder what Prentiss will have to say."

She shook back her head, raking fingers through the tangled chaos of her hair. "He'll wonder why you didn't just kill him. Turk, I mean." Then she turned back toward McQuarry's. "Can we get out of this rain?"

He caught her wrist and dragged her a stop. "He's a master gunner, is why. Besides, there's one man dead because of you already, even if he is no more than cannon fodder. How many more do you want?" A thoughtful pause. "And what will you do when it's Prentiss?"

The last fumes of wine had long vanished, but she was dazed still, and defensive, and wetly bedraggled. Her eyes narrowed. "What do you mean? Should you have let him finish what he started?"

"I dunno. It might have taught you a lesson. Stay where you belong?"

"If I'd stayed where I belonged Dick Prentiss would be a sentimental memory with a stretched neck. For both of us," she added.

"If there had been some other way, I'd have used it. As it is…"

"As it is, Master Fitts," Molly declared, holding her ground. "You'll have to learn I'm not leaving him, not for your reasons or anyone's. When he wants me to go he'll tell me himself, and even then I'll fight to stay." She relaxed a moment, her face softened with recollection and strain. "Don't you understand, you bloody fool. I love him."

"So do I, darlin'," Jimmy Fitts said as the sky opened up around them. "Which is why I'm not going to hate myself for this in the morning." Without warning, his fist flashed and struck her jaw, and her world went utterly dark. Lightening cracked over the harbor, and the thunder crashed directly overhead, as with a muddle of ruined lace, she slumped into Jimmy's arms.

Rather later, in a cheery corner at McQuarry's, Davy York, who was generally more sober than he looked, sat fast in conversation with two other captains, talking business and ignoring the crash of weather outside. There being nothing in it of interest to himself, Prentiss lurched to his feet in search of Molly.

The room was emptying, the conversation lagging, and the rum turning sour in his mouth. Might just be best to find his girl and take her home. That much he could be sure of in the warm, charged air.

Before he could find the doorway, Lily found him instead. Black-eyed, lurking in the shadows dancing under the trees of the deserted courtyard, she presented her body and her mouth to him in a single, sensuous move. Irritably he tore her arms from his shoulders and pushed her away.

"Not now, Lily, dammit. I need— I mean, have you seen Molly?" When she sniffed a negative, he went on. "Well, Jimmy Fitts then? Where the hell is everybody?"

"Ah, *oui*," she pouted. It had worked before. "I suppose I am nobody, then?"

"At the moment, aye."

Searching the front courtyard over her shoulder, he managed to look everywhere but at her. Still, there was no flash of auburn hair, no spark of gilded laughter anywhere. Lightening crackled through the air, lighting up the yard, but she was not there.

As the thunder rolled into the yard Lily leaped into his arms with a timid shriek he did not believe, and this time he hardly moved, chilled with disgust.

The pout returned, slyly. "If you care for her so much," she said. "Why do you let her slip away?"

"She's a free woman, Lily. Like yourself. She can come and go as she likes."

"She is a child, Prentiss. She wants watching. Or to be left at home with her nurse."

"Don't be stupid."

Roughly sober now, he deigned at last to look into the high-boned, exotic angles of her face. She was, he decided, not nearly so pretty as Molly. There was a hardness he had not noticed before, and even a touch of cruelty lurking in the over-ripe lips, nothing generous about them. When she ground her body into his, his only response was revulsion. Roughly he picked the brown arms from around his neck again, and thrust her away.

"But it is like you, Prentiss, to say a girl is free to go or stay, but if she stays, you leave. You tease a lass's heart till it breaks, eh, then run away. Wait a few hours and you'll forget her altogether, *n'est-ce pas?*"

"I suppose you mean I've broken your heart?"

She dropped her glance in a coy imitation of modesty and said nothing.

He barked with disgust. "God save us! You haven't got a heart to break, you bitch. Come, what is it you missed most about me while I've been gone? My pretty face? Or my sense of humor?"

For a moment, somehow, she dared to imagine he was hers again, and being seduced she met his eyes and said, "Neither one," and made to touch him.

But this time, he stepped aside and his eyes were hard. Cold and angry, he said, "Exactly. Look, 'tis different this time, Lily. Special. Understand? Now get out of my way."

"No, wait!" In dismay, knowing what she knew, Lily tried to stop him. "Prentiss, please, listen to me. You cannot see what she has done to you! How could you!"

All at once, he grabbed her wrists and shook her. "For godsake, Lily, what is this sudden concern for my bloody welfare? You've never cared a day in your life for anyone but yourself. And nothing you can do or Jimmy can say, or ..." A single chilling thought stopped him short. Silently, he cast her away and stepped back, fists closing.

"Where is she, Lily?" he said with awful quiet. "What's happened? You know, don't you. And Jimmy does too." The terrible realization awoke. "They're both missing. Damn it, you lying whore, what have you done!"

Panic breaking his voice shattered the cheery complacency of McQuarry's into brittle silence, punctuated only by the tapping rain and the aching flash of lightening. Half a hundred men and their women turned to stare as Prentiss, wild-eyed and despairing, cried out. In terrible confusion, he pushed past Lily not even hearing her babbling out confession and vilification together. Betrayed and abandoned, he thrust himself back into the common room, elbowing a path through the smoky, drunken crowd.

"Davy!" he cried.

But into the madness came another voice, high and shrieking. Not Molly, crying for rescue, but the broken yelp of the forgotten secretary, MacBean. Out of nowhere, he stumbled drunken and streaming out of the rain screaming for vengeance and brandishing a brace of pistols. When one discharged, the whole place ducked and stared at the principals from cover, waiting for the finale.

"Prentiss! Davy York! Ye bleeding bastards," the little Scotsman squawked, stumbling over benches and tripping on a fallen ale cup. Someone ventured a laugh. "They've taken her! They've stolen my master's child, y'poxy whoreson bastards!"

"What are you saying? Who has her!" Prentiss heard his voice break and didn't care.

"You know it well enough, ye swaggering gommerel. That beanpole friend of yours, that Fitts. Not enough to steal her away to be your whore, but then to sell her off, her that trusted ye!" The remaining pistol leveled shakily at Davy.

Another shot rang out, but the pistol fire that echoed around the stone walls came not from MacBean's hand. The little man dropped with a strangled gasp, a gaping hole red in his throat. Attention swung toward the door where stood Jimmy Fitts, ashen-faced, mud-streaked, and grim.

"What in God's name!" York was on his feet at last, mercantile thoughts chased from his consciousness. "Fitts, have you lost your mind?" But his question drowned in the sudden surge of excited voices.

Prentiss turned on his friend with fury and loathing written in his whole frame. "In God's name, aye. What in God's name do you think you've done, you swine?"

"Killed a flea," said Jimmy, tossing the spent pistol aside. Ned's pistol.

"You know what I mean."

"Do I?" He started for the door but Dick's hand fell heavily on his shoulder. "I know the mad bastard was shouting and waving a gun at Davy. What more should I know? Suppose I should have let him fire?"

"Davy can look after himself. But before you stopped him, he said…" But Prentiss choked on the words as their meaning suddenly sank home. "You're too late, see. He named you already. You've taken her. You've *sold* her, haven't you!" he hissed.

Madness overwhelmed him as he clutched Jimmy by the shirt.

"Haven't you, you filthy… Damn you, where is she!"

"That's enough!" Colder than he had ever felt, Jimmy caught up his friend's wrists and carefully plucked the hands from his linen. "I did the only thing I could do. Thou'lt thank me one day like you thank me for Madame Serena's, or the Polish general's widow. Look at 'ee!" he sneered, his face an ugly twist of scorn. "Torn up and raving over a doxie. What's next, picking flowers and singing hymns? What kind of way is that for a man to act?"

And so saying, he pushed away and flung himself into the stormy night, trying to swallow the ugly lump in his throat. He had done the best thing, he was sure of it. The only thing he could do. Prentiss would get over the wench. He'd be a man again, and everything would be as it should be. And that was that.

Prentiss's crowded thoughts were not so sublime.

Molly did not want to think about anything, and that was fairly easy. When she managed to force open one eye, she seemed to be underwater, so shimmery was the light. Colors undulated, waving like fronds of sea weed, but in colors she had never seen. Her stomach hated the effect, and heaved. Closed eye was better.

Years later, she woke again, filled with hazy dreams both light and dark. Still groggy, the last memory of Tortuga might have overwhelmed her with horror, as the pain and the terror came flooding back, but the drug kept all at bay.

If I could wake up, she thought, I could faint.

Part of her smiled, perhaps her mouth. It was so hard to tell, when she could feel so little.

What the gentleman watching her saw was a foolish grin, like a child's. More worldly than she, he returned the smile, although she was still altogether unaware of him. She would be surprised, he thought, when she woke. Almost as surprised as he had been to find her, at last; the object of his search purchased at random from a pirate.

He wondered what she would say, when she knew that the man who had sent for her was her friend of friends, almost but never quite her first lover, Armand de la Valier de St. Juste. And he wondered, too, what made her smile in a drug-fogged dream. Almost anything might. They would have used opium, of course. Stronger than hashish and longer lasting, easy to maintain. And quite pleasant, if used in moderation.

"Why do you smile, Armand?" Eugénie, whom he no longer loved. The corners of his mouth turned down as he leveled his gaze on her. The once cheerful, mischievous face had lost its sparkle, the colors faded. Even the black curls that whispered across her forehead seemed without luster. This frontier life had not suited her. And he despised her for it.

"A better question is why you are here? Did I not leave orders to…"

"She is my friend, too." The voice was timid, almost stammering. "Is she going to be all right?"

"Of course. That blackguard has too heavy a hand with his drugs, and she has been badly handled. But it is nothing past help. A slave could keep watch, but I prefer to do so myself."

"I still don't understand why she is here at all."

With an impatience barely concealed, Armand sighed. "I told you, I have been looking for her since we arrived. You told me her parents lived on Martinique, and that her family was here. That seems not to have been the case."

Desperately, Eugénie wailed, "I did not lie to you, Armand. I swear it. It was in her last letter, but that was a year ago or more." The lie was so old she no longer remembered the truth.

Having brought her to the edge of tears, he graciously permitted himself to show a gentle mask of forgiveness.

"I know it, my dear. It is not your fault. How could it be? Of course, if you had answered her letter then, you might have had another, and more news."

Her pointed face, already pale, went altogether white as she gasped, "Oh Armand, how could I! What could I have said? That I had finally taken a lover? And that it was you?"

"Enough. Go to your room."

"I don't want to."

"Don't then. Stand here and be childish. But if she has heard you, what will you tell her?"

At that, Eugénie gasped again, and fled the room to be instantly forgotten. Her brother's attention turned at once to Molly, who murmured and stirred, then settled again. Perhaps the crisis was past, for she seemed to be sleeping at last instead of drugged senseless. A little while then, and she would wake.

For Molly, the dreams had lost their shape again. There had been a quick and detailed recollection of a wild chase through city streets, with laughter at the end of it. And the sparkle of blue eyes and tender conversation. Then came the awful drift into exhaustion, and a fatigue that filled her mind to its limit and her body to the bone. And finally, a lightening of that, although the blue eyes did not return.

And now, voices, Sweetly and maddeningly familiar. Part of her wanted to sleep forever, now that sleep seemed possible. But curiosity and plain English stubbornness forced her awake instead.

The gentleman in the stylish shirt and curling black hair, dyed to cover the encroaching grey of middle age, watched as her delicate auburn lashes fluttered open over the smoky jade he had waited with such longing to see. He nearly laughed to see how they widened, first with disbelief, then with delight.

"Armand!" she cried, her beautiful voice a joyous croak. She tried to reach out for him, but fell back to the pillows, betrayed by her drug wracked body. Grinning, he took her hands, urging her to calm. "Armand. It is you. Oh, it is you."

He laid a cool hand on the pale brow and pushed aside the damp fringe of ringlets, dark with sweat. Tears sprang to those green eyes as his elegant fingers touched her cheek and lips. "Yes, *chérie*, it is I," he said to her weeping. "I am here. Hush, *ma petite*, I am here, and so is Eugénie. As always, little Molly."

She reached a hand to touch his face. "Oh, Armand, I was so frightened. What has happened? Why am I here? What are you doing here? And ..." Her voice caught as she stared widely, seeing the room for the first time. She seemed to hear clearly now the voices half heard in her sleep. "What, what am I doing here? I was on Tortuga. I had ... And there was ... Oh, Armand, I have had such awful dreams."

He was far more taken with seeing her again than he had anticipated. So much so that he nearly cast aside his plan and told her the truth. Nearly, but not quite. Instead, he turned her hand in his and placed a soft kiss within it. Then bent to touch his lips to her trembling mouth.

In that moment, he overwhelmed her will. This was the kiss she remembered, had longed for through so many lonely months of passionate regret. She was not strong enough to return all the fire she felt, but it was there, restored to all its burning intensity. And Dick Prentiss's blue eyes flew from her mind.

She sighed from some awful, hidden depth of soul when they parted. His eyes, brown as chocolate, melted through her as though seeking a home. Finally, hoarse with desire, he spoke gently.

"So you are still my girl?" She nodded, incapable of speech. "And there have been no others who might have taken my place in your … heart?"

She gave a fleeting thought to Prentiss, and all the pain that loving him cost her, and shook her head. If greater delight than her own were possible, it showed in Armand's aristocratic face.

Molly said breathlessly, "Am I still your little sister?"

With a small smile, he shook his head. "Not any more. That was a little girl I knew long ago. Now you are … Now you are exhausted and must rest. You have been very ill, *chérie*." Reluctantly, he tucked the counterpane around her again and touched her cheek. "But the fever has broken, and you are ours again. Rest is all you need."

"Fever? But no, Armand, wait." He turned in the doorway, waiting. "Tortuga. I was on Tortuga with … with Captain York. And there was music and the Turk … I mean, he hit me. And it was raining. There was a storm. And I, I…"

His brow creased with concern, he raised a finger to his lips to quiet her.

"Nightmares, my love. Fever dreams. Do you not know?"

"No, I…" She gasped, and simply shook her head.

"You were indeed on Tortuga, a hostage of York's pirates. My men rescued you and brought you here. But ah! Perhaps it is just as well the memory is clouded. So long as there is nothing to cloud our wedding."

She shot straight up, almost but not quite distracted by the sensation of linen and lace in which someone had wrapped her. "Wedding!"

"Hush, now. Get some sleep, or you invite the illness to return."

"But …!"

"No more!" He snapped out the words, unaccustomed to being crossed. Since he was clearly in earnest, Molly said nothing more, but watched in mute amazement as the door closed behind him.

Well, she thought. Fever, rescue, and wedding. Has he always thought I was this stupid, not to know my own mind? My own life?

Desperately she wished to fling back the covers, find some real clothes, and get out of here, only the deadly weariness meant her limbs would not answer to her will. This was madness! Except—and the exception was considerable.

Except, was this not the man she had wanted. Longed for? Surely that kiss had been genuine. Nothing she had done in the past year had been free of his memory. Even Prentiss. Ah yes, Prentiss. The laughing center of her life. How much of him did she really have? And her honest heart answered back: More than anyone.

What did Armand want? And why lie? For he was certainly not telling a whole truth. His men had rescued her from Turk? But no, that was Jimmy Fitts. Who then knocked her unconscious himself. And then ... and then ... what?

Darkness. Hazy darkness and dreams that left a bitter tang in her mouth. Drugs, not fever. She had assuredly not been a hostage. That was going too far. But did that mean Jimmy Fitts was in Armand's pay? Or that Davy was?

It was surely too much to consider with her mind still spinning and—stretching catlike for a yawn—with the bruises on her cheek and her arms still tender.

Bruises.

The terror of her last waking hour on Tortuga came home all at once, pure and unaltered by time or drugs. Overcome, she turned her face into the muffling pillows and wept.

When she woke again, it was morning, the sunlight breaking pure and clear through crisp muslin curtains ruffling in a light breeze. The shifting shade of palm leaves made a lace against clear blue sky, echoed in deep black on the carpet. A moment later, birdsong trilled outside the window, and the salt tang of the sea was strong and clean.

Clear headed at last, Molly smiled tentatively at the sure beauty of the day and thought she might be hungry. The evil dreams were gone.

At a sound, she turned to face the wizened visage of an old black servant standing nearby. No, a slave she supposed.

"I tell Monsieur you awake, Mamazelle," the woman said in French. "There are clothes for you here in the wardrobe. I will send one of the girls to help."

Then, "Wait!" said Molly. "You can answer some questions?"

The old woman paused, expressionless, in the doorway. "Don't know nothing."

"Who is your master?"

The woman blinked and said, "Monsieur le Capitain Armand de St. Juste, Mamazelle. Don't you know that?"

I know less than you. "What has he told you about me?"

"What should he tell me?"

"Servants always know everything. Answer my question."

Molly thought the aged face went a touch sly.

"Slaves don't know nothing, Mamazelle. I can't tell you nothing you don't know. Ever since he come here last year he been looking for you, Mamazelle. He say, in France you are his fiancée, *oui*? He say you come to the islands and get lost, he try to find you. Dat's all. I go now." She paused one last time in the doorway, though, to whisper. "But I think you should not be here. Nor the young mistress, neither."

"Eugénie? Eugénie is here?"

The door clicked shut in punctuation.

The old woman was right: she did not belong here. Armand was neither what she had imagined nor what he claimed to be, and he did not have her best interests at heart. Something was happening here that was founded on lies and filled with secrets.

But how to get away?

Well, she thought. None of this would be decided standing here. She needed to know a good deal more and her head hurt.

Rapidly, she stripped off the lacy nightgown, so pretty but limp with her fevered sweats. Even the gay blue ribbons were soiled. From the oaken wardrobe she chose a dressing gown of palest rose, heavy satin garnished with silver ribbons, the short wrists cuffed with creamy lace.

The bruises she dared to look at might have been fading. How long ago, she wondered, for bruises to have risen and be fading already.

She ignored them and slipped the gown over her shoulders, tying the ribbons snug across the bosom. The ruffled lace mostly covered the worst marks on her arms.

"Oh, if only Prentiss were here," she breathed, then realized sourly: "If only he knows where I am! He owes me a rescue, I think."

There was irony here, which she appreciated. How many times in the past had she conjured Armand's name for advice or aid, or to admire her accomplishments. How often had she relied on her memory of him, and now it was Prentiss's name that stirred her. His voice she longed to hear laughing her name, teasing or in passion, earnest or playful. The love against whom all others would be compared.

She paused before the huge looking glass in one corner of the little room, long enough to wish she could wash her hair. Her face was drawn, the jade eyes dull and prominent. She had surely lost weight, and a bruise was yellowing over one arched cheekbone. With an effort, she tried on a pleasant expression. "It will have to do," she sighed. Trembling a little, she stepped out.

The house was very large, quite as big as her uncle's in Port Royal, and seemed to be filled with trees. Palm, banana, some strange bamboo, and others she could not name claimed a broad central courtyard. Hummingbirds whirred past her and big blos-somed flowers nodded red and garishly erotic around a clear pool filled with exotic fish and fed by a little waterfall forced indoors.

The effect was shocking; the world of Man was supposed to be ordered, with the green anarchy of Nature controlled and restrained. Not this chaos brought indoors, blatantly invading. It was far less like a European country home than a Turkish seraglio. The comparison made her think once again of Turk, and a wave of nausea almost overcame her. She leaned against the wall, fighting the dizziness until she won.

Then she was aware of voices below, and remembered her goal: breakfast and information.

As she stepped to the courtyard path, the voices became clearer: Armand and—she smiled with real warmth—Eugénie too. The friend of her youth, companion of her schooldays. Shyer and of a quieter beauty, she had given her whole heart to Molly in the old days. But she had loved her handsome brother with an idolatry that

Molly, infatuated herself, had only faintly echoed. And now she had followed him even to the Indies.

But what were they saying, there in the dining room? Molly paused, trying to listen.

Facing Armand across the length of a huge mahogany table, Eugénie was successfully maintaining her temper. There would be no further display of weakness, she had decided. If her lower lip trembled a bit, and her eyes were the slightest bit damp in the corners, at least it was no more than that.

Sipping at watered wine, she waited while Armand finished giving the day's orders to the staff: housekeeper, plantation manager, overseer, and a fierce looking villain with mustaches who was probably one of his tame pirates. Idly, she crumbled a honey cake between long fingers, no longer imperially slim and elegant. The nails were gone, the knuckles swollen and white with tension. She no longer wore rings since her hands had gone so puffy.

It was the heat, she thought. The stifling air, heavy with moisture, like a perpetually impending thunderstorm. How she longed for the cool nights of Paris in the spring, the gentle summers in the countryside, the crisp air of a snowy winter. When she looked at Armand, she saw it all so clearly again, and knew that it was gone forever. She had given him everything and gotten this exotic prison in exchange.

She loved him still, in spite of everything, but that love was poisoned, sinful, and addictive as opium. Watching his face, strong and competent, she could almost remember why she had admired him. No, loved him. Be honest. Just as in her mirror she could still see some tired bits of what had called him to her. A year ago, two years—no, longer. Before Molly's mother died; before her friends had abandoned her; before Eugénie truly understood that Armand's sister would never be Armand's wife, not even here at the back of beyond.

Her attention wandered, lost in thought. Both Molly and Eugénie had been at least a little in love with the dashing young officer, almost 15 years older than either of them. He was only a step-brother, in truth, which should have made everything all right, except that it was still wrong. Eugénie realized she had been hoping for a marriage as sometimes happened, to solidify the union of their families and fortunes. But Armand's father had died without such an arrangement, and Armand himself was of no mind to marry. They had been so close, she so much younger, it must have seemed indecent to him, to anyone.

Then how had he seduced her? On a dare from the other wild young officers of his company? A birthday kiss too fond, a Christmas embrace too ardent? Had he forgotten in that moment who she was? And then to excuse, to explain that it was only a corrupt and discredited Church which said they must not. The natural attraction of man and woman was the only law, he said. And she, overwhelmed, believed him.

Now here they were, trapped in the convolutions of their secret, their lives a lie that he was about to wrap her friend in it as well. More lies and more secrets. Did he imagine Molly would not know? She, who had been as close as a sister herself? It could not be borne.

St. Juste stood up from the table, pushing back the heavy chair with startling shriek of wood on tile.

"Armand, we have to talk," said Eugénie.

He gave her a patient look and sighed. "Now?"

"I cannot let you do this to Molly."

"I have no desire to discuss this with you, now or at all."

"Armand, please."

He seemed to think for a moment, then let a smile touch his mouth. Moving easily to her side, he took her hand, and kissed it. Gently, he turned it and kissed the palm; she shuddered and felt the blood rise, flushing her bosom with color. Then he bent hungrily to her lips while one long fingered hand traced the lush curve of her breast with delicate nails, trailing fire where they touched. The tiniest sound escaped her throat as he broke away.

"For the last time," he whispered. "There is nothing to discuss." At once, he straightened, almost sighing. Tears sprang to her eyes, of shame and hatred. "I am offering her marriage, and I am sending you back to France. Mercier has agreed to your fortune, what's left of it, and you will be an honest woman again. I had thought that would please you at least. God knows, nothing else does."

"I can never marry!" she hissed desperately. "I thought you understood that. Not Mercier, not anyone. I'm no good for any man but you. And you! Can you take your filthy soul to the altar beside that sweet girl!"

He said nothing at first. His expression never changed. He said finally, "What I do is no concern of yours. You will take a husband, and make what you may of it. I will take a wife."

"Wife, indeed. When we have no priest. And when you tire of her ..."

"There will be a priest. There will be a wedding."

"She is my friend!"

"She is my ..." He strangled the rest. "Will you stop me, little sister?"

She meant to speak. She meant to say she would kill him first, but the words caught in her throat. His gaze locked on hers until her eyes filled with tears and dropped. When she looked up again, she expected to find him gone.

Instead, there was the shock of seeing Molly in the doorway, framed by exotic flowers and trees. The smile on her face was open and generous, though she seemed perilously pale. She could not, must not have heard. Armand was at her side in a moment.

"My dear!" Eugénie exclaimed, rising from the table "But you should not be out of bed!"

Molly brushed by Armand to sweep into her friend's arms, tears spilling freely onto silk and taffeta. When they parted at last, she held Eugénie's hands and searched her face. There was trouble there, and deep sorrow. A puffy redness about the sunken eyes told of constant weeping and sleepless nights, and refuge taken in wine. The porcelain complexion, once the pride of Paris, now stretched coarse and hot across rounded features. The once delicate hands were swollen, barren of jewels.

"Armand, you are a vicious brute," said Molly. The chevalier stiffened; Eugénie tried to turn away. "Honestly, to bring this delicate girl into this climate. I suppose you've been making her cook for you as well. My poor Eugénie! Your beautiful hands!"

Eugénie tried to speak, but Molly stopped her, recalling some manners, as always, too late.

"Oh, my dear! You must forgive me! What a heartless bitch you must think me, to go so long without seeing you, then to be so unkind."

"I do not make her ride, or play the spinet, or manage the house, or anything at all she does not wish," Armand said smoothly, and guided Molly to a chair. "And it is you who have been ill. My dear, you must rest. Eugénie is well enough, now you are with us."

The other girl forced a smile into her voice. "I would not let him leave me behind." She met the hard black gaze briefly. "I am so happy now you are here!"

But Eugénie could not force the smile into her eyes, and Molly noticed. She also saw the change that came over Armand, the strain in his manners and Eugénie's. She had not understood everything she had overheard, but something here was horribly wrong.

Servants brought her fruit, sweet bread, and bitter chocolate while they chattered of Paris and their schooldays, remembered friends, adventures, and happy times. Eugénie seemed, if anything, even more wistful in her memories of Paris than Molly. The laughter was strained as Molly recounted the day they dared each other to run with rampaging students through the old city's ancient streets. It almost made her want to tell her about Prentiss, but a native caution and hard-won discretion kept the story back.

Finally, Armand rose with a laugh and said, "Truly, Molly, you are a tonic! Eugénie looks happier than I have seen her in some time, and in better health as well. It is too sad that this reunion must be short-lived. She returns to France at the end of this month. Our little girl is to be married."

"Married! How splendid! Is he as handsome as our bold Captain Armand? Ah, but that could never be. Oh, you must tell me everything."

The Captain intercepted one last time, "Unhappily, my dears, I cannot sit with you all morning, as one of us must make our living. But you must entertain each other, so long as it does not exhaust Molly."

He raised her hand gently to his lips for a chaste kiss, but the look in his eyes spoke promises of other pleasures entirely. A sharp look to his sister warned her against any untoward confidences, then he was gone.

Free at last, they strolled chatting through the spacious house to the drawing room: rosy walls printed with leafy shadows from the exotic plants that invaded everywhere. As they sat on the divan, surrounded by the alarming indoor jungle, Molly took her friend's swollen and feverish hand, and frowned.

"Eugénie, please tell me," she said. "What is the matter? What has happened to you? To both of you?"

The dark eyes dimmed once again. Her friend forced her mouth into a tight smile and looked away.

"Your islands, Molly. I should never have come. But Armand, well. He does expect me to be stronger than I am."

"But why is he here at all?"

"Papa died. There was a little money, but not enough for Armand to live as he thought he—we—should. So he sold his commission and bought this place, and *la!*" She shrugged once-lovely shoulders with a nervous laugh. "Here we are."

"But why does he say we are betrothed?"

Her friend seemed startled. "But you are, of course."

"Do you suppose I would forget such a thing?" Molly tried not to sound too harsh, but they were trying her patience with this nonsense. "Armand wanted my hand, and other things besides, but he never mentioned marriage, I'm quite sure. Even when he might have done so, and I might have said yes. I always imagined he was looking for something else in a wife, though I could never tell what. Perhaps a humbler spirit! Marjorie—well my mother would not have liked him much, I think."

She was laughing a little, more thinking out loud than conversing with her friend, until slowly she realized that Eugénie was weeping. Silent, miserable tears spilled from her eyes in sparkling counterpoint to a long, bitter sigh. Comfortably, as in the old days, Molly put a friendly arm about her waist.

"There now, I've done it again, haven't I? Forgive me darling, I am so thoughtless. But can you just tell me, remind me, how I happen to be marrying Armand?" Perhaps it would be simplest to play along for a while. "Please, sweetheart? I have had a terrible bump on the head and I'm quite confused."

But Eugénie could scarcely keep her voice from breaking. Resting her head on Molly's shoulder, she whispered, "Don't you remember. Just before you left Paris. Armand was with his regiment, and could not be home in time to see you off. He wrote begging you to stay, but you were in such a state after your mother died, you hardly read the note. But you said, *'If he loved me, he would give me a reason to stay.'* And then you said, oh, I remember it so clearly, *'I will never love anyone but him.'*"

Molly's eyes grew wide, their brilliant green clouding. She sat up and a little away from her friend, withdrawing her arm. "Eugénie," she said quietly. "No."

"I know I should not have told him, but he was crazed when he came home to find you had gone."

"Eugénie, it was you. You whispered in my ear, *'I can never marry. I will never love another.'* And I didn't understand. What did you tell Armand?"

The dark girl sprang up, pacing the room and wringing her handkerchief. "Nothing. Just what you said. How much you …"

"But I didn't"

"Yes you did!" Eugénie turned on her, eyes wild. A bitter laugh escaped her, with an edge of hysteria. "What could I have meant by such words?"

"No wonder he tells such a curious tale. But my dear, he has never asked for me. There is no contract, no betrothal."

"But there is! I have seen the letter from your uncle!"

Molly fell back, silent. Her thoughts reeled, refusing to sort any of this into any sensible order. This letter—if there were a letter—was certainly false, an outright lie. But whose? Armand's or Eugénie's? And to what purpose?

"Oh, don't you see?" the other girl croaked. "He wants you. He says he will marry you, and he is sending me back to France and away from you both! Armand always gets what he wants! Oh, why ask so many questions?"

And losing all control, she fled the strange room in a rustle of taffeta and tears.

"Well," said Molly. "This is a puzzle. Oh, Prentiss, where are you!"

She stood up slowly, a slight dizziness returning, quickly willed away. Then she realized that once again she'd been left alone to entertain herself. At least this time she was not locked up in the pilot's cabin. Still, "It's an island with no door and no key and the wide sea to keep me in it. What am I going to do?"

St. Juste rode out with his overseer to survey the land clearance on the southern edge of the estate. Pushing back the jungle was no easy task when the land was so rich. Everything wanted to grow back as soon as it was burned away. But St. Juste could not bring himself to mind. There was more land here in Martinique for a single owner than any ten men of his class might covet in France. And now, all was beginning to look like perfection. When it was green with sugar cane, it would be heaven.

The man, Dauzet, spoke little as they rode, which left Armand free to consider his plans in detail. So many things had changed. He chuckled a little to think of it. All he had really wanted was a new mistress. He had retained Jeremiah Peace with that intention alone.

The search for Molly had been a ruse from the beginning, a way of beguiling Eugénie away from family and friends. But she had only become more nervous, not less, the bitch. And more shrill, and more demanding. And fat, besides. The luxury of unrepentant sin might have its cost, he felt, but the ceaseless weeping had become too much. And so came about the arrangement lately concluded with his friend Mercier.

Dear Mercier. His true preference was for pale young men, but as his father's only heir he needed a wife. Armand, in a similar situation though less troubled by it, was only too willing to sell Eugénie like the outworn mare she was, just to be rid of her. Mercier would not treat her badly, or trouble her much at all once he had done his familial duty. And he would certainly be discreet.

All Armand wanted was to have her gone, and replaced by a fairly regular stream of young, pretty, and inexperienced girls. Thus the arrangement with Captain Peace for a new one every few months if possible. It made him sigh in happy anticipation as he rode.

Molly, however, was an unlooked-for prize. He had desired her since the day she came to live with them. Thirteen years old, with a merry, heart-shaped face almost hidden in bronze curls, and breasts just budding on her girlish chest. She had always held him off, laughed at his seductions, challenged his manhood. And then! What a creature she had become: courageous, and bold as a man but still as delicate as a wild rose. But her presence now, here, did affect his plans.

Perhaps, he thought warmly. Perhaps I shall marry the girl. A prosperous gentleman should have a lady.

His thought lingered warmly on the touch of her lips, then moved to imagining her hands, her body, all the things he would teach her to do, to put that adventurous spirit of hers to good use. It might take quite a long while indeed before he tired of her.

"You see what I mean, there, Monsieur," said Dauzet. They cantered to a halt at the edge of a rise. The overseer's voice grated harsh in the captain's fantasy, but brought him back to matters at hand. Getting down to business, he put women out of his mind.

Dick Prentiss had been angry enough to kill, crazed enough to try. At the edge of panic, he had demanded to know where Molly was but Fitts, from safety across McQuarry's common room, claimed not to know. He ducked in time to save his head from the wooden mug that came soaring through the air, but not his shoulder. The massive purple bruise was yellowing at the edges and the Madeira smell if not the stain was almost gone from his blue shirt.

For days while the weather raged, Jimmy had not been safe while Prentiss drank and swore and bullied any who crossed his path. Then someone found Black Thomas's body, stripped of valuables, and that story came out. Jimmy narrowly dodged a pistol ball, and walked more carefully after that. The Turk, wisely, seemed already to have disappeared along with Ned Courage, holed up in the caves some said, or shipped out with someone else.

For Dick himself, the days were a black nightmare. Davy had not actually locked him up, though he had threatened with perfect sincerity to do so. Then Jimmy disappeared, to everyone's relief, and Prentiss cooled to a glacial calm. He drank with quiet intensity, fending off all offers of sympathy or good humor, until even the toughest girls left him alone. The sympathetic had already given up. When Lily reappeared with a handsome black eye of her own, McQuarry himself ordered her brusquely out of his sight.

After an hour in his own room, still rich with the scent of her, Prentiss locked his door and walked away from the house. He settled down to wait in the furthest corner of McQuarry's palm shaded courtyard, though he could not have said for what.

The squally weather matched his mood. He slept sporadically, and ate less. Habitually clean-shaven, he was growing a beard by neglect. He hardly spoke, until even Davy lost patience with him. But the only words he wanted were questions that had no answers, demands that could not be met. He could hardly bear to hear her name, but it was the only syllable in his thought.

Drinking helped. Steadily applied, it left him floating but not actually sick; his speech slurred but not incoherent. At best it numbed the mind, and at worst it could not quite blur the pictures that whirled there of red hair gilded with sunshine and eyes as deep, as green as the sea. Nor could it dull the memory of her voice, of her presence. The flicker of a skirt at the corner of his eye could make him start, imagining for a wretched moment she was there. Twice, near twilight, he plainly heard her speak his name: once playful, once almost desperate. That, at least, the wine could drown.

If the sun rose and set, it was of no consequence, because Molly was gone. Weary, hating life, he laid his head on his folded arms. Before his senses left him altogether, it occurred to him to wonder at the size of the hole in his being left by her absence. It was too much, too much to consider and once again consciousness left him.

But the world would not go away, nor could he fade out of it. Abruptly, in fact, it interrupted in the form of his captain.

"Hey, Pilot," Davy bellowed jovially, kicking the bench where Prentiss sprawled. "Time to sober up lad. Work to do. A fortnight's lovesickness is all I allow." And with that warning alone, upended a leathern bucket of water over Dick's head.

With a roar, Prentiss was on his feet. And abruptly sat down again, blinking stupidly in the morning light. Water sluiced through the tangled mane of his hair, through the thickening beard and the coarse fustian of his clothes; beaded on the tips of sun-bleached lashes that blinked with astonishment over eyes more red than blue. The rest of the crowd at McQuarry's who had long since stopped noticing him, thought it an especially good joke.

"Bloody hell, Davy!" Dick shouted when he could find his voice. "Bloody fucking hell!"

The rest roared even louder, while York just radiated exuberant good cheer, and sloshed a second bucket in his pilot's face. Prentiss coughed, sneezed, and whipped water and dripping hair together out of his eyes and mouth. "Christ Almighty!" he added, and commenced a series of expletives of diminishing intensity. "What are you trying to do?"

"You stink, lad. The girls have been complaining. So have the rats. I thought you should have a bath, is all."

Prentiss was not to be humored. "I suppose this is for my own good," he glowered.

York shrugged. "What else?"

"I'll thank you to leave me alone, you damned interfering bastard. I'll—"

"Jimmy's back."

That caught him in mid-oath, and he turned up a sidelong glare at his friend. "Am I supposed to take some comfort from that?"

"And he knows where our Molly is."

"What?"

"I thought that might get your attention. The *Mary*'s ready to sail. Are you?"

Still at the edges of despair, he looked down at his clothes, felt at the maturing beard, and ran his fingers back through the unruly knots of unwashed hair. He smiled blearily. "Better if I shave. I can't seem to remember eating anything. Have I?" Almost at once he was better, as if the sun had come out after two weeks of rain. Molly was within reach again.

Davy beamed. "That's what I wanted to hear. Lucky then Keaton's Annie got supper and a bath waiting for you. Annie swears says she'll even barber ye, just to get rid of the lot of us!"

"How much time have I got?"

"Couple of hours, no more. DeRoet can take us out, but I'll want you at the helm by the third watch. It'll take some days, if the weather stays fair, which I doubt. Still I don't want to leave her where she is any longer than we must, and the evening tide will suit us fine."

Dick took a deep breath, and let it out slowly. He nodded, thinking, almost sober, making plans. Trying to make plans. "So, where is she?"

"Martinique," said Davy, suddenly grave. "And I wouldn't leave my dog in the hands she's in, if I could help it."

"Jimmy still isn't safe, you know."

"Leave it be. He's trying to make it up to you. And her, I'd guess. Now go stuff your gut, have your bath, and let's go get her. God's death, man, Molly'll probably kill 'im in any case."

13

A HAY FOR THREE

THE LONG SUMMER days passed in a hot Caribbean haze. Storm clouds gathered on the western and southern horizons, but passed by with no more than a sporadic, soggy rain. The jungle both within and without the house only seemed to grow closer, while Molly fretted. Armand was unremittingly courteous, but firm in his assurances that their marriage was imminent. He begged her to set the date, but assured her he would wait only so long before setting it himself.

She found herself longing uneasily for the release of the drugs again, but knew it for a false desire. Just so, the daily pressure of Armand's presence, the sensual terror he evoked strained her whole body so that recovery from opium, fear, and an almost constant nausea seemed impossible. Each evening's conversation taxed her wit and invention. Every morning was a joyless arising, facing the tense hours and the underlining fear. Overwhelmed with apathy, Molly slept away the days, too tired to imagine escape. From Prentiss or any of her friends there came no word, nor seemed hope of any.

Eugénie was poor company, forever red-eyed and sad. They talked each day, but their conversation was animated only by

Molly's reminiscence of their school days. The older girl added very little except a nervous smile. With shrill persistence Eugénie maintained that she would not return to France until she saw her brother and Molly wedded. Any other mention of marriage she tossed aside with a careless flutter of her hand. They both drank a good deal of wine, as strong as they dared, and pretended to do needlework.

Behind the house were gardens, surprisingly more chaotic than the wildlife indoors, where Molly could walk while her health ostensibly returned. There slave gardeners went busily about their tasks, answering her idle questions but impatient to return to work. Each cast an uneasy glance toward the house when she stopped them.

She could ride if she liked, but her health looked never to improve, which taxed her temper even further. The soggy, oppressive heat of the Caribbean summer, together with her enduring illness contrived to sap her vitality quite away. She hated the feeling, but could not drive it off, and began to suspect something in her food.

A week passed, and then another. Hurricane season enveloped them. The southern sky was filling with black, curling storm clouds, promising rain but no relief from the oppressive humidity. Molly had now spent yet another idle afternoon admiring the gardens and trying to chatter with her friend. Eugénie wanted to plan the wedding. Molly could not bear to think of it.

At last, pleading faintness, Molly almost ran from the garden to the questionable shelter of the muggy shade indoors. Green eyes dazzled, she was briefly blinded as she entered the sudden darkness of the atrium with its pattering waterfall and trellised ceiling. Shy bougainvillea, insolent orchids, and fat, heart shaped, nameless leaves of all sorts dangled like tentacles from the close-woven screen overhead, dripped their shadows across her face like the clouds of the steadily darkening sky.

"Molly?"

A hand touched her shoulder out of the dark, and she skipped back. "What!"

A man's shape loomed in the shadows, tall and angular.

"'It's me," the shadow whispered. "Jimmy."

Slowly the shape took on depth and form, and the troubled, pock-marked face of Jimmy Fitts materialized before her, stiff with apprehension.

"You! *You?* You bastard, what the hell do you want?" Automatically, she swore at him in French, then caught herself and repeated in English, for good measure. "Get away from me before I scream."

"Be best if you didn't."

She said nothing, but her fist snapped up with intent.

"I know, I know," he added quickly. "It's all my fault, and I've been an ass."

She could only blink rapidly in frank astonishment. The fist opened like a deadly flower, and she slapped him, putting her shoulder into it, though she had to reach high overhead to do it. He flinched under the echoing sound, as well as the blow.

"You've *what?*" she hissed. "*What?* You planned and you waited and you arranged with some pirate no one else will sail with. You waited till I was drunk and alone, then watched me beaten but not quite raped. Then you knocked me out, filled me up with drugs, sold me to God knows what kind of whoremonger, who dragged me away to this, this seraglio, where a man who was like a kinsman to me lives in wanton lechery with the sweetest maid alive, who should have been his dearest care, and yet expects me to marry him whether I will or no. And *you.*" She stopped at last to inhale. "And you have only been an *ass?*"

He could not let her turn away but taking her shoulders thrust her struggling into an alcove cushioned with philodendron, darker even than the rest of the room. "Listen to me."

"Jimmy Fitts, by God, if I were a man … No, if I had a sword! I'd make short work of you, and you know it. Let me go!"

"You've got to listen to me. Jesus, Molly, we're trying to rescue you!"

That stopped her at once. She glared at him in utter fury. "All right, where's Prentiss then?"

"He's not here."

Her eyes went wide with disbelief. "He sent you in his place?" she spat. "What am I, a lost cat? Are you so much smarter than he is? Or, no." A thought made her gasp. "He doesn't still trust you!"

"Look." He coughed an impatient sigh. "Do you want to see him again or not? God, woman, it'd be easier to leave you here than get you away."

She twisted again under his hands, and dropped her diction and her words to the clipped, coarse accents of the street, to something she thought he might understand. "I don't believe this. We're friends now, are we, you and me?"

As Prentiss had done before, he jerked a little with the change. By her own design, the lady under his hands addressed him like a dockside whore, nasal and mocking. "Go on, my darling! Tell me about your change of 'art."

He had the grace to look ashamed. "That's it, just. Losing you made him crazy. He nearly killed me."

"And?"

"And like that he's no good to anyone, no good to himself. So Davy and me, we decided …"

"*Davy* still trusts you?" she hissed in the same tones.

He pressed on with commendable restraint. "I wouldn't say so much, no. All right, truth is Davy made me find out where they'd taken you. No, he doesn't like what I done neither. I made a mistake. I was mad, all right."

"You never liked me."

"I still don't," he snapped, as weary as she. "I mean, no, that ain't true. 'Tis what you are, is all. We was partners, me and Prentiss. No place for a girl like you in a life like ours. I told you before."

"Aye, you did," Molly said, and sighed with some disgust. "A girl like me." She clucked a little and shook her head. "As if you knew what kind of a girl I am." She glanced pointedly at the hands still on her shoulders. He stepped back. "And now?" she said.

Now he reached into his jerkin to pull out a long knife, hilted in black briar and capped in silver, and watched Molly's eyes widen in the dark. "I found it for ye. Thought you might be missing it."

"Dear God!" she breathed, stunned back to her natural voice. To a conversation already punctuated with telling pauses, she added another while she stared and stared, taking in the meaning of the gift. Then she nearly snatched the old dirk out of his hand. The steel gleamed golden in the half-light as she drew it smooth from a new sheath.

"I had thought it was gone for good." She looked up into the scarred face and saw what she had missed before—a glimmering of acceptance. "This was Rafe's, y'know."

"Aye. I know. I knew him, y'know, a little. Met him before the... well, I should have known you'd be ... well." He had to stop; there was too much to say that was not his to tell. "I put a new scabbard on it The old one was rotting away. No good for the blade." Neither of them mentioned the silver fittings he'd added as well.

"I see."

The feel of the hilt in her hand again, the balance and weight of her father's last gift lifted her heart, and she realized suddenly that Jimmy was embarrassed. It was easily the longest speech she had ever heard him make. If awkward and mainly aside from the point, it was surely sincere. And the gesture was beyond reproach.

"Thank you," she said. And because there was only one thing left to say, she added, "Peace between us then?"

Jimmy nodded tightly, and jumped as she leaned up to place a light, devastating kiss on his cheek.

He looked away suddenly, listening. Around them, the air was cooling slightly with hints of rain in the fading afternoon. The house would be astir soon, busy with servants readying for supper.

There! Boots crunching on gravel, too close by. Molly heard it too.

She said, "You have to go. Tell me, where's Prentiss?"

"The *Mary*'s anchored round the point. Prentiss and Davy, everyone, plus the new lads."

"All right. Good. All right," she said again, half to herself. "Yes. You must go. Now! Before Armand gets back." She paused a moment longer, then said firmly, "Yes, all right. Come at dawn. With Prentiss, you understand? And as many men as Davy can spare. There's no real defense here. We can overwhelm them with no trouble, I'm sure. Don't worry, there's plenty here to make it worth while." She laughed, just short of hilarity. "Something for everyone, not just Prentiss. You tell Davy I said so."

"Wait a minute." This didn't sort with his orders.

"And here!" She slammed the dagger back into its sheath and thrust it into his hands. "I have no place to hide this now, and I don't want to leave it behind again. Keep it safe for me, all right?"

"But Davy said ..."

"Will you do that for me?"

"Yes."

"Then go!" she hissed, and forced him at last away. "Tell Prentiss…" There was no time. "Oh just go!"

As he slipped back into the shadowed dark, Molly's brain whirled with possibilities, suddenly charged with invention. Prentiss was coming! He was here! She had back her father's dirk, her talisman. And enough of her friends were on their way to bring her out when Armand would not let her go. But not for hours, yet. No, not for hours. She must find some way to fill the time, cover her excitement, and or else risk the whole game.

One ironic notion made her smile. For the first time since her arrival, she had something to look forward to, but no way to share it

So now, eleven nights and a thousand miles from Tortuga, *Jealous Mary* rode at anchor within sight of St. Juste's vast estate, but not yet in the welcoming crescent of his harbor. The sun set sulkily behind the island's bulk, ragged with jungle. Off shore a light breeze smelling of green just ruffled Prentiss's hair across an expression of tight-jawed determination where he leaned against the ship's rail. The jaw itself was freshly shaven, his old, befouled clothes changed for immaculate new ones. The blue brocade of his waistcoat, had he realized it, exactly matched his eyes. Paul DeRoet held the watch at the tiller, while Dick permitted himself a pipe and reflection.

The men themselves were relatively quiet and orderly, smoking, even singing on deck. Owen Jones's fiddle urged lively thoughts to do with dancing or fighting. And since they had just come away from six weeks ashore with their wives, legal or otherwise, sentimental contemplation was a not popular attitude. Mostly, they had not been this sober in days, and if they were somewhat subdued, they were also ready for action.

Davy liked them best this way. Trusted them. Turk's desertion was a pity, in its way, for he was their best gunner, but others were more reliable. And Ned Courage was no loss to anyone.

When Jimmy Fitts reported his mission ashore, a moment's deliberation let him consider the *Mary*'s strengths over all.

"Dawn?" he said at last. "The sun'll be in our eyes."

"She said dawn," Jimmy Fitts answered.

"She say why?"

"No. Must be tides. A reef? Maybe she wants one last night as a rich man's mistress."

Prentiss threw him a long, hateful look, then turned his face again to the sea.

"None of that, now," Davy went on, noticing the exchange. "All right, we passed that entrance yesterday, and the approach is smooth as glass and broad as Keaton's bum. Not much defense, but plenty of warning to the house."

"She's expecting us at dawn."

"Well we don't always get what we expect, now do we. I tell you, I know about this St. Juste, and he's as miserable a villain as I've met in a lifetime of villains. They say the 'wife' he brought out of France with him is his own sister! He's been nosing around for slavers amongst the Brotherhood, and that isn't right. We want Molly away of there now, you see?"

Jimmy agreed sulkily, while Prentiss only seemed to grow more still. "*Armand de la Valier de St. Juste,*" Molly had said before, taunting him. His hands gripped the portside rail showed knuckles white with tension. "What then?" he said.

"I like the sound of midnight myself."

"She was sure."

"Who is doing the rescuing here, lad? I say the evening tide will do us as well as dawn. We'll still have dark for cover, and all the house in bed besides."

Jimmy shrugged acceptance and went to join the others.

"You're the captain," Prentiss said.

"Aye, lad, I am."

"You should have let me go to her!" He whirled off the rail, the long hair whipping back in his face. "Why did you send him? He might have sold us all. Probably has done."

Davy nodded, "I suppose. So I'll not let him out of my sight once we're ashore. On the other hand, love makes a man foolish—making no accusations, of course. I didn't trust you not to be a bloody hero."

"Hero!"

"Look, you blistering idiot. I needed someone to cock an eye, make sure she was alive, and discover the best way in. Which is what Fitts does best, if you remember."

Reluctantly, Dick knew it was true. Hadn't it been Jimmy he asked to find Molly's house and the way in for him, not so long ago? "Aye."

"And, though I don't know why I'm explaining myself to you, he wasn't likely to try to bring her out by himself."

"Am I?"

"Aren't you?"

Prentiss stared at his feet, pushed the hair back behind one ear, then sighed. "You don't understand."

"Of course not. You'll see her soon enough. Christ, if this crew can't take one godless son of a bitch without losing you both then we should all bloody take the veil."

Dick ran frustrated fingers again through his lanky brown hair, now quite clean but tangling in the breeze. Took a breath and let it out again explosively. Opened his mouth to speak.

"Enough." Davy snapped. "Who's captain?"

"You are."

"And why's that?"

Dick arched an eyebrow in surprise. "Because you're always right? Or because you're a heartless bastard?"

"And don't forget it. Get some rest."

The revelry gained in intensity as Davy went to join in, resting far from his mind. There was little enough rum about; he wanted them more or less rational for a rescue mission. Dick looked after him in some puzzlement, but settled himself to wait. Another few hours and it would be time to hoist anchor.

Maybe Jim and Davy were right. She did make him foolish. Maybe that made him reckless. He did want to run in and steal her away in one grand gesture, sweeping all his enemies before him. It might even work. More likely get them both killed.

He smiled a little ruefully and stared out toward the dim hulk of Martinique. He desperately wished he could ask Jimmy for information. Did she look well? Had they mistreated her? What did she say? How did she sound?

He could hardly ask. It would only prove their point, and it would mean being civil with Jimmy. One thing he was sure of: when he got her back, everything would settle down. Things would be as they should be, a fair balance of excitement and simple happiness, and the not-inconsiderable fortune to be had and spent along the Spanish Main.

Just knowing, accepting, how close they were freed him from despair. With some of his old jauntiness returning, he jumped down to the gun deck to join his wit and humor to the others.

Early in the evening, fresh from a scented bath, she sat before the looking glass with a hairbrush, clad in a loose gown of sparkling silver-grey taffeta. The auburn masses of her hair falling wantonly over the textured shoulders, she frowned into the mirror, unhappy with nameless flaws only she could see.

When Armand came with a brief knock into her room, he brightened to see her so. Again, she allowed him to misunderstand, to think she was making herself beautiful for him. as plans began to form behind her sparkling eyes.

"Armand," she said sweetly, and rose to his light embrace. She even found it possible to return his kiss as eagerly as she had at first, when she was still too ill to think. When they parted, there was wonder on his face.

"What change is this, *ma chère?*" he said with awe.

She laughed that lilting bell-like sound that Prentiss loved, and said only, "I am very happy."

"I have not seen you so cheerful since, well since Paris. What change has come over you? Or," his face clouded with mock concern. "Have you taken another lover while I was away?"

She hated to lie, then her humor made its own decisions.

"What other man could so please me, Armand?" How pleased was she? Bile gathered in her mouth.

Hearing only flattery, he kissed her again, more than ever aware of his desire for her. Even the thought of her with another man sent him wild with proprietary jealousy, and increased his craving. When he released her this time, he thought she might almost to be laughing at him.

"Don't mock me, my girl," he said, a little fiercely. "Not about that."

That tinkling laugh again. "But Armand, what other man could own me? How can you doubt?"

Half the laughter was at herself, raining double meanings in the unspoken answers to every teasing question. No one could please her so well as Dick Prentiss. No one owned her. Prentiss was here. Armand could not doubt himself for a moment, but he was wrong.

Delighted at her own cleverness, she maintained the comedy.

"Armand," she said, coyly entwining her fingers into the short black curls at his neck. Lightly, she kissed his lips again, murmuring as his hands moved across the grey silk falling loosely over her breasts.

"Now stop, this is important."

"You are trying to seduce me, Molly. I assure you, it is not necessary."

Now she only smiled up at him, tolerantly, as at an eager child.

"Seduce the master? No, my dear. At least, not yet. No it is something else. A favor."

She moved slightly, still standing in his embrace, and felt the desired response through the loose silk of her dressing gown as his yearning hardened. He might indeed promise her anything, in such a state. "We have not talked about our marriage, about the wedding."

Startled, he drew back. "But you have not wished to discuss it! How have you come to change your mind? Or do you remember at last how much you love me." Pleased with the course of events, even if puzzled, he broke his hold and led her to the chaise under the garden window.

With a rustle of silk, she sat comfortably on the rose-colored velvet, dappled with leafy shadows in the deepening twilight. "You know," she said. "When I first woke in this house, in this room, I was afraid."

"Yes."

"Of you, of this place, of everything."

"I know. You were a silly girl, but I understood."

"But now." She looked him straight in the eye and let him take her hands in his own. "Now I am not afraid of anything."

If he had known her at all, he would have realized that the curious glitter in her smile came from fighting a terrible impulse to laugh. Instead, he sighed with shuddering passion to surprise even himself. Surrender so near!

While she held his eyes, he raised her hands to his lips. "And my favor?" she asked.

Without hesitating, he began nibbling at her fingertips and said, "Anything."

"A small thing, really. There is no time to send to my aunt and uncle, I suppose."

"Eugénie leaves in ten days, so no, I hardly think so."

"Then just so I may have some word of them. It's been so long since I was torn from my home by those evil men." A shudder ripped through her at the thought of Turk, which Armand could interpret as he liked. She would have her revenge soon enough. "May I see the letter you have from Uncle Roger, agreeing to our marriage. Eugénie told me you had it." He seemed hurt.

"I suppose I should not tell you," she went on "that he never said of word of such a thing to me. If you had mentioned it sooner, I might have …"

"Oh, Molly, I have been a fool! Of course you may see it."

Was the surprise genuine, she wondered. Certainly such a letter was a forgery. It would need no skill to convince only Eugénie. What would he show her?

It had slipped her thinking that he might rather distract her with his advances now, and decide later what to do about a false document. And inexorably he was pressing her back to the welcoming softness of the velvet couch, his mouth hot at the hollow of her throat, at the strong pulse in her neck. He bit delicately at her ears, brushing aside the golden earrings with their swinging emeralds, his gift.

She tried to stifle a sigh as his mouth moved along the line of her hair. Old desires flooded back, her girlish fantasies nearly overwhelming the rational part of her mind. She turned them aside with the image of Prentiss in her window.

Now the hard mouth covered hers, hard tongue pressing open her lips. The tiny whimper that escaped her throat must sound like passion but all she wanted to do was gag. Well, let him think what he liked of it.

Long minutes passed, filled with smacking kisses and harsh sighs, while behind closed eyes she called up the memory of Prentiss peeling a dusty cover from a dreadful Spanish mirror. The laughing eyes in her mind made her close her arms without thinking on Armand.

Smirking with success, he sat up and shrugged out of his coat, opened the ties of his shirt. Then one by one he began to untie the bright blue bows that closed her gown.

A sentimental corner of her mind argued for cooperation. How long ago it seemed that she had wished for this moment. She had wanted. He had promised.

He had lied.

Instead of relaxing into thoughtless lust, the stormy eyes snapped opened wide and cold. It was easier to remember who and what he was with his haughty, possessive face clearly before her, thick with passion; a coarse ordinary man with a square face and rough hands, not a whirl of heat. He was not looking at her eyes.

Hard fingers prodded soft flesh, and she gasped, frowning with pain. He laughed with no sympathy, and no apology. So far she had not sought to touch him at all, though apparently he expected that by now she must be longing for him.

"Shy with me yet? You'll learn better in time. I shall instruct your liking. For now, I suppose, we must make some show of daintiness." So saying, he gripped the edges of the gown and wrenched them apart. Appalled and defenseless, Molly cried out.

"Oh *ma chère, ma chère*," he sighed in frank appreciation, and closing his eyes, put his hands to her wonderful breasts and gathered them like scented pillows to his face.

Lying back on the chaise, one arm thrown over her head, she sighed and hoped it would be quick. She would allow this if there was no way out, because she needed the time, but she would do it in cold hatred. Except for the weight and damp heat of his body, stifling in the humid air, she felt nothing but loathing.

When his teeth closed around one nut brown aureole, hot fingers shaped her waist, traveling over hips, belly.

"No!"

He ignored her.

"Armand, no! Please!" It was too much. She had thought she could, but no.

The questing hands withdrew. Instead, still clad in gold-ribboned breeches and silk shirt, he hauled his body up between her resisting legs, scouring the silken skin with gold embroideries, tassels, buttons, bullion fringes while he sought her kiss.

When she protested again, he snorted and sat back, breathing harshly.

"Isn't it one of your English poets who warned you virgins to make use of time?" he said. "I will teach you to make use of this, I assure you." And he wrestled open the wide breeches till swollen cock met air.

Delicately alarmed, she turned her face away. Mainly she wanted to laugh at him, with his shirt rucked over his manhood, bruised with desire, as if she should be overcome with rapture at the mere sight. Forcing her lips into something he would take for a timid smile, she whispered.

"But Armand, surely that is for our wedding night. Please, do not do this!"

With a sneer, he leaned forward awkwardly, half on the chaise, balancing somehow on the floor, and pushed her knees apart, and slammed them shut again over his swollen member.

Oh sweet Jesu, she thought. Oh Dickon! He is going to do it anyway!

A push, a graceless grunt, a sweaty spill of stickiness under her thighs and he was done. He rocked back, apparently smug with satisfaction. In another moment he had gone, growling his contempt, clothes left behind like a conqueror's banner.

Loathing bridged into irony with the closing of the door.

"So!" she sighed aloud. "That is famous seducer? No wonder he is so fond of virgins." Ruefully she lay back and chortled with suppressed laughter. "Good Lord, I'm all over black and blue! Oh Dickon, don't be late."

Then she got up to start again on her ravaged toilette.

Just before eleven o'clock that night, the *Jealous Mary* lifted anchor and slipped noiselessly into the broad bay at St. Juste's front door. No more than a shadow hanging on the stormy horizon, they anchored again, dropped the pinnace with a splash, and slid away. Under its one triangular sail: ten men, including Prentiss and Fitts and their captain himself.

They came ashore within sight of the great house, all its red brick a looming shadow against the jungle dark, and ablaze with light. Servants swarmed about, and the windows glowed, silhouetting a dancing couple tracing the stately figures of a sarabande.

"Damn," said Davy from the rustling cover of leafy foliage that surrounded the house.

"Midnight sounds good to me," Prentiss answered with a note of sarcasm. "Shall we join the party, or wait for the cover of morning?"

"You shut up."

"There's no one else there," Prentiss went on in some surprise. "No one else dancing. No one else in the room. What kind of a ball is that?"

"Well, it's not the Saracen's Head when the fleet's in, is it?" Jimmy whispered. And got an answering chuckle from Prentiss, which startled them both.

"Maybe," said Dick, "this won't be so hard after all."

"Aye. Pity," Davy said. "The lads are looking for some fun." Agreeing murmurs answered from the others, hidden in the darkness. "Look, there's someone else."

"Another girl. Christ, which one is Molly?"

"Don't be stupid. The one that's dancing, of course."

"You would be able to tell at a distance, wouldn't you?"

"On my mother's soul, I'd expect to know her if I was blind and deaf in the darkest pit of Hell." The passion in Prentiss's voice was simple, unadorned, and absolutely devastating.

Jimmy blinked.

"Well, then," said Davy. "Let's go."

The usual late supper was, for the first time since Molly's arrival, positively gay. Armand was pleasantly charming, aglow with good humor, wine, and new conquest. Eugénie was almost light-hearted, some unusual spices in the wine working a singular magic to overcome her accustomed strain. She had put on a pale blue gown of watered silk that set off her dark hair, and floated through the room, resplendent with golden ribbons.

After supper Armand called for tobacco and pipes, an generosity seldom extended. Though he was used to the exhilarating effect, the smoke made both ladies a little giddy. Molly inclined to giggles and Eugénie wanted to sing, when she had finished coughing. By midnight they each seemed to become almost unbearably witty, and Eugénie said something to make even her step-brother laugh out loud.

It was determined that singing was in order, so they retired with brandy to the music room. Molly sat at the spinet, which she managed creditably once she remembered where her fingers were—even brilliantly, considering the tobacco was slightly cut with hemp.

Then Eugénie played while Armand led Molly out to dance, adventuring first the stately sensuality of a sarabande, then a sprightly allemande. The last turned out a bit too sprightly, for Molly missed her step, and fell with a muffled shriek in a heap of emerald satin and silver lace petticoats. The giggles turned into near hysterical laughter, as Armand gallantly tried to help her up and fell to tickling until he lay almost in her lap.

Taking immediate advantage of the situation, he rolled her into a smothering embrace, plunging a laughing, lecherous face into her bosom.

Molly shrieked, still intoxicated but suddenly frightened.

A hard discord crashed on the keyboard.

"No!" Eugénie was on her feet, all humor vanished. "Armand, no! I won't have it."

He raised a drunken sneer to the girl he had seduced and was trying to abandon.

"Leave us!" he snarled.

With a gasp, Molly rolled out of his arms and tried to scramble to her feet, but he clutched at one ankle.

"Come back, *ma petite*," he sang playfully, and dragged her down again. The hand that pulled her now slid up her ankle and thigh beneath the clutter of petticoats.

At once Molly was sober and angry.

"No, Armand," she said coldly. "Not here."

And just as suddenly his mood changed again. Laughing it off, he pushed her away and got up himself. "Ladies, ladies, my little dears," he soothed, mollifying. Oh, he was almost all charm tonight. "We are celebrating. Come, let's have more brandy."

Just drunk enough, Eugénie had already forgotten why she was on her feet. The thin lips sketched again her uneasy smile, as if even happiness were painful. Laughing at the edge of something like hysteria, she cried, "Yes, more brandy! Come, Molly. Another glass for you. Or something sweet. Sherry perhaps? I remember you always liked … mmm, the sherry! And maybe just a one more pipe, Armand?"

He nodded, magnanimous.

"Yes that's it. Please, Molly. Please!"

Molly September took a deep breath, composing herself with the memory of friendship and a reminder that this need only last a few more hours. That indeed, if they tarried here cheerfully together all night, she might even keep out of Armand's bed—or wherever. And by dawn, when Dick got here, Armand would be in no condition to resist.

A new, sunny smile creaked into place, and she shrugged in tipsy acquiescence where she sat. Her friends laughed, good cheer restored, and Armand helped her, if a little clumsily, to her feet.

"Yes, more wine, by all means," she said. But no more for herself, no.

"Do you know," she said, as a fresh glass appeared in her hand. "I have not had a fencing lesson yet from you, *cher* Armand." She tossed her hair, the extravagant curls gleaming russet in the candlelight. "I have missed our practices."

Seeming artless flirtation covered sudden dismay. There was a disturbance somewhere outside. They couldn't be here already! Had Armand heard?

"Ah, but you have not been well." St. Juste sat back comfortably in a padded wing chair, his back to the door.

"I suppose I never was any good."

"Not altogether bad. For a girl," he nodded, and drew on the freshly loaded pipe. "I would not be ashamed to say I taught you. Women, of course, do not have the stomach for real fighting. But for the basics, not bad."

He had no idea.

St Juste's thoughts, like the blue smoke wreathing round his swarthy head, roiled in lovely patterns. Such a delightful vice, tobacco, whatever the moralizing and self-righteous might think of the leaf's unmistakable decadence. So relaxing. No, so stimulating. And so profitable. The extra touch of wild hemp in the blend made one feel so, so powerful.

Then someone shrieked high and desperate, echoing across the house.

"Qu'est-ce que c'est?" he shouted. "What's that?" Was that a noise in the atrium? Another cry. *"Qui est-là?"* Who is there?

He listened, but when nothing followed, he waved it away. "Never mind. Dauzet will deal with it. More brandy? Or coffee. Shall we have coffee?

He peered blearily at Molly. Why did she seem so distracted? Even agitated? Perhaps smoke did not suit her after all. It had certainly made Eugénie nervous, that slug of a girl. Slut. No. *Something.*

He leaned back in his chair, eyes half closed, almost catlike with drug-induced bliss.

"I think you should give me lessons again, Armand," Molly said as if nothing had happened. "Would you?"

"Molly, don't be ridiculous," Eugénie answered. Pallid, she stared past her brother's shoulder into the long, tree-shadowed atrium. Shadows seemed to move above in the gallery. Men's voices muttered, guarded and low. Someone gave commands in the dark.

There was a scream from the kitchen. Eugénie yelped in terror. "Armand!"

More low cries, and the quick hiss and distinct bang of musket fire! Men shouted, and others ran.

"Pirates!" St Juste cried suddenly, and tried to shake the fumes from his brain.

Molly was on her feet so abruptly she knocked over the decanter and its tray with a crystalline crash. She bolted around the spinet, and a wrought iron stand of candles tumbled flaring in her wake to spill flaming wax across the fringed cover and cross the carpet to velvet draperies.

This was the moment, yes. But hours too soon! *Men!*

Behind her, Armand was shouting. The servants, the slaves, the house, awakened like an ant hill, began to scurry in shadow and torchlight.

Then out of the dark a tall, tolerably attractive, slightly rakish figure appeared suddenly in the doorway, cutlass in hand, a stained brown buff coat belted over his best silk shirt. His face was flushed, his curling brown hair governed under a scrap of cloth as blue as his furious eyes.

"Molly!"

"Dickon!" Sobbing with relief, she cannoned into his arms like a desperate child.

Eugénie shrieked; Armand's bellow rumbled unheeded after. The embroidered point lace of the spinet cover began to crackle along a fiery edge.

"You idiot, I said at dawn!"

He didn't dare kiss her yet, or touch her. There would be no stopping when he did, and they were not finished here. He could hardly bear even to meet her eyes, or his hands would tremble.

Instead he stepped back and said, "Overruled again, Sweet. You can guess how. I take it this is the famous Armand, who was almost your first? Did you tell him it was too late?"

Finally, St. Juste shook off his daze, and shouted for a sword. When there came no answer, he plucked one off the wall and advanced. Eugénie shrieked and clutched at him then collapsed gasping when he shook her off.

Molly said, "Yes, it is. I'm sorry."

Against it all, Dick was impossibly cool. "Really! Well, you were very young," he said tolerantly. "Ah! Behind me now, love. Have a care!"

Just in time, his sword swung up to meet Armand's descending rapier with a clang, and they closed.

Nicotine, with its curious ability to both calm and stimulate, surged through St. Juste's trained body, pricking both anger and icy determination. But Prentiss's strength had been stored on melancholy and fed on outrage, and his temper was absolutely in check. He fought across the room like a champion.

Unfortunately, of course, so did Armand. The years of experience both in the *salle* and on the battlefield were evident in his every move. On his best day, Dick was not as good as Davy, and he knew it. And Davy would never be as good as Armand de St. Juste. In a short while that became all too clear.

"This will not serve," he said, when he could catch a breath. Firmly, he grabbed Molly by the arm, and retreated into the dark and treacherous atrium.

A light rain, hardly more than a mist, had begun to fall through the trelliswork high overhead. The smell of storm was everywhere, damp and urgent. Fat drops that collected on the greenery spilled leaf to leaf into each other to become a steady trickle. The tiles were slick already, the gleaming yellow and red Spanish enamels deceiving the eye with reflected candlelight. No, that was firelight. Boots slipped.

"Which way?" Prentiss gasped in a moment's respite.

Molly had become so used to speaking and thinking in French, it almost took too long to remember, let alone answer, in English.

"Here," she breathed at last, and ducked into a brake of some spidery bamboo overgrown with vines. It was dark here, and clammy with mist and sweat.

They dared not speak, but when she caught the look in his eye she trembled to think it was not only the deliciously masculine joy of battle that glimmered there, but something special that was all for her. Maybe he too was remembering the first time they had hidden together in the dark.

And maybe his only thought was for this particular desperate moment. All about them men were shouting and others laughing. Above it all scraped the unforgivably bright sound of a fiddle playing a jig. Slaves were disinclined to stay and defend the house, but other men had found weapons and were using them.

Dick caught his breath, frowning in frustration. He wasn't afraid; he just hated hiding, cowering in a corner like a cur, but he also knew he was overmatched. As much as he wanted to murder the bastard, the task was to get Molly and go. He waited, one hand on his sword, the other desperately on her wrist, while a sphere of silence gathered around them. *Now!* he thought, and started forward.

Nerves tingled *No!* Molly grabbed him back.

They heard St. Juste before they could see him, a hunched dark animal stumbling towards them almost sightless in the gathering firelight, swearing a steady stream of abuse. The Frenchman ran into a square of light, paused to wipe his eyes clear of mist, then charged away toward some uncertain enemy. Maybe the darkness, maybe a surprise?

Damn it! Prentiss had what he came for. Why couldn't it just be over? He had what he wanted, and St. Juste could go hang, if only he would. But no. He …

"I take it we intend to get out of here?" Molly whispered.

Recalled to the moment, Dick nodded shortly. "Look, I can't handle this bugger alone. I don't know where Jim and Davy have got to. I'm going to go find them."

"Don't leave me alone!"

His grin glowed in the darkness as he handed her his cutlass and said. "Here, you keep this. You'll be fine."

"What about you?"

"Trust me."

"Dick?"

"Hm?"

"Are you never going to kiss me?"

Dick had been trying not even to look at her, but he dared to now. Most of the lamps had been doused long since, and the music room was a flower of flame, but he thought he could read by the light in her face.

"Not yet," he said, though his resolve was close to slipping. "Not until there's all the time I want to take."

At last, he took the courage to stroke her downy cheek with one light finger, and was rewarded to feel her tremble under his touch.

She took heart and said, "Be safe." He nodded, and vanished into the murk.

In the dark, Armand shouted for aid, but most of his servants were gone or dead, and he had no allies within ten miles, or a thousand. Even the overseer, Dauzet, did not answer the desperate cry. Only Eugénie, forgotten, wept and lurched uselessly after him and called his name.

Was it getting lighter? Dawn was still hours away. Dawn, he thought, when the witch might have had him so besotted as to be utterly at the mercy of her buccaneers. He would deal with this, and then with her.

Nostrils flared at the smells of burning varnishes and cheap brocades. He pivoted back toward the music room, and saw to his dismay the sulfurous yellow glow, tinged with red, flickering in the gloom. The sound of crackling flames and spinet strings snapping, twanging discordant in the red heat, rose under the revolting sound of someone sawing at a fiddle.

Wild-eyed pirates surged past him, carrying away bundles of rich clothes, jeweled boxes, a brass-bound trunk. Everything, everything he owned, everything he had salvaged from a disorderedly life, marched down to the beach in the arms of laughing Englishmen. A gold and crystal mask a hundred years old fell from someone's hand, and shattered into splinters quickly kicked aside.

Dazed, angry, raging he called out for them to stop. Only one even paused to laugh at him, answering in a bastard French.

Eugénie caught his arm, but he shrugged her off with a curse.

"Please, Armand, we must get out of here!"

"Hang off, you whore! Damn you, get away from me! Don't touch me!"

Irritated but barely distracted, his anger focused on her, and he shook her off, lightly he thought. She slammed against the wall. Briefly he met her eyes, his utter loathing unconcealed.

"Don't you understand, you hopeless bitch?" he hissed through clenched teeth. "I hate you. You disgust me." The rapier rose silver in his fist.

She recoiled in sudden horror, trying to melt along the pretty, flowered wall to the floor. "No!" she wailed, reaching for his hand.

But with a shake, he dropped her at his feet like a terrier finished with a rat, and brought the sword slashing down on her unprotected shoulder. The blade rose and fell again, gleaming darkly wet in the glow of flames. Still enraged, he struck once again, ferocious even when her voice had stopped, the interminable whining halted at last.

"Armand!"

A voice. A shape limned in fiery haloes, as if the wonderfully scented masses of her hair burned in the night. In her right hand, the glinting shadow of a sword.

"Molly?"

All around them, most other sound seemed to fade away, except the growing roar of the fire as it caught a music box, an ebony god, a gilded picture frame.

"That's quite enough."

"So there you are," he said pleasantly. "Where have you been, my love. I have been so worried, looking for you."

"Were you?" She answered in English as cold and sure as she had ever pronounced. "You have a curious way of demonstrating your concern, Monsieur."

He stepped carelessly passed his sister's silken corpse, shoving it aside with a thoughtless foot. "What do you mean?" His voice was husky, roughened by anger and the hot, smoky air.

"I used, for example, to think you loved my friend. I even fancied you might love me."

"And I do!" He reached a hand toward her, his face twisted into a portrait of bewilderment. "Molly, I do!"

The shapely shadow seemed to quake with harsh laughter. "I shall have to write that down, your definition of love, and teach it to my children. If I want them to be whoremasters, or sharks."

Still lightly corseted, she had stripped to her shift and stays over a single petticoat, kilted up and shining; the silver lace reflected in bronze the shadows of the growing blaze. Strange, almost bizarre, she seemed to his dazzled eyes more beautiful, more desirable than ever. Utterly misunderstanding, thinking she wanted him, he took a step forward. The cutlass snapped up in her hand, cocked and ready.

"Come for me, *maître*. Find if your lessons will serve me well enough to see Eugénie revenged. Or kill me too."

"No!"

But he was within her range. As he took one further step, she dropped into the fighting stance he had taught her, as nimbly as a dancer, and made her first attack. He parried artlessly, almost thoughtlessly. How could a gentleman take such a situation seriously, fencing with a naked girl? But she pressed him, seriously or not, and finally succeeded in nicking the wrist of his sword hand.

So now his pride was engaged. Suddenly he was quite sober, aware and irritated. He cut forward to riposte, then lunged expecting to skewer her easily. But lighter-heeled and less debauched by far, she danced away out of reach. The teacher, however, was not to be outdone. Irritation increased to anger, if not yet to the madness that had left poor Eugénie dead on the Spanish tiles.

Balance recovered, he pursued her, pressed her into the flame-licked doorway. The heat and smoke made her cough, which broke her concentration and her balance, and his next, professional slash cut a trough across her arm as she dodged. Stunned eyes widened, she stared at the arm, then let it pass.

The pain would sink in later, his sword was that sharp. Now there was only the weight of the blow, a good deal of blood, and quick understanding. Tight-lipped, Molly remembered at last what kind of sword she carried, and what other lessons she had taken.

She changed stance, dropping into the crouch Prentiss had taught her, no longer governed by the strict rules of the *salle*. Boldly, she presented the whole front of her body, but low to the ground and, cat-like, pressed the attack again. He fell back a little before her, and had time to notice what Davy had seen before: the single-minded determination that drove her to keep on, blow after stinging blow, even when common sense would have told a man to pause, regroup, breathe.

If I stop, I will die. A young woman, less-experienced, smaller, lighter, of shorter reach, she would take every advantage and expect to give none. She could not expect to win, especially now that Armand seemed to have taken up her challenge in earnest. But she did not plan to kill him, only to survive.

She knew that even with a change in her tactics she was far over matched. Very well, she thought, she could choose the direction of her retreat, falling out of the blazing music room towards the door. Firelight leaking from the rooms above lighted the shadows under the stair, and that way lay safety. If only, damn it, if only she could hold him long enough.

Where the devil was Prentiss?

Wheezing, she withdrew.

Calmly, Armand backed off, black eyes reflecting light like soiled windows. She could tell he was breathing harshly, as she was, weighing the situation. Her sword was heavier, her arm less strong, but she had youth and too much to lose. He was 15 years older, debauched and out of practice, but far more experienced. Her left arm was on fire. She had marked him and so had Prentiss.

She dragged a sooty wrist across her face to wipe away the sweat that had begun to cloud her eyes, and winced. There it was, the deep pain of the gash screaming along her arm. There were others, each a light bleeding touch, a scratch deep but not lethal, meant to annoy and weaken, not to kill. Each now ran with fire.

"I suppose you are just toying with me," she said.

"You started this, *chèrie*." Their conversation resumed, peculiarly bilingual, as though language were part of their fencing. "I intend, of course, to finish it."

"Do you?" she said between gulps of air.

"You know you have never beaten me. I have always been toying with you."

"I've had other teachers."

He nodded, betraying a little weariness after all. "I thought as much, for all your maidenly protests."

A haggard smile trimmed her gamin face. "Maybe I never was."

"You know I was Eugénie's lover?" A vicious grin, hoping to shock and disarm.

In her turn, a slight, tired nod. "She told me. Or she tried to. Did she tell you she was pregnant?"

"You're lying," he snapped.

"Maybe. What matter? You killed her. And what place is there in the world for the a child of incest, the bastard of a discarded whore?" The word was its own condemnation, but it carried no weight with him.

"I loved you!"

"Now that's a lie." She flipped the errant curls back out of her eyes and sneered. "You are too disgusting to live, Armand. I should not dirty a sword on you."

"I will kill you, you know."

"Forgive my presumption, *maître*, but I think not."

"Can you stop me?"

"She doesn't have to, actually."

Behind him, above the roar of gathering flames and crashing ceilings, Dick's voice rose steadfast and cheerful. A pistol flared, and without further conversation, defense, or threat, Armand de St. Juste crumpled to his knees then to the floor with cry and a neat hole in the back of his shirt just behind the heart.

The rapier rang against the tiles as it dropped, doubled by the song of Molly's cutlass cast away, and the pistol itself landing with a splash in the pool under the little waterfall.

"Oh God, I thought you'd never come!" Molly wept, and rushed into his arms.

There were no more words. Only his hands in her hair, on her face, her body. Only her arms desperately circling his waist, clutching at his shoulders, as if they could melt into a single loving mass. Mouths locked in such a kiss that Molly knew she would faint or melt quite away if they didn't stop, and she didn't care. As if they had never kissed before. As if they had never done anything else.

"If you two have got a minute," said Jimmy Fitts. "We'd best get out of here before the whole place goes up."

The dry, sensible voice, tinged with inescapable urgency, finally reached them. They moved apart as two doors to a single room, and stared at him.

Then, "Here!" Jimmy threw and Molly snatched Rafe's long black dirk out of the air with her good hand. "You'll be wanting that, I guess."

Prentiss raised an eyebrow but chose to focus on the immediate problem. "Right," he said. Then looked down into Molly's eyes, the cloudy jade ringed with fatigue. The blood on his hand was seeping swiftly from her arm. "Sweet Christ, you're hurt!"

The dear face screwed up in a wince as she nodded.

"Can we go now?" she said, and collapsed. Jimmy held her while Dick dragged the scarf from around his throat and tied it round the wound, then he took her into his arms and out of that terrible house.

Under a thunderous sky, the pinnace fully laden was waiting just off the beach where they had left it. In the end, only one hapless cook was injured, and almost no one died. It was the looting that cheered the men as they took the place and everything in it they could carry. Some treasures would be doubtless left on the beach, but no matter. This was private vengeance, and none of it belonged to the King.

Their escape was lit by the great fire now roaring through the mansion, leaping to the outbuildings, and licking at the edges of the mangroves. It would spend itself soon enough, hissing out as the light rain turned into the storm that had threatened since dinner time. The noise of it faded as they rode the choppy waves around the headland.

Prentiss kept the tiller while the others rowed back toward *Jealous Mary* where she lay festive with lanterns, just beyond the point. Molly settled against his knee, sheltered under his free arm, awake but dozy and comforted though numb with pains large and small and sick with the charred smell of smoke. They did not speak the whole way, content with the simple contact of bodies and minds.

"I'm sorry," Dick said when they were safely aboard and tucked into bed. "I never meant to leave you alone so long."

"I can get into a lot of trouble in a little time, it would seem. Even without you to help."

The new barber-surgeon, Hughes, had cleaned and patched her arm. She would steal a little fresh water for a proper wash when the morning broke, but it would be a day or so before she could clean the stink of smoke from her hair. No matter. For now, hours of gentle reunion later, she lay in Dick's arms in the lamplight of the wide sailing master's cabin, completely happy at last.

" Was it so bad, all the time?"

"Yes. Worse because I thought you would never find me." She smiled sleepily into the shadowed indigo eyes. "But you did."

Prentiss held her close, careful not to press her bandaged arm, and marveled. It was hard to believe this little girl had coolly fought a much older, more experienced swordsman to a standstill in the midst of chaos and fire. This woman had proven herself as courageous, as cool under pressure, as any man Prentiss had ever known. And without knowing it she had, finally, taught him the truth of his heart. In the end, it was more than he could bear.

He looked down at her, nestled in the crook of his arm, so small, so vulnerable, and stopped resisting the feelings that tore at him.

"I've been such an idiot," he said thickly. "Have I never told you how much I love you?"

In shock, for she could not answer that without her own voice breaking, she simply shook her head, *no*. A faint, embarrassed pause.

"I do, you know. I love you."

She could hardly think for the hammering of her heart. When she found she was holding her breath, she could only let it out in a broken sigh while salty tears filled the corners of her eyes and spilled onto his chest.

"God's death, Molly, what more do you want of me?" He was laughing. "I have just put my heart into yer lap. Do ye not love me a little?"

She turned in his arms, still speechless. Her hands slipped through his hair, petting the long strands away from his face, tracing the firm, strong line of his jaw, so he kissed her just once, lightly, but she was still staring at him as though he had dropped from the moon.

"Of course I love you, you great loon," she said. "From the first time you looked at me."

Impulsively, he brought her face up to melt on his kiss, taking more care this time to make his feelings plain. She was so sweet, he thought, on his lips and in his heart.

The wind luffed in the sails as *Jealous Mary* started to fall slightly out of the midnight wind. Automatically, he listened for Paul DeRoet to make the necessary correction, and relaxed when the flutter stopped.

Adjusting his arm under his lover's shoulders, he said lightly, "We could get married. If y' like."

Molly's thoughts, overwhelmed, caught in her throat with a sound too much like a sob.

"Oh!" she whispered against his chest.

"Have I said something wrong?"

"Oh my dear," she said, and slipped in his arms to meet his eyes again, shining in the dark. "What a fool I would have been not to love you. Yes, I would like that very much."

He started to laugh, then his mouth came down hungrily on hers in a kiss that left no room for such a question, or indeed for questions of any kind for a long time.

Much later, Dick answered a passing thought. "You said you wanted to go home."

"Hush," she breathed. "I am home." And consciousness slipped away.

Damp eyed, he brushed the tears from her face, then fell asleep himself. In other hands, *Jealous Mary* set herself into a course away from the storm.

14

NUTMIGGS AND GINGER

SUMMER PASSED INTO autumn between dangerous excitement and more work than Molly had imagined. Skirting the storm that harried the islands below Martinique, Prentiss took them down along the warm, indigo waters of the Lesser Antilles then up across the Spanish Main itself, where any Englishmen were understood to be outlaws and heretics, any English ship a pirate. Blithe nevertheless, *Jealous Mary* sailed out of the squalls of the French-held islands and into the Spanish roads to scout for merchantmen dawdling behind their escorts.

From one they took pale green porcelains and new-minted gold doubloons, sacks of black peppercorns and pungent spices Prentiss couldn't name.

"Grains of paradise, these are," Molly said, breathing in the sweet tang. "Galingale in that one, I think. Ahh, yes. And oh, nutmegs! Oh yes, I'd call this precious goods!"

The men stumbled under the burdens of rich woven carpets, casks of pearls, and gold thread silks from the Philippines; the treasures of China and the Eastern Indies, the spoils of Peru and Ecuador, bound for Havana, thence to the palaces of Spain, the bankers of Venice, the garrisons of the Netherlands. This one, true enough, would never see another Spanish port.

There was more.

Stacked in one corner of another hold they found crates of tiles, cobalt blue with gold sparking in the glaze like lapis lazuli, and packed in straw. Prentiss and Jimmy exchanged glances over the first opened box, and smiled. "Parlor floor."

The Spanish commander, an *hidalgo* of exalted rank and extraordinary mustache, was relieved, along with his sword, of a vulgar quantity of emeralds, lately ripped from the mines of Colombia. Molly thought they matched her eyes. Prentiss quite agreed.

The surviving crew were left north of Curacao with their small boats and their aristocratic officers, but two well-placed rounds from Matt Christy's cannons sent the galleon *Santa Martiana* to the bottom in gilded Hispanic splendor.

On the *Nuestra Señora* a week later, they found boxes loaded with good Spanish muskets, brand new, plus powder and shot. They also found sixty English seamen condemned for piracy and heresy, being transported to the Indies as slaves. Davy left them in possession of the prize ship and half its cargo, most of its food stores (never mind the mice), a keg of rum, and the headings for Port Royal, Tortuga, and Southampton, to choose from as they might. When they parted company, days after, the all-English crew of the newly re-christened *Mary's Fancy* were healthy and singing, and the *Jealous Mary* sailed on, hungry for more. Davy kept the muskets.

Throughout the energetic days Prentiss never let Molly out of his sight; seldom took his hand entirely away, wherever they were. Few words of any kind passed between them, though they were always in concert, as they were always in touch. A smile, a breath seemed to be enough.

And somehow, the crew dealt with this equably, as if she had become their mascot to be pampered and cosseted, even in spite of her taking up boys' clothes once again. As her wounds healed, and the singed ends of the beautiful hair were trimmed away, they brought her gifts: carved toys, a bawdy joke, a song.

It helped perhaps that many of the lads were new, coming aboard just before leaving Tortuga. They all knew about Molly, of course, and most had watched Prentiss's obsession as it grew, and who knows, may have signed on as much for curiosity as for Davy's reputation as a lucky captain.

The new men were, like the others, of all sorts: the master gunner, big Matt Christy, and his picked cannon crew, who replaced Turk and his cronies; the barber-surgeon Hughes who doubled as ship's carpenter, the tools being much the same; an Irish fiddler to team with Owen Jones; and a boy with a drum. Keaton's Chrétien had wanted to come along to rescue *Tante* Molly, but Annette said "you can rescue her next time", and Keaton agreed.

Jones, in fact, came and sat at her feet and played love songs and dance tunes by turns, whether the lads were at their work or not. He knew, because Molly had told him, that it was his music, all unwitting, that had drawn her away from the others that night and let all the rest happen. He hoped, in some small way, to make it up to her.

Her arm still aching, Molly felt useless in action, so when they went after the *Santissima Trinidad* she sat in the sheltered helm out of Dick's way, with pistols primed in case of misadventure, and waited it out, flinching at the noise. Then she stood when he locked down the tiller, and watched between envy and terror as he leaped down into the fight himself.

Between times, she set herself to learn the charts and divine the subtleties of sextant and compass, and to tell fixed stars from planets. There was, as Prentiss showed her, more mathematics in navigation than she had supposed, but in that she discovered a talent that all her teachers of embroidery and sketching and the spinet had never required. That would be her father in her, Davy said.

While she stood her watches, she picked up the tricks of the brigantine's rigging that made her so maneuverable, and marked how it shifted and adjusted with weather and time. She couldn't climb aloft yet with the rest and she hadn't the strength to haul on the lines when the rigging wanted adjustment, but she could watch and learn. And in their idle moments, Jimmy set himself to remind her fingers of the sailors' knots she had learned as a child; Keaton, to watch the weather like a living thing; and Davy, to load and fire a musket with speed.

When Davy was content she could name all the sails and the lines by their yards and their uses, and answer the commands with the right responses, he let her sign the *Mary's* Articles in strong, Italianate strokes, after first striking out the ordinance against women.

Then, twenty-nine days after Martinique had dropped away behind them, and skimming under the green intimations of Nicaragua, they picked up a shadow. Pacing the *Jealous Mary* off her starboard side, just within the limits of the lookout's vision, the swelling sea now masked, now revealed another ship, schooner-rigged and black against the sky, flying English colors. It lay under the whitecaps perhaps four hours distant; less, if her master knew his business.

Next day, Davy trained his spyglass again on the phantom shimmering like fool's gold in the distance. "Bloody hell," he said, and slammed the glass home.

"Well?" said Keaton.

"Well now I just don't know, do I!" Davy snapped.

His lieutenant stepped back in alarm. The captain had been all out of his usual spirits for days, and the West Country vowels went round in his mouth. Now he was etching finger prints into the polished oaken rail where he gripped its jealous rim.

"Might be friends, maybe. And it might just be the pissing Inquisition or the Royal bloody Navy." He stopped to breathe unhappily between imprecations. As if talking to himself he added, "I don't like the way she's just hanging in the air out there. She must see us as well. She knows we're here. So run or fight or hail us, damn yer eyes! Till she stands in closer … " He spun away from the side.

"You lot!" he shouted at whoever happened to be lying about. "Sure ye've aught to do besides idle yer stringy carcasses in the sun drinkin' my rum! The damned cat does more work. If I find that lower hold's not squared away by sunset I'll have yer tripes for supper."

While they scrambled, Davy slammed towards his cabin, then changed his mind and pivoted, marching back amidships where he stopped, brooding. Once again he turned to glare at the horizon, gray and layered with storm.

Green season, they called it. *Hurricane season*, they meant. Sudden squalls, deep heat and sullen air. A smear of rain perpetually hanging in the distance. A phantom stranger lurking in plain sight.

"Bloody hell," he muttered. "Bloody strangling god-forgot hell."

Something was wrong, utterly wrong, but he couldn't seem to catch it. It was, he thought, as if a door in the air somewhere were standing open, just waiting for the right decision, the right action. A moment was waiting for him and he was captain, he should know what it was. Not a feeling to make a man easy in his skin.

He spat with distaste, and raised his voice: "Master Prentiss! Master Keaton! If you please. *Now!*" And dragging his pipe out of his pocket, he shifted his heading once again toward the privilege of his own quarters

From where he still stood at the starboard side, Will Keaton turned a sorry look up to the helm. Molly had been sitting cross-legged at Prentiss's feet, pouring over some book or other and sometimes asking questions. The wind kept teasing their voices away as it teased up the wisps of hair she held out of her face with one hand, while bracing fluttering pages with the other.

As if he had always meant to, and belike he had, Dick was handing off the con to Paul DeRoet, who glanced down at Molly and with an evil expression rapped out a question like a Dutch schoolmaster. She squinted up at him, frowned, then snapped back an answer.

The two steersmen exchanged doubtful looks. DeRoet asked another, or possibly the same again, rephrased. Molly reeled off a longer answer, and smiled when she was done, and cackled with delight when they laughed and said by God, she was right. Prentiss snatched up her hand and kissed it, and hauled her to her feet.

The quartermaster almost sighed as he caught Prentiss's eye and waved him down. A very pretty picture, aye. Very lively. He was getting too old for this.

"I know," Molly was laughing as they joined him. "Next you'll be asking me for the principal exports of Madagascar, and the capital of China."

"That's a trick question, love. There is no capital of China."

The image of light and life, the two of them, busy in their busy universe. Ignoring the warning in Keaton's look, they ducked under the abbreviated passageway into the restrained elegance that was the captain's personal domain.

The sailing master's quarters that they shared with Keaton and DeRoet were, as Molly had noted before, fine and well furnished, to be sure. The captain's cabin, she now marked, was as near to palatial splendor as any Englishman was likely to get while floating in a wine-dark sea. Spacious, flanked with glazed windows under the stern castle, beveled glass and lead and ivory, with a colored panel of some libidinous exercise in the middle; rich with dark woods. Florid but declining any indulgence in saints or coats of arms, it was the office of a gentleman adventurer who knew what he needed and what he liked, and who declined, if you please, from further ostentation, the instructional stained glass aside.

"If the lesson is quite finished," Davy said acidly He had planted himself in a chair at a massive table of some dark wood, and was apparently dealing a hand of primero for four. He frowned over a queen, noting an annoying resemblance to someone else with red hair, and said, "Did I invite you?"

Molly jumped. "Captain?"

"I think you heard me." He glowered briefly, then heaved a dramatic sigh. "Never mind, never mind. Sit down, all of ye. Aye, you too, lass, God save us." The last card snapped to the table like musketry, face down. "Report, Mr. Keaton. Stores?"

"Fresh water's getting low, Captain," said Will smartly, dragging up a chair and relieved to be merely businesslike. "And the supplies we took off the *Trinidad?* That'll last a while longer, if we're careful. Crew's galley stank like a midden, but the Dons ate well enough."

"Bloody Spaniards," Davy growled as if it were a new observation. Impatient, he gathered all the cards again and flexed into an elaborate shuffle. "Prentiss. Where are we? Exactly."

Dick rattled off their position by degrees and hours to his latest reckoning, then cocked an eye at his captain's clearly intolerant expression, cleared his throat and added, "Aye, sir! Five days out of Portobello, sir, nor any reason to go there. (Once was more than enough, thank you very much.) Eight days at a dead run to Jamaica."

"Are we rich enough to go home, d'ye think?"

"Hold's just half full, Captain," Molly said at once, though he hadn't called on her. Davy twitched, but nodded her to go on. She had picked up the cards dealt in her direction and was considering them. With a smack to Prentiss's shoulder, she held out her open palm without meeting his eyes. "But that half is worth at least as much as you brought in last time."

Dick produced a gold doubloon and three silver shillings. She claimed them all sweetly from his palm, and slapped down the silver. "With all those spices, it'd be best to get them warehoused."

"You *are* Rafe's girl, aren't you," said Davy over a diamond trump.

She grinned outrageously and played a six. "I'll wager I know what we've got as well as Will does." Drew a card and sweetly pushed the gold piece forward. "Likely better." Then she folded the cards into a single smug trick in her hand. "What's going on, Captain?"

"In a minute." He fiddled with his cards, suddenly at risk. A glance at Keaton whose cards still lay untouched. Five Spanish *reals*, an English angel, and a Venetian ducat rang on the table. "All right. Prentiss. What do we know about this stretch of coast?"

"Aside from it being a right motivation to practice our Spanish?" He was laughing while he fished Molly's next wager out of his purse. Three gold florins and a Bohemian dollar. "No towns, but there could be savages, and they're not likely to be impressed that we're the heroes of English sovereignty." And a golden English sovereign, just for the irony.

Davy reached behind him to fetch up a very good bottle of wine and a clutch of silver cups from a shelf under the mullioned windows with their rainbow view of the ship's wake poured as he noted:

"Marry, my lad, you mean to say there's no clear place nor friendly to drop anchor and take on fresh water between here and …"

Slug back the wine and pour again. Discard a knave and a deuce in diamonds. Draw two cards and scowl as the girl pushes the golden angel into the game. *Ten shillings, on my life.* And takes up the two besides.

"Between here and Port Royal, no," said Dick, fascinated. "Not friendly, exactly, though I seem to remember—"

Then he glanced at Molly and stalled. Things he had not told her loomed close again. And no, maybe they weren't important, not secrets, exactly. Just things. He noticed her noticing. A last florin hung in the air between them, snatched up by the girl who gave him back a wolfish grin and slapped down her cards.

"*Primero 62*, Davy. You're mine."

Prentiss objected. "You can't keep him!"

"Remember what?" she said.

Prentiss twitched, misled, belayed and betrayed.

"I remember," Prentiss said. "That there's an inlet—never mind you're a devil at cards as well, my girl, there's still a thing or two you don't know—two days and a bit, this side of San Lorenzo. Conning the entrance is a jade's trick but it's a good harbor, hard to see from outside, easy to set a watch. Pretty little place, besides. Broad beach, easy hunting, even fruit trees and such like. The spring's no more'n a hundred paces inland. And far enough away from the mouth of the Chagres not to start me shivering again."

"The Chagres?" In the midst of dragging her winnings gleefully to her bosom, Molly halted on the word, but Davy intervened.

"Just a river, darlin'. We fought there once, no matter. Spaniards?"

"Not last time I was there."

"And we know how long that's been!"

"Aye," Dick said soberly. "We all know. Just tell me where ye want to go, Davy, an' I'll put us there safe and sound, sure enough."

"All right, here it is then. (*Damn you girl, just shuffle and deal.*) It's my mind that our shadow out there is Royal Navy. Our papers are in order, aye, but I've no mind to be boarded and risk losing the richest prize we've ever brought in so's some wet-nosed Midshipman with delusions can take the credit and cheat my men out of their fair shares. (*One of ye cover this hand or y'are both dead men.*)"

Cards down, money out. Davy gave himself time, this time, to think. Before he spoke, he was sure. Two bright new-minted gold doubloons rang on the table. "I had a contract to join up with friends, but it's been some while past since we should have seen 'im. And if it was him back there, he'd have showed himself. So (*Ha! You bitch!*) we're on our own. Your wager, madam," he added smugly.

"What friends?" Keaton said.

Davy barked a laugh. "Aye, well no true friend of yours, if I mind me. Last time you met Preacher Mendez, Will my hero, he tried to baptize you!"

Keaton grumbled an uncharacteristic growl. "I thought I saw you talkin' t' that pratin' Dutch bastard."

"Dutch?" said Molly. "*Mendez?*" Discard an eight and, oh, the nine, draw—nothing of consequence. She considered pouting, and threw in a shilling for the hell of it.

"Aye, his mother's family was English who went to the Spanish Netherlands for their religion, then she married some Calvinist, or maybe it's t'other way round. Whatever the truth is, (*Oh draw again, my beauty. Draw again!*) he hates every Spaniard ever born for the heathen murderers and bastards they are. An' he confesses every Catholic he finds till they turn them from the Bishop of Rome..."

The other men sang out like altar boys at the choir: "*And all his detestable enormities.*"

"Aye, you have it pat. When he takes a Spanish ship, or a French one, he preaches 'em a sermon before sending 'em to the bottom. That's his baptism."

Molly played her queen and laughed to cover a shiver. "Best if I fail to mention my year in the convent, then!" Now it was Prentiss's turn to raise an eyebrow. "Oh, aye?"

"Later!"

"My little nun!"

She thumped his arm and snatched the pipe from his mouth. "I suppose he'll call me names and tell you I'm the whore of Babylon. Damn!" Silver coins collected in the middle of the table, but her cards failed of their promise even as Davy's seemed to improve. "As if you cared."

"More likely add you to his harem! Though if you treat him as you do your loving captain, Molly mine (and it's 'Mary', in sooth, ain't it?)" He ducked. "Some other pastime you won't like nearly so much."

She did not like the sound of that at all and her hand, Davy noted, tipped a little forward.

"Well, never mind," Davy said. "You'll find out soon enough. In the mean time, Pilot! Let's see if yer as good as you think you are. And how fast you can get us under some obliging cover. Keaton! I want *Jealous Mary* as quick and as lively as the day she was launched. Dress 'er up in all her petticoats, man! As much canvas as she can take. Clear that bastard off my horizon! Let us fly, my bonny lads. Fly!"

Hissing "*Maximus!*" Davy slapped down his cards and drew the gleaming treasure of the table singing into his hands. His temper, his luck, and his resolution were back.

So they flew.

Keaton shouted orders and the crew sprang up to haul on the lines and shift the rigging to its most lively configuration: square rigged here, fore-and-aft there. Scrambled aloft and released every inch of canvas from every yard.

He shouted again and one by one each sail thundered open with a roar as it filled, engorged, belled and caught the wind. Under Prentiss's expert hands once again, *Jealous Mary* leaped forward like a harpy, and the phantom that had haunted them fell quickly behind and vanished into the haze where sea met leaden sky. Somewhere out there a storm was edging past them, spattering the *Mary's* deck with incidental rain, but the wind of its passing lent them speed as they heeled over and ran west. Once out of sight of their shadow, though, *Jealous Mary* drove south, determined not to leave an obvious course behind them.

The sky cleared to dark blue then black under a paper white moon, and glittering stars for Prentiss to fix on winked between the shredding clouds. Confident at last and exhausted with calculation, concentration, and maneuvering 300 tons of ship and cargo for hours through rocky seas, Dick, hollow eyed, returned the helm to DeRoet and himself to Molly's care.

Then with the stars, a compass heading, and a sure and certain knowledge of the coast, they ran all night before the wind, so instead of two days and a bit, it was late morning the next day when Prentiss flung himself shivering up to the main deck with Molly close behind.

He had heard the *Sail ho!* in a dream, turned over and cursed, but as he dragged himself to the helm he discovered the truth clear in the unsubtle noon. There, out there, just there within moments of rescue lay what might have been the shadow he knew he had left behind in the Bay of Mexico. He knew, he was sure; it was gone; laid behind him like absolution and remorse.

But instead like a nightmare, a sloop that could not be there, slung low to the water, rigged for speed and flying English colors presumed to trade fire in baroque and enameled silhouette as fine as martyrdom, as clear as spring, with two Spanish galleons. In the ordinary way of things, such ships would have surrendered comfortably, lacking the escort long vanished and under-gunned besides, but they perceived an advantage of numbers and meant to press it.

The *English Testament,* as she seemed to be, was at a clear disadvantage given the double target she had chosen. The defenders, Spanish or not, might very well have been correct in choosing to fight back, thinking themselves beyond capture. But they had reckoned without Fate and Richard Prentiss.

The *Jealous Mary* sailed into the fight screaming on the wind, dragging up her gallant sails and slamming shut her cannon ports. Fresh again and utterly expert, Prentiss heeled the *Mary* about in a maneuver most pilots would have guaranteed impossible to a vessel her size. He brought her about nearly on a skid as fine as a silver penny.

Wind shifted across Molly's face where she clung to the ratlines; breath caught in her throat. The groan of massive timbers vibrated through her own bones and muscles. Molly stood fast, and watched the man she trusted above all others lean the *Jealous Mary* into a perilous curve to the windward of three close-quartered ships.

Stresses grew and changed focus, orders called, men moved in quick competence and Molly felt herself lay over with the ship as if it were part of her, the pressure of each change profound on her own body and mind. Fear and exhilaration skipped up with flying sea spray until she closed her eyes and wondered if she remembered how to pray.

Then, first gently then all at once, the brigantine leveled out. Crew hauled on the halyards that shifted the great sails yet again, and scrambled to the quartermaster's orders so she skated into place, her port side now sliding parallel along the enemy's idle gun ports. The crew all around gave up a startled, ecstatic, slightly hysterical cheer and jumped to their boarding positions.

Dick Prentiss, author of the miracle, allowed himself a strained smile and graciously acknowledged the praise of his fellows and their own part in it, though every muscle ached with leaning on the tiller and his voice had vanished straining into the wind. From here on, any orders he needed to give would be relayed to Keaton through Paul DeRoet who stood behind him, but the hardest part of his work was nearly done. The trick now was to keep the *Mary* clean against the target in time with the gunners' volley.

On Davy's order, Matt Christy flung open his gun ports and uncapped his cannons, a bleak grimace on his broad Northumberland face. A pause. A breath. Match set to the first touch hole, and the first shot was away, the big gun rocking back on its limber. Then the next and another as they set off the running broadside till ears rang with the half a dozen explosions and the air filled with bitter, eye-assaulting smoke. Owen Jones and his new partner struck up a jig while the privateers hurled cheers and insults over the side with the shot.

As before, Jimmy Fitts anchored himself at Molly's left hand. Almost idly, he looked to her, corrected her stance, her grip on the cutlass, said: "Pistols primed? Show me."

She rolled her eyes but sheathed the sword to pull both pistols from her broad blue sash, and showed him. Locked and loaded, primed and ready. A sharp nod approved, then a reluctant grin. Overcome with something like brotherly impulse, Jimmy reached out and tugged the loose curls gleaming against the buff deerskin of her jacket. "Ye might just do, at that."

Before she could answer, Mr. Keaton on Davy's signal bellowed "Drummer!"

Derek May's big drum rolled into the thunderous cadences of battle.

"Grappling hooks away!"

On the other galleon, the *Testament* did the same. Briefly, the defenders rallied to hack away the offending lines, only to be discouraged by a few firm shots from swivel guns. And the privateers were once again swarming onto a foreign deck eager, hot-eyed, and screaming for the wild exhilaration, the fear and anger, the unexpected skills that sprang to life.

Behind them on the palm-flattered Main, a hidden volcano puffed white as a coffeehouse pipe, and before them two proud merchantmen took a deep breath and shrugged down their colors. The Spaniards had surrendered. Time to round up the crew, isolate the officers, and discuss ransoms, terms, and parole. And hurry. Hurry. Because Christy's gunners were simply that good and the *Eulalia* was sinking.

The familiar process began. Molly jammed her weapons home and made first to identify the quartermaster. Then while the man stared in mixed horror and fascination at the brash young woman—a woman, *por Dios!*—she asked politely in her schoolgirl Spanish for the ship's manifest. And as always, the poor startled officer in question laughed and essayed some vulgar compliment, until the muzzle of her swift drawn pistol leapt into the hollow of his throat, and he gave in. In minutes, Molly and Keaton were

Maggie Secara

below, directing the salvage, identifying the most valuable, the most marketable, or otherwise most useful items. Time, as so often, was in shortest supply.

By the time Molly got Keaton's word that whatever they had was all they were going to get, and if she was coming out she'd better be quick about it, she was up to her knees in sea water and drenched in the streams pouring in from all corners. There was nothing left that mattered, and no time to retrieve it, and the last of her men who might have taken it were urging her up the ladders.

She'd found the Peruvian gold, the elaborate silver plate, and 26 barrels of beer, not to mention two pipes of very good wine for the *Capitano's* mess, which she'd sent up first of all. The lads had moved smartly to bring it all out as she directed, while Keaton, whose job this was, concentrated on getting it all stowed. At last she slogged up into the light, soaking wet but merry, with a box of ivory combs under her arm. Jewels were all very well, but a girl did need a comb.

"Molly!" Prentiss had shouted himself hoarse but he called anyway from the *Mary's* deck. "Are you coming, or do you mean to swim to Costa Rica?"

"You mean it might be too far to walk? I thought we were on the doorstep!"

She tossed the box to him, which he caught along with his breath as she dashed across the last catwalk. Barefoot, she scrambled lightly across, reaching out with a balancing hand to just touch the last grappling line, then fell into his arms while the last of her lads crowded over and around them cheering. On the other side, Keaton had already clambered with Davy over to the *Testament*, now raucous with victory.

Prentiss spun about and started to shout for DeRoet to pull away from the wreck before they were caught and sucked down with her, but his voice was worn to ribbons. Happily, the stocky Fleming knew his business and had been waiting only for a signal. Orders went up, the wind held true, Paul hauled on the tiller and drew the *Mary* off to safety. Dick turned back to Molly, shining.

"I think, my lass, that you've found your calling," he rasped as he kissed her.

"What, Davy's housekeeper?" said she, a moment later.

"I'll tell you Keaton's impressed. He and Davy meant to write this one off. But you knew where to go and what to do, just. Of course, we did what had to be done, but you kept it from a total loss."

She blushed a little and waved aside the flattery. It was no more trouble than organizing a pantry, and she'd done that more than once. "I did like taking the look off that Señor's poxy face. But you! You, my lad were brilliant! I thought sure... well. Good lord, but what's become of your voice?"

"Too much saying your name all night!"

She meant to protest but she was too busy kissing him. Excited, exhilarated, she wanted the thing she always wanted after a fight. "How long," she murmured between kisses. "Before we come back about to meet the rest? Do they need us? Is there time?"

He stopped, held her away a little, and sighed, though the sapphire light in his eyes betrayed him.

"Not nearly enough to make you happy, you heathen. Besides, Davy's taken Keaton over to the *Testament*. That leaves me in charge on deck."

She frowned prettily. "Hardly seems fair."

"Now get on. You've still work to do, if you mean to be petty officer. Ye'll be wanting to get things ordered below, before the lads get distracted."

"Distracted?"

"No questions, now. You have your orders."

She looked at him sideways but decided to go on. "Aye aye, Pilot. May I pick my own team, sir?"

He shouted over her head. "Molly needs three sturdy fellows here!"

All over the deck things hit the deck with clangs and thuds and a dozen men at once threw hands in the air, calling with lecherous grins. "Disappoint someone, will you? I still need a few to sail the ship. And be crafty down there, if you please. If Mendez knows exactly what we have, he'll decide what parts of it are his and we'll never see it again."

"Will he so? He can fetch it up himself then!" She turned and started away, calling out names. As the lucky few jumped, she turned back and said, "This Mendez. He's some kind of priest? A preacher or something?"

A single eyebrow flared to mock her. "Or something, aye."

"Ordained and all?"

"So he says."

"D'ye think he knows a wedding service?"

A wry smile twisted its way across his lips. "You know someone who longs to be married?"

She let her own dazzling eyes grow very big, and cocked her head coyly. "Mayhap. Let me think a little longer, while I'm cannily managing the stores."

Managing took longer than expected and required more than three men and her own lively self. The spectacular racing tack that had brought them about so ferociously had wrecked havoc below decks, and boxes and barrels were everywhere. Two crates of celadon porcelain had shivered into sea foam crumbs and had to be tossed; and a keg of rum had smashed, which made the air itself intoxicating as well as ruining a Chinese carpet of uncommon quality. She sent the carpet up to be spread on the forecastle deck to dry and air. It would bring no cash, but someone's pounded earth floor on Tortuga would be made more glamorous by a silken rug.

By the time they were done, storage was not only ordered but well organized. Molly and any of half a dozen young men—no one more surprised than themselves—could have put their hands at a moment's notice on any single piece of gold, casket of jewelry, or sack of peppercorns below *Jealous Mary*'s decks.

The hard currency lay furthest in, uneasy to hand and all but invisible to casual inspection or idle hands, and the jewels and jewelry lay within that. Things they might actually need or want while voyaging—beer, rice, rum, biscuit, the last of the oranges—went nearest to the hatch. Behind them, rolls of cloth and carpet made a rich but impenetrable barrier to more glittering prizes. The muskets she sent to be racked on the gun deck as if they had always been there.

Now Molly stood back in the dim filtered light, drenched in sweat and deep satisfaction, paved in dust, some sparkling silver and gold, some red as saffron. The whole cramped space smelt of rum and ginger, but she breathed it in as happily as if it were roses. Perhaps the dear nuns' lessons in housekeeping hadn't been completely useless, after all.

The men slumped or lay collapsed over tidy barrels and crates and passed a bottle of rum, tired but finished. With a look she gathered them to her: Jimmy Fitts and Gil Denham, young Billy

Mariott and old Dan Rhys, Jeremy March, and little Muggs who had not ceased complaining but worked nearly as hard as the others, though he may have sat down more often. Owen Jones, too, who had kept them going with lively tunes and bawdy choruses, and distributed the rum on Molly's knowing glance.

She stood back and admired their handiwork, battened and braced and swept so tidily away even the rats had retreated in dismay. "Now look a' that, then," she said in the common voice she kept for them. "T'will be a pity almost to unload it when we come to Port Royal, eh?"

She had teased and cajoled and ordered them about all day, and they laughed comfortably with her now.

"What d'ye mean unload it!" said Jimmy in mock alarm.

And Owen Jones added, "That's never coming apart, now, look you. A bloody work of art, it is!"

"Might as well say, thank 'ee lads, now you've built Windsor Castle for us, I think I'd like it in Yarmouth instead."

The mocking and grumbling played light and welcome to her ears as a dance tune. What, she thought, would Rafe think of her now, sergeant of her little band of cutthroats, fiddlers, and engineers.

"Not unload it?" she nodded somberly. "Very well. I take your meaning. But, aye now... ye mind that smallest box of jewels," she asked, playing out the joke in her broadest accents. "The one in the very midst?"

They groaned and nodded. That had been the first argument, and she had won it as she'd won nearly if not quite all the rest. "Ye mind Jimmy here set it on top of that barrel o' fine French brandy. So ..."

"Hey!" They pretended weakly to start digging towards it, but collapsed exhausted and aching in seconds. "It'll wait," they agreed.

"Now all we've left to do..." Savage groans erupted. She'd started more than one sentence with that reflective phrase, as well. "All we've to do, gentlemen, is somehow crawl ourselves out of here and secure the hatch covers before they pack us in here with the onions."

Weak cheers and a stumble for the ladder.

Molly kissed them each in turn, then Jimmy swung her lightly up the ladder to the open sky. As she emerged into the long declining afternoon and the freshening breeze that swept them along the coast, the shock of clear air struck her over-heated body like ice. The air, like the sea spray dashed up from the bows, pricked her skin like fairies dancing over her eyes and arms and soaking clothes, and on it a rich green smell like the flowering forests of all the world.

Paul hugged the coast watching for Prentiss's hidden cove, and the starboard horizon erupted in green untended forest, white beach, and smoking mountains soaring overhead.

The wind caught her as it caught the great sails, her knotted hair, the wet folds of her shirt. She whipped the sodden scarf from her throat, and flung out her arms and stretched in magnificent agony. Quick applause pattered down from the watch riding aloft in the fighting top, and others hugging the yardarms, taking in canvas. She smiled with easy grace and curtseyed like an actress.

Her work crew swarmed out of the hatch behind her to the good-natured jeers of their mates. Four hours in the dark with Prentiss's girl, eh? A display of blisters and an invitation to trade places nearly started a fist fight, but the smell of food was in the air as well, and they really were too tired. Molly moved to intervene, then waved it aside with a shake of the snarled auburn head.

"Aye, aye," she said in what was left of her best quarterdeck voice. "In the dark for four hours, and still hungry, by God! Strike me, but anyone wants me will have to make an appointment!" They whistled at her bawdiness, and let it drop, all grins. They were hers.

Who'd have thought it would come so easily? Easy! Her hands were burnt and pricked with tiny splinters from grabbing ropes and balancing rough hewn crates. She hadn't the strength or the reach to match the men, but she could see the shapes and the patterns, think and plan, and by the bye: *Now hold this while I secure that. Now tie that off!*

Just a hand right here, miss.

D'ye ken a running bowline, Moll?

Aye, well enou', let go.

Easy, forsooth!

The warm well-being that attended happiness unlooked for made her dry lips twitch up dreamily and her weary mind wonder what had become of Prentiss.

Ah! Jolly male noises from the captain's cabin, and one or two strange faces lurking nearby. That would mean visitors at the captain's table. So they had started without her. Well, they could live a while longer in the same poverty of her company. On such days as this she had two cravings, only one of which, lacking Prentiss, could be fulfilled just now, so she ducked into the galley to find her supper and a very large cup of wine indeed.

Besides, there was still one more task.

She filled a bowl with what Toby Millikan swore was stew, being made up with rice and fish and dried peas, flavored with small beer and chilies and looted cardamom; and for pity took another up to the helm where Paul DeRoet stood the dog watches alone. It must be nearly three o'clock, she guessed, minding the hard black shadows of the yards that fell across the golden deck.

A high fair sky streaked with clouds blew overhead, peeling the eyes from her head, stirring the color in her cheeks and chapping her lips. "Can I ask you something?" she said after a bit.

Paul nodded and gulped down a spoonful of the questionable mess with thanks. "As you like."

"Is it only you and Prentiss? Pilots and steersmen, I mean?"

He shrugged. A swallowing pause and a slug of thin wine. "Davy can take a turn, of course," he added in his deep, flat voice. "Captain has to be pilot as well. Master Keaton, too, though he is a better quartermaster. Better than most. Of the rest, aye, most can at need. Prentiss or me, we can set *Jealous Mary* under a star and leave nearly anyone alone, if they can stay awake and the weather does not change, and it is a straight line. Easier to reef sails and drop anchor, mainly, for nights. But aye. Me and Prentiss—Davy says where he wants to go, and we take him there."

His direct unclipped diction always brought out her best voice as well. After a day in course tavern accents, it was even a pleasure. As his student and as the lady she used to be, she asked, "Could you set *me* under a star and leave me alone?"

The spoon stopped half way to his mouth. Grey-blue eyes slipped sidelong to see if she meant it, and drew no sound conclusion. "Not this voyage," he said carefully.

"Good," she said. When he lifted a single expressive brow, she added, "I knew if you said yes, you'd be lying."

"A man would be very foolish to be false with you, Mistress."

"But one day?"

He stared down into the compass box, tapped it as if it might be lying, and shrugged again. "I think me you are not strong enough,

Molly, in your arms and chest. Pretty chest though it is." He permitted himself a small, pleasant smile which she wantonly returned. "But aye, one day you will know the stars as well as your father did. And how the ship sails, and why. I think it is in your blood."

Again, as always, a hint, a wink, but no more. What was it! "You think so?" she said mildly. And after a stretching moment, added, "It's odd. Everyone says I am my father's daughter, but they never quite say what that means."

It seemed he might say something else but he scraped at his bowl instead.

"Did you know him, Paul?"

Overhead the wind sang in the sheets and gulls cried. Below in the cobalt sea that matched her eyes, dolphins danced beside them, calling out and laughing at the great dark being that swept their waters but would not play.

"There is something out there," he said suddenly, peering into the smoky distance to the east. "Look there. Do you see?"

She turned as he directed, expecting no more than sky and the back edges of hurricanes and the low black shape of the *English Testament* following a few points off their side now under a plain red ensign. Why would no one say more about Rafe?

"Nay, it is gone now. I think."

She hardly knew Paul DeRoet, certainly not so well as she did Prentiss or Davy. Or even Keaton. The weeks of their acquaintance had been mainly questions and corrections, just like school without the nuns. She liked his tutoring. Where Prentiss in his fondness might be inclined to let her live with half a good answer, Paul DeRoet had set her proper lessons when she begged for them, and waited for proper answers. And if he had expected little from a woman and a light wench at that, he had seemed quietly content with her progress. But they were not close, no.

Younger than Prentiss but older than she, he had no past that she could discern, and no light chatter. She had imagined that a direct question might produce direct answers. With the momentary nerve storms and false alarms aside, she tried again, hoping not to sound like an importunate child.

"Did you know my father?"

He stared still at the bruised horizon over his right shoulder, steering not by sight but by the tremor of the tiller under his hand,

and the sighs of wood and sail about him, and the taste of the wind. Something was out there, he knew it, which did not belong.

"I did."

"Am I like him, then?"

He glanced briefly into her eyes, glowing deep green under the wild, gold-dusted hair. "I suppose."

Acres of silence.

"DeRoet. That's Dutch, isn't it?"

Her swift redirection bent a smirk into his seamed, sober face. "I thought I was the schoolmaster here. Yes, it is. Flemish, rather."

"You don't sound Dutch."

An expressive shrug. Near enough as makes no matter.

"We are an adaptable race," he said. "I sail with Englishmen, Irish, Welsh. If I sailed with Jews or Chinamen, I would sound like them too, I guess."

"They say that Mendez fellow is Dutch."

"A damned Walloon," he snapped. The eyes went hard without changing their distant focus. "And the Devil like him is a Spaniard. Steer clear of that one, *schatze*. Look, there again!"

She looked. Nothing. Maybe? No. The subdued intensity in his voice and longsighted stance, though, gave her pause and made her look again, training her sight into as much distance as her dark-adapted eyes and mind could reach.

Maybe.

A dark fleck against the patched sky might be a sail. It might as easily be a cinder in the eye or a flock of gulls hunting in the deep swells flung out by ranks of thunderstorms. It might be a ship going anywhere. It might be anything.

"Shall I get Davy?" she asked softly.

He coughed and put out his hand for a gulp of her wine. Wiped his mouth on a sleeve and shook his head.

"Nay, not yet. Look, girl, you had best be off. My thanks for bringing that, and the wine. You have had a long day too, I hear. Your man will be looking for you."

Oddly obedient, she gathered up the bowls and cups and spoons, "You aren't going to tell me about my father, are you? It's all right, you know. Someone will." She stretched to place a small kiss softly on a wind burnt cheek.

Wide eyes stared from under the fair hair fringing his shoulders. The broad Flemish nose reddened as, to Molly's utter amazement, a furious blush bloomed over the ruddy face.

"Here now! None of that. If Prentiss murders me, Davy will be not be happy. Get you gone. I have work to do."

She winked shamelessly and strode away, letting her hips swing in the loose serge breeches she wore with the deerskin jerkin and dust-streaked shirt, but he had already returned to his business and no one else noticed.

Still no answers, but another friend, perhaps. Eventually.

Eventually. And eventually someone would have to tell her something about the laughing, bright-eyed man who had taught her to see pictures in the stars and held her when the great winds stormed across Barbados. Someone would tell her how he died.

Well enough. She had business of her own. This excursion into supper had been an incidental whim, a restorative physic to a congested day. But her last job wanted solitude, and that as a rule was as hard to find aboard a ship as a Christian among the cannibals. Fact was, she had all day carried in her belt, softened with much handling and streaked with salt, the manifest of the *Santa Eulalia.*

The idea was simple and all her own. Someone eventually would expect to see that manifest, and Molly meant to govern quite precisely what they saw.

She slipped therefore from the sheltered helm to the main deck, unremarked and unremarkable in her new-found fellowship with the *Jealous Mary's* crew. Swinging by the open galley she stopped just long enough to scour her bowls with sea water and a handful of white sand set by for the purpose. She also nicked a bottle of Canary wine from stores she had sent up herself, and sauntered to the refuge of the sailing master's cabin with its handsome desk and the quire of good paper recently liberated from one Spanish ship or another.

Home at last, and altogether alone. The solitude was uncanny. The first time she had been truly alone in weeks and weeks.

First thing, the stiff, filthy garments came off, flung into a corner. Naked to her small clothes, such as they were, she grubbed around in the carved black chest for anything else. A silk shift, she fancied, would make her feel better. Better still, if put on after a quick bath. That thought made her smile. *Right.* Home, indeed. She'd ask Dickon to wash her hair tonight, sluicing all the dust and strain of the day away with a pitcher of fresh water. Well damn, they'd be refilling the water casks in the morning. Surely, she could waste a little now.

So assured, she stripped down to her own pink flesh, splashed water into a blue and white Chinese basin, and wrung out a saffron sea sponge. Face and hands, shoulders and neck could be clean, at least, and here and there as well. The top layers puddled muddily at her feet. Cool water over hot, wind-crisped, dust-harried skin was relief enough to shock her out of the weariness that had been growing since emerging on deck.

Attention wandered.

Energy faded.

Such a day. What had changed? The reflection staring out of the looking glass at the pink and brown woman she had become seemed quite strange. For one thing, to her dismay, she'd broken out in freckles. Everywhere! Not many, but the dainty dusting across her nose was new and all thanks to her recent career in the sun. Well, her mother had always said nothing good came without a price. But it was more than that.

Her breasts seemed softer too, the belly more defined, like a goddess in a Nuremberg folio, or Eve after the apple. A woman's body, no longer a girl's. Odd to look at herself so, one hip cocked, bare feet poised like a dancer's, head tilted thoughtfully. One fine gold chain knitting up the fine hairs at the back of her neck dropped between those breasts, her only ornament.

What, she wondered, did Prentiss see?

Even the cabin looked different, for some reason. Less foreign, more her own. She stretched and drank in the smells of sea wrack, old leather, and Prentiss's things, and the mainland riding so close on their starboard side she could almost reach out and pluck bananas from the trees. Something had happened, was happening, changing. Coming on deck, exhausted and exhilarated, had felt yes, like a birth, she thought dreamily with the sponge poised under one rosy nipple. A rebirth, yes, out of the depths of *Jealous Mary's* ...

Bright eyes flew open.

"Christ, girl, just get dressed!" she snapped at the reflection.

At length, dry and chilling even in the gilded light falling from the mullioned window, she threw on the silk shift, with the Flemish lace cuffed at the elbows, and over it the old blue gown. She'd had enough of men's work for the one day. Dickon might even like to see her in skirts again, and the silk was a gorgeous luxury. As it fell in sensuous folds over her skin, she shivered with wanton pleasure that survived even the layers of rosy petticoat and fustian frock. And if she could keep the lace out of the ink, who knows, she might even be presentable.

Out there somewhere, hiding against the horizon, lay trouble. The thought intruded, dredged her up and away from self-indulgence. Searching for her slippers she found resolution and thrust all other fancies aside.

Chair.

Desk.

Paper.

All right, and a velvet-covered foot stool which, since her feet did not quite reach the floor, was hardly an extravagance, even if it was embroidered in gold and silver with the arms of a Cardinal. With a glass of pale Portuguese wine, a fresh pen and good black ink, Molly settled in to amend and copy out Spanish documents in her own fine English hand.

When Prentiss came in, he found four closely written pages accounting the complete if not quite true contents of the ship they had taken hours before, neatly ordered under a pair of crystal earrings at the edge of the desk. Nearby, the ink pot capped, the pen cleaned and laid aside, and Molly sliding into sleep with her gaudy head on her arms.

"Come, Sweet," he said, though it tore at him to wake her. "Someone you've got to meet."

He filled her in quickly as she went to splash water on her face and hook the jewels into her ears again.

"We sank her without his help. We'll keep her without his permission," she said, just as Prentiss flung upon the hatch and ushered her into the pellucid glare of the great cabin.

Suffused with the day's dying light, the room felt crowded and smelt of pork, spoiled scent, and unhygienic guests. She had paused to let her eyes adjust when out of dust-moted silhouettes a thin, high Netherlandish voice cried, "So dere's women here after all!"

A vast caricature of a buccaneer leapt up from Davy's table, blinking and exclaiming.

"Ach! York, thou knave, you have kept this dainty for dessert. Praise God for His handiwork! *Zulks men konden vrille strootje te gulde, eh?*"

A shout of ugly laughter from the two other villainous strangers now conspicuous at the table. "I said that I wager you can spin straw into gold," he translated with a vulgar wink. "Say now, *vrij meisje*, are you saved?"

Molly blinked owlishly but without interest, in no mood to concede the advantage of surprise.

So this would be the legendary Mendez. A huge yawn she could only wish to have planned exploded over her face. She waved a hand at it out of habit, wiped sleep like tears from her eyes, and blinked.

He was taller than Prentiss, she noticed, but not nearly so well made. A thick, doughy chest and limbs strove against a skirted coat of flattened mockado that had once been solemn black, now sunburnt brown and red, streaked filthy with tallow grease and ancient dinners. From an almost bald crown, long pale hair strayed in greasy strings to the vast, once-crimson sash straining over his equally vast middle. No one could call it a waist.

Sallow, unwashed skin and colorless eyes stared back, clouded with drugs and drink. Behind him, two or three of his officers, she supposed, of no better sort, smirked in support. His teeth were bad, and his breath stank.

Molly cocked her pretty but resourceful head, fluttered the almost invisible lashes over bright, widening eyes. Prentiss, recognizing the lapidary quality of that glance, stifled a sudden impulse to laugh while Mendez, who really should have known better, took her silence for shyness, thus falling in step with all the men before him who had mistaken her youth and beauty for light-mindedness. He laughed again and lurched for her hand.

The lady's knife sprang up like a live thing poised over his chins. His officers bristled as he froze, but minded how thoroughly they were outnumbered.

She said, "We saved your substantial arse today, Captain Mendez. That should be enough religion for one afternoon."

"*Ja ja*," he snorted but retreated half a step. "Your captain has saved my treasure for me. T'at is a true sign he is among the Elect of God."

The long knife glinted but did not waver. "I have told Davy, and I will tell you, *Mijnheer*," she pronounced crisply. "*Santa Eulalia* was a supply ship. Salt pork and rice and green beer. But no gold, no goods, in short, no treasure."

"I am to accept a girl's accounting? Ha!"

She handed the new-made pages to Davy with one eyebrow slightly flared, and added, "You may review the manifest, if your Spanish is up to it. Otherwise you must be content to take my word."

"And now I must take a woman's word!" His sneering face bounced just inches from the blade which still held steady. "What world is this? A honest woman, and one who can count! I am to believe two wonders in a single day!"

Prentiss was already in motion but Davy put up a hand. "Question her, ye question me," he snapped, which was not quite the same as giving his word, and stuffed the papers into his belt. He added quietly. "That's enough, now, lass."

The blade lingered a moment longer then floated away to its home at her back.

"Ah York, you haf your wife well trained, I see." The man held her under a bold, appreciative stare but withdrew his advances.

Davy barked a laugh and, as the tension relaxed a little, said, "Mistress Molly September, I have the honor—if that's the word—to present Captain Pieter Mendez. Preacher Mendez, you may call 'im."

"September?" The piggy eyes narrowed even further. "Not…?"

"Oh, aye!" The customary surprise and affirmation.

"Ah! A lady then, *zij zit?*"

"Aye she is, so mind yer heathen tongue."

One day she must get someone to explain this almost magical power her father's name had on everyone. "When it suits me. But you, I'd guess, are always a rogue."

He chortled greasily and said, "And so I am, *schatje*. But I think you like a rogue."

"That's as may be," said Prentiss, surging forward at last. "But she has one already."

The humor twisting up the ends of his mouth did not extend into his eyes as one arm settled proprietarily over her shoulders.

"*En zo*! The girl is not York's wife then, but yours, the long vanished *Miester* Prentiss?"

"Near enough."

"But how now! A woman aboard and not a wife!" He leered as if he thought the expression charming. "You will pardon a godly man while he tries to understand the minds of the sinners who surround him. Is this according to the Brotherhood?"

"No one has so far thought to ask," said Davy quietly. "She's a signed member of my crew, if that's of any matter to you. Neither a whore nor a captive."

The matted mockado slipped carelessly over a shrug. "As a sitting governor of the Brethren of the Coast, it's my place to ask. I like to know who it is I fight with— or over." The thin, stained smirk crept back toward Prentiss, holding in his neatly capped temper. "Near enough, says t'ou?" Dick nodded curtly. "But *waarom verwijl*, you dog? Why delay? I am much in favor of weddings. I am myself married dozens of times, and all of them in their righteousness follow me everywhere."

Prentiss spat. "I say we get us ashore first and divide up what's to be divided, then we'll worry about the Brotherhood. I'm content." He directed a confirming glance to Molly. She nodded, tight-lipped. "She's content. And Davy…"

"Is Captain of this ship, and there it is," Davy said. "We're agreed. The *Santa Eulalia* is ours by right. *Felipe* we share. 'Tis time we moved on."

Mendez chuckled in his high, woman's voice and adjusted his sword baldric to no apparent effect. "*Jawell*, keep your rice and beer. The other boat we can share! Of course, you will have to trust *my* accounting. It is only fair." Then the pirate gathered up his men with a look and, shouting a final obscure injunction from the book of Proverbs, they were gone leaving a ringing silence in their wake.

"Davy," Prentiss said quietly, still staring after the oily smudge of Mendez being lowered to his own boat, swaying and cheerful in the bosun's chair. "I do not like that man."

York nodded, thoughtful. "Aye."

"Long day."

"So it has been. Much further you think?"

"Any time now. Can I kill 'im?"

"You may not."

"Rather clean up your own messes?"

"Aye, I would."

Molly snorted with unladylike derision. "I suppose that means 'tis up to me."

Finally, Dick dragged his gaze back into the cabin to lie open and unguarded on Molly, all cream and red-gold and fierce in her faded blue gown and defiant freckles. Her eyes spoke, and all at once there she was, waiting and warm in his mind.

"Look, Davy," he said in the same, off-hand way. "Any ship's captain can marry people, aye?"

"So he can, on his own ship at sea."

With frightening care, Prentiss took her hand and raised it to his lips, then drew a long breath without looking anywhere but in her eyes, "Belike you'd do us the favor of wedding us, then, this girl and me. Right now."

Molly shuddered under a wave concocted of awe and gladness.

"Good lord, sir, I am only seventeen!" she murmured in the words she had given her uncle in anger only weeks—no, months—before. "Wait, that's a lie," she said through a considering grin. "Nay, an error in my accounting."

Grins all round. "A woman who can count?"

"I have had a birthday somewhere in all of this. I am eighteen!"

"The law says that's old enough to decide for yourself," said Davy. "And God knoweth we are law abiding privateers. Unless …"

"Nay nay," she waved away the frown. "No special issues in my legacy. No pre-contracts. No lawyer's exercise in writs and properties, nor waiting till I'm five and thirty, nor the right man choose the right casket. *La!*" she exclaimed. "*Ma foix*, Prentiss, I suppose that is your plan? Marry the heiress, secure the fortune. And in a day or two… "

As if there were no one in the room but the two of them, as if the room were the pillars of Hercules and they facing the precipice alone, he dragged her fierce into his arms and stopped her at once.

"No more," he said. "No more of that game between us."

She pulled her face up out from under his firm, taught-muscled shoulder; dragged out her hair caught in the incidental grasp leaving tweaked strands behind, unmindful. Her green eyes settled again on his blue, so wonderfully blue, and in this moment all pretense dropped away. In the wreathed smoke and tension and anger and urgencies of the last night and day, she too saw no one but the man who, loving and longing, held her between his two hands.

"No," she said. "No more. If we have not faith in each other, we have nothing. So here we are."

"As we must be, as I never expected to be."

"No jealousy, no mistrust."

"Nor doubt nor barrier of truth or fancy."

"None, before God," she said.

"None before God, from this day till … well." He stopped, suddenly self-conscious. "Davy, say something!"

"You've started, you'd best finish, lad." York held out a hand to Keaton, who put a bottle of wine in it. No help from that quarter.

Dick cleared his throat and took the dare. He had meant to plan, to anticipate, to bring flowers or something but here of a sudden the moment rushed toward him and would not be denied.

"From this day forward you are my wife," he said with rough clarity, overwhelmed that this girl, nearly half his age for God's sake, had claimed his mind and heart. "No matter what may come."

It was not the wedding service laid out by the church—any church—but the truth of his words unrehearsed and impulsive sang in her blood. Molly listened and understood at once that out of the moment just recently ringing in anger and clever invention, she was just as young as her objections and sailing into marriage nevertheless. True marriage, as it had to be, the meeting of two minds as well as hearts, more than four feet in a bed. Sword and shield as well as music and flattery.

She heard his words, no less amazed than at the moment he swiftly disarmed her in a cheap back room in Port Royal, nor when she entered his sanctuary of books and thought on Tortuga and saw him truly for the first time, or when he dispatched without heroics the man who would have killed her out of hand and she knew she would not die so long as he was near. No less stunned than at any of those moments, she caught her breath and his hands and said, to her own wonder, "Aye. Whatever else may come, I am your wife, and you my husband." Alive and free of choice, she stepped into her wedding vows awake and sure.

Even more than he, the words nearly caught in her throat before stammering forth alive and fine.

"I love you," she said, which she had contained so long. He had, she realized, already said the awful words weeks ago and she, laughing, had pushed them aside for his sake, or for her own.

Davy knew a cue when he saw one and now stepped between them, took their joined hands in his, and said rapidly,

"By the power of my office as captain of this vessel upon the high seas, and with Will Keaton here to witness, I declare this romantic nonsense to be valid and binding till the sea takes ye either of ye, or the sun falls into it, or this scrawny bastard is found face down in a Portsmouth ditch."

He stepped back then to survey them, red-gold hair and sun-streaked brown, oblivious to all but each other. "I don't suppose in all these tons of treasure under our feet there's a ring?"

Prentiss glanced at him with brief hilarity, then reached into his jerkin and pulled out a soft leather bag and from that, a carved circle of Russian amber, cherry red and unfamiliar in these waters.

"You've diamonds a-plenty," he whispered, almost as if Davy had not spoken. "This you can have only from me."

His eyes only now broke from hers so he could with ease slip the dark red gem, petalled like a rose, over her finger.

Surprise, and yet again surprise. All she knew for sure was how much she was in love and how much she trusted the love offered in the perfection of the impromptu ritual. She had thought herself too young to marry, but now.

Now.

Now she understood in one instant the choice her mother had made, and its value no matter how costly. She felt her mother, poor Marjorie, smiling behind her, and knew it was right. Prentiss's joy sat solemn on his face as midnight on a quiet sea, but she could feel the deep happiness radiating from him as warmth from a summer sun. She thought briefly how much more romantic men were, and how they took such care to hide it. And in that realization she loved him even more.

Out of some unremembered dream, her father's face and shadowy form hovered ungently into the room, leaning with old familiarity on the varnished oak and burnished leather of the captain's cabin, bulkheads and bars. So Molly thought at any rate, dancing on the trailing edge of her childhood with Rafe's last laughter suddenly in her mind. She shivered but said nothing and looked down at last at the ring on her hand, and glowed in surprise.

Different, yes, this deep red amber, glowing like an aspic and fragrant with the warmth of his body. Gold might be perfect, but this in its very frailty would be the blazon of their life together.

Prentiss too felt a shudder, a passing of scented air, and an odd sense of something. Approval? But not believing in ghosts, he added it only to the utter sense of happiness complete. With utmost care, he met her lips with a kiss, gentle at first then wild and deep with joy.

When she could see clearly again, she stepped away a bit, still holding both his hands and fighting the urge to laugh. Merrily, she asked "Will you still love me when I'm old and gray?"

"Good God, woman!" He flipped long sun-gilded hair back off his shoulders like a lion ruffling his mane. "You can't imagine there's much chance we'll live that long!"

And the moment swelled again into a salt-smelling and indigo day with work to do and panics to quell.

Davy rolled his eyes and allowed as how his quarters were parlous over-crowded and if he must, he'd throw them after Mendez himself.

"Ye're not out of this cabin in five minutes more and I'll warrant ye both die young. Man and wife, indeed! So you are. Now let your friends kiss the bride, silly bitch that she is, before I decide I only need one pilot. I'll grant you half an hour. Half an hour, mind. You've still got to con us into this famous harbor of yours and you might want some daylight for it."

Will Keaton had not stopped grinning for these long solemn minutes and was already planning how to explain, celebrate, and extend his own long suffering marital bliss to Prentiss and his girl. If it was anyone's turn, it was his peripatetic houseguest's who now might, please God, find it was time to build his own neat little place up or down the golden path from the stone house under the date palms of Tortuga.

He pried the girl out of Prentiss's hands and kissed her brow sweetly, then handed her to Davy who kissed her mouth quite soundly indeed.

The moment shattered entirely when Jimmy bounced in to request the captain's presence on deck, just in time to catch her as Davy let her go. Still grimy and sun red under his scarred face, he glanced from Prentiss to Molly and back again, and said doubtfully, "All right, what've you done?"

Dick shrugged. "Had to keep her out of Mendez's greasy clutches. Just seemed best to marry the brat m'self. I'd have told you, but there didn't seem to be any time!"

"Do you mind too much, Jimmy?" said Molly, standing quite still between his hands.

"Nay, not I." He lightly brushed his cool lips against hers and returned her to Prentiss. "I've just lost 30 shillings, is all."

"How's that?"

"Aye, did ye not know? There's been a lottery going since Martinique. I had you marked for tomorrow, on the beach, at midnight."

Molly realized they must have left the captain's cabin because she woke comfortable as a kitten in her own corner of her own quarters. Paul DeRoet was rolled into a hammock slung from the opposite bulkhead, which meant Prentiss—her husband Richard, Dick, Dickon— was again at his post and she was now, if she would be, Mistress Prentiss. Molly Prentiss. Molly September, Master Prentiss's wife. The pilot's wife Molly. Nothing had changed, and everything. She was no different than she had been this morning, and nothing like.

Nothing like.

Davy had said half an hour, which had turned into an hour and somewhat more. Only Paul's weary banging on the door, coupled with friendly but earnest threats to life and limb, finally brought Prentiss, groggy with love and his own long day, back to the world and duty. Dick had kissed her lips and eyes and breasts and this and that, then grinning left her.

Now through the layers of the *Mary's* hull she felt the anchor chain shudder and fall to a sandy bottom. Sails would be reefed, the deck stacked with supplies and tools to take ashore. The first long boat banged against the side, then dropped with a flat splash into the green waters of the lagoon. Then another, loaded she knew with men and empty barrels to take on the fresh water that Prentiss *my husband* had guaranteed would be there.

Wavelets slapped the wooden sides and rocked her where she lay, still and calm at last. She could hear the calling voices on deck, the rough laughter, the give and take of the ordinary business of sailors. Listened like a small child sent to bed while older children play in the twilight street outside, calling down the night—a little envious, a little tired, but sweetly languorous as when a fever passes. The thought came blatant and awful. Supplies?

They were handling her supplies!

"Wait!"

15

MOST MEN DO LOVE
THE SPANISH WINE

IT WAS PARADISE. It was the garden men dream of when they dream of peace, of release from pain, of blissful old age, of love. Barring the mosquitoes, it was exactly as Prentiss had described, a multiplicity of green.

Less than a hundred paces from the beach, indeed, tiers of waterfalls stepped over and out of a hillside high overhead, like sugar spilling from a hundred bowls, into a blue garlanded stream that looped away to where it must inevitably broaden to the sea. The sound of it rushed like a passage of wings over the green-crowded riverbank, background music to the rainbows thrown up by the perpetual mist. In amongst the green, Molly saw that other things decorated the world: orchids of extraordinary delicacy, fruits she had never seen, flowers that had no English name. And noises! The scream of a jaguar, the chatter of parrots, white faced monkeys crashing through the canopy.

Fringed with soaring palms, the secluded lagoon was deep enough and wide enough for both the slender *Testament* and the more massive *Jealous Mary* to ride comfortably at anchor and hide safe from passing storm or naval sloop. There was beach enough for both crews to spread out and drink themselves silly without stumbling over one another more than once or twice each, this first night. After that, the more enterprising would move up off the beach to cut stakes and broad leaves for old-fashioned buccaneer's huts tucked under the trees.

After weeks at sea, the word of the day was Play.

To his credit, Keaton did make sure the water casks were filled, tamped tight, and stored before allowing the rum to be off-loaded. Most of it, anyway. And Mendez cooperated by keeping his women aboard the *English Testament* until the greater part of the work was done.

"His women?" Molly shrieked in horrified, unladylike delight while a boat load of blowzy, cheerful women, some none too young but certainly enthusiastic, jumped ashore exclaiming like starlings and rattling with jewelry great and small. Her sense of the absurd was pricked, to say the least.

A platoon or two of the men, urgent duties accomplished, stooped like kestrels to the shoreline to bring in the *Testament's* plump and fulsome pigeons. By the time the last prosaic foot had stepped across the tide line, a half dozen commercial transactions and two fist fights had already been resolved.

The next launch carried Mendez's bandsmen, a gruesome lot who hammered out a tuneless clangor with Christian zeal but very little else. If you listened closely, you could more or less make out the strains of *Come Ye Thankful People Come*. If you were not musically inclined.

The whole expedition had become by then more than Molly could bear.

"His *women!* Preacher Mendez? The new Calvin? Last champion of sanctified wedlock?"

She collapsed cross-legged to the sand and could not, would not, stop laughing even when the shallow wavelets bubbled to her toes. Prentiss had to pick her up and haul her like a sitting Buddha to the tree line, coughing but still lightly hysterical. He dropped her in the thin grass under the first sheltering tree he could find, and dropped himself beside her. Helpless to do more than chuckle along with her, he watched her fall over backwards in another fit of giggles.

When she stopped choking long enough to listen to him, he added a correction. "They're his wives, actually," he said. That was an error. She screamed again and rolled over in the leafy detritus of paradise, and buried her head in her arms. Every time she tried to look at him, or the beach, at the horizon or the ships in the lagoon, or anything, she bubbled again into helpless laughter, swearing in three languages or maybe four.

"*Madre de Dios! Merde!* Oh God, oh God, *ma foix!*"

Prentiss just stared, shaking his head, one eye on her, the other more or less on whatever else was going on around them in the long gathering dusk. Keaton had the *Mary's* crew in orderly hand. Jimmy was settling a small disagreement over a half dressed pair of thick ankles draped in gauze and jangling bells. Davy stood with his usual good nature and a stout cudgel right in the middle of things, the eye of the storm. Paul was probably dozing aboard the *Mary*, and that was as it should be. Owen Jones seemed to be giving a fingering lesson to the *Testament's* band master, and something like music began to assemble.

Watches had been posted, stores were in hand, cooking fires were springing up near a circle of smooth stones high above the tide line; all good order as daylight crept away. Some of the lads were cleaning muskets and daring each other to go hunting in the dark. In other words, Molly exploring her lunatic side was as much as Prentiss was required to mind.

He would gladly have stood under the guns of Panama again, instead. Not that he wasn't enjoying the sight of her so completely overcome with merriment, but it was hard to know what else to do with her. So he waited, pushed the hair out of his face and enjoyed the light on-shore breeze that flipped it back again, and the bell-like music of her voice, and the smell of the air. The last time he had stepped up this beach had been the beginning of a nightmare but that was gone, all gone. Now, his cheeks ached with smiling at her, at Molly, his wife.

Gradually, she caught her breath (barely) gasped and tittered again, wiped at her streaming eyes and wished she had a handkerchief. She gulped heavily and collected her wits just enough to speak.

"So," she stammered at last. "So, what do they do, all these virtuous wives? Cook and clean? Sew his buttons on? Gather them rosebuds while they may?"

"That last, I think. Maybe not rosebuds, all of them."

"Oh nay, not that one. Look you, the one fancies herself a Mughal maid, with the breeches under the petticoats, and all the veils. Except she's coming right out of that little bodice! Oh dear," she hiccupped. "Toby seems to have ripped it."

Prentiss peered down the slope under a lifted hand. The shade was thickening toward twilight, but the rattle of bells picked out the girl she meant.

"Oh aye, her. She calls herself Lakshmi, when she's not too drunk to pronounce it. But she's just plain Nan from Plymouth."

Molly managed to stifle most of an explosive giggle. "And she's one of what, a dozen wives? Do they all come with costumes?"

He nodded, still amused.

"Aye, mainly, and their own virtues too. There's Faith, see. And Charity," he counted off on callused fingers. "And Prudence who says she used to be a nun, and that might be true. The tall one with the determined expression, that's Long Kate—the smart one. The little pink one is Dolly—no wait, Dolorous Strife or some damned Puritan thing. And the black one is Divine Grace, I think."

"You think? Don't you know them all?"

A doubtful brow lifted, answered by a shrug, but his hand slipped over hers, fingering the red amber ring with meaning.

"Not all." His eyes locked into hers as he raised that hand to a lingering kiss. "And not any more."

She accepted that and went on. "And they're all married to Mendez? Is that allowed?"

"Oh aye, so he says, and he's the preacher, I guess he knows. It's his church."

"You suppose he knew Rafe?"

"Sweet, every seaman from Barbados to Cockburn Town knew your dad. Sure every man I ever knew wanted to sail with him, or for him. But he would never have signed on with the likes of Preacher Mendez, not for fortune or glory."

"And why's that?" she said gently, the amusement still present but the mood subtly altered.

"Because the Preacher is a proper jackal, the old pirate. At peace or at war, with letters of marque or without, and an English ship as much a target to him as Spanish or French."

"And Rafe?"

"Ah, Rafe was a gentleman, love. No Spanish ship was safe from him, and he had a solid right fist, I can tell you that." His jaw ached slightly in recollection. "But he was English, by God."

Distracted, he had forgotten almost who he was talking to. Well, it was not so bad after all. She loved him; she wouldn't mind maybe. Maybe later.

Idly and wonderfully, he played with her pretty fingers and threaded his own through them, and brushed light lips across her hand again and sighed. "I wonder what we'll all find to do if the King's ever done fighting with Spain and France?"

She was drunk on her laughter, and intoxicated with Prentiss, so she accepted the evasion. And well, she learned a little at a time. Perhaps that was as it should be.

"Won't there always be work for an expert pilot?" So many other questions she wanted to ask hung unspoken in her mouth.

"Aye, there will. But the life won't be the same. Nor the rewards."

He shifted his grip to swing her round easily, gently into his arms. Fitting him neat as a jewel in a fine setting she leaned into his chest, a warm and pleasant burden that made him thoughtful. "What shall we do then, I wonder. Should we become merchants ourselves, eh Moll? Go back to London, buy a stall in the Exchange, get some thieving clerk to run it for us and rob us blind while we sail out to Madagascar and the Indies ourselves?"

"They say those waters are full of pirates!"

"Oh aye, heathen bloodthirsty ones, with not a word of English amongst 'em. But I think we know how to handle that."

"I don't suppose the children will be quite safe."

He looked down with careful speculation but her eyes were elsewhere. "Children?"

"Eventually, you know, there will be children. Happens to married people all the time."

"Ah well, not Madagascar, then." A silly grin softened the look he turned back out to sea. *Children!* "Jersey, maybe. Or the Isle of Wight."

"England, is it? Not Jamaica?"

"Come along, wife," he said suddenly. He scrambled to his feet, dislodging his congenial jewel. "Not bloody likely for Spaniards or French to stop being bastards, so it's idle to think about."

He dusted himself ineffectively of leaves and jungle carpet, then took both her hands and dragged her up as well, and rocked a little as he did so. Lacking the constant movement of shipboard, the land was annoyingly still.

"Oh, but I like it here," she protested. "'Tis a perfect view, if a bit dark."

"Ah," he said, tipsy with a day and night of tension and skill and marriage. "Already contrary. I should have known. Sweet, it's dark. Night's come. There's supper, and some dancing later, I expect. And all on our account."

"So we're not going back to *Jealous Mary* tonight?"

"We are not."

"Am I going to meet all these famous Mendez women?"

"One or two. Most will be busy through the night, I expect."

"And... ah!"

He drew her to him, burying his face in her hair, almost drunken with her voice, the peculiar fancy of having children, her body locked in his, the honey-scented labyrinth of her mind. How long had it been since he had sat with her alone like this for thirty minutes altogether, he wondered. And awash at once in love and salt air, he said, "Hush, love, hush. Someone wants to give us a party. Be thou gracious."

Her whole body, her whole mind dovetailed with his, what could she do but smile in the lowering dark, nod, and whisper, "All right."

So cased in love and strange new thoughts they went down into the firelight and the music.

Music, moonlight, firelight, deep, deep shadows and deep red wine from Portuguese hillsides. They had cheered as Prentiss brought her to the cluster of cook fires, and crowned them each with a garland of vanilla orchids and passion flowers. The scent filled her head with impossible sweetness, and cheered her heart. A pale yellow gown appeared from somewhere. One of the less frivolous wives, tall and pleached with irony, helped her into it, in front of God and everyone without God nor the girl nor no one else realizing that somewhere in the process the pretty wench had briefly been naked to her knees.

From the same hands a bottle green coat appeared for Prentiss, and if neither garment was as pristine as the tailor made them, their flaws were concealed in the forgiving glow of torches and rum. Long Kate Riley, who did these things as lightly as she breathed, then got efficiently back to her cooking and everyone else's well-being with snapping voice and snapping eyes.

Someone else had ferried a pair of Davy's fancy chairs from the *Mary*, and these they sat her in and Prentiss too because, someone said, they approved of marriages, and weddings were even better if a girl had a proper place to entertain her guests.

Rather than sort out that curious logic, Molly allowed herself to sink into the wine, the chair, and the parade of presents. It was astonishing how the corners and lockers and secret niches of the *Jealous Mary* had been rifled for wedding gifts.

A old-fashioned jewel that had begun as a huge fresh water pearl strung from golden chains and fancifully set in gold with emeralds and diamonds, colored enamels and carved, fragrant ambergris so that now it was a galleon of the treasure fleet under the protection of a great sea god with sparks of sapphire lodged in two grey pearls for its eyes.

A table-cut emerald the size of an actual table—nay, a mere fancy, that; it was no more broad than her own little hand, and magnificently flawed with streaks of lightening—had once had hung, so Davy said, from the turban of the sultan of Singapore.

A golden enameled pipe-tool made like a tiny pistol was neatly set with rose-cut emeralds and hid three steel tools in its belly for poking and tamping and cleaning.

A long, low casket of wrought gold indiscriminately paved with hundreds of colored jewels, each in a bevel lined with black foil to let every sapphire, emerald, and blood ruby catch and fling back the light, had been a gift to the king of France from the Grand Turk himself.

At that Molly sputtered: "A pencil box! Paul, you shouldn't have."

And more wine to feed the laughter.

Wild pigs turned on huge spits till they cracked and sizzled. The hunters had quickly been successful, and others less energetic had climbed the trees so that pyramids of mango and guava, banana and papaya were within thoughtless reach of anyone alongside the piles of rice flavored with cumin and cinnamon, and the startling turtle pie. Clearly someone besides Toby Millikan was cooking, and enjoying themselves at it—that would be Long Kate who had survived more than one cruel siege on invention alone—and there was plenty and all of it good. Between the music and the laughter and the intoxicating perfumes of roasted meats, the very air was charged.

Except that it was on the torch-lighted beach instead of a busy, lantern-lit courtyard, and there were fewer women—and it being nearly a thousand miles way—the party might have been any night at McQuarry's. If anything, there was more music. Owen Jones and Rob Thomas, his new partner, never seemed to tire, so long as there was rum or even beer quite near to hand, and somehow there always was. Young Derek May, whose huge drum boomed over a battle and roused them to war had pulled out instead a flat Irish bodhran, more suited to the occasion. They found one of the *Testament's* lads had a whistle he actually knew how to play, and the night swung toward dance. If they took a break to eat or piss or handle a girl, there would be more to eat and more to drink and a string of terrible jokes until, properly adjusted, Owen would re-tune, give brief, knowing instructions to the others who presumed to play with him, remind them of some other night when they had gone so beyond themselves, and start in again.

Molly sat in state, crowned in flowers and splendid in diamonds, until she could sit no longer. The music snatched at her soul, and when she looked at Prentiss, she knew it had caught him too. Eyes and minds met. He leapt to his feet and bowed over her hand. "Madam?" he said, and in an instant the bottle green worsted and the gay primrose silk took their place at the head of a forming set.

The wild improvisation on an old familiar theme wound down and out, capped by a roaring shout and vigorous applause on the last sawing chord that echoed in the jungle behind them. Then Owen caught Molly's eye, and waited.

"You know Mr. Playford's dances?" she said. He smirked. What nonsense. Of course he did. "The *Whirligig*, then, if you please."

A nod, a wink, and eight-for-naught to set the pace and trigger the brain, and the dancing began in earnest. It was not for the faint of heart. They skipped up English measures and jumped through Irish reels, and when they were too drunk for the busier dances, kicking up sand with their heels and casting off in all directions and screaming at each other (*Other way round, y'fool!*) they pulled back to simple things—round dances for as many as will, with names to make them laugh like *Gathering Peascods* and *Cuckolds All A Row*, and the hornpipes they could all do in their sleep.

Molly danced until she couldn't breathe or think or wonder about anything, and all she knew was how perfectly happy she was.

Little by little as the hours passed, as the circles of light and laughter grew smaller and collected into one, those who could do so paired up for other entertainments, and those who could do nothing else lay snoring where they fell. At last she threw herself at her chair, and missed, and fell in a hiss of primrose silk and azure ribbons to the ground.

"Oh dear," she said. "Oh dear! Dickon!" A thump and a curse and he was face first in the silks at her bare feet, looking dizzy and delighted. "Where'd everybody go?"

The music had stopped. The fires all burned low and the shadows above the beach were littered with bodies in various states of collapse. Some low conversation still murmured at the edges of the light and further off, coarse giggles and a chink of bells.

She saw as the world stopped spinning that the circle about her had closed and contracted, till by midnight the company had come down to a last few of her friends, an odd stranger, and Owen Jones bowing to her, exultant over a last jack of rum. Then he packed up his fiddle, clapped Rob Thomas on the back, ruffled Derek's hair and yawned. The tall girl who had been waiting for him all night stepped out of the dark and drew him away.

"Everyone that matters," Davy said pleasantly out of the rosy glow. "Is right here."

Everyone, whoever they were, were largely obscured by the sullen glow of a fire too near her eyes, but she expected it was her friends, the *Testament* crew having more or less withdrawn to their own corners. But Davy was here, yes, and Keaton nodding with Matt Christy over a shared bottle of wine. Jimmy had been away but sauntered back towards them now looking pleased with himself. He plunked himself down on Molly's other side and hazarded a quick kiss on the cheek.

"So you two've made up, have you?" said Keaton, as if he had just noticed.

"Bugger off, sir," Jimmy replied affably, and reached for the wine bottle. "I've worked as hard for her as for you these two days past."

"He has that," she said. She scrummed about a bit, looking for a comfortable position to sit in the sand—the delicate gown and its fine embroideries would assuredly be rags before the sun came up—and settled Prentiss's head on her knee.

"And a right bitch she is to work for, I can tell you," Jimmy added with a grin.

The wine came to her, then Dick who had started singing, reached up a hand for it and she sighed. "You'd best sit up, my lad, or you'll have wine everywhere."

"Born to give orders," said Davy, reclaiming the bottle. "Just like..." A breezy silence filled the pause, punctuated by the distant crash of waves and a set of ratcheting snores, much too near. "Like her whole darlin' sex."

Molly looked away, hardly listening, used to the hesitation.

At the other end of the long curve of the beach, almost the opposite horn of the moon-bent crescent of the lagoon, another fire blazed up, freshened with new fuel, and a sharp honk, Molly thought, of wicked laughter. Mendez, apparently, since she had not seen the villain for hours. Truth to tell, she had not seen much to remember of anyone except the world-filling presence of Dick Prentiss, of her husband.

Now that she had settled, it was hard not to keep glancing toward the other light, so she tried harder. Over her shoulder, curtains of mist pleated into the ridges of the mountains. Out in the still waters of the lagoon two lights bobbed, the only sign that two ships anchored there, straining with treasure. And overhead, like party decorations, ran a sky littered with stars.

Gaping into the wide dome of heaven she caught her breath and said, "Remind me, Dickon. What constellation is that? That one, is it the Lion?"

"You know it is, love," he said, peering into the wine bottle instead of the sky. "You've marked the zodiac out to me a hundred times, and all the others besides."

"Then tell me, is it supposed to be coming apart?"

Four other dozy heads tipped up and gasped with pleasure and awe. And with cause. For leaping out of the rising constellation of Leo came a radiating rush of shooting stars, not merely one or two, but a dozen, and then a dozen more spinning out from the constellation like a Catherine wheel, and filling the sky like diamonds flashing on a contessa's ball gown.

Davy hummed and smiled. "Ah, yes. Aye, of course. Damn, Prentiss, what's that thing DeRoet always says?"

Striding step by crunching step from the dirt path to the sandy edge, his fair Flemish face pinked in unaccustomed smiles, Paul DeRoet stopped and stared up and recited in what sounded like bad Latin.

Then breathing in the merely terrestrial scents of night, the schoolmaster added: "Or as you would say, not being a 14th century Portuguese: *a movement of stars such as no men never saw nor heard of. From midnight onward, all the stars began to move, some in one direction, and others in another. And afterward they fell from the sky, and so thickly together that the sky and the air seemed to be in flames. Those who saw it imagined they were all dead men, and the end of the world had come.* That was 400 years ago, almost. We're wiser now. My lords, ladies, and gentlemen." He bowed and retrieved the wine bottle. "May I name to you the Leonid meteors, as men of science call them."

"How long does it go on?" Molly breathed.

"Oh, the rest of the night, I should think."

"This happens all the time?"

"Mm-hmm. Every year."

"Paul?" said Molly in a small, stunned voice. "You can keep the pencil box."

They watched, utterly silent, until it seemed the world and all that lived hung suspended on a line dropped from the center of a nursery of stars. Of old convent habit, Molly crossed herself from forehead to breast, shoulder to shoulder, and without thinking, Prentiss did the same. A chuckle broke from him, thinking how long it had been since he had seen the inside of a church of any religion, and the spell was broken.

Even cosmic grandeur will surfeit the senses in time, and there was a bottle of wine more to open, or two or three, and songs yet to be sung. A few others were wandering back to Molly's congenial salon, tapping another keg of rum, retrieving a small Italian guitar, and gaping in their turns at the spectacle in the sky. Under the weird light that rendered all things wonderful and strange, an empty keg made space to throw dice, another supported a chessboard. It was again like McQuarry's, only quieter.

Shuddering like a pagan, Davy swore and stirred up the fire to drive back the uncanny, quivering starlight. "Not as if we haven't seen it before. Give us a song, eh Jimmy Fitts?"

The guitar that came to Jimmy's hands broke into a familiar aire that made them think of home, and which Prentiss hummed bits of in Molly's lap while she combed long fingers through his curling hair, stroked the lean line of his jaw on down to the sun-browned chest still cooling under the linen. Under that touch, the caress drawing along his body as far as she could reach, then starting again, he shivered with pleasure. Sweet melancholy and fire in the sky, the thick green smell of the rain forest, and the rich scents of her body filled his mind till he could barely think except to understand that now, for once, he was completely, perfectly happy.

"Y'know, Davy," he said when one song ended. "I think it's time we turned for home."

"And why is that, pray? Some urgent appointment?"

"I feel like spending some money on my wife And we all know there's no better place for that than Port Royal."

"Well," said Molly absently. "There's, oh, London. Paris..." Distracted, she was watching Jimmy's hands, shocked and mystified.

"In November? Too cold."

Jimmy modulated from an old *villancico* into the cheerful seduction of *Watkin's Ale*, and the night swept into song as the last hangers-on, and those who could not endure that music should proceed without them, came in for the choruses.

Her color waxed wan and pale
From taking too much Watkin's Ale.
This proverb is well taught in schools:
It is no jesting with sharp edge tools!

Dick sat up again and drew Molly protectively across his chest. Easier to sing sitting up, anyway, and this way he could kiss her during the verses, when she wasn't laughing and blushing herself.

As was the custom, when Fitts stopped for water thinned, as it were, with rum, he offered the guitar to the next in the circle, which happened to be Prentiss who only laughed and would have given it across to Davy, but Molly stopped him. "May I?"

The instrument came into her hands as it had so often in times past, alive and familiar although the last time she had played it, those hands had been rather smaller.

Glances traveled around the fire as she trued up the tuning. "Sea air's no good for an instrument like this, but we can at least try." She could feel an intense quiet settle catlike around her, waiting. "Yes, yes, I know," she said without looking at them, listening for the G. "You may as well say it. Just like my father."

Almost idly she picked through a melancholy progression, not brilliantly but with skill.

"I knew him very little, aye, but he taught me a good deal, the whiles he stayed with us. And as it happens, he taught me some of it on this very guitar, did you know that? Look you here, on the third fret? I put those scratches in it when I was nine years old. A right little cat I was then." A few uneasy chuckles. "I never thought to see it again."

A few more plangent chords, and the hint of a tune. Pause to correct the low E, head cocked to the sounding board and still not making them meet her eyes.

"'Tis the oddest thing, though. I'm like him, you all say, but y' will not say what that means. I am surrounded by the men he lived with, sailed with, commanded—ah yes, you thought I couldn't tell—yet no one speaks his name. There are no tales in the night watches that include him, at least none in my hearing. Why is that, I wonder?"

Now her eyes lifted to each of theirs in turn, from Davy to Keaton and Matt Christy, around to DeRoet and Jimmy Fitts, and settled at last on Prentiss who chose to stare again into the flickering starlight. So she lifted the late-night remains of her pretty voice instead and began to sing:

As I roved out one morning
One morning in May
I spied a pretty fair maid
And unto her did say...

The delicate, hard-worked fingers slapped the strings to silence, making her listeners jump in their discomfort. "God's death!" she swore gleefully. "Is there no song in English that starts without those words!"

Shaken and uncertain, they broke into laughter as she meant them to and, compassionate, she flung them into something bawdy instead, an old echo song that let her nudge Prentiss into balancing her wine-shot voice with his easy baritone.

The keeper did a hunting go
And under his cloak he carried a bow
All for to shoot at a merry little doe
Among the leaves so green-o.
Jackie boy!
  Master!
Sing ye well?
  Very well.
Hey down!
  Ho down!
Derry derry down
Among the leaves so green-o!

When they were done chasing the doe through thinly veiled coverts of innuendo, and done watching Molly and Prentiss make faces at each other, she thrust the guitar back at Jimmy and fell helplessly giggling into Dick's long kiss, hardly aware that her very foolishness had released their tongues. The Spanish wine sailed round again and the stories began, at first tentative then gaining confidence augmented with melodrama.

Did everyone remember, Davy asked, about the time Rafe September saved Sir high and bloody mighty Harry Morgan's arse at Puerto Principe when his poxy French bastard partners deserted him? The tale came out in fits and starts, changing voices as each man who was there, or knew someone who was, told the bits he knew or thought he remembered, or had been told, or must be true.

Then there was the time, said Keaton, that Rafe rounded up all the whores of San Hieronimo and saved them from being burned alive when the city fell. From over the freshening firelight, Long Kate stepped up to agree in skirling Irish accents.

"True for you! And don't I know it myself, for I was one of those whores!"

The men roared, knowing it was so, and bade her join them.

"That was your dad?" she added. "God save 'im, he was a fine lookin' man, too!" She sat down with Owen Jones, who looked contented and pleasantly unstrung as he drew her onto his knee and dragged her arm round his neck.

The crowd that had been dwindling began to swell again. Some came from the ships to change the watch, wondering what they'd missed beside supper; others from their makeshift nests to complain of the noise, only to be brought up short by their captain's eloquent glare. Still others simply knew a good party was worth a night's sleep. Wide awake or merely philosophical, one by one they strolled in, broached a new keg, and picked at the last of the cold meat and yams and fruited rice (nodding gratitude once again to Long Kate), and dragged more wood to the tumbled circle of rocks above the wrack of the tide line.

Most of the *Testament* girls had returned to their own crew mates at the other end of the beach or slept wherever they had last made arrangements. Others like Kate came along as their more sentimental partners wandered down to add their part to the stories and tell their own, or to do no more than listen. Whether remembering or hearing for the first time the tale of Lake Maracaibo where Rafe blew up the Spanish flagship, they fell silent at Davy's telling, rich with danger and mad heroics.

Forty great guns the *Santa Magdalena* had, and all of them wasted when Rafe piloted that fire ship into place, Davy recalled with relish. With a skeleton crew of twelve brave men, himself and Prentiss with him, Rafe had rammed the *Magdalena*, which then blundered toward the 30-gun *San Luis* so that her captain had, gibbering, run her aground while Morgan boarded and took the only slightly less imposing 24-gun *Marquesa de Cartagena*. And somehow Rafe and Davy, Dick and Will Keaton had come away in spite of wounds and pain and overwhelming dangers, with 20,000 pieces of eight, diving to safety before the *Magdalena's* magazine blew.

Twenty thousand? What, in their teeth?

Keaton shrugged. "That's how Rafe told it He could tell a good story, could Rafe. I'm not sure he could count, God save 'im."

"A question!" Molly cried, a long way to the comfortable side of a lot of wine. "I have a question!" she said.

They waited, a dozen or two grins rosy on as many pairs of rosy cheeks

"I want to know." She gulped back a hiccup and giggled. "I want to know how *Jealous Mary* got her name!"

A pentagram of exchanged looks, one slight frown, a shrug, two lifted brows and some resigned laughter.

"I thought everybody knew that," said Prentiss lightly. "Rafe called her after his little girl. Screamed like a banshee every time he put to sea. Jealous as a six-penny whore, he always said."

The delicate pool of silence that started to form included just the few of them: Molly—who was christened Mary—and Davy, Keaton, and Paul. And Dick Prentiss. Who sailed Rafe's ship, and had married his daughter.

Then out of nowhere, like a gift from some peculiar god, or an uncanny spiral of stars, a cracking belch devastated the moment. Molly gaped and buried her head in Prentiss's shoulder, choking in embarrassment, and forgot the question. He smiled foolishly and held her. Again, the laughter rolled in around them to bury the last filament secrets in tidal waves of noise and good cheer, till there was no room for melancholy or mysteries.

Other tales stopped and started, some with Rafe in them, others about Morgan or L'Ollonais, or Rock Brasiliano, or how Jack Morris sacked Villahermosa after a 50-mile inland march. In a hurricane. One even told of Francis Drake, dead these hundred years, as if it had happened just last summer, and they laughed and thumped each other's shoulders as if it were true and they had been there themselves. All the while overhead the meteor shower slowed but never stopped, shedding on everything a quavering glitter, as much light as a full moon but filled with magic.

"My favorite," Molly shouted into the next break, flushed with wine and an image of her father she had never thought to see: courageous and skilled, profane and randy, even silly. Indeed, rather like herself. She swallowed and started again. "My favorite is the one where Rafe September ran away with the governor's green-eyed daughter."

"I know that one!!" cried Prentiss, and folded her into a fierce embrace while the others roared their approval, whistled and gave up their applause.

She kissed him and kissed him again, all other things forgotten, reveling in the feel of his arms holding her and his body crushing hers; and the kissing turned to passion, and passion to need. Eye to laughing eye, gleaming with desire and exhaustion, her hands framed his face in a tiny cave, close and damp and hot, where she knew she had time to say just one important thing. So she did.

"Dick Prentiss, if you don't take me to bed this minute, I swear I'll never speak to you again."

"And rightly so, wife! And rightly so." He winked, met her lips once fleetly, and jumped up. "D'ye hear that, my lads! Her favorite story!" he cried, flinging her up to stand, however unsteadily, under his arm. "And time to show how history repeats itself! Say good night to your guests, my lady."

Wide-eyed and disheveled beyond belief, she staggered a curtsey, opened her mouth and popped out a much smaller, more ladylike eructation, and blushed when they cackled with rowdy good cheer. Seizing the moment, Prentiss grabbed an armful of her long skirts and thrust it into her care. Jimmy tossed him a torch which he caught with surprising ease.

"Now!" Then he snatched her free hand and under the flaming sky they raced giggling up the path to the waterfall, away from noise and ghost stories and the hovering past. There was more they had not told her, more he had been relieved not to tell, but it would wait now. It would wait. Before he gave her that particular tale, he would show her again how much he loved her.

Sober and stone-faced in the midst of merriment, Davy watched them go, a spot of color brightening the last hours before a hard grey dawn. One day soon they would have to tell her how Rafe died. But not tonight. No, not tonight.

The first passage was swift and fierce, as if the whole evening had been leading to that moment, as if waiting any longer would consume them. Unsubtly, he took an impatient knife to the laces of the gay yellow dress, already shredded from hem to knee.

"Here is the maid all tattered and torn," he murmured with sober delight, now caressing the bodice and ribboned sleeves from her shoulders. Another quick slash opened the gown from the waist and the whole thing fell away from her body in rags while she shivered, bright-eyed.

"Shall I milk the cow with the crumpled horn?" She had heard him, and loved him for the childish joke.

He tipped up a lustful grin from somewhere near her knees. "An thou wilt."

The light shift that was all she wore beneath it split up its center seam with a touch, and the whole rich, sweet-smelling tumble of lace and linen and silk became their bed. And when the first frantic waves had crested, and they cried out together in splendor, he drew a deep breath and began again, slowly. Hands and mouth and mind bent entirely toward her pleasure, all other thought, all other trials driven out by love and need.

They moved together as the music had moved them throughout the night, seamlessly in time with each other's rhythms, and utterly in tune. The chatter and bubble of the stepped waterfall just outside their door counterpointed the intricate simplicities of love: her fingers in his hair, his lips on her mouth, her knee at his hip, the impossible perfection of her breasts in his hands, all enclosed in a lopsided canvas room roofed with broad leaves and floored with two hacked pieces of a vast silk Chinese rug, lightly scented with the faintest tang of rum and salt air. It was all the room they needed.

Just before dawn they slept, having driven hearts and minds and oh yes bodies over the brink so often there was no counting. The morning complaints of women fetching water and young men coughing and swearing they were too old for this life filtered through to them vaguely as they drifted finally to sleep, still caressing and exchanging small kisses.

Soon enough that hard dawn leeched the night from the eastern sky, and the sun lurched red and resolute straight into the eyes of everyone sleeping on the beach or near it. Long Kate had already dismissed Owen to stand his morning watch on the *Mary*, while she kicked Toby Millikan up to get fires going for thick sweet coffee and strong tea, and for the less adventurous, a tot of hot rum. For those who could stand—and Kate's estimates were routinely sound—last night's pork became this morning's gammon, fried up in an iron cauldron with butter and sour white potatoes, six apples, and a small armful of wild onions. At her word as much as their captains', hunting parties headed into the interior to replenish the larder. But later, much later, when heads and stomachs were more to the task.

It would be a rather quieter day than the last.

Rather later, Molly wakened in the drenching heat of afternoon. Beautifully, wonderfully, Prentiss slept still beside her, limbs awry and tangled in the ruins of the yellow dress, as careless as a child. Joy warmed her all over again with a wholly different heat from the stale air of their precious hideaway, warmed her so that she started to reach for him again, when the body's simpler demands made her rise. And gradually, the creeping awareness that had been beyond her last night, now made her look around at his wedding gift.

He had with his friends built her a little house to keep out the damps and prying eyes, so that for the first time in months they could make love in utter privacy. There were tasseled pillows on the ruined Chinese carpet; they had cut it into at least four pieces and built the hut to fit, layering the pieces to keep out the damp. In one corner sat a smallish chest with some clothes, should she decide she needed any. Another box was filled with wine bottles, conveniently opened and re-corked, and a pair of jeweled goblets. By it, a low table with a plate of fruit and cold meat tight-wrapped in waxed linen pockets. A pitcher and basin, a comb and a silver hand-mirror made her smile at her own well-known vanity.

Hanging from a cross beam, two long loops of cord, knotted at intervals, racked their weapons against one canvas wall—swords, pistols, powder horn and shot—because nothing in life is certain, and God hates the unprepared.

Suffused with affection for them all, Molly ran her hands over the plush pile of the carpet, peered doubtfully into the mirror, and dragged the comb over her hair then, trembling slightly, splashed harsh red wine into a goblet worth more than the school fees for the most refined ladies' academy in Paris. The jewels bit into her fingers. Every texture, every sensation tingled as if it were brand new.

She explored the chest again and, grateful, found thick linen towels under shirts and shifts and breeches and petticoats and a sad old blue gown. Water tipped into the basin, the corner of the towel sank in the water, and a brief bathe wiped away the residues of night and sleep.

There was more. The door was a curtain of jeweled and embroidered satin meant for a marquesa's gown, and as she saw when she drew it back cautiously, just outside it sat the marquesa's gilded and padded close stool, her chamber pot. She almost laughed out loud. Long Kate, certainly, had been here too. That would also explain the towels.

When she ducked back into her bridal bower, so lovingly made, Molly woke Prentiss up to thank him. Graciously, he accepted and returned the compliment, two or three times over.

Dick had sited the cozy hut of spare sail canvas and palm thatch near enough to the river but far enough from the main path that, if they chose not to be seen, no one could tell another soul lived there. And for that night and that day and another night, they chose not to be seen at all. Davy and his officers knew where they were; and Jimmy, who with Prentiss and DeRoet, had built it; and Long Kate because Kate always knew everything. Of everyone else they were free.

Jimmy kept an eye on them, made sure to take them proper food from time to time, and since he had forgotten it, Dick's pipe and tobacco. And from time to time bowls and spoons, properly wiped down, were set out for exchange. Fitts shook his head and decided that everything had turned out all right after all. He wouldn't have minded keeping a girl of his own, maybe, but for now the Preacher's easy marriage-by-the-hour plan was keeping him in trim, and he was happy enough. Besides, someone had to look after these two until they got back to their senses. And what was a holiday for, anyway. Call it a honeymoon, and be damned. It wasn't as if it could last.

The others saw Prentiss and his roaring girl sometimes in passing, at a distance: swimming in the river, climbing the face of the waterfall, hanging from a tree tossing down fruit and once, when Molly stabbed a banana spider the size of her fist, they jumped to Prentiss's hoarse cheer. In the late afternoon there might be a riotous shouting and the crash of swords, or the crack of musket fire, as they played in earnest And at any time, other sounds less violent but just as intense would come from somewhere in the trees, but that might be anyone, so who could say.

For the rest, there were those for whom, old or young, one unsheltered night ashore was plenty. The more experienced men gave impromptu and marginally smug lessons in the art of raising huts from whatever materials they chanced on. The oldest of the men had started out this way, when buccaneering meant they hunted wild cattle and pigs and smoked the "buccan" meat to sell among the island settlements. That was before the demon Spaniards had made their trade impossible and forced them into piracy. Not every man was outraged.

Still, in those old days they had cheerfully hunted and butchered and hung the meat to smoke, and if it looked a deal too much like work now, still for a few days they could do it again. It was practically nostalgic. The rewards were sweet enough: Kate's cooking only got better, the rotation of the available girls seemed fair enough, and the rates for both were reasonable, if unorthodox.

That is, Mendez swore he would not abide fornication among his flock and so, in a burst of generosity, agreed to set aside his marital rights, on condition. Crocodile tears streamed from his pouched eyes as he gave up each wife on request to one man after another on an hourly basis. A public service, he said it was. Weddings were brisk and dowries cheap, and no one seemed to mind the spontaneous adjustments to the sacraments.

It was practical.

It was paradise, and it could not last.

16

UP A DOUBLE AND BACK

ITCHING TO LEAVE before he had been there a single day, the Preacher reminded Davy over and again of their bargain to join against all flags. He blustered. He threatened. He said he would gather up his men and sail out alone, if need be, and leave his perpetually squabbling women behind as just punishment. He had a hold full of silver and gold to be divided, but would not hear of a sharing out before the next phase was agreed upon.

Davy cheerfully countered that he would make no plan at all unless he had discussed and found it amusing once sober and once drunken. And drunk or sober, if it did not make him laugh out loud, he would never embark upon it, whatever it was. An eccentric requirement, yes, and enough to bustle the grotesque Preacher into a fury that communicated itself to his crew.

What Davy meant and would never admit was that he was simply not in the mood. His hold was full, one of his officers was on honeymoon, and the bargain had been violated weeks ago when Mendez failed to show up at Martinique. He had no intention of including English flags among his prey, and he himself was having a fine holiday watching the games played out under a deceptively clear Costa Rican sky. The sooner Preacher Mendez tumbled to that fact and sailed away, the better.

Besides, it was clear that not everyone found the arrangements charming. To the Preacher's women, already inclined to harem jealousies, the exclusive attachment of Molly to Prentiss was not natural or even, they thought, entirely decent. His crew, cut of a more desperate mold than Davy's, were openly hostile. A pretty girl was a commodity who, by the articles under which they sailed, ought to be open and available—if not technically free—to all. And any man foolish enough to fall under the spell of a tart deserved mockery at least, a good thumping at best. Lacking Prentiss and Molly to harass directly, they turned their snarls and cat calls and lewd suggestions on the rest of Davy's crew. Attitude, lubricated with generous lashings of rum, led to daily fist fights, brief and pointless, that Mendez saw no reason to discourage.

It only confused the issue that, while hating Molly for nonspecific sins, the *Testament's* women found the *Jealous Mary's* men more generous than their own, and a change from the peculiar world the Preacher imposed, part perverted religion and part sea dream.

So for fourteen days in resonant discomfort—virtues, costumes, and all—they shrilled and bickered like a border town brothel until Long Kate, who was nominally their senior, flung down her household book in tightlipped annoyance, and marched up to the waterfall. If she wanted to listen to hens scratch and cackle, she muttered for all to hear, she could have stayed in Ireland.

At the base of the hissing waters, she stopped to draw a long breath and swear roundly in her own patched text of Gaelic and English, with some Spanish for color and six good words of German for pure grating vulgarity. Then she tucked the hems of her stained old green gown into her belt and stepped down into the stream, delighting in the endless sprays that prickled her face and arms. The cool water ran over the plain, common toes and stole away the temper.

She stepped carefully, testing each stone under foot, at the same time listening from long practice to every level of sound around her for cues and meaning. Aye, somewhere above and just to her left, above the bird calls and under the sighing waters, a duet of suppressed giggles rattled her knowing ear.

Without so much as looking about, she raised her best field voice and said, "Sure, the both of ye. And haven't I enough trouble on your account, without you making light of it?"

Delighted laughter, and Molly dropped from an overhanging branch like a descending fairy. Kate nodded shrewdly and added, "Aye, and yourself too, my hero!"

"A hero, am I! Will ye listen to the darlin' girl!"

With a happy shout and a good deal more crashing, Prentiss swung to the ground as well, vivacious as a new day. A few paces further on, hidden by ferns and the fans of low palms and guarded by a violently-colored spill of bird-of-paradise, the makeshift little honeymoon lodge lay in splendid isolation. She had entered their sanctum, as she very well knew.

Rolling her eyes at the theatrical entrance, Kate clambered astride a warm grey rock, dangling her long, long legs in the water.

"Cross of Christ about us, milady, I might have expected better manners of Rafe September's girl."

"She will keep calling you 'milady'," said Dick. "We can't seem to make her stop."

"Don't be taking it too much to heart, milady. A habit of speech, only. Funny, ain't it," she wondered, settling the soggy hem comfortably above her knees. "You wouldn't expect an old whore to be such a creature of habit, would you?"

"Not so old, love," Prentiss said sweetly.

She beamed and paddled her feet in the water, minding her manners. The rich chestnut hair knotted on her crown was threading with grey, which she would see to when she got to some civilized place again; and the figure was less trim than it had been but still fine, she knew, at thirty-two. True, over one breast, just visible above the neckline of the gown, was the still angry scar from someone's knife who no longer had the use of that hand. Nor was the face quite perfect: the snub nose looked to have been broken once leaving it misaligned over a mouth twitched up with mockery. But the skin, though coarsened from weather and the irregularities of her life, was Irish cream and faded roses, and the dark eyes were merry.

"I haven't thanked you," said Molly.

Comfortable in loose britches and Dick's old shirt, she sat cross-legged on the grassy riverbank with shining eyes. She'd not met Long Kate till now except for the one time across the firelight, but already she knew and liked her. She realized suddenly that she did not in general care much for the company of other women, but this woman—this unapologetic whore—was different from the usual: intelligent, resourceful, and something she couldn't quite name. That alone made her fascinating. More than that, Kate had known Rafe, at least a little.

And Molly was in her debt. "I know my lads, and I think I can tell where they left off building my little house, and you began. I am grateful to you."

Kate waved her off. "I think I know your lads, i'faith, and enough like them. If I'd let them, you'd have had six crates of wine and a razor case, and not a button more."

"Not quite true," said Prentiss, indignant. "I'd have found her a button."

"Aye," she drawled cynically. "I know what you'd have found." She let them exclaim and blush, which made her uncomfortable. Blushing had not been in Kate's lexicon since she was twelve, except as a tool of her trade. "Enough of that! D'ye think y'might be ready to come back to the world the rest of us live in, so?"

Slightly ruffled, Dick said, "If we must. I expect that's up to my captain." Then realizing there was more to the question, he added, "You said you've had trouble on our account. What trouble?"

She whipped off her head cloth and dragged it through the stream. When she had wrung it out and settled it dripping around her neck, gasping at the coolness, she said, "It's half mad they are, Preacher's men, aye and the women as well. They'll tell ye Miss Molly thinks she's too good to be a whore like the rest of us. It's just that true, milady, for I knew your Da and you *are* too good to be a whore like the rest of us. Well—"

A dismissive shrug indicated the camp. "The rest of *them*." Molly giggled and nodded the odd compliment. "And you, ye sentimental bastard, with yer wedding rings and honeymoons unsettling my girls! Though it was a grand *ceilidh*, to be sure, I'll give ye that. Still isn't the camp all a-grumble and a brawl waiting to happen from morn till night since then!"

More exercised than she had meant to be in this pleasant dell, Kate stopped to draw breath and scoop cool water up over her hands and arms, and splash more over her face and throat. The green stuff of her gown, already heavy with water in the skirt, grew dark spots over the sun-streaked bodice and rolled sleeves. Soothed at last, she focused on Molly.

"I know my lads as well, milady, and a vicious lot of ill-tempered bastards they are, like their captain. Villains, that they are. And if my girls get loose, well … there will be blood under someone's nails before it's done."

"Is that why you came up here, to tell us this?"

"I came to find a moment's peace!" She swore again and kicked at the river. "Why should the two of you be the only ones free of their shite the day long? So here I come and if I should happen to notice either of you hiding like the Devil in an apple tree, belike I'd give you the last good piece of me mind. If that captain of yours (God save him) hasn't been to tell you aught, belike 'tis that he's a man and pays no mind to what goes on about him, so long as there's rum in his fist and a handsome wench on his knee, and thinks all others the same. And so too, he's happy enough to spend a few minutes each evening knocking the teeth down someone's throat defending you."

Surprised and troubled, Molly's eyes met her sweetheart's and their thoughts collided once again.

"I suppose it's time we tear this all down," she sighed as she clambered to her feet. "It's been lovely, but there it is."

Prentiss blinked and made a decision. "Pack up," he said. "Perhaps the lovely Kate will of her courtesy lend a hand."

Kate cocked her head quizzically and blinked like a sparrow, which Prentiss caught. "Aye, courtesy is expensive. I'm good for it, as you've reason to know. And I'll send Jimmy up with a team to bring it all away."

She winked and blew him a kiss. "Good lad."

"And you?" asked Molly while considering that last exchange. "While all this labor is going on without you?"

"I, Sweet," he said with the hard consonants of a rich brogue all Irish in his own mouth. "I will venture into the wide world and lend our valiant captain the last good piece of Kate's mind. And see for meself what's toward."

At that, he hopped up from the bank himself, placed a swift but perfect kiss on Molly's mouth. "I love you," he said, and headed down the seaward path.

"Another thing, too!" Kate called cheerfully. He checked, and waited. "Preacher expects to be leaving tonight!"

He nodded and jogged on.

"And it's about t' rain!"

He waved.

"Leaving?" said Molly. "You're not leaving?" Astonishing, she thought, how much she would mind. "But you can't! I mean—"

"Can't I?" said Kate, then she laughed and relented. "Never fear, milady. Preacher'll be leaving without me." And reveling in the effect of that remark, she added. "Aye, love, yer darlin' Captain Davy is taking me back to Port Royal, it's that much he loves my kitchen."

Knowing from experience just how much Davy loved the idea of women aboard his ship, Molly gaped. "You talked him into —"

"Talked? Nay talkin' was not quite the means. Oh, he growled, the dear man, but the thought of four or five more days of my cooking, plus a promise to teach that cannibal Millikan a thing or two on the way, was as much as he could bear. Ah, ah, my youth is all but gone! There was a time when my smile alone would have been enough, so!"

She sighed with sweet derision as she drew long fingered hands provocatively up those long legs with just a particularly distracted tilt of the chin. Then she chuckled deep in her throat as she slipped off her dappled grey rock into the water and waded out rosy and smiling. "'Tis a good thing I can cook. Come you, girl, let me look what a mess you've left of all my hard work."

Molly grinned, knowing exactly what Davy's terms had been.

Shadows were indeed tiling the path. Prentiss looked at last to the sky when he was sure Kate could no longer see him taking her orders. And yes, clouds gathered over the treetops, sun gleaming off the high tops of thunderheads in blankets as red-gold as Molly's hair over pockets of black, wicked-looking shadow. He should, he guessed, have suggested leaving the canvas walls and roof up till morning, just in case.

Such thoughts vanished as he nearly crashed into Jimmy Fitts stalking grim-faced up the path.

"And not before time!" Jimmy said, as Prentiss took not just his hand but his arm in a startling embrace. Their eyes met for a long moment in judgment and consideration. "Look, Dick…"

The uncomfortable pause was unavoidable, no matter what he might have intended, no matter what services he had rendered.

Shocked them both, too, since Jimmy hadn't called him "Dick" in years. Now words spilled from him on their own, words he meant but had not meant to say. "Look, if ye're still wanting to call me out, I understand."

But Prentiss waved the idea aside with a lightly startled expression. "Are you mad? Molly'd kill me."

That made Jimmy brighten a bit, still raking nervous fingers through damp, tangled hair, and shivering under a passing cloud. "I'm still surprised you haven't. I know I was stupid, and worse."

"You were that. But man, if Molly's forgiven you, it's more than my life is worth to carry a grudge she's already put away."

"Aye, but ..."

"Jim, enough!"

This business was making him squirm. From a gesture as seemingly trivial as the return of an heirloom, he'd seen Molly's acceptance grow from reprieve to something like friendship, until now she treated Jimmy like a fond older brother to be poked at and bullied and relied upon.

Under that assault of good will, his friend had been apologetic and powerless. What could he do with his own anger except let it go. "'Tis past and done. Now will y' tell me what's going on?"

And it was done. They had been friends for ten years, they could be friends again, and the odd discomforts that had infected their time together in the last two months disappeared.

On a breath of deep relief, Jimmy said, "Right. Something's got to be done about Mendez and that poxy scum he calls a crew."

"Aye, so I'm told."

"Oh? Ah, that would be Kate. Oh aye!" He laughed at Dick's raised eyebrow. "Ye're not the only man that women talk to, my lad. Did she also tell you he's been sinking English ships all summer, and there's English silver in his hold, and that's enough to hang us all. Come on then. Keaton says it's time you an' him took this to Davy, before there's a mutiny!"

In two careless weeks the makeshift camp had spread like a carnival fungus along the tide line, extending crablike up into several smallish clearings in the trees along the river. One was base camp for the hunters and their smoke houses, another an improvised common room, a third for Kate's efficient kitchen and stores.

A hundred violent men and a dozen weary women sharing a makeshift kitchen, a spring, and each other must eventually reach their limits. Even Davy's mellow discipline declined as the heat and humidity rose and unpleasant passions flashed. Arguments flared over whose turn it was with Lakshmi, or whether there was too much pepper in the stew. With tempers short and weapons near to hand, it was pure luck that so far no one had been killed, although many were nursing bruises and one, at least, a broken hand and a motive for murder. Descant over everything, the skirling of outraged female tempers, and *continuo*, the low murmur of their scheming punctuated the air.

In the last few days it had become common for Davy or Keaton to interpose his own body in amongst their squabbling friends—and those other people. Even Jimmy had been dragooned into sergeant's duty. The Preacher's officers were no help, and worse, were as likely as any to be found in the midst of the fray. Even to have started it, which is how Prentiss found them as he and Jimmy broke into the kitchen clearing.

Two men were fighting, more were cheering while women shrieked or wept It looked like a tavern brawl in Port Royal, with the neat addition of white sand and fresh air among the grass and black basalt.

As they emerged from the trees, Prentiss pulled up short and laid a hand across Jimmy's chest to halt him. He frowned and took in the scene, counting the participants by groups from old practice.

Most of the women were here, yes. He supposed the late afternoon was their idle time for napping or mending or plotting against one another in shaded corners. Having spent the fortnight apart, he had to guess at the arrangements, but he knew a little about how a brothel operated. He'd housed in one, a time or two. But where were all the men?

"What's the matter?" said Jimmy. "That's our German Jack. He can take care of himself, certain. An' that's Williams, Preacher's bosun who doubtless deserves it, whatever it is. Davy said to let these barnies work themselves out, so long as no one's killed or crippled."

"Hmm." Prentiss wondered, still scanning. "Did hunters go out today?"

"Not today. We've been hanging and smoking wild pigs and a couple of cows for two days, and we're near enough done as makes no matter. I was just back there. A pair of snoring drunkards—both ours—and a girl poking the fires, is all."

Prentiss leaned back against a convenient tree, arms folded, watching the blows and bodies fly amid the cast iron and crockery.

"Jimmy, how many men does the *Testament* crew?"

"Oh, forty mayhap. Plus the girls."

"And our sixty-five, so call it a few over a hundred, hundred and twenty say."

"Aye. Less the twelve on the *Mary* to keep the watch, and two on the headland for lookout. Maybe another ten snoring somewhere or working on their gear."

"And six at watch on the *Testament* because Mendez is an idiot. Davy's aboard, is he?"

"Aye, and Master Keaton, Matt Christy, and Paul, plus the watch crew. Some of us have to keep working while you take your holiday. They're waiting for you, come on."

"No, stay a bit. Look!" Dick gestured. "Even allowing some are sleeping or idling somewhere else, how many should there be? Isn't that the smallest bloody brawl you've ever seen for what should be sixty or seventy men. Hell, most of them are our lads! Jimmy, where are the Preacher's men?" Astonished realization swept them both.

"Christ! No one is supposed to know we're here, and they've gone out pirating, or God knows what else. Partnership!" Prentiss spat. "Give me your pistol."

Jimmy grinned "Going to need covering fire?"

"Give me the damned pistol." Fitts drew both from his sash and handed one over, checking the priming first, by habit. "Now you walk 'round their other side, by the stone circle. Watch for my signal. And Jim? Fire in the air, this time, can you?"

"I still say that was an accident!"

"Go on!"

With a wink and a mischievous mind, Prentiss waited while Jimmy moved into position, then strode into the clearing. Marriage was a wonderful thing, he acknowledged, but putting these bastards in their place would do near as well.

Calmly, he lifted the quarterdeck voice that governed *Jealous Mary* through storm and battle. "That's enough!" The pistol rose in his hand.

The few watchers nearest him looked up and registered the hard eyes and the grim, humorless smile, and the gun. A few backed away, snatching at their fellows, but the principal combatants continued. Dick stepped back and as they rolled toward him, made a show of wincing when the next punch landed on a cheekbone, striking blood into the air as the thick braided head of German Jack bounced off Kate's best cooking jar.

The tempered red clay rang, teetered, and crashed. Williams snarled and dragged Jack to his feet with one fist baled in the fabric of his jerkin, the other cocked for the next blow.

A nod to Jimmy. The first pistol blared. Except for a final rebellious shake from the massive Williams, everything stopped.

"That'll do!" He kept his own pistol in reserve, and entirely visible. "Put 'im down, Taffy. I said put 'im down, damn you!"

Staring at Prentiss, the Welshman opened his fingers and Jack crashed back into the crockery.

Now that he had everyone's attention, Dick said pleasantly, "And who is going to tell me what this is about?"

The women, who did not know him in this mood, seemed inclined to volunteer all at once and at volume. That would not do. The pistol in his hand discharged into the air. They jumped, and twittered to a jingling silence.

"Look, Pilot!" Williams growled

"Ah, a volunteer."

"'T'weren't naught, Pilot. Just play, look you."

Prentiss surveyed the wreckage of what had been a nicely ordered camp kitchen, noting along the way that Jimmy was well into reloading. He shook his head. From behind, still hidden by the deep greens of the forest, came the sounds he was waiting for: the long, determined stride of a very tall, very angry campfollower, accented by the more rapid pace of his daintier but just as remarkable wife.

"That's so, Pilot," Jack added.

"I see. And you're going to explain to Long Kate that you've torn her kitchen apart for fun, are you."

Both Williams and German Jack looked about them stupidly, taking in the broken pots and the scattered baskets of fruit and wooden dishes in the dirt, and the cauldron on its side, and Kate's one decent work table splintered into kindling. Fearless men though they both were, they swallowed hard.

"Now gentlemen," Prentiss went on in the same charming mode. "I have to meet just now with my captain, so I can't stay to make you put this all to rights." He counted evenly backwards from five and watched Jimmy's face split into a grin as Kate burst out of the slope behind him. "But I know who can." He could feel her sputter to a halt in cold fury.

Before she could take a breath to give voice, he turned smart about and gave her his most elaborate bow. Molly, stalled in mid-stride herself, had to stifle a laugh, recognizing the gesture but not wanting to spoil the effect.

"Madam, if you will allow me!"

Long Kate Riley, calling on her extensive experience with men and their taking ways, was not, he noted gratefully, screaming yet but there was no mistaking her temper as she surveyed the damage.

Prentiss said, "I offer apologies on behalf of some of our men. They are idiots." The men bristled.

Bright-eyed as Mad Maudlin, she nodded tightly, arms and hands folded firmly under her normally friendly bosom.

"If you will give me an accounting, I assure you I will cover the costs of their errors—out of their shares." Slowly, the generous mouth began to soften, just slightly. "In fact, I expect as ladies of quality often do, you may be inclined to undervalue the things you use every day, so mark you, whatever value you specify on any item, I will double it."

"Pilot!"

"Triple, or they'll find themselves walking home!" There was no mistaking his humor at all.

"Aye, Pilot," Jack grumbled though Williams said nothing.

The suggestion of a smile in Kate's wild Irish face broadened into a proper grin.

"Moreover," he went on, reveling in this. "They will clean it up, with the help of their fellows here who joined or in any case failed to stop them."

More low grumbling, but neat white teeth began to show in Kate's smile, and even some of the women began to appreciate what he was doing. "Under your supervision, of course, Madam. Jimmy Fitts! You'll leave your pistols with the ladies."

"I will do that, Pilot!" Jimmy said crisply.

"And ma'am, if you will accept one more suggestion?" She nodded once, waiting. He knew perfectly well that no one ever addressed her as a gentlewoman, so he had to end this soon. In a moment she would be laughing outright. "Though 'tis not for me to tell you how to run your household, I say let your girls stand easy until it's done. The men have created this mess, they can clean it up themselves."

Wild high laughter burst at last from Molly and Kate both, and the rest of the girls besides, while the men shouted their dissent It wasn't fair! It wasn't right! The volume rolled towards a roar.

Prentiss tossed a nod at Jimmy Fitts and again the pistol report ended the argument. Someone yelped and grabbed an ear. Jimmy shrugged away Prentiss's swift scowl and reloaded.

"Not fair? Not right? Women's work is it!" Dick snarled, flinging aside the genteel façade. "God's Blood! You dogs have fared better in these fourteen days than in yer whole worthless lives! You will do as ye're told, and pay what you bloody owe, or I swear I'll leave you to her alone! Is that clear!"

It was clear.

Kate kissed him as he handed over the other pistol, now double-shotted. Molly kissed him adoringly, which added cream to the sweetness of command. She nodded as he whispered instructions in her ear. And without looking back, he and Jimmy shoved one of the *Mary's* small boats into the water and rowed out under squally skies.

Confronting Davy was not as pleasant as it sounded—if anyone had thought it sounded pleasant—especially after the lengthy report on the Preacher's latest sins. In all, Dick and Keaton, Christy and DeRoet were uniform in their opinion: Davy had contracted as far as they were concerned with the Devil's own lieutenant for the high seas, and they were all going to hang. *Jealous Mary* was an English privateer, by God, respecting English flags; Mendez was an out and out pirate, respecting nothing: nor flag nor gender nor good intentions. What the devil, they wondered for an hour of steady drinking, had Davy been thinking of!

Davy had, in fact, no good excuse but bluster and a thin tale about what if they maybe had needed backup at Martinique, which they had not.

"In other words," said Will Keaton, who had credit enough, he hoped, to get away with it. "You were blind drunk."

"Was I, damn you?"

Keaton, disgusted and entirely too sober said, "Aye, and besotted with two of the Preacher's women besides."

"The habit is contagious," Davy said, glaring hot-eyed at each of them. "Blame Prentiss."

"I learnt it from you, Captain mine. But I," Dick added, kicking back his chair in agitation. "Well damn it, I was— I am— in love, you bastard. You were thinking with— God knows what you were thinking with. Next time I'm in Port Royal, I swear, I'll take out papers to have ye sent to the Bedlam. If they don't hang me first for piracy!"

The fist that commanded them all slammed to the table to make the cups rattle. "Enough!" he said. "Ye've had yer turn. Pretend just for a moment that I am still the captain of this ship. Your captain." They variously sighed, hissed, or blew their displeasure but said no more. "You have been content to follow me so far, and for some long whiles, aye?" Reluctant agreement. "And to some profit. Have I ever steered any of you into shoal waters?"

"Not me," said Matt.

Prentiss pulled a terrible long face and said, "You're new."

"Bloody hell!" York cried, already half way over the Spanish table and reaching for Dick.

Keaton yelled "Matt!" and one big powder-burnt hand came down like iron on his captain's shoulder, while DeRoet grabbed Prentiss. "Can't let you kill 'im, Davy. Right or wrong."

"Christ almighty! I will not explain myself to you! Any of you!"

Dick willed his fists to open as Paul's strong hands forced him back into the chair, and he drew one long uneasy breath.

"All right," he said. "You are my captain, aye, and my friend too, I hope. Not to say ye've never been wrong! And I'll back you all the way to Execution Dock, just for the asking, never doubt it. But when that bastard sells us all to the Devil, I reserve the right to say I warned ye."

York growled but backed off. "Fair enough."

Silent, he dragged the cork out of the Madeira again. More wine splashed into each chased silver cup, letting the silence develop.

Whatever devastating move he was planning, it was crushed by a light tap at the door and Molly in the room. "Captain?"

"God's Death! Can I have no peace even in my own bloody quarters? What is it, damn you!"

"Gentlemen?"

With flower-like innocence she stepped into their testy circle. Five grim faces failed to change as they turned, though Prentiss managed a tight smile.

"I left thee with orders, lass. What is it?"

"So who's to be murdered? If it's Mendez, I'm with you, and the crew as well I dare say. But you'll have to chase him."

"What's this!"

"Just after you left, Dickon, they came ashore for the girls, bags and baggage. Kate isn't at all happy, I can tell you. When she said she wasn't going, Williams just pushed her down and walked away."

"Molly!"

"I've just told you! They've gone."

"Gone?"

"Warping out of the channel even now."

Chairs scraped back, tipped and fell as all five men scrambled over each other to get on deck. There she was, the *English Testament* low and black on the water a mile off their bow, leaving a grimy trail in her wake. As the first fat drops of rain smacked his face like angry tears, Davy swore. "And everything off the San Felipe with him."

"Including two boxes of silver meant for the garrison at Port Royal, so Kate says."

"Bags of silver shillings with good King Charles' face on 'em. God, no wonder he didn't want to share out, so long as I kept saying no English targets!"

"The thieving bastard."

That made Molly smile but no one else.

"Who the devil's on watch up there! Christ, I shouldn't have to wait till someone rows out from shore to tell me the news!"

"They had no orders to report anyone leaving, Davy. Just arriving or passing by."

"You must have heard them. Both crews hooting and firing charges off the swivel guns, and whistling kisses. I never thought to see our lads so happy to say goodbye to easy women. Didn't you hear them?"

"We were, ah, bit preoccupied," said Will Keaton.

"The isle was full of noises," Prentiss muttered cryptically.

"What's that?"

"I said it's time we ran for home, Davy."

"Oh home, is it? And which home is that, now that we're pirates, eh? Preacher Mendez having made off with our reputation, as you are so blithe to tell me."

Indulging in an arch look while the *Testament* showed them her gilded tail, Prentiss explained.

"Here it is. What if we leave some of what we've taken right here. We found some lovely deep caves, Molly an' me, back under the waterfall up there." He had failed to notice the color leave Molly's face at the mention of home. "We lighten our load, see, and trim up the manifests, then skip on to Jamaica lily-white and virtuous."

Pale, and now trembling, Molly said weakly. "I can't go to Port Royal."

She had not been afraid of anything, anything in the world, mere moments ago. Not Spaniards or cannon or loss of love. But home meant her uncle, the law, the implacable Captain Benning. She had thought never to return.

That was nonsense, of course. Port Royal was *Jealous Mary*'s home port. It was where they all spent most of their shares drinking and gambling and wenching, knowing there would always be more out there on the seas, so long as the king and his wars lasted. That was fine for everyone else, but the thought of it terrified Molly to her soul, and no one even noticed.

In the end, Prentiss's idea carried. Molly and Keaton supervised the choosing and disposition, repacking, and transition, in blowing rain, of crate after crate of money, jewelry, and plate. Even the cases of muskets, cleaned up new and repacked in oiled cloths smelling slightly of cumin, were ferried through the downpour to safety behind the waterfall. At the same time, another work crew under Jimmy Fitts retrieved all the meat from the smoke houses and wrapped it up in banana leaves, brown paper, and old canvas.

Then through the evening and half the night, while the men groaned from their labors and inhaled Kate's stew with their grog, Molly and Davy sat down to realign their paperwork with the contents of their hold. It needn't be exact. No one would expect it to be. It wanted only to have started out clean and careful and in Spanish, and it should show some handling and a little weather. God knew, the weather was easy enough to provide. Davy thought he could provide some handling. Molly made him promise not to wipe his bum with the pages.

By the time they were done and the old papers destroyed, the new ones filed away, the sky had cleared again to a moonless sky pocked with stars. Though the rain had stopped, it was too muggy to sleep aboard ship if you didn't have to, so except for those assigned the night watch, most of the men flung themselves down on the beach as they had the first night, with smudgy fires to keep the mosquitoes at bay.

Kate disappeared about the same time as Davy, although everyone knew the Captain was in his cabin with all the windows open and his own store of wine, so in fact no one had disappeared at all. Keaton stayed aboard as officer of the deck, as if they needed one, and Paul took advantage of a last night with the sailing master's cabin all to himself.

For their last night in paradise, Dick Prentiss took his young wife to bed in the hideaway he had created for her a hundred paces from everyone else. The rain and the work and the strain on her Spanish vocabulary had left her edgy and cross, but Prentiss let it go. The day had been long and filled with crisis, so he blew out the candles and reached for her.

"Bastards," she muttered in the dark.

"Hmm?"

"Nothing."

"Ah," he whispered, and let his hands speak the rest.

Because Kate and Molly's packing had been interrupted first by riot then by buried treasure, there were still domestic affairs to conclude, and Prentiss was up before her, gathering their last things together in the wet drippy morning before the sun broke into their seclusion and turn the pleasant grey mist to steam. He had collected all the bits and pieces into baskets or tidy piles of what could be left behind and what must come away, and now was taking the walls down, untying points and collecting the canvas neatly into measured pleats that could be stored away and used again. His mood was so light that he whistled, thinking of nothing but the work at hand.

Green eyes fluttered open over a sleepy smile. She loved to watch him like this, to study him while he worked, exploring with renewed wonder the etched soldier's profile thrown into relief against the steely sky he revealed with each re-folded panel. The sun-streaked hair fluttered birdlike about his cheeks under a bright kerchief and his workaday felt hat.

Even in the sullen morning light, his eyes never lost that extraordinary blue, as if an English summer day had taken up residence.

She approved again the breadth of shoulder, the line of strength in the corded muscles of his arms leaning into this simple work as surely as they did on the *Mary's* tiller, or the curves of her body. The strength, she thought, and the mind that drove it, understanding and reading from moment to moment the shifts in sea or men's tempers, or herself. It was that strength, she knew, that drove her mad with excitement every time he touched her; that mind that called to her.

She startled as a flock of red and yellow macaws screamed overhead, executed a precision turn in flight and soared off on business of their own. In counterpoint, a bright green hummingbird buzzed into what was left of the doorway, hovered, then went straight for the broken fruits left on the low table last night.

"You know what I miss?" Molly said quietly.

He paused in his work to smile his good morning, and nod toward the table where wine and the last of the bread waited for her. Steaming next to them sat a covered pitcher filled with hot water that Kate had sent for washing. "What's that, love?"

"I miss plain ordinary birds." She sat up to consider, drawing her knees up under the linen. "Sparrows, starlings, nightingales. Plain flowers, too. Like daisies and forget-me-nots. Or roses. I do like roses. Compared to parrots and orchids they're all quite dull, I suppose, but at least I know all their names." The hummingbird floated up to stare her in the eye, then swept away as if it had never been.

"Is that all? Nothing else? No one else?"

Rubbing the morning gum from her eyes, she sighed. "I miss my parents. Sparrows and forget-me-nots I can find again."

The linen sheet slipped away from her pretty breasts, sweetly rounded, but she paid that no mind. Instead, she took a deep breath and spoke with a deceptive calm. "Morning, Dickon."

"So it is, Sweet." He winked at her over armfuls of wall.

"I was awful to you, last night."

"Don't be daft."

"Well I'm sorry anyway. It was the hurry, and the rain, and —God!—trying to remember what the English is for *aguja*."

Stillness first, so that she wondered if he had even heard her, though in profile she saw the startling eyes glitter in thought as he hesitated, his arms laden with dusty, rain-pocked canvas.

He said mildly, "*Aguja* is needle." With sure hands, he untied the last supporting knot, checked and tucked two wayward folds. Then the wonderful eyes met hers again, and she simply had to say it.

"Dickon, I can't go back to Port Royal!"

The fear she had almost conquered last night now filled her face and reached into trembling hands, and it was too awful for him to let pass. Without another thought, the canvas slipped unfurling to the ground, and he was on his knees at her side, folding her into his arms. Dusty and careful, he held her until the tremor subsided.

"I know you're afraid. Nay, Sweet, listen to me. And yes, I do know why!" She shook her night-tossed curls without conviction. "You think I don't pay heed, but I do. Fact is, we can't avoid Port Royal, and you know that. We must drop off the King's share, or we lose our letters. But there's no reason for you to meet your uncle, or anyone you don't wish to.

"Love, no one can hurt us! When Davy's business is done, sure we're rich enough, we can do anything we want. Find us a neat little house anywhere you like, and raise fat children, and grow coffee. I know, we'll buy that place behind the Saracen's Head, shall we? Give Driscoll some competition by selling real rum! Maybe sail to Madagascar!"

He clung to her, his own emotions swelling with the urge to protect her. "It will be all right, I promise. I love you. I promise." And he sealed that promise with kisses, as if in the whole world only kisses were true.

Finally, when her panic had subsided, one last awful thought occurred to him, which did make him stop and swear even as he grabbed her about the waist and tumbled her back into the bedding.

"My Christ! Settle down? How ever will we tell Davy!"

The troubled breathing had just begun to turn to sighs when the sky exploded over paradise.

"Dickon!"

A second pair of explosions rang through the sheltered grotto, and screams began to rise from the camp.

Swearing, Dick was on his feet, scrambling back into his clothes. "Damn it, where's my sword!" She nodded to where all the weapons still hung from their improvised rack, swaying in the shock wave. He tossed Molly's to her and snapped his orders. "Get dressed. Load pistols."

Then he snatched up a musket, unwrapped the lock and checked the priming, said "Wait here!" and was gone.

17

A New Ground in D minor

THE ENEMY HAD SAILED in out of the sun, silent but deadly and virtually invisible. The watch should have noticed, but the white glare made Billy Mariott yawn; he had just come on duty, and there had been nothing to see for days. The first chain shot took him down with his lookout perch and the *Jealous Mary's* reefed foretopsail, which tangled and ripped like a knife through the rigging as it fell, and crushed two men under the spars. Flung into clear air with a view of three volcanoes, Billy fell howling to the deck and died.

The next shot ripped through a staysail and snagged around another. Then at last out of the smoke the villain came on into the rippling green waters of the lagoon, the black demon frigate that had haunted and harried them into cover, flying the king's colors: His Majesty's ship *Blackbird*, out of Port Royal.

They were offered no challenge nor a chance to surrender, but in minutes *Jealous Mary* swarmed with grim-faced strangers in the long red coats of Royal Marines. Then the *Blackbird*, having deposited her raiding party, heeled away, presented its guns to the shore, and began to fire.

Davy roared out of his cabin half naked only to find it was too late. Keaton was already down, skull cracked, face a wash in blood. He seemed to be breathing but at his feet, Paul DeRoet lay broken under the fallen sail. Sobbing with rage, Davy set off two pistols point blank at the red-coated bastards nearest him, then cast those aside and drew his sword. Even blind with hatred and sorrow and revenge, a small corner of his consciousness thanked God that Kate had gone ashore already.

Gone ashore. With Prentiss and Molly. Where the *Blackbird's* cannons flared and trees exploded.

To the men breaking down their huts or playing football on the beach, it was as if all hell had come upon them. First the horror of watching the *Mary's* maintop explode as if by an act of God, and young Billy tumble to his death on an awful cry. Then the helplessness of watching her boarded, still shrouded in mist. And then, out of the sun and bitter smoke, the familiar, unmistakable sound of cannon's roar.

Round after round kicked out in flame and shot that blew up the sand or bounced and crashed into the forest, or shattered the hospitable palms into shrapnel. Screaming, they dove for cover, those that could move, and found no safety. They knew their muskets were no use at the range of the 9-pound guns. Still they grabbed their weapons and stumbled blind deeper into the forest. They could stand and die, or they could run. Some fell before they could get to their feet. One just disappeared in a mist of blood and sunshine.

The stone circle where they had built their bonfires and danced, and gotten drunk, and reveled in their freedom and their pilot's wedding, blew up under an iron ball and rained down death in knife-edged splinters of rock. Kate, early in her kitchen and giving tea to the most timely, heard the first shriek of the round shot sick with horror.

"Not so!" she breathed in Gaelic, and stood stark still, staring up. "Not again." She fell to a crouch and covered her head with her arms, knowing there was no shelter.

Then came the explosions, and the retching screams around her, and the showers of sand and gravel. In the reloading pause, she ran, not toward the beach where horror waited, but up the path toward the waterfall, out of range and even, she could hope, out of sight of whatever raiders had found them. But timing was not in her gift today. A round crashed into her cooking fire, and one shard of her last good cook pot slammed across her side as she ran, followed by another, each raking away wool canvas and linen and flesh, and spinning her to the ground, which saved her from the iron kettle that sailed through afterwards, and smashed instead through a low lying palm tree.

When the next ball buried itself in earth yards away, she was already flung on her face in the grass and blasted earth, spilling blood into her old work gown, unconscious but alive. All around her the wounded and dying moaned, and the firing went on. A flock of red and yellow macaws burst from a tree.

The air filled with acrid smoke and suspended sand and the dirty leaf mould of the jungle floor, blinding and gagging those who could still stand, who stumbled in retreat. The rising sun in their morning eyes flinched golden through the smoke and again a line of cannon flung death at the killing ground.

He could keep fighting, Davy knew, but they would lose, and in the meantime men under his command were dying in their safe harbor. Here aboard, he was less than twelve to their, what? It had to be thirty. Overmastered with four military issue sabers poised at his chest, Davy sank to the deck, his back to a wall. Bleeding from a dozen places, speechless with fury, he tried to see through the blur of smoke and furious tears just who he was expected to surrender to. It certainly looked as if he was meant to surrender, since they could kill him right now but chose not to. They seemed to be fighting no more than a holding action, but what did that mean. To terrorize, but perhaps not to destroy? Whatever, he had still taken out three of the bastards before he fell.

And there beside him, sweet Jesus, lay two friends. Christ, he had been through a hundred fights with Will Keaton. How was he going to explain this to Annie? And DeRoet too, steady and endlessly reliable Paul, the quiet teacher, killed stupidly on his own deck with tiller locked down and pistol still primed in his hand. Who else would he have to account for? Who else had he lost—and to Englishmen, for godssake! No, to that bastard Mendez who had sold him out.

Right now all he could do was stare at his blood-drenched hands and hope to save whatever might be left of his crew.

"Your sword please, Captain York." A reedy, hideously familiar voice whined above him. "Get up, get up. I do hate to receive a surrender from a man on his knees." A smug little laugh. "Unless of course it is the only way. Get him to his feet, Alcott."

Davy threw off any help, and struggled sliding up the wall using his slashed hand and the battered old sword as a prop. It was a shuffle, a humiliating slip in his officers' blood and the tangle of gear, before he could meet the other man's pale eyes.

"I know you," he spat at the dandy in the gaudy uniform. The elegant black wig was beginning to whiten, pocked with bits of flying ash.

"I shouldn't think so," said Sir Simon Benning. "Nay wait, strike me, but I do remember seeing you, the last time you came to make your scurrilous report to the patient Sir Roger." The sly face hardened. "You understand the rest of your men are under attack? Your sword, please, Captain, or the cannonade continues."

Snarling, Davy flung the weapon as far as his remaining strength would allow. "You take it, y' swine!!"

At which dramatic gesture Benning, who still expected to marry Molly September, flung the back of a scented fist across the bleeding, insolent mouth. Then pouted to find two flecks of blood offending his perfect lace cuff. He was, but for the ashes he had not yet noticed, pristine and might have been going to a ball and not a fight in which men died, or a slaughter in which no one was permitted to fight at all.

"Good enough." He turned his back pointedly. "Lieutenant Alcott, put him in irons but leave him here on deck where what's left of his crew can admire him. And oh yes, when you've done that, you may signal the *Blackbird* to cease fire, there's a good lad."

"God's Blood! Who the hell do you think you are!" Davy cried. "(*Make haste boy! Hurry!*)"

"I am the officer arresting you for the kidnap of Molly September, niece to the King's Comptroller for Jamaica, in connivance with one Dick Prentiss, a known thief."

"Kidnap! I never saw the girl!"

"That is a lie." He lightly smashed York's face again. "She is with you, and if she is not aboard at present, we may hope for thy sake that she is out of range ashore."

The eyes flickered a bit. If she was not here, that meant they were firing on his fiancée. Well, no matter. The silly cow's own fault if she would not be rescued. "In the meantime, there is the rather more infamous charge of piracy."

"Ha, piracy, say you. You're the pirate. My letters are in order, you dog."

"Thy letters, y' base-born scum, give 'ee the right as a privateer to harry and attack the enemies of our most gracious sovereign his Majesty King Charles. But I have evidence of a formal partnership entered into with one Pieter Mendez, also called the Preacher, a Dutchman who is an undoubted pirate preying on all flags. His crimes are therefore your crimes."

"Mendez, that bastard! I'm an Englishman, by God, you think I'd join with him in such hunting? (*Go on, lad, go! My Christ, they're dying out there!*)"

George Alcott, already white and sickly with his first engagement, tugged the leg irons and pocketed the key, then raced away to signal the cease fire.

"Ah well, there it is. I say there is proof." A single trumpet rang out over the last thumping rounds, and silence sprang up. "Thou sayest not. The court will decide just as soon as we return to Port Royal. A court presided over, be assured, by thy sometime sponsor, Sir Roger."

"Thou'rt a poxed, lying, whoreson bastard ..."

Benning struck him again with the opposite hand. This time a great ring laid open Davy's cheek.

"I'll have no more of your filthy manners. Incidentally, I have also a warrant for the arrest of another known thief, one Jim or Jimmy Fitts for the murder of Sir Roger's employee, James Cridden MacBean. This Fitts is also known to be one of your merry band."

Mendez had been thorough, you had to give him that. The fee must have been huge. He had all the stories, knew every name, had taken every detail through nights of sitting by the fires and days of selling his women by the hour. Those viscous, clacking bitches! And then the damned pinnace went out that no one noticed, and made contact with Benning by some plan, and gave them over to this evil butcher. They were all going to hang.

Prentiss, if he were still alive, was going to be insufferable all the way to the gallows.

Pushing down the rising sense of panic, Prentiss hurried along the upper path that ran against the river instead of the usual one that led down to the sea. That way lay madness and death, surely. This way, an animal track worn clear and broad by two weeks of men's adventures and women's needs, pushed past hunters' rough huts and the buccan sheds, and connected the clearings they had occupied in common. Musket in hand, he loped along as swiftly as possible. He paused to duck at every new explosion that roared like the wrath of God, waiting for the leaves to settle and the echoes to clear.

He found men stumbling in retreat, clutching their weapons and their friends. They called out to him, and there was nothing else to do but muster them together, cajole them to take cover and wait, while he went on. Matt Christy found him, looking pale and grim as he hauled a terrified Derek May into the trees with one hand, the boy's drum with the other. Derek would not come without it.

"I take it the guns aren't yours, then," Dick said acidly. "Do we know who it is?"

We did not. With a few words, Prentiss left him to collect and organize the men as they struggled to assemble. Jimmy was still out there somewhere, dead or alive.

And so he was, sitting flat dazed but apparently unhurt within a few feet of Long Kate, a mug of tea still warm in his hand. Scattered about him, three other men were groaning and picking themselves up and examining small wounds. Owen Jones, Rob Thomas and Hughes the surgeon had been caught in the explosion of the cook fire, and their faces were red, Rob's hand scalded. German Jack seemed to be dead and Kate was unconscious and bleeding ten paces away.

"Jimmy!"

"Bloody hell!" Fitts shook off the confusion and with Dick's help, stumbled to his feet. "What the hell was that!"

"All signs point to our being under fire," said Prentiss. "And by now I'd say they've got our range."

"Agreed, but who's doing the firing? Not Matt running artillery practice in the fog again, is it?" The mocking grin returned. The glaze on the brown eyes cleared.

"Not Matt, no. Now come on. Everyone who can is falling back. We have to move." Kate would be all right, he found. Her breathing was shallow but steady. The bleeding had slowed, and the wound would be more painful than deadly, from the look of it.

Careful but firm, he pressed a stained kitchen cloth against the hole in her side, and snapped out her name.

"Kate!" The midnight eyes came open, sullen and angry. He chuckled darkly as she swore, and picked her up. "That's our girl!"

"Who?"

"Hush. We don't know. No more questions."

"Molly?"

"She's fine." He frowned. He'd told her to wait, but would she? Odds would not seem to favor it. "For now."

"Christ about us, that hurts! Feels like it's on fire! Where's Davy?"

"Don't know. Now will you be still?"

"Then who...?"

"Jimmy. Take her, will you?" With as much care as he could manage, he set the woman protesting on her feet and into the other man's charge. "Join up with Matt. See what weapons we've got. Try and figure out who's missing. And for godsake get under cover. I'll send anyone I find to you. I'm going to—" But the words were cut off by the next salvo. "Bloody hell!"

Downhill was death. The only possible safety was by the river.

As for waiting there, Molly had no more intention of waiting for fate to catch her than had any other woman of spirit since time began. Swiftly she threw on a shift and dragged on breeches and tied back her hair. Then she sat down cross-legged with four pistols and the powder horn in her lap, and one by one with trembling hands somehow got them loaded and primed. As soon as she was done, she scuffed into her low-heeled boots, thrust all but one of the pistols into her sash, and swiftly left the shambles of her house. On second thought, she came back for a spyglass, and started again.

The boom and thud of cannon had stopped only briefly. Reloading, she thought. That meant only seconds, but she was little and quick and she could take advantage of the lull. Keeping off the path itself, she moved through the brush until she had a view of the sea, framed in leaves and obscured by whisping smoke and the glare of sun on the water. here should be just one ship in the lagoon, her own. But a low black frigate was firing broadsides at the coastline and behind her, *Jealous Mary*'s foremast was shattered at the fighting top, the forward rigging a mess of tangles.

"All tattered and torn," she breathed with forgivable irony. She slipped open the spyglass and trained it on the unknown vessel. The sloop rigging had made her think it must be the *Testament* returned for some pious reason of its own, but no.

"Why, Sir Simon Benning! How very flattering! Pity the price of flattery is the lives of my friends."

The cries of the men on the beach and in the woods began to reach her, distant and removed. A few angry voices seemed to rally the others, but mainly it was panic and fear. Then the next rounds came in and there was no other sound at all.

Prentiss had not returned, which meant, she hoped, that he was gathering the men together. He would want to know what she had seen. Her mind racing ahead, she had an idea that knowing might not be enough. The men would try to fight on Benning's terms; she must be ready with a tack of her own. She slammed the glass home and waited for the next lull, then warily turned back to what was left of her little house.

When she found Prentiss and the lads huddled under the riverbank and flinching with every blast, she was dressed in her old blue gown and petticoats, with a scarf around her throat. She had wrapped a new silk sash twice about her waist, knotting the ends to hang properly, and brought the pistols wrapped in canvas instead. Dick was not delighted to see her, no matter how she was dressed.

"I thought I told you to stay there," he growled as she ran into his arms.

"And so you did, precisely as if you meant it," she shouted back, raising her voice over the explosions.

"One day you're going to have to learn to take orders." Some of the men smiled, and one of the married ones said, "Get used to it, Pilot."

"I was hoping to have a wife long enough to get used to it."

"And if my husband is going to die over me, I hope not to be the last to know of it!"

Then the firing stopped again, and they waited while the silence grew, almost as nerve-wracking as the bombardment.

Molly breathed at last and said, "I thought you might like to know who it is out there."

"And you have found this out. While you were busy disobeying orders."

"As it happens."

He waited. "Today?"

"Do you by any chance remember Captain Benning? Sir Simon Benning?"

The face she loved stiffened into the angry planes she saw on him only at war. "I remember you were supposed to be wed to that swine, aye."

"He seems to have found us."

The jaw only tightened further as she made her report, the glitter in the eyes grew harder. Out of fifty men ashore, they had lost ten for sure, with at least as many wounded, and who knew what the state of affairs aboard ship might be. It seemed likely that Davy and the others must be dead, or how could any of this be happening? That he could lay it all at Benning's door was almost a relief. It was not some random attack, and it was someone he already hated. Very economical. He would mourn Davy after avenging him.

The silence grew longer. Odds were good that meant a shore party. Benning, the infected pillock, must be coming ashore to reclaim his bride, presumably with armed troops.

"If I tell you to stay behind this time, will you do it?"

She shrugged a little, then nodded. "If you don't leave me too long. You know how I hate it."

He let a swift smile invade his face and kissed her, then called for Jimmy and Matt. Plans laid, weapons in hand, they each took ten men and moved forward slowly. Everyone went, even the wounded; even Kate, tight-bandaged and light-headed but not to be left behind. When Molly complained, it was Kate who silenced her.

"This whole business is Preacher's doing, milady. That means treachery on as many counts as the devil can whistle up. You say they're here for you? Then the last thing we must show him is you, d'ye see? Now you bide here and if there's nothing for a bit, then you can creep up and find some good place to watch if it's safe. But let the bastard not see you. If Davy's lost, as your lad says, we're likely all done for ado, but let's not make it easy, milady, eh?"

Molly didn't care much for this argument, especially since it made so much sense. She agreed at last, and so lay flat in the grass under the trees to watch them go, the remnants of her friends, her crew, her family deploying across the battle ground that had been their home. As long as she could, she trained her glass on Prentiss, though his form shifted and bobbed amongst the others, and disappeared first of all.

More silence. It seemed like hours. Then shouting, and the clatter of firearms, so much less than cannon but noise enough, and the breath of gun smoke began to drift toward her. More shouting as Jimmy brought his men in from the left, with Kate's skirling Gaelic battle cry rising above the baritone and tenor of men on the field. Then from off to the right where she knew Prentiss had taken his section, desperate cries, clashing swords, and all at once, silence. A single voice, unintelligible.

It was too much. Was it over? Had they won? Was Dick all right? She could wait no longer. She shoved the glass into her sash so no reflection could betray her. Pistol in hand, she ran across the clearing, and slipped into the laughing trees where she and Prentiss had sat and talked about children. As before, it gave shelter with a long, angled view of the beach.

The tableau that unfolded before her first made her weak with the same terror she had felt at the thought of Port Royal. They had lost. Well and truly lost.

In the distance the *Mary* seemed to be coming about and making for open sea, while down on the sand, the remainder of the crew was being rounded up, cruelly battered and manhandled into place. Hands were tied and a guard set while more boats from the *Blackbird* made into shore. Even Kate, who had weathered so many sieges and battlefields and survived so cheerfully, was cringing. That sight alone frightened Molly almost more than all the rest.

An officer was shouting orders. She realized with a start that it was Benning himself, just as foppish and just as brutal as she remembered. More so, perhaps, because the exquisite fashion plate he affected was so at odds in this rough place: the long scarlet coat in a fine wool velvet flaring over looped and skirted breeches, all thick with gold braid and dozens of buttons; the lace at his wrists and throat; the ludicrous wig; the gilded sword. Even his garter tassels were fringed with bullion.

But worse, far worse, he had Prentiss bound before him. They were snarling, she could see, like dogs, although the cross-breeze carried the sound away. Whatever Sir Simon said, she knew it would be disgusting, as if he believed it reasonable to decide whether to broil or to roast a prisoner before lunch.

Benning did most of the talking, of course, with occasional barks from Dick that only infuriated his captor more. In fact, he seemed to be holding Dick partly off the ground by his collar; as high perhaps as Benning could quite manage unaided. When the answer did not suit him, he struck his prisoner across the mouth.

Molly nearly cried out but only bare whimpers escaped her control. Angry tears would wait. At least he was alive.

She knew he must be trying to protect her. Even now marines were trotting down the long path with bits and pieces from their house, evidence of her occupation. The jewelry would be already in their own pockets, of course. That was fine. She could spare it. The jeweled wedding goblets she had already flung into the jungle, for spite. They would not have looked for the treasure back in the caves, and they had not found her. It was possible, she thought, just possible if she were clever to come out of this losing no more than trinkets. If she were shrewd enough.

In any case, this had to stop before Prentiss or anyone took any more damage on her account. She moved down and along the slope as delicately as possible. The same breeze that had carried away the voices masked her movement just as the blue gown and mottled light concealed her presence in the leaves.

The voices were clearer now. Benning was demanding her surrender, Prentiss denying she was there.

"She had a fever." Dick said as if for the hundredth time. "We left her on Tortuga. She may be dead by now, for all I know."

"And I tell you I know that is a damned lie." The fist poised to strike again.

"Let him go!" Molly stepped out from the trees, blatantly alive and well. Her one pistol rested lightly but with interest in one hand. She lifted and pulled back the cock with an ominous click. "Let him go!" Released at last, Prentiss folded grateful to his knees.

She would so much rather have worn breeches and sword, with the effect her fighting costume always had on unsuspecting men, but as it was, Benning hardly knew her. In fact, he looked twice at the pretty strumpet who stepped out into the sun.

"Molly?" For a moment the refined gallant was almost a schoolboy.

Her hair flew loose in the breeze, spangled with sunlight, her color high and her breath rapid, which enchanted the old shift and worn gown into something rare. The dusty freckles were new, and the fine gold chain that slithered around her neck and dove into the delightful cleavage.

"Faith, Molly, you are even prettier than I recall. The sea air must suit you."

Little and oddly garbed as she was, she drew herself up to her full pride, and spoke as though she were dressed to meet the Queen, gracious and even slightly condescending: "Do not, I pray you, presume on our acquaintance, Captain Benning. I think I am still Mistress September to you."

Prentiss twitched, but she quelled him with a thought. Safer that Benning not suspect she had changed her name and her status, if her husband were to survive the voyage home. Mendez might have told him, but the Preacher had never thought her wedding any more real than the ones he performed every day, so perhaps not. Just to be sure, she had knotted the precious red ring with other jewels and coins into the ends of her swaying sash. Her hands were naked.

"Whatever you like, my dear. I—"

He had finally worked out what had confused him, aside from the pistol which he chose to ignore. The dress she wore was no better than a rag, an abomination for a lady whose fortune he meant to marry.

"'Sblood, my child, what are you wearing! This is monstrous! Ah faith, never mind. Happily, your most charming aunt made me bring along some of your own clothes. This indignity need not last."

She wanted to spit on the ground as Davy would, or do, oh, something Kate might do if she had the upper hand, but the playing field was too fragile. Too much in one direction and all the others would close. So she contented herself with a delicate sneer and said only, "I can imagine. But 'tis all one, Captain, for I am not going with you."

"Is that so?"

"It is. I am of an age to make my own decisions, and I am doing so. Now release my friends and cast off for home."

"I'm afraid I cannot permit that, ma'am."

"I think you have no choice, since this pistol points straight at your heart."

"I admire your faith in the weapon, your skills, and the weather, my dear." She blinked, but nothing more. "I fear that if I leave you, then you should have to stay here alone, you and this ... woman."

"My servant," Molly snapped.

"Of course." He slipped a wink at Kate who only closed her eyes on pain and a desperate thirst. "Your servant, with whom I have no issue. My orders are to return these men and their ship—with its logs and all its ill-gotten treasure—to Port Royal for trial. Kidnap, murder, and piracy are not to be set aside at the whim of a young girl, no matter how handsome."

"My uncle—"

"It is your uncle's complaints that are the source of my orders. And the governor of Jamaica, Lord Vaughn, under whose authority the warrants are carried out. If it were up to me, I should far prefer to leave these villains and take you alone, but I fear the decision is no more mine than yours."

The pretty nose wrinkled with delicate distaste. "You are such a liar."

"Ah, you wound me!"

"Give me but one excuse, Captain, and I most certainly shall."

Sir Simon was tiring of the game. The sun was high, the jungle steaming, and the beach littered with bodies both alive and dead that already made this conversation unpleasant enough. His beautifully tied cravat was wilting. Worse, the gold braid of his uniform seemed to be curling in the heat.

He said, "My child, this will not do. Certainly I cannot return to Port Royal without you, and I cannot let these men escape justice. Since you persist in this nonsense, you leave me no choice."

With a sudden violence she had forgotten was his, he snapped his fingers. "That one!"

A raised musket fired, and Jimmy dropped like a broken doll with a bubbling oath and a hole in his shoulder. Molly screamed.

"If you prefer, I can simply execute them all here!" Benning shouted, a gleam of pleasure in his eye. "All of your lovers, here and now! This one is a murderer, that one a thief, even your serving woman is a whore. All of them are pirates. Fine company you keep, madam."

His gaze lighted once again on Prentiss, whose long hair fell forward over his eyes. Benning snatched at Dick's collar again and jerked the hated face into the sun. Molly whimpered to see the bruises already beginning to rise, but held her tongue.

"Aye, what of this one, the one who stole you away, eh? This drunkard, this petty thief, and a clumsy one at that!"

The mocking eyes shut tight against the glare, and Benning let him go, shaking the pilot like rubbish from his fastidious hand.

"Aye you, my fine lad, you cannot face me, can you. For I know your tricks. Was he teaching you his trade, Mistress, when he foolishly made me his target? This Dick Prentiss, this swinish son of a dockside whore, this seasoned voluptuary." He loved the way the words filled his mouth, the loathsome accusations rolling like arsenic into wine. "This filth, this heartless despoiler of young women?"

"No!"

"Did you not know that, Mistress? Did you know that is how your pretty, light-fingered paramour spent his days in Port Royal? And elsewhere, I've no doubt. Seducing honest wives and decent widows. Charming silly young girls away from their families and out of their fortunes? A nice career your friend has had. Piracy and whoring, thieving and riotous living. Now pimping as well, I see."

"Stop it! Stop it! It isn't true! He was a friend of my father!"

"Is that what he's told you? Aye, well I suppose it may be so, for your father was no better. All the more curious then, ain't it, your father dying as he did."

"You lying bastard!" Prentiss shouted, struggling to stand. "Molly, no!"

Pushed beyond belief, she had pulled the trigger. But the flint snapped, sparked. The powder hissed. And failed. Prentiss groaned and buried his face in his bound hands. In the shocked silence, Molly could only stare and cry out in horror, "No!"

They had been neglectful. Last night's rain had gotten into the powder, and nearly every charge had failed. Their whole effort to meet Benning on a fairly armed footing had been nothing but disaster, like the whole rest of the day. The only guns Molly had heard were the Navy's.

Sir Simon sneezed, then barked his sharp, nasty laugh and turned his back on them all. He would have liked to go on. Heaven knew there was more to be said. But he had wasted enough of the King's time on his own business. It was perishing hot, and the tide was turning. "Take her," he said, and sauntered toward his launch. "Oh, and do bring the rest."

18

MARQUE AND REPRISAL

THE *JEALOUS MARY'S* CAPTAIN sat on his quarterdeck exposed to the noonday sun, and seethed while his own men cleared away the carnage and the litter of his broken ship under a humorless detachment of marines. He watched grim-faced while young Billy Mariott, Will Keaton and Paul DeRoet were put over the side without ceremony, with no words spoken over them, like traitors buried at a crossroads. The lads who came to take up the bodies wept openly and would not meet their captain's eyes for shame. He was not a man given to sentiment, and what in another man might have turned to tears was in Davy York nothing but cold, awful anger.

After a while Davy found himself transferred under guard to the *Blackbird,* to watch from another man's deck while his ship was sailed away under a green lieutenant he'd not have trusted with a rowboat. Sailed away dishonored like a prize of war, her treasures to be paraded in triumph in Port Royal, her men stripped of the fair reward for their pains in the service of their King. It nearly broke him to watch her go. The *Jealous Mary* had been his for four years, by Rafe's legacy and the will of the men who had voted him captain on a blood-stained beach in Panama. She'd been damaged before, and had seen her men die, but not like this. Never like this.

Sorrow and anger resolved in him like an icy chord. He would salvage his ship and his reputation, and what there might be of his luck. Then Sir Simon Benning would die. In the meantime, all he could do was watch from the swaying fo'c'stle deck while the bastard rounded up his people on the coastline. His men, dammit. His men and two women who should not even have been there.

So they found him, still staring blankly when they were brought aboard. Molly screamed "Davy!" and ran to him. Prentiss shouted and Kate only scowled through her own pain, though it was glad she was to see himself alive after all.

The marines, just soldiers who happened to draw this assignment, had no orders about the girl and let her slip through, but there was to be no disorder among the rest. Muskets barred the way, and those who declined to cooperate were clubbed to their knees.

"Prentiss, don't!" was not enough to stop him. When Dick slammed cursing to the deck under the brass heel of a musket, all Kate could do was *move along here!* with the rest. The redcoats would drag him up eventually.

Speechless with relief, Molly ran to Davy who opened his great arms with the black chain looped between them and closed her in. It was good, he thought, that Rafe's girl had made it through. Before they all died, he had things to tell her. She wanted to know, and he owed it to Rafe.

"Molly," he said, patting her shining hair, then he stood her away at arm's length. The feel of her was a comfort, and he had no use for comfort. "What lass, no weeping now. What would yer old man say?"

She looked up into the hard grey eyes and gasped just a little. She knew him in his anger, but not in this lightless, chipped-flint rage. If Simon could see this, she thought, he'd be wise to kill them all now and be done with it.

"Davy, what is it?"

He had things to tell her, but first things first.

"It looks as if I'm not to talk to my officers, what's left of 'em. I'm sorry, lass, but you get to deliver me the butcher's bill. Report now, if you please."

Slightly in awe but with graceful economy she laid out the tale, named the dead and the wounded, and described without excuses what they had tried and how they had lost. He said only: "So Prentiss is all right, then. And Kate too. I'm glad. That's one good thing." If he swallowed a little heavily, there was no reason to mention it.

"Davy?" He looked down as if finally seeing the pretty, troubled face; as if hers were the first eyes he had met in a hundred years. She said, "Your report, if you please, sir."

Unaccustomed as he was to taking orders, he nodded heavily and filled in his part of the story, which proved harder than he'd expected. He was no nearer tears than before, but he could only speak because the anger was damped, compressed and tucked into a corner until it could be applied to effect and with force, so the words came hard to him. Mercifully, it took little time to rehearse the tale and tally the dead. Of how it felt to lose his friends, and his ship, there was nothing to say.

To Molly the tears came easily, laced with anger of a warmer kind. In finding him alive, she had assumed, they had all foolishly assumed, that everyone else would be safe as well. She swore bitterly in English, then even worse in French, and he put his arms around her again, banking her rage with his own, until armed men came and presented Capt. Benning's compliments ma'am, and would she be pleased to come in out of the sun. She started to tell them what she'd be pleased to do, but her captain let her go and said sharply,

"September! Go do what you must for now, and that's orders. See you mind them for a change."

The voice that acknowledged him was hoarse but steady. "Aye, Captain."

As correct as a countess, she nodded her courtesy, untangled herself from his chains, and allowed herself to be led away.

Life had not been silent these past months. Music and cannon fire, the yells of battle and the occasional quarrel in steel do not make for quiet moments. Even five uneventful days had their share of argument and outcry, orders shouted, scuffles broken up, and the sullen slap of blue waters against the *Blackbird*'s hull cutting the sea smartly under a fair wind for Jamaica.

But silence is a relative thing. Even with all these incidental noises, nothing could match the ring and shout of Port Royal that reached out to meet them. A hundred great ships rode at anchor in the harbor, and a double handful of smaller ones, lighters carrying merchandise and plunder to the warehouses on Thames Street; pleasure boats and island sloops and Naval frigates like the *Blackbird* that patrolled the waters round about the island, the one English jewel picked loose from the Spanish crown. The harbor was a forest of masts.

The *Blackbird* passed under the grey stone ramparts and awesome guns of Fort James, and docked and tied up in the usual tidy way. To her larboard side, *Jealous Mary* dutifully limped into place. George Alcott, looking surprisingly efficient, carried a handful of neatly copied and cannily adjusted manifests between board covers while, just as if he knew what he was doing, he crisply ordered the unloading. It meant dragooning the *Mary's* own crew for service under the eye of a modest detachment from the fort.

The soldiers were not here to supervise a perfectly ordinary cargo, but to seize and arrest David York, Richard Prentiss, and Jimmy Fitts for crimes upon the high seas. At their head of the arresting party, Colonel Rhetford waited where the *Blackbird's* gangway met the dock. He did not look happy.

Waiting on the fo'c'stle deck in layers of pale green satin, Molly sighed for the hundredth time. At her elbow, the ever-practical Kate agreed.

"So," she said, adjusting her new mistress's point lace and arranging her cleavage with appalling familiarity. "At one jump I go from head bitch to lady's maid. Is that a promotion, do y' think, milady?"

Molly just stared fixedly at the complement of redcoats poised to meet them, almost at her feet, and at the Colonel gravely waiting to come aboard.

"The pay is better but you don't get to lie down as much. Christ, Kate, it's as if I had never gone! Everything looks exactly the same as it did, only a little smaller." She added, shifting slightly in her clothes: "And tighter."

"Stop squiggling, milady. The price of beauty. That dress looks damned fine on you. 'Twould be silly as holly at Lent without the stays, and you know it."

"Never felt silly in stays before, that's all."

"If that's all, then your life's a fine thing, milady, and hardly worth the complaint."

There would be no winning this, that was clear. Besides, to be fair, Kate was wounded herself, and still wearing the same dress, roughly patched and fiercely rinsed, that she had nearly died in, and had no better. Molly knew she should be more grateful.

She gave something like a shrug but less committed. "What next," she muttered. Now Rhetford had come aboard to meet Benning, exchanging salutes and a few tight words. "What bloody next?"

Kate sighed and thumped the girl. "You mind that tongue, milady, or the whole thing falls apart."

"Ah yes. Four months of proving that I don't have to live as they wanted me to, and now the only weapon left to me is the one I hate most. And it's broken. These freckles are hardly ladylike. And good lord, my hands! I look like a laundress! Aunt Henrietta will have two fits. God is laughing at me, Kate." She clucked in something like humor. "How's Prentiss?"

"He adores you. Now hush, and let the bastards have their say. Here he is."

"Oh, God!"

She had not been permitted to see him. She only knew he was alive because for a while Davy had been brought to dine with Sir Simon and herself, out of some perverse courtesy, and with oblique and charming double entendre he had passed a little news. Dick was well, unhurt, beside himself, hopeful, and he loved her. Davy put himself out considerably to present, as Molly did, an urbane and confident air, and somehow they managed never to mention Prentiss by name while in truth they talked of little else. If Benning knew some kind of code was passing between them, he did not have the key to it.

But after the first few days and a blistering argument, Molly dined alone with Kate and that avenue closed.

Kate having more latitude, however, had also time to smoke a pipe with the crew, and flirt with the officers, and insinuate herself into corners that let her pass messages more directly.

The one time Molly tried, she had been found and returned before she could do more than touch his fingers and hear him once say her name through a barred window. After that, Benning made it very clear that the price of disobedience was Kate's safety. Long

Kate Riley, the long-legged whore from Kerry, for whom he had no warrant but Molly's friendship, which he could use even if he could not fathom it. Molly couldn't bear to tell her how she was being used.

Still the sound of Dick's voice, two syllables no more, was precious. They hadn't harmed him especially after that first morning. It would be all right, something would happen. And now, almost at her feet, there he was stumbling up with Davy and Jimmy blinking into the hard light of morning, unshaven, stinking, and looking inexpressibly weary. Jimmy's shoulder sported a wrapped bandage of sorts, filthy but marginally better than nothing. Prentiss's face looked swollen with bruises, and he seemed to be limping.

"Oh, God! Dickon!"

The words leapt from her, lost she hoped in the din of the wharf. But he had heard.

She saw him jump at the sound of her voice, then steadily he turned as if to speak to Davy and lifted glittering eyes to where she stood. He looked awful, he looked wonderful, their eyes met and he was there, deep in her mind with assurance and love. He lifted his bound hands to his lips in a gentle salute, then someone corrected the liberty with a blow.

"Oh, Kate!"

There was a shout and a scuffle below, and everything changed. Without warning, a redcoat was crashing to the deck and Prentiss had a knife between his hands. Davy's ropes parted, then Dick's in turn and Jimmy's at last.

Weapons appeared out of the air, and Benning might have died right there, except both Prentiss and his captain wanted him and had never reached an agreement. A musket fired from the dock before Rhetford could stop it.

"For godssake, hold your fire, damn you!"

But the target was moving with the swell of the sea, and the ball sang past Prentiss's face.

Rhetford's pistol had already vanished as had Benning's under the clever hands of the street thief they had come to arrest, and both now pointed back at them, cocked and ready, like Davy's mocking grin.

By the time Molly applauded, crowing with triumph, her husband and his friend were perched over the starboard rail, hanging precariously from the ratlines sporting idiotic grins and a pair of naval issue cutlasses in their capable hands. The crowd that had formed set up a cheer. Arrests and hangings, those were good entertainment, but making the soldiery look ridiculous? That was a treat. Prentiss as always knew his audience, and played to it now.

"If you please, gentlemen!" he announced with a flourish and an energy belying his looks. "It's been delightful, but I fear we cannot stay. Molly, love! Watch for me!" He blew her a kiss and loosed his grip.

In that frozen instant, a dagger they had not reckoned on spun out over the watching crowd dead straight for Prentiss, and buried itself in his breast.

"Dickon!" Molly shrieked. Jimmy cursed and reached for him, but there was no help.

His face a mask of blank surprise, Dick's desperate fingers clutched at the lines an instant longer.

"Bloody hell," he said thickly, clawing at the knife. He flung a desperate look to Molly even as the tenuous grip gave way and he fell, not quite as he had meant to, into the welcoming sea. Covered with horror and a spray of blood, Jimmy too let go with a growl. A double splash, and nothing more.

Molly howled for someone to for godssake give her a sword, and sprinted for the main deck where Simon Benning slouched smug but not perhaps surprised. She was half way there, a fury of green silk and ribbons, before long-legged Kate caught her up bodily, lifting her off the deck, her own wounds opening like fire for the effort, and wrestled her down.

Kate would have killed the poxy bastard herself and cheerfully, if she could, but all she could do now was rock Molly in her arms and mutter imprecations in Gaelic, a litany to the tune of her own astonishing tears.

While Molly screamed her despair, a voice in the crowd cried bitter disappointment in Turkish even as hard brass-butted muskets beat him senseless. He'd been aiming for Jimmy Fitts and the bastard had escaped him. Then a misjudged blow that was supposed to break Turk's nose instead pushed bone into brainpan, so that his last fleeting thoughts of revenge failed along with his life.

When the soldiers rolled the tattered body into the water, their sergeant cursed them for the careless scum they were. Didn't they know the bugger they'd just pummeled to death was the one who had given evidence against these here pirates? Then with an ugly laugh, he swore they had earned an extra ration of rum for saving everyone a lot of bother, and formed them up again.

Davy was over-powered before he could surrender, as he had meant to do all along. Yet another plan dismantled. He spat full in Benning's complacent face, and for his pains took one unchecked blow across the mouth. There would have been more but for Jack Rhetford's sharp intervention.

Davy said nothing as they marched him smartly away under a tight escort excited with death, eager for the rum that made this duty almost bearable. The cheerful bastards even congratulated him on a valiant effort. Might have worked, sir, but then you never know, eh?

Others peering over the dockside or examining the waters between the *Blackbird* and the stone piers reported no further sign of the pilot or his partner, neither ripple nor bubble. There was no reason to suppose that the one wasn't dead or that the other could swim. Well, that was that, then.

Crude jokes were already circulating on the dock as the crowd, frustrated of either further gallantry or continued mayhem, sorted itself into its ordinary patterns. The disgraced men of the *Jealous Mary* stood numb, staring across both decks frozen by this last disaster. They had to be flogged to take up their work again.

Kate did not know Jack Rhetford, so when he presumed to kneel and take Molly's hand, she snapped at him as she would at any impossible man.

"Will ye not leave her be! Haven't ye done enough, for the love o' God!"

"Someone has, I can see that," he said. Molly's face turned up to him in deep anger and bottomless pain. "And more than enough."

"I suppose you want to arrest her as well!"

"Not at all. Molly, my dear, I'm here to take you home."

"Ye bastard, she was home till five days ago. Who the devil are you to take her anywhere?"

Molly made the effort, tried to say who he was, but the tears closed her throat and she waved them away. If her life was over, what difference did it make if anyone misunderstood anyone else.

So he introduced himself, as gently as he could considering he did not ordinarily account for himself to women such as she. Then he asked, "And who are you?"

"I am Long Kate Riley from Kerry, and you touch my lady at your peril." Her nose was red and her rosy cheeks were sticky with tears she never shed. Never. Embarrassed and angry, she would have defied the King himself and yet not been able to tell you where they had come from.

Rhetford smiled a little, knowing now exactly what she was, but still puzzled. Well, explanations would wait. Clearly there were stories to be told, but not here.

"She's an extraordinary girl, your lady, isn't she?"

Kate rolled her dark eyes as if that were the most foolish thing she had ever heard a man say in a lifetime of foolish men. Then as her clever brain moved finally away from unfamiliar sentiment, she began to see him for what he was.

"You're a friend of hers, so," she said tentatively. "Not like that *gombeen* bastard yonder."

She liked that his lip curled at the comparison. It was clear, he was in fact a proper soldier and a gentleman, well dressed but no powdered fop like that other.

"I am her friend, yes. And her family expects me to take her home. To their home," he added when she drew breath again to object.

All right, he spoke well and even, knowing what she was, politely. "I'm to go with her, mind you."

He nodded. "Of course."

She decided to trust him. "Come now, milady," she said, unwrapping Molly's arms from her own. "Come love, what cheer! The colonel says it's time to go. I think me we'd rather not spend another minute aboard this slave ship, aye?"

Molly could barely hear through the anger and panic roaring in her brain, and conning the words that came to her was impossible. She also had no mind and no care at all for what happened next, and so she allowed Jack, patient steady Jack, to help her stand, and waited dumbly while he even gave a hand to Kate, who thanked him.

She also gave no resistance when on impulse he lifted her into his arms, an incongruously frothy package in tear-stained satin and ruined lace, and carried her away. Sir Simon actually tried to forestall him, expecting to make some cavalier's gesture to his departing guest, but Rhetford pushed past him.

He took two steps and without looking at her said, "Don't do it, Kate." The woman had her skirt balled in her hands, clearing the way for a scouring kick to Sir Simon's knee. "Ye'll only make yourself dirty."

She blinked, scowled, and settled for calling the villain three filthy names in her native tongue, before striding to the street where the Colonel had hired a chair, God bless 'im, so Molly needn't walk at all.

The water was green, jade green as a girl's eyes and perpetually cloudy with silt. Five fathoms down, the sunlight failed even at noon. Which was why, still crashing in a cloud of white bubbles and the accumulated trash of the docks, Jimmy prayed he had marked how Prentiss had fallen and where, and prayed just in general for luck. Luck was the only chance they had now, and the faithless bitch had been remarkably shy of late.

Still sinking, he reached out to his right and he fancied, but perhaps he was drowning after all, that a light hand took his own and guided it. The mocking laughter in his ears was certainly his own delusion, but against all chance, the solid shape of a linen-cased arm filled his fingers, and long dark hair not his own billowed like kelp in the green green haze. Blue eyes stared unfocused and still surprised.

Lungs burning, he pulled Prentiss into his arms and with no hope at all, kicked toward the surface but not too near, then dragged them both along the barnacled side, savaging his one free hand and a leading shoulder, but keeping to the curve of the hull.

"This is the last time, mate," he thought haphazardly as he made his goal, the broad swaying shape of the rudder. His head broke the surface just under the stern where none would be watching. Though he wanted desperately to sob a great breath, he managed somehow to stay quiet. It was, he thought, perhaps his least appreciated talent. "The very last time."

It might well be. Dick wasn't breathing and there was still that knife in his chest, though perhaps not so deeply as all that. Wedged a bit on a rib bone, maybe, but mainly anchored in the thick deerskin of his old buff coat. Threads of blood wafted out of the wound, teased into ribbons by the slap of the water under his chin.

Jimmy's own wounded shoulder burned like a bloody bonfire, but he'd had worse. Never mind that now. They'd always managed before, and there was no time to dither over a sudden change of plans. There was space to be crossed between the two ships in silence and in speed. Mind that, and nothing else.

Salt stung eyes scanned up. *Right.* Guards posted, but concentrating elsewhere, focused maybe on whatever had become of the last bloody hero and his last bloody flourish. On hustling Davy away. On whatever terrible thing Molly might be living through, giving them all a show. Good as a hanging any day, he thought, and lurched into a clumsy side stroke for the *Mary's* swelling hull.

He could swim. Of course he could swim though many sailors could not. Jimmy Fitts had grown up in London along the river where boys earned bright shillings for retrieving a gentleman's hat or a lady's gilded fan, or their silver goblets tossed away in a pretty temper. Or diving for survivors when a troupe of gallants on a drunken dare offered the boatmen a bonus to shoot the bridge, as they said, in the dark with the tide against them. And sometimes they dived for the gold sovereigns which other more fortunate gentlemen tossed in the tide just to bet on which boy came up from the sludge first.

Boys on the river learned to swim. Sailing men, who knew how slim the chances of rescue at sea could be, did not. The crowd could be forgiven their assumptions, even thanked.

The strokes were awkward but blessedly few. The *Mary's* tiller by some lucky chance had been locked down properly so the whipstaff lay still in the water, giving him a slippery but otherwise steady purchase. He fancied for a moment even that Prentiss's chest moved, almost as if he had found a shallow breath. Maybe their luck was turning after all.

Better late than never, Jimmy thought. Hearing again the odd laughter in his mind's ear, as you might say, he slipped them both round the old girl's rudder, then checked the dockside again. Not a soul seemed to look, never mind notice. Bloody odd, but he didn't like to question it.

Was Prentiss breathing at all? Sure he wouldn't have been able to hold a breath as he fell, so he'd have taken some water on that first tumble and the long crawl afterwards. But how much?

Covered in shadow, Jimmy took a chance and put his hand to the dagger, an ugly thing but wickedly sharp. Yes, the very tip seemed to have caught on bone but it was the swelling leather holding it in place. If he drew it out, the wound would hurt like hellfire but might not be as bad as it looked, and shouldn't kill. The salt sea would cleanse the wound and if... *yes!* Just as well Prentiss was unconscious, or the scream would have been mortal for them both.

And look at that! They'd both left their cutlasses, so neatly won, in the sea but now they had a knife. That was something. Jimmy passed it to his other hand and, taking yet another chance, thrust the thing into the bobbing side of their ship. It stuck, and gave him a hand hold where he was instead of twenty feet away in sunnier, more visible waters. All right, now if he shook Prentiss, shook him hard and thumped his chest! *Yes!*

Dick hacked, Jimmy thought, like cannon shot but nothing against the noise of the town. Shaken some more, he coughed again and spewed green water, gagged on it and vomited while Jimmy held him under one strong arm.

"Jesus!" Prentiss gasped and swore again, with less elegance. The voice was coarse and raw, but there.

"You are," said Jimmy, "the laziest bastard I ever knew,"

Eyes streaming, Prentiss coughed again and turned a rancid eye on his friend. "Aye," he rasped. "And the next time you can take the knife."

"Nay, squire, I took the bullet last week. Still hurts like bloody hell. Your turn."

"Ah, well there it is."

"I don't suppose you feel like a swim?"

"Not especially."

"I'll just be leaving you here then?"

Dick looked half-drowned but vaguely thoughtful. With a hand on Jimmy's good shoulder for balance, he let himself slip under the water just long enough to come up again, this time with his hair slicked back behind his head instead of in his face. "On t'other hand, since you've gone to all the trouble."

"Again."

"Pity to waste the effort."

"Specially as they've failed t' kill you, and all."

Dick nodded soberly but with real gratitude. "So it seems."

With new wounds and old irony they managed, as a dozen times before, to slip through the net that had been set for them. It wasn't exactly the plan they had settled on, but near enough as made no matter. If Prentiss could keep from fainting, they'd be fine.

Keeping to the *Mary's* side, heads barely breaking the waterline, they slid like otters under her bow and under the wharf, under the feet of everyone who might have wondered where they were, or might have wept to see them, and moved with painful slowness from beam to tarry beam, landing to landing in the shadows. An aching hour later they came ashore just a quarter mile away on the careening sands below the King's Yard and the Governor's House, almost under the ramparts of Fort Carlisle. Since they were dead, no one cared.

By that time everything hurt. They slogged up onto the beach and sat in the sun comparing pains in the comparative shade of a galleon being chopped and remasted into a brigantine. Workmen taking their midday meal with round bottles of beer jeered and offered to share their dinners with the ragged deserters who'd washed up on their shore.

Too exhausted to eat, they each accepted a long mouthful of beer, then lay back and fell asleep in the shade of a stretched mainsail, oblivious to the hammering and the grind of saws and the creeks of pulleys, the shouts of workmen returned to their labors.

The sun was falling toward the sea long after the day's work ended when they roused stiffened joints and wandered into town. Strange to be in a city again, elbow to elbow with five thousand people in perpetual riot. As they turned their steps for Huggins Street and the familiar shadows of the Saracen's Head, Prentiss prayed that Driscoll hadn't let out his room.

And in the corner of his ear, as you might say, he heard a bell-like giggle that made him turn around.

"Moll?"

Jimmy started. "You heard it too?"

Eyes met, brows furrowed. "Not Molly, I suppose."

"I swear I heard it before," Jimmy said. "Back when you was trying to drown me. I couldn't see you or anything, then by God, there you were under my hand. I could've—"

No. Heads shook the thought away, and they left it alone. If Luck, their fickle goddess, had decided to flirt with them again, best not to mention it.

They resumed their painful progress through the alleys and side streets, giving the lockup and Fort James a wide berth, and stopping too often to let Prentiss catch his breath. The Lime Street market was shutting down as they cut across its northern corner, rolling away from a half dozen soldiers taking their ease. Prentiss idled long enough to pick a straw hat off a counter behind Tiny Pepper's back, and shuffle into the next alley. The skill was in the shaking hands, but just barely.

"This is going to be bloody," he said.

"Minor setbacks, no more," said Jimmy, covering for him automatically.

"No, this here!" Dick slumped exhausted against the shaded wall, letting his head roll to one side. His good hand pressed coat and shirt over the gash that burned like burning match in his chest. "It's bleeding again, and I think…"

Against his will, a wince and a gasp escaped from him, and he swore.

Jimmy Fitts frowned. It wasn't like Prentiss to notice a little wound. Something was wrong.

"Look, The Bull's just here. We can get us a drink, rest a bit." Find a surgeon.

"All right," Dick breathed. "But send to the Saracen's Head, eh? Let someone know we're on— on the way. If Molly … If … Christ, I hope Driscoll hasn't sold the rest of my clothes!"

At least his sense of humor was intact, he thought, even if his chest was split open.

The warrens of Port Royal would hide anyone who wished to disappear, and they had friends everywhere who would keep their secrets. Now, dead or alive, they let the back streets swallow them up.

The air in King's Lane was not so free, no matter how much cleaner it might be. Lady FitzRobert wanted a proper homecoming to welcome their lost girl to the bosom of her family, and of course to proceed with the marriage plans so rudely shattered. She did not care much for Sir Simon Benning herself, but he seemed to have changed his mind again. Did that make him unsteady? Henrietta thought not.

The pity was that Molly did not seem happy to be home, rescued from those despicable pirates. And that woman, that bog-

Irish Riley woman, was impossible, but she must be borne, if only for peace in the house. Four weeks had passed in civil quiet, for the most part, it being Port Royal. Now all at once and past all bearing the world was upside down again. Henrietta bustled to return her niece into decent society.

Molly did nothing. She rose as bidden each morning and dressed dutifully with Kate's help. She sat at table with dish after dish in front of her and from time to time agreed to force a bite past her lips. The tears had dried but she moved in a daze. The neighbors called, and all the young people. She had become in some tawdry way a sensation.

Captured by pirates, tortured surely and tormented, subjected to who knows what indignities, and finally rescued by the gallant Captain Benning! It was all too exciting, and they wanted to know everything. Had she been raped? They looked almost hopeful.

She tried to tell them a little, which made the girls giggle and look shocked behind their fans. It hardly mattered what she said. Everything was astonishing, alarming, not to be believed. They were delighted. Even this new maid of hers, outrageously Irish, bespoke some outlandish series of events.

Wedding plans were whispered and dresses planned, young gentlemen compared who might escort them. They sat, the young ladies of Port Royal, with Molly in the bright morning room, an aviary of silk and ribbons, sucking down tea and sweet cakes and chattering as if she paid them any mind.

"You do know I cannot marry Sir Simon Benning?" Molly said without preamble.

Brittle silence descended, then shattered in a partita of shrill laughter. "Oh, *ma chère amie*, what a wonderful joke!" French tags had become the rage in her absence.

"No, no, I cannot. I—"

"Molly September, you are the most cunning girl!"

"My name is Prentiss," she said plainly, and examined minutely the porcelain teacup in her hands, one of a set she had liberated from the *Santa Martiana*. The sounds of cannon fire and Spanish curses rang in her ears. "I am Molly Prentiss now."

That made them laugh more heartily, and if possible more coarsely. So droll!

"So it's true, *n'est-ce pas?*" The accent was as awful as the manner. "You actually went through some heathen ritual with one of them? Some form of marriage, my father said, but hardly binding."

Molly turned a dead gaze at Celia Trout who, God knoweth why, expected to be her maid of honour. Carefully she said, "I made my vow."

"Oaths taken under duress are not binding, my father says. So it ain't a proper marriage, is it? Lord, how could it be with one of *them*. Besides, I heard he was topped by one of his own men, or some such thing."

The delicate cup crashed to the floor, splashed cold tea on a half dozen hems.

"He is not dead!"

Watch for me, he had said. She had watched him fall. *Watch for me.*

"I said my vows, I have a ring, and the captain—"

"Milady!" Kate's sour voice cut through the jumble in her brain, and she stopped. The only voice she needed to hear was Dickon's, and the only one that made any sense was Kate's. "You promised."

She sat down again in a descending fog, the image of Dick falling from the rigging clear before her.

At last, sweetly she focused and resettled the mask of respectability with a dull smile. She said, "Oh dear. I pray you forgive me, Celia."

Collecting all those startled, puffy faces with her cloudy eyes she added, "You have all been very kind. Life has been—disordered, lately, you see. So many changes."

Celia, now that she had an understanding with Drake Ffoulkes, felt quite the *doyen* of the young set once again.

"Ladies," she sniffed, not altogether unkindly. "We can see how weary the poor creature is. Such an ordeal."

She had been reading her mother's books and waiting in the afternoons upon Mary Morgan, Sir Henry's lady, so she had all the good manners money could buy. "I believe we should withdraw."

Then she stood, and the whole giddy flock like a lake of flamingos rose fluttering with her.

Molly had one good grateful look in her catalog still, and turned it now on the appalling young woman who presumed to direct the company. Would it do? A glance at Kate seemed to confirm. She did have some care for those around her, out of habit and general good nature. But this was no longer her world. She longed for the open sea, the lift of the deck under her feet, the perpetual wind, and the warm steady light of Dick Prentiss.

She accepted airy kisses instead from each young woman and had Perkins show them to the door. The silence that closed in after them was clear and pleasant. Birds sang in the garden, and shafts of sunlight angled into the room, comfortable and bright.

But she had had enough of little chairs and little cakes, little courtesies. So she thumped a tasseled cushion to the floor and kicked it straight into the sunbeams, then sat on it cross-legged like a boy, a disordered bonbon of changeable rose and gold taffeta. Remarkable for a girl in stays, she slumped over her knees, a collection of sighs. If he wasn't dead, where was he? *Watch for me.*

"Dear girl!" said Kate, and dropped beside her and lifted the troubled face to meet hers. "Hush now. Look at me."

When Molly's eyes came up, they were dry and certain. "Kate, it's not true. If he were dead, I would know it."

The older woman took a breath to consider the wisdom of pointing out that every girl waiting on the edge of her first battlefield thinks the same. She leaned away to pick up the glittering shards of teacup, and said it anyway.

Molly bridled. "And you think that's what this is, a camp girl's wishful thinking?"

"Bless me, lass, but I do," Kate sighed. "I know you loved him, but he's gone. You loved the adventure he gave you, but it's over. Ye're luckier than that camp girl, I can tell you."

"And how's that?"

"You've come home."

"To this!"

"Aye, to this. Mark you, luckier than that girl whose handsome soldier is a rag of blood and offal, the laughing fellow she followed from her village in South Kerry? She has no money to speak of. She has the clothes on her back and an evil reputation among honest women. Her parents won't want her, if they wanted her at all. If she's strong and lucky, if she can cook or make friends, she'll be all right. She'll have another man in a day or two, and he'll be dead or have left her by the next summer."

"She didn't really love him, then."

"You're wiser than me, milady."

"How can you know? You don't even believe in love!"

"There's so little evidence for it in the world, lass. 'Tis better not to."

"And I at least have all this." With a theatrical gesture she caught up the finely appointed room, the clothes, and jewels and more.

"And so you do."

"Kate, what am I to do!"

Long Kate gathered her into capable arms, and rocked her like a child for another moment's sympathy. A moment was enough.

"Let him go, my girl." And her voice now was firm. "Let him go. Easy or hard, there's other men to think of. Captain Davy, God save 'im, goes to defend himself tomorrow, and he'll hang unless you remember your part."

No matter what else, Davy still lived and it was Molly's job to keep his head out of the noose. That much had not changed.

"Come along now," Kate said giving her a shake. "Remember what you are!"

"I know who I am," said Molly with a stubborn toss of those bright curls

"Aye, but what are you? Ye're the canny lass that adjusted the accounts in two languages, ain't you? You're Rafe September's daughter, and queen of the western isles."

"They'll believe me, won't they?"

"What virtuous maiden would speak for the pirates that took her against her will?" She could not help the smile. "And subjected her to all manner of insult."

"All manner!" Molly agreed, with a genuine blush. "You're right, of course. If Davy's innocent, so are the others. My God, if Prentiss were alive and anyone knew of it, Kate! If Benning knew!"

Kate nodded, betraying only a little of the relief she felt. "He is dead, *mo criodh*, and you must believe it, so."

She did not add that for the girl's own sake, they must also get her safely married.

Watch for me!

Somewhere, perhaps just outside the garden window, a tinkling laughter ended in a kind of chirp and the clash of little bells.

Davy York had been idling in relative comfort deep within Fort James, rolling dice against himself in silence. The food was acceptable, though not Kate's. She'd only been allowed the one visit, bringing news and a pie, but since then, no word had come from anyone.

At least the jailers were courteous company. They were not permitted to explain the charges against him, but he knew perfectly well what they were. He had no recourse to lawyers, but he also had no need of them. If Benning had his way, and FitzRobert would see to that, he'd be swinging from Execution Dock by nightfall. Except for Molly, on whom everything depended.

By the time they escorted him through the crowded room in Government House, he'd begun to give up hope of that. There had been no word; she hadn't come or sent Kate. He supposed Prentiss's death must have unhinged her mind, though he had hoped she was stronger than that. Still, a woman was a fragile thing, even this one. More likely she was cursing his name, and rightly so. His men were his responsibility, even the blistering mad ones like Prentiss. And maybe it was fair payment for other sins besides.

When they hauled him into the Governor's chamber it was over-crowded, hot, and sticky with humidity though the December sky outside arched clear and blue, untroubled with cloud. A little breeze made its way through the gallery of open windows on the one side of the garden level chamber, but the crush of velvet and good wool gabardine warmed it up again.

A dozen stout gentlemen of indeterminate function stood about, cuff to gilt-edged cuff, fine copies of one another in their long curled wigs and high heeled shoes. Sir Simon Benning smirked glossily among them. Someone, doubtless a bad-tempered whore, had lately scored his cheek though the red wheals were powdered over.

Even so branded, the villain presumed to take the hand of a remarkably pretty woman sitting to one side in a cloud of cream-colored moiré satin and lace, prinked up with silk ribbons and a sash the color of her eyes. Her golden-red hair was knotted prettily at the top of her head, with the curls fluffed out at the sides and back spilling onto creamy shoulders. Other fashionably curling wisps floated on a clear brow powdered to disguise a dusting of freckles. She did not, *good girl!* seem to care for the fellow's intimacy. Then the knowing green eyes met Davy's, and deliberately, remarkably, winked.

Smoothly he removed his gaze, stunned nevertheless. *That* was Prentiss's Molly? God's death, no wonder...

Perhaps there was some hope after all. The wink should mean she was here to refute the charges as planned, not confirm them, unless her composure meant she didn't care. He made an effort not to hope. Whatever her intention, she was certainly a dazzling sight and if it was to be his last one, then at least he had that.

At the other end of the room, FitzRobert looked nastily triumphant, with a posture less indolent but just as smug as Benning's. He shuffled some papers officiously at the Governor's desk, then took a seat in one of the only other chairs. It was no courtroom, only an office. Even Davy had no prisoner's dock to separate him from the rest. No real trial then, but a summary review. The judgment already made had only to be delivered.

And here was Lord Vaughn, the Governor himself. The letters of marque stolen from Davy's cabin had been signed by the Duke of York but approved by Sir Henry Morgan before that prince of privateers had been recalled to England for his own review. Doubtless that would be enough for Vaughn to find fault with them, as he had everything else, apparently at FitzRobert's direction.

FitzRobert. Davy wondered what the fat bastard had on his Lordship to make him so powerful.

At least Molly had had the wit to begin covering his backside long before the need arose. Clever girl, perhaps letting Prentiss keep her had not been a mistake after all. Except, of course, for getting him brought up for kidnapping.

Davy stepped up, and squared his shoulders to look as much like his honest self as possible. Colonel Rhetford, who was a decent fellow for a soldier, had at least let him send for his good blue coat and britches, although regretted he could not allow Davy the privilege of his sword. At least he could present himself as a gentlemen, however great his anger and abiding sadness. He missed the sword.

Lord Vaughn began to speak, a thin voice that barely carried even in the close-packed chamber. There was little to say, of course. The charges were clear. Davy demanded to hear them as was his right. A murmur ran through the room, something like surprise. Did the fellow not know his place?

FitzRobert looked offended. Benning stepped forward to inform his Lordship that the prisoner had been read the charges on his arrest. Vaughn frowned his displeasure. It was not the rule. Benning drawled his apology, bowed, and retired.

"My lord, if what Sir Simon chose to tell me is the charge—that and nothing more—then I should like to reply in my defense," Davy said in refined accents he seldom used. Behind him Molly's eyes widened, her turn for surprise.

"You can answer any of these charges, Captain York?" Vaughn sputtered. He had been assured this was cut and dried, open and closed, there and back again in time for a nap before dinner.

"If they were true, my lord, no. But they are each the most preposterous nonsense."

The mutter in the room became a rumble. It was not a jury. Not one of them was his peer, never mind a friend. None of the other captains in port had been included. He had no support, and probably no hope, if they would not let Molly speak. He had to give her the chance.

The Governor's long, thin face wrinkled unhappily. Barely begun and already not going well. Dyspeptic and annoyed, he pushed back the elaborate wig to scratch a grey stubble, then slapped it back into place.

"You may proceed, Captain. But I warn you! These are serious charges, I will listen to no foolishness, and no lies."

"Of course not, my lord." In other words, he was not to cite personal malice on the part of FitzRobert or Benning. Very well. "I should have thought my reputation alone would have been enough. I am a good servant to His Majesty, as you all have cause to know."

He recognized them now, the merchant sponsors, and raised his voice to include them. "Every one of these gentlemen has profited from my trade, and from many others'. They have not been cheated."

"You have cheated me every time, you lying rogue!" FitzRobert shouted.

Davy's hand twitched for his sword, which of course they had taken from him. He turned back to Vaughn, controlling the swift anger. "My lord!"

"Now, now, Sir Roger," said Lord Vaughn. "I will have order here. This may not be an ordinary court, but neither is it a tavern, and will not become a brawl. Proceed, Captain York."

"I know you have the papers from my ship there before you, d'ye not, my lord?"

FitzRobert glanced away just as Vaughn looked to inquire. "Papers, Sir Roger? You did say there were papers of some sort."

"A log full of vague entries and half-truths, your Excellency."

"And the original manifests of six or seven Spanish treasure galleons and merchantmen!" Reserved surprise began to replace the grumbling. "They should be easy to find, Sir Roger. They are in Spanish." And a low laughter.

"I suppose you've kept only the ones that suited you!"

"You have but to inventory everything removed from the *Jealous Mary* to find there is no more than listed, and no less. If your Spanish is inadequate, Sir Roger, you'll find there is the English for each list also among my papers."

Scrambling with some decorum, his lordship identified at least one matched pair of manifests and quickly scanned them.

"My Spanish, as it happens, is sufficient to the task. And if the records of the *Santa Eulalia* are an example of the rest, then I'm afraid you will be hard pressed, Sir Roger, to prove this charge."

At this, Simon Benning roused himself. "But how do we know that these are true records? He had more than enough time to alter them!"

"But why, my lord?" Davy asked, suppressing a laugh. "I had no warning, and have never been so accused. Likewise, if I were in the habit of cozening my sponsors and my king, and getting away with it, why should I spend the time, why bother?" He added with an evil grin, "You know what lazy villains we sailors are. I can assure you, that scribbling vile hand belongs to some canting Spanish priest, not to me. And if the manifest is a lie, then where, I pray you sir, is the rest of the treasure?"

"My lord," he went on grimly. "Captain Benning's men brought the *Jealous Mary* home, crippled though they had made her and short two good officers murdered at his order. There was surely time to open every seam from stem to stern. If there had been anything to find— If the good captain says he found anything of value which is not in those lists, ask him where it is now?"

One. The smile he turned on Benning pricked even into his eyes. Benning surely would have converted some of what was found to his own use. Molly's lovely forgeries would show up the differences. Oh what a beauty that lass was! Rafe would have been proud. Pity Morgan wasn't here to appreciate the joke as well.

Lord Vaughn hemmed and scratched under his wig again. The sturdy fellow had a point, although he might not have followed it exactly. The fellow certainly could talk, better than FitzRobert and without Benning's whine. Was he merely clever, or was there truth in all this?

He was beginning to suspect some personal motives here after all, though he still did not wish to hear it. Only ten o'clock and already the day was unbearably hot. What had he done to deserve this posting?

"Let us leave this point for now. Sir Roger also accuses you of kidnapping his niece. And since she was found among your men, I have no choice..."

"But it is not so, my lord," said Molly, her sweet voice clear but reserved.

With becoming grace and a rustle of satin, she stood. The whole warm room rocked to a stunned silence, giving homage to youth and beauty. Some junior courtier began to speak a line of verse, but took a senior elbow in the ribs and stopped. Still the stories had gone round, and perhaps, some thought, the modest gaze was instead a practiced device.

Vaughn, however, had been protected from rumor in this case. Sir Roger had declined to soil his niece's reputation while marriage negotiations were still fluid. So graciously, his lordship motioned the lovely creature forward.

Every nerve in Molly's body wanted to leap up and shout, but long hours of correction with Sister Alonzo's ruler and book simply took over. A dainty hand twitched up skirts just far enough to permit small steps, steps that never revealed so much as toes under the hovering hem. She might have been floating.

Two astonishing seconds, and she was rocking back and down into the full courtesy of the Court. A pause, calculated to the exact degree of the gentleman so honored, and she rose again, hands modestly folded at her waist.

"If you please, my lord," she said in the merry voice Prentiss adored. "I was never kidnapped!"

FitzRobert roared, "How now, you jade!" While the room went wild, and from just outside the window came an unbridled hoot that had to be Kate, waiting with the servants.

Davy wanted to applaud, but a pleased smile had to do. "As I said."

Not quite done, but there would be no going back now. It would not bring back his men, but it would put him aboard his ship, the last point against him being too ridiculous to carry.

"I think you must explain yourself, mistress," said Lord Vaughn wryly. The ethereal vision before him could hardly have run away on her own, but there she stood, insisting most charmingly that she had. He nudged a sputtering FitzRobert, *"Get her to Court, man, and the King will make your fortune!"*

"I should like to explain, my lord," said the girl, "but my uncle seems to have my answers ready made!"

Roger scowled, a vein in his forehead throbbing purple with rage.

"Of course she was kidnapped! My God, does a decent girl run away to sea like a beggar! A girl with prospects and fortune?"

She waited for the echoes to die, then spoke slowly with imperial poise.

"Does a decent girl deny that she has been kidnapped, if she has? Would I seek to protect the villains who so insulted me, violated my honor? Or would I rather demand to be revenged on them. If this man had offered me violence, would I not pray to see him hang? My lord, it may have been foolishness, but it was indeed mine own inclination to go to sea." Molly smiled tolerantly, a dangerous gleam lurking under the pale lashes. "Instead I must tell you of Captain York's unfailing courtesy to me, and his care for my welfare."

"But he did sail away with you!"

"I am old enough to govern myself, my lord. Although of course with the advice of my family and friends who mean me only good." Someone coughed. "Still, I fear I have been somewhat willful."

Both Davy and Sir Roger snorted with the understatement, but only one was laughing. "I went aboard the *Jealous Mary* in disguise."

"With the connivance of this, ah, Richard Prentiss, I see."

"Nay, my lord." The solemn denial caught in her throat for a moment, but she would have his name clear, alive or dead. "On my own. A trick of a cloak and a false voice, pretending a cough. I slipped past the lieutenant whilst all looked elsewhere." Past Keaton, who could not deny it. Davy in truth had not seen her come aboard, and no one here had a better story.

Sir Simon thought he might. "That is impossible. Can you imagine for a moment my lord, that this lovely young woman could be mistaken for a sailor, no matter how well cloaked? Of course she had help. I saw her with that rogue in the streets!"

"*La*, sir, in the streets?" The charming laughter tinkled from her like Mass bells. Davy was going to owe her so much for this! "I wanted to go to sea as a privateer, like my father, not become a common thief. I wanted to sail with my father's mates, on his ship. Sentimental, I suppose."

She shrugged prettily. Men sighed against their will. "Then once we were at sea, Captain York had very little choice, I'm afraid. Isn't that so, Captain?"

Davy nodded soberly, just managing to maintain an even demeanor. "Her uncle will agree, I think, that the lass can be somewhat, ah, difficult." Molly had the grace to blush.

"She was so good an actress then, can you not see she is acting even now!"

"So now I am also a liar? Or perhaps I have been bewitched? If this was kidnap, why did no one ask for ransom? Goodness, Simon, you cannot make up your mind but that we all must be guilty of something! I must say that puts paid to any thoughts of our marrying, you and I. Surely there is a streak of madness in your bloodlines."

"Your Excellency, you cannot listen to this, this balderdash! She is not to be believed. She…"

A limp waggle of one lordly hand waved him off.

"Ah, but I do believe her," said Lord Vaughn, a fond if not quite grandfatherly haze softening his bloodhound countenance. "I fancy, sir, that if this lovely child told me the Moon was visiting in my garden, I should put on my best coat and ask it to tea. And if the same child asked to me to take her to Far Cathay or Cambalu, I fancy I would raise the sails myself."

His lordship admitted a small sigh for his own youth, long vanished. "Captain York, I should agree you had little choice in the matter."

Two. It was working. They were laughing, all but FitzRobert and Benning. The bastards were going down, six fathoms under!

From outside, Davy could hear voices rising, including one pleased, womanly shriek, into something like a cheer. No time to listen, though, for with an incoherent growl Benning pushed across the room, his silver-tipped walking stick raised to strike the insolent bitch.

Then his feet went up and he walked hard onto Davy's fist and doubled over it. Molly screamed. A second blow put Benning on the floor. Davy wanted, oh he wanted to go on, but the restraints of the day and his guards held him back.

"My lord, I protest!" he shouted as hands were laid on him from all sides. "For godssake, my lord, the lady was in danger!"

"And I never saw you dance better, Davy!"

A huge voice bellowed from the arcade, and Sir Henry Morgan strode in, red-coated and black-wigged, to change everything.

"Let him go, you bastards! Bloody Christ, Vaughn!" he roared. "What business is this!"

Behind him came Jack Rhetford, who had brought him, and the throng of henchmen from the garden, and one fine, tall campfollower.

"Harry!"

Davy no longer bothered to contain the big grin and the hearty laughs he had been husbanding. He shook off the hands that held him, and they backed away, nerves dangling. It was over. It was all over, or it would be in mere minutes.

The common understanding was that Henry Morgan, the admiral of Portobello, Maracaibo, and Panama, was as broad-shouldered as a great oak and twice as tall. So legends accrue to men who are in their own time larger than life. In truth he was not so tall as Davy, and not quite so sturdily built, but with the same dark hair and grey eyes of the Celt. Though he came from Llanrhymny and Davy from Penzance, and Davy's hair had mostly frosted, as they embraced they looked like twins trying to merge.

It was also true that Morgan took up more than twice his share of space in any company, and so he did just now.

"Go on, Vaughn, explain all this. The lads here and, ah, this very handsome female." Eyes twinkled in Kate's direction, which made her laugh again. "They were mixed in their opinions. I'm inclined to believe the woman, but that may be my weakness. Davy, the blister there is getting up."

York's sturdy boot connected with a gold-trimmed rib. "Sorry, sir."

Benning went slack again, whimpering.

Davy couldn't stop grinning. Revenge was going to be so very sweet and, with luck, neatly violent.

On his feet and shouting, FitzRobert fulminated as Lord Vaughn, who really had thought this all cleared up, scratched under his wig again. "Morgan, what does this mean? Why are you here?"

"Didn't think to see me again, eh? Well fear not, it will not be for long. The king and I are friends again, you see. You, on the other hand... And you, you green pustule!"

He snatched Sir Roger by the buttons and flung him to the side like an afterthought. "You are both commanded to wait upon his Majesty just as soon as ever you can get your arses to England. If you delay so much as a day in departing, I am to hang you both for, ah, irregularities in your accounting of the Crown's shares in privateering, and for permitting the growth of piracy in these waters!"

"But, but..."

"Bugger your buts, both of you! And oh yes, I am returned to my office as Lieutenant Governor, so you may get your buggery butt out of my chair, Vaughn."

"Sir Henry, I protest!"

"Do it from over there! Davy, what the devil is all this about!" Gorgeous and profane, Morgan was still capable of striking to the heart of the matter once he had made up his mind to do so. "FitzButtocks, why aren't you packing!"

Still sputtering, Roger scrambled protesting to the door where Rhetford set him firmly on his way home.

"They say I'm a pirate, Harry," said Davy, meekly.

"Oh now, that won't do, man! I've got fresh commissions from the King to put down piracy! Can't have one of my best captains swanning around, damaging the King's peace, attacking the King's friends."

"They say I had a contract with Preacher Mendez to sail against all flags."

"And did you?"

"Harry!" That was wounding. "Have you ever known me to serve such a notion!"

"Times change, man," Morgan shook his head sadly but with a glint still in his eye.

"And that wig has boiled your brains, Harry Morgan, if you don't know me."

"The charge is false, Sir Henry!"

Molly had faded behind all the prosperous gentlemen, furious at not being able to defend herself against Benning, and aching with unladylike passion to kill the slimy bastard herself. If she had stayed nearby, she'd have given herself away. So she had watched the awesome entrance between the gold-braided cuffs and curled wigs, until now she had to call out to be heard.

All heads turned again to the vision who had so captivated them already, and a way was made for her. As gracefully but more swiftly she swept to the fore, but this time stood firm, adjusting her voice and manner yet again to the setting. Even Sir Henry Morgan was startled to silence.

"Sir, the contract Captain York made with the Preacher was to come to my rescue. A contract the Preacher failed to honor, since he never appeared."

"What's this?"

"'Tis too long a tale, sir, unless around a mug of ale," she said with a pale smile. "Through no fault of Davy's, I was taken by surprise from Tortuga. I was overcome with drugs and sold by someone called Captain Angel to a Frenchman on Martinique. Davy brought the *Jealous Mary* and his crew to bring me safe away. We met Mendez some weeks later, but never sailed with him nor shared in any prize he took."

"And who would you be, my lady?" Morgan frowned slightly. She reminded him of someone, but who? All beautiful women reminded him of each other. "Do I know you? I hope you will tell me that I do."

With one boot still planted in the small of Benning's fashionable neck, Davy spoke with the sobriety of a Court chamberlain. "Sir Henry Morgan, I have the honor to present Mistress Molly September. You may recall her father."

The black brows went up with delighted surprise. "Strike me! Rafe's little wench? Well, there it is! It is clear this gorgeous creature wouldn't lie to save your ugly hide, so it must be true. You are no pirate, Captain York, nor never have been."

Three.

Every charge from top to bottom dismissed. If only Prentiss were here, Davy could gloat.

19

FAIN WOULD I

WITH THE SHOUTING ended, the good triumphant, and the bad disgraced, Sir Roger was at last on his way to England. Lady Henrietta, loyal wife, had gone with him to write importunate letters to every well placed relative, every acquaintance of any consequence, and the King himself. Having missed the point entirely, she even briefly imagined Molly to be coming with them, away from this den of thieves, to stand with her uncle. The possibility that Molly might volunteer to improve all their fortunes by charming the King and perhaps even displace the current mistress may not have crossed the virtuous Henrietta's mind, though it did occur to others, including Molly, who rejected it out of hand.

Instead she waved a heartfelt farewell to her difficult relations and became, in her tempered misery, the mistress of the house called The Arbours in King's Lane, Port Royal. She had confronted her enemies and vanquished them, but the elation of that triumph was empty and short lived. The profound melancholy returned, if anything more deeply than before. When her thoughts were clear, she toyed with the idea of shutting up the house and going to sea as

Davy kept suggesting. Then the image of taking up that life without Prentiss overwhelmed her with its folly.

Into that fog moved Jack Rhetford, taking charge when she would not, governing her life with a grave authority so different from the riot of the summer. He had turned off most of the household servants, there being so much less house to serve: the cook and a scullion, the butler, two grooms and a parlor maid would do. And Kate, of course.

With the grim hand of his office, the Colonel also firmly dammed the flood of gentlemen young and old who flocked like importunate sparrows about poor Mistress September who, together with her notorious fortune, was so clearly in need of protection and wise counsel in her investments. Exercising a lighter touch, he even managed to keep back the giggling girls, who were if anything more thrilled and slightly envious than before. At Rhetford's direction, Kate returned invitations with regrets but without explanation, although from time to time the young ladies were permitted, in pairs, to call. To himself he had sworn that she would always, in his company, be safe, and so a subtle barrier of attendant soldiery sprang up at her doorways to enforce the limits that would keep her so.

Since he understood, as others did not, that she was in mourning, he sat with her through the long silences waiting, patient, for the awkwardness to dissipate. The courteous reserve won Kate over, the necessary hurdle if he was to continue to wait upon her lady. Then Molly began to see through the solicitous friendship to the genuinely decent man behind it, and was touched. Still, the fogs remained. She moved through her days as through a colorless dream.

After the inquiry, Davy came to visit full of boisterous good humor and succeeded in making her smile, and eventually to laugh. His fortunes had been restored, and all the lads as a consequence got their shares and were busily squandering it in the taverns and stews of the town, while *Jealous Mary* got tricked out in new main mast and rigging. From that bounty he brought a huge carved box filled with gold coins, a pouch stuffed with pearls, and a fistful of sparkling gems that made up Prentiss's share and Molly's—in her own right as well as her widow's compensation, according to the *Mary's* Articles.

Davy also had found somewhere the glittering Turkish pencil box, Paul DeRoet's wedding gift, which he laid on the spinet without comment. She stared at it, and at Davy, both recalling a black sky filled with falling stars, then she went back to playing. Later, Kate would take it upstairs.

Even Kate got prizes: strings of pearls and chains of golden bangles, which she immediately looped along both arms, and spent the rest of the day clashing against each other to hear them ring. Then she put them away for "just in case". The next day a parcel arrived for her from certain of the crew, forty gold sovereigns as belated recompense for her kitchen, plus a carcanet of golden rosebuds tipped with rubies, in general gratitude. She promptly went out and spent part of the money on good knives and kettles and a decent iron griddle for the next time she might have need of such things. And a new dress. And a hat with two feathers. The necklace, she wore every day for a week.

Davy thought, too, to bring Rafe's guitar and made Molly play it whether the mood was on her or not. Better still, he brought new stories of the improbable Sir Henry Morgan. Most of his time in this first welcome week of freedom had been spent renewing their old acquaintance, both telling and listening to stories neither of them believed and drinking like sailors. Which, as they both observed, they were.

Sir Harry, he said, was most ardent in his desire to meet "that damned pretty woman" again, although Davy admitted that he wasn't quite sure if it was Molly or Kate the old pirate meant. Either way, he made her laugh again, even if nothing could chase off the image of Prentiss's death that hung like *Jealous Mary's* broken rigging between them.

To drive the shadows away, he had brought rum and made her drink it in the twilight garden until she giggled. He told stories with Rafe in them, or Keaton and the others, and even some where Prentiss played the hero's part, and he chided her brightly for tears. When that was done, he thanked her briefly but sincerely for saving his neck.

And then, because he had promised himself, he watched while a round of her rare and lovely laughter slowed and said: "You've been wanting to know how your dad died." He was not prepared for the reaction.

"Davy, no!"

He blinked and set down a chased silver cup he particularly admired. "No?"

She sat up straight and a little wild, but quite, quite sure. "Was it shameful, how he died?"

That caught him back a bit. Some answers were clearer than others. Then he shook his head. "Nay, but I ..."

"He was a good man, wasn't he?"

"The best of us all."

A pale hand, the freckles and all the hard-worked calluses fading, pressed his own dearly but the jade eyes glimmered like torchlight, even in the glow of late afternoon.

"Until that night on the beach," said Molly. "I only knew Rafe as a child knows the wind: a big voice and broad shoulders, full of laughter and power, but not quite real. You—you all—you gave him to me as you knew him: your own captain, brave and alive and fine. You even gave me back his music." The sweet lips twitched in something like a smile. "I don't need to see him die through your eyes, as well."

"You don't understand, lass. Me and Prentiss, we..."

"He's dead, Captain." Both of them, dead. "It doesn't matter."
Watch for me.

He sat thoughtfully for a bit, uncomfortable with a secret now that he'd made up his mind to tell it. He'd made a promise. On the other hand, since he wasn't mere heartbeats away from dancing a jig on Execution Dock, wasn't it better to content her whim than increase her burden. It had waited this long.

"We're lifting anchor for Tortuga on Sunday next. Are you coming?"

Eyes softened gently, as if tolerant of a foolish but well-intentioned child. "Oh, my dear."

"Come on lass, someone's got to keep my stores in order! God's truth, you're the nearest I've got to a petty officer. Oh, I can find others, aye." Another thoughtful pause. None who had been his friends and shipmates so long and so well. He shook that off. "Besides, the lads are asking after ye."

"Are they?" She smiled. "They expect I'll bring Kate along to cook for them!"

"There is that."

In silence, the small, well-made fingers crumbled a biscuit idly to dust. "You're going to have to tell Keaton's Annie," she said suddenly, diverting the question.

He was not to be parried. "It would come easier from you."

Now she waited, looking away, considering the colors, scarlet and yellow, of a macaw perched in a banana tree just beyond. "Ask again in a day or two?"

"You said that two days ago," he grumbled.

The insubstantial hand pressed his sleeve again and retreated, and he realized she had not met his eyes in some while. "I know, and I'm sorry. I even know how hard it is for you to ask."

Her pity was alarming, and too much for Davy, who had no faith in tender moments. In something like panic, he hurried to his feet. Fumbling for words, he kissed her cheek and went away, brushing passed Jack Rhetford in the garden gate.

He recalled himself long enough to offer his hand and thank the Colonel like a gentleman for getting Morgan to the hearing in such good time. He'd had no opportunity to say so, till now. Without Morgan's unexpected intervention, even Molly's clear version of their story might not have saved him. Of that he was certain.

Graciously dismissing the effort as no more than justice upheld, Rhetford's finely-drawn features said quite plainly that Captain York had no further business here. He bowed. Davy did likewise.

Shivering slightly, the captain perceived an urgent need for a cheap drink and low company, and fancied he knew where to find it. Life amongst the gentry might suit Harry Morgan, but Davy had had enough. The girl would come if she would, or not.

Somewhere just ahead, mocking laughter teased him towards Huggins Street.

The days wore on. Not so many of them, in truth, but filled with long hours. Reacting to Molly's distress like Perseus defending Andromeda, the Colonel managed without entirely neglecting his duties, to find time each morning and an hour of most afternoons at the big brick house in King's Lane with its garden of entwined rose trees and its shady walks. With Kate's support, he often he stayed to supper, encouraging Molly away from sorrow with his steadying strength.

Part of almost every evening saw him leaning on the spinet, encouraging her to play, or joining his surprising tenor in a duet he'd forgotten he knew. And when, overwhelmed and speechless, she slammed down the cover and wept, he gathered her into his arms and held her in wordless comfort until the storm passed.

It takes so little time for a comfortable thing to become habit. Like a patient recovering from a dire wound begins to notice degrees in the discomfort, Molly's awareness of him grew, and of how much a part he was of every day, her attentive Jack. She began to look for him at his regular times, grateful for a friend who had no part in her lost world, and to miss him if he stayed away or was detained.

As for Rhetford, the tempo of the relationship suited him. He had never been a comfortable suitor, had let marriage pass him by as he became more gruff and set, as he supposed, in his soldier's ways. He had come to Jamaica a young, ambitious captain twenty years before to take the island for Cromwell, and survived to hold it for the King. He had weathered every change of religion and Parliament with fortitude, but remained too honest to make a fortune out of it all. Simply a good soldier, a good officer, and a patient survivor.

With nothing but virtues to offer, the proper wife, the shrewd match, had eluded him. But now. Oh, but now this bold, tragic girl had conquered him, utterly, until he came to imagine, to hope, that once her grieving had passed, there might be room in her heart for an aging Colonel of Foot in a backwater posting without influence or prospects, who cared for her.

When he stopped under the rose arbors and asked her to marry him, she caught her breath and shook her head, and he tried to apologize, but she stopped him.

"Oh Jack!" she said, with the same awful pity and terror that had so undone Davy York under the same rose trees. She felt, quite suddenly, quite old. "My dear! You cannot want me. A wife like me? What can I bring to a marriage but a flawed and melancholy affection and a damaged heart? You deserve better than a silly girl forever in love with another man."

In that moment, he realized what her conversation with York, just now, must have been like. The look on his face must be the same one. Even so, he dared to take her little hands in his hard ones as the disquieting words pushed out of him, sticking on air almost too thick to breathe.

"Look, Molly," he said with as much courage as he had ever needed under fire. "I am a soldier, no more than that. I have no great fortune, no path to glory. That you might come to love me, even after a long while, is more than I dare to hope for. Nay, let me finish. I only wish— only want— if you will let me care for you, give you a place in the world. Even, perhaps, to give you children for your joy. Molly, my dear, I find the thought of you at my side, on any terms you like, to be such...." He swallowed hard, foundering on the shoals of poetry. "Such an..."

She had not yet lifted her face to his. A tightness gripped his heart like iron bands, disturbing and almost indecent. Stammering was altogether too much. The air under the trees was soggy enough without the messier emotions clogging it any further. Despairing at last of uneasy sentiment, he retreated into the brusque manners he knew best.

"Look, Molly, I know I'm an old fool. If only you would permit me to care for you, as your husband—I would ask no more."

Molly could hardly bear to meet his eyes, knowing that her own were dry. He would think her heartless, or worse, angry when it was only the lingering uncertainty, even now, that Prentiss might be alive, might at any moment saunter through the gate with the last glow of day magical behind him.

Watch for me!

She had kept watch, and still there was no word, no sign, not even a rumor. She had seen him fall. And over Jack's shoulder, lurking in the shade as twilight closed over them, Kate clearly knew what he had asked and she nodded, tight-lipped and sure.

"Not so old," Molly said, looking up at last. The eyes she met, thank God, were brown.

Prentiss woke on a Sunday as the first bells of Port Royal's churches rippled across the morning air. The long weeks of summer had taught him to find Molly curled under his arm, and so even now, he did. When the place beside him in the still, narrow bed was cold, and the light slanting weakly in from the alley was not the sun careening off the sea, he groaned and nearly wept. The Saracen's Head: his old room, and the remnants of wine sour in his mouth. *Damn.* A fever dream and nothing more. Nothing more.

There had to be more.

The plain gold ring on a thong around his neck dragged at the strings of his hair when he turned his face. The headache that rolled with it had an un-liquorish feel; more like a sleeping draught, he thought curiously, with the sour aftertaste of a tincture of opium. That must mean something. Point by point he examined the evidence:

The growth of beard that colonized his usually trim chin had been there long enough to go soft and start to curl. The thin seam of pain worrying his chest was certainly not new. Neatly stitched, husbanding its bruises, a deep cut had stiffened his side for lack of use; so much so that the first burst of activity forced a low mew from his throat as he dropped back to the mattress. He would have to hoist himself on the other elbow to look around if he meant to avoid screaming. That was no dream.

A plain gold ring? *Yes!* His marriage ring. Dick folded light fingers around it and fell back, blinking with relief. Very well. So. So he was alive, and indeed married. He was recovering from some new disaster in spite, as always, of the odds against any of it. If he tried he could, with extreme care, throw aside the thread-bare blanket and stand; pick up a book and put it down; walk to the grey window, and wonder where Molly was.

Wait, of course. She would be at her uncle's house, pretending to be a dutiful child, speaking up for Davy, and waiting for her husband to reclaim her as soon as it was safe, as they had planned. If the plan was still in effect. Unless the plan had already failed.

Another tour about the room. On a pallet near the door, the comfortably familiar sight of Jimmy on his back, snoring lightly, with one arm looped in a sling. Fitts, obviously, had saved the day and Prentiss, one more time, was in his debt.

Dick let out a hoarse breath something like a sigh. It did seem to be Jimmy's fate to keep pulling Prentiss out of the fire, whatever it was.

So perhaps the images spinning through his brain were part memory, part wishful thinking, and the usual dose of mere truth thrown in to keep him honest. The musty smell of the room hinted reassuringly at how long it had been closed up, even how long he'd been back. That, added to an inescapable stink of infection and noxious remedy, prompted him vulgarly to recall just why he was back in this ratty old bed. Someone had tried to kill him, yet again, and come damned close. Days must have passed.

In a moment, staring blankly into the muddy alley, some flash of color—or a woman's scent, a child's shriek, some trick of the half-light—recalled the moment when everything went wrong. Or no. There had been too many of those to count, and each on top of the other.

All right, the last he could remember: the curved dagger bedding itself like new fire in his chest. Half an inch either way and the blade would have missed the rib—which hurt like every corner of hell, by the way—and opened a lung, and the pain would have long been over.

He had a vague recollection of dancing, of drowning, of the taste of beer, of something clumsily stupid like lifting a brimmed hat from someone's booth. Fainting in a doorway?

Christ, not again.

He felt like an old and poorly managed dung heap. Wasted fingers raked through unwashed hair, cringing almost at the touch. Odd how for weeks at sea these things never mattered. Ashore, thinking about a girl, one missed the niceties. The finer feeling urged him reluctantly towards more active curiosity.

All right, how long had it been, and where the hell was everyone? Why wasn't his gilded redhead, his wife, cooing over him in deep concern; his captain pacing and profaning his parentage and his skills?

Start with something simple, then. *What time is it?*

The morning was dim, certainly, but in this room that permanent twilight had long been a fixture. Ah, from the dew still on the bricks, it must be morning, not long after sunrise. *Now what day is it?*

Whatever the time on whatever day, he was sure of one thing. Jimmy Fitts had slept long enough. The hole in the other man's shoulder was older than his own by a week, and neatly cauterized besides by gunshot, so how much could he mind being kicked awake. Gently. By a friend. Who was at the same time shouting and dribbling a conveniently stale jack of beer over his head. Hell, were they friends or not?

The roar that rattled the glass in the window frame was Jimmy Fitts exploding wet and furious off his pallet, fumbling one handed for sword or pistol, in the end staring about wildly for enemies. The glitter of lightning that followed was Prentiss's *sang froid* shattering into hysterical laughter

Dick sat down hard and yelped from the pain that rocketed from shoulder to groin, until he hiccuped with tears but could not stop cackling. Jimmy frowned, wiping sour beer from his own thickening beard.

"And this is the—"

"—thanks I get," Prentiss wheezed. "Aye. God's death, man!" In a minute or two he was nearly capable of speech. Well, willing to try. "You know how to stop it happening, of course."

"Next time, leave you in the water?"

"There you have it, son."

"I've a better idea. I'll spend ten days hiding you in a plague-ridden pest hole whilst nursing you back to health, then tip you out of a window."

Standing over his oldest friend in the world, Jimmy briefly considered kicking him, just for good fellowship, in the wounded side. No, he'd only have to waste another ten days, not counting the money spent on drugs, rum, and Driscoll's cooperation. Besides, Molly really wouldn't forgive him this time. "You look like a hundred years in hell."

Dick peered up from unkempt, sick-room hysteria with a glitter that was not, at last, from fever.

"Where is she? Is she all right? She's been here, aye, or sent someone?"

On this point, Jimmy Fitts was less eloquent. Defensively, he shrugged. "Dunno."

"Come on, man. It's been days, hasn't it!" More silence. "She doesn't know?"

"No one knows."

"No one?" said Prentiss bleakly.

"Not even Davy. It ain't safe. Davy has his own worries—or did have. They say he's free, and Morgan's back. You and me—well, you've been mainly unconscious. Me too, the first few days, so Jesse says."

"You couldn't get word to Molly? My God, she'll have my head!"

"I tried, I swear it!"

Blowing a sigh, Jimmy dropped to the floor beside him. As an afterthought, he reached to fetch a rum bottle from under the low table. A quick swig rinsed his mouth, then he spat it into a corner.

Prentiss, more finicky, winced and took the bottle from him while Jimmy went on.

"Rhetford's put a guard on the place to keep out the riff raff—that would be me, and all those lads lining up to marry her money."

Dick frowned. "She can't marry anyone. She's wed to me!"

"Not if you're dead, my lad." Jimmy sniffed and pulled a sour face. "God knoweth, ye smell like a corpse."

"And you like a grave robber," said Dick. "And since you've used up all the beer—"

"Hey!"

"I reckon I need a good bathe, a decent razor, and maybe something to eat. And... Christ! Who sewed this up? The pig butcher?"

He poked an exploratory finger at the perfectly decent stitching under the padded linen, marveling at the rainbow of bruises that roamed out across his chest. When he looked up again to meet Jimmy's eyes, all the lightheartedness vanished. "Then I've got to see her."

"You ain't been listening." Fitts grabbed the one good arm with his one good hand. "You can't get to her, Dick! No one can."

He should have known better. There was no mistaking the set of Prentiss's jaw or the steady light in the deep blue eyes.

"I can."

The wedding was set for Sunday at eight in the morning, in the hope that the day might still have something cool about it. But December in Jamaica is very like June, except that the hurricane threat has lessened. Hot humid days gave over to hot nights only slightly less muggy. The great window in the southern wall of Molly's room stood open as it had in June, it seemed, a thousand years before. And as before, the fine muslin curtains stirred softly in the late night breeze, freighted with the scent of the sea and with it, the free life she had sought and briefly found.

Her thoughts rested on that night when, as now, she had lain sleepless and alone between fine linen sheets. On the charming scoundrel from the marketplace who she flirted with, then hated, then adored, then married. The long, fine figure, strong and sturdy; the firm chin just slightly cleft; a straight and noble nose dividing long, almost exotic blue eyes that stared merrily out of a sun-browned face. A rogue, certainly, but honest and intelligent, skilled and sure, and dear God, the man she loved.

It hardly seemed possible to have accepted his death, he was still so clear and present in her mind. Lying shrouded by the pale hangings of her maidenly bed, she stared fixedly at the shadowed window frame, willing him to appear, and counted the hours that he failed her. Another moment, another moment surely, and he would be there.

Watch for me!

So she watched, terrified of sleep, of the dreams that brought him to her every night, only to be snatched away as invading sunlight knitted up the path that had opened for him.

But Kate was right, of course. The dead might walk in dreams, but they were still dead. Even when she could feel the weight of him pressing the mattress beside her, his hands warm on her body, his tongue a flame in her mouth, what could it be but dream and wishful thinking. And tonight, of all nights, when she needed most for the dream to come true, nothing changed.

When Kate shook her awake before dawn, she clambered up from unwilling sleep, from sweetly desperate longing to bitter anger, cross with the world. She stood disobliging and uncooperative while Kate pinned and poked and tied her into her wedding clothes.

With no time and not quite the nerve to order a new gown from George Alcott's mother, they had settled on the best dress she owned, the height of Paris fashion two long years ago: palest rose moiré like the edge of a sunset far out to sea. The shimmering skirts drew back from a silver petticoat and came together again at the back, almost behind her knees, all new-dressed with golden sash and rose-gold ribbons. Just off the shoulders, a course of Flemish lace dashed across the bodice cut low across sun-kissed décolletage.

Fat pearls tear-dropped gracefully from her ears, Jack's gift. In a way it was pleasant, she thought, to have new jewelry someone had actually paid for. The Chinese pearls at her throat, for example, and the diamond bracelets, she had liberated herself. She thought too of all the treasures she had left on Tortuga, in Costa Rica, at the bottom of the sea that she would likely never see again. Gold and diamonds, friends, the husband of her true heart.

Satisfied at last that the gown hung with proper modesty for a modest bride, Kate left to see to other things and abandoned Molly, no happier but less choleric, to her mirror, dusting pale powder over the evidence of an unladylike familiarity with direct sunlight.

While the new maid crimped her hair with hot irons and tugged and fluffed it *à la mode*, Molly betimes would frown and begin to speak, then stop. Simply by passing, every minute provoked a heavy sigh as it sped, crawled, or stumbled by turns toward the wedding she did not want and could not avoid.

She tried, she truly did, to take an optimistic air. Jack was a good man, to be sure, and she was fond of him. And it was her own choice, as she kept reminding herself. It was the right thing to do. It was.

A woman really could not live alone in the world, no matter how romantic it sounded. No unmarried girl could sign a contract, give her oath, invest her own funds, or manage her own property. While a widow might, sometimes, continue her husband's trade, what trade could Molly claim? Besides, at her slender age in the world, who would expect her to be more than some great man's plaything. The adventure was over.

Jack Rhetford's offer was sound and sensible, and even if it did mean he now became almost her owner, he was at least honest and kind. He would keep her well, give her a family, and ask nothing of her that she could not give. A good marriage was a partnership, and in time, well, who knew what might come. Few matches were made on as solid a ground as this. If there was no passion, there was at least friendship. No sensible girl desired more; few expected as much. And yes, Kate, she had been given her heart's desire, her romance, but it was done.

As much as she knew she was doing the sensible thing, even the right thing, the awful feeling of disaster patched the bright and airy room, like her mind, with darkness.

Every time she looked into the mirror, she saw reflected the window in which Dick Prentiss had come to her, insufferable and adorable. A trick of new light threw shadows on the curtain that made her catch a breath, almost believing she could see him at last, lithe and mocking in the window seat. Then the light shifted, and the quick flash of hope became a thorn in her heart as sharp as the tormenting, erotic dreams.

This girl, this thick-fingered maid that Kate had found somewhere, finished the knot at the back of Molly's hair with jeweled pins set with emerald and pearl. Another long and miserable sigh shook her as the woman switched implements of torture and proceeded to pluck and shape the perfectly shaped brows to widen the wide eyes. That lasted about two minutes. Then Molly jumped from her seat, kicked back the stool and, swearing like a dockside whore, slapped at the intrusive hands.

"*Assez, assez!*" The last time she'd had a maid poking hot irons and pinchers at her, she had been speaking French, and hated it nearly as much. "Enough, damn you! The Colonel will think he's wedding a bewildered sheep. Stop it!"

In a fury, she turned and snatched the long tweezers out of the girl's hand, and spun them in her fingers into a weapon.

The girl leaped back, babbling apologies in, what was it, Italian?

"*Avanti, puta!* Oh, just go away!" Tears she would not shed lurked behind her fury. "Get out!"

"Milady?" Kate stood in the doorway, arms folded, surveying the trouble. Clothed in efficiency and a good russet gown, she delivered her own message first. "I've given Perkins your orders. The staff are on their way to Sir Harry's house to help with the wedding breakfast and all."

Then she came in, and took the flustered maid by the shoulders to steer her out of further trouble. "Go on home now, lass," she whispered. A few bright coins passed hand to hand and the girl, one frightened glance over her shoulder, ran from the room.

"You couldn't help that, I suppose," said Kate.

"The bitch scratched me," Molly grumbled.

Turning, she flung the tweezers against the paneled wall, where they stuck, thrumming like a tuning fork.

"Very nice, milady," said Kate, and retrieved them without comment. "And I'm sure she did not."

"She was clumsy."

"She is one of Lady Vaughn's personal maids."

"Kate, I can't go through with this, I don't care how sensible it is! I can't! What am I to do?"

"You are to stop being so foolish and collect yourself, madam," Long Kate said sternly. "Then come downstairs, where the carriage is waiting to take you to St. Dismas's church, where you will marry

Colonel Rhetford, good man that he is, and put your life in order as you were meant to. I can't take care of you forever, y'know."

"But Kate!" Without meaning to, she took desperate hold of both of her friend's hands. "What if— Oh God, what if he is still alive?"

Melodrama always made Kate impatient, the more so in the mouth of someone she had judged to be above such nonsense. What good were all her lessons if they went begging?

"I thought you were settled on this," Kate scoffed lightly, but did not drop her hands. "*Dhia*, lass, we would have heard! The town cannot keep secrets, not for love nor money. Davy would have heard."

"Jimmy wouldn't let him die!"

"Jimmy was hurt himself, so he was. Who was to save him, then, so he could save your man, eh?"

From somewhere out of the clear dawn air, a mischievous giggle erupted, then doubled on itself with unmasked delight. Two auburn heads, one golden and one dark, turned sharply to peer into a fold of shadow beyond the billowing gauze of the bed curtains.

They had each a flickering, not quite identical impression of a young barefoot girl in kirtled petticoats and loosened stays, laces flying, with a jeweled goblet in her hand. Hair light or dark, streaming unbound in all directions, blue eyes or brown—they would never agree—she danced into the dusty light on a jingling ball like a gypsy. A chime sounded, or the bells on her fluttering clothes: naught but the striking clock in the hall, surely.

Fortune looked up, and for a moment met their eyes, then turned on her translucent heel and fled across the window seat and faded into the brightening air, leaving a trail of laughter and the scent of chocolate. They thought for a moment that the gilded, jingling ball bounced twice from the window, and hit the floor, spun through the middle of the room, and stopped at their feet. When Molly moved one slipper towards it, the ball glittered into a single beam of sunlight, and the music was gone.

"Mother of God!" said Kate most sincerely.

Molly's eyes shone. She breathed, "He is alive!"

"You can't trust her." Kate was shaking her head over their still joined hands.

"Nay!" Molly said, imagination soaring. The sweet voice soared with excitement, daring to consider the fantasy. "Nay, what if, what if she's had her fun with us? Now think! We had nothing but luck all summer. All summer, everything! How many ships taken, how many storms skirted, against the odds? But now… but now!"

She gasped, flushed with fear and childlike hope. "Kate," she begged, wringing both their hands. "It could be, couldn't it? Or what did we see? Do you believe in such things?"

"Don't be daft, I'm Irish! Of course I do. Besides…" A tingling, pregnant pause before Kate went on, ashen with apprehension: "I've seen her before."

At last they dared to meet each other's eyes, blinking away the after-image of square, white windows and glittering girls. Newly shaped brows lifted. "Tell me?"

Kate felt suddenly very old. Luck had turned on its heel so many times, it was hard to explain. Complaining about it made it worse. Accepting the twists and counter-marches didn't make it better, but the bruises became easier to bear and led to philosophy. It did not lead to hope.

"Better not, *mo criodh*."

"Tell me."

The sound she made was not entirely impatient. "I've given you the better part of it already. That girl I told you of, with her drummer boy. A lovely lad he was, milady. One day he stepped in the way of a cannon, and he died."

"Oh!"

"Men die in the wars." As Prentiss surely had died.

"But you loved him."

A crooked smile sketched under Long Kate's weary eyes, and she nodded slightly. Just now, she needed to sit down. So she took Molly to the bed and sat on the edge, drawing the younger girl to her side like school girls sharing secrets.

"Aye, I suppose I did, for the most part. He was a good lad, too." A melancholy laugh bubbled from the slender throat. "Truth to say, I can't even tell you his name! But y'see, the night he died, when I thought my life was gone with him, that same mad little whore danced through the camp, laughing like, well like what we both heard, just now. Next day I married a sergeant, milady."

"She's Luck returning, then."

"Of a kind. She leaves without warning, and wants a gazette when she comes home, the jade."

Green eyes dropped, suddenly doubtful. "Or mayhap we're only over wrought and wishful. Or we've had too much sugar in our tea, or hemp in the tobacco, or—"

"Hush, now! 'Tis not to be made light of."

"He's alive," Molly said, glowing, whole, and sane.

Reluctant as a virgin bride, Kate nodded. "All right, he's alive. But where?"

Molly thought she knew. "He was hurt. So was Jimmy. Oh God, why didn't I think of this before? If Driscoll hasn't given away their rooms, they'll be up there drinking themselves stupid and dosing themselves with God knows what. He'll have left money somewhere; he has friends everywhere."

She laughed suddenly, gloriously, and flung Kate's hands wide apart. "A dozen women will be spilling blood to take care of him! Both of them."

"Driscoll? An Irishman, is that?"

Molly explained what little she understood of the peculiar nature of Huggins Street in general and the Saracen's Head in particular, feeling oddly nostalgic for a place she'd spent so little and such uncomfortable time.

"Irish, I guess, aye. In Port Royal, they might be from anywhere, men like that. Or nowhere. But if, well, if we're not both mad together and seeing things—"

"Hush! Don't say it, or the bitch'll take it away. Right now, you must get in the carriage and betake you to the church. I'll go to Huggins Street."

"Can you find it?"

Almost shyly, Long Kate place a light kiss on her remarkable mistress's cheek. "I can find the campmaster on marching day; I can find your tavern."

The bricks savaged Dick's hands and tore at his knees. The wound in his chest wept with every stretch of that arm as he clambered from hand hold to painful hand hold up across the bricks and up the trellised wall. He had made this journey before, but in pleasurable excitement, not in agony.

At a sound he froze, waited in screaming silence with all his tortured weight hanging from his shoulders. The red-coated soldier walking guard below paused, alerted by a scratch, a dribble of mortar from the bricks, the disgusting crunch of a snail shell collapsing beneath careless fingers.

Good God! With all the pains and perils of this island duty, the fellow was far more conscientious than the average drunken soldier, damn it. All right, all right, Dick's thought sang like an incantation. As long he didn't move, the fellow wouldn't look up, all would be well.

A wild growl and a rattle of ivy. A brindle cat burst from cover near the kitchen door, tussled with an imaginary rat disguised as a leaf, then vanished into the silver-laced grass at the sunny edge of the path. The redcoat bent for a rock, and stood to toss it after the animal with a laugh, then he shouldered his musket and moved on. Dick let him clear the far corner of the house before climbing again, faster now, where fingers of ivy threatened ruin over the half-timbers of the second story.

One hand caught the sill, then the other, where a fine sprigged muslin curtain billowing in the light breeze spilled across his ravaged hands.

Leg up, knee over, and the habitually jaunty pose arranged itself deliciously in the window, as once before, if breathing a little harder. The scent of powder and rouge and perfume breathed at him over the hot metal smell of goffering irons left in a brazier. All the detritus of a young woman's bed chamber tumbled sweetly about the room, without her.

He caught his breath and stepped down into the room, ears tuned to every household noise. Silence. The word, according to Jimmy who (when not comatose) always had the news, was that old FitzRobert and his lady had gone. That would mean Molly alone, maybe with Kate. It should be perfect. Even so, there should be servants.

Carefully, he tried the hallway, then on soft shoes pattered down the stairs. Even the kitchen was idle, ovens cold, pantry locked. Dining parlor and morning room, music room, rooms he had no names for, all stood scented of her but unoccupied.

Sick with loss, he ran light hands over her furniture, stared at her paintings, touched a bowl of flowers she must have touched and knew she had gone, perhaps only minutes ago. Vanished, but where.

His stealthy tread had become a determined march by the time he slammed out the kitchen door and into the garden.

Gone. Golden sun stung his eyes, refracting the bitter light before him into diamonds and hexagons, as tears would if he were crying. Where the devil was she? Couldn't she have waited? *Watch for me,* he had said, and meant it even as he fell, expecting to die. He would survive and come for her though Hell should bar the way, did she not know that?

He came to a halt in a brake of white roses, not quite sure how he had come there. The last time he'd been in this garden, it had been to spy on her while she sparred with that pimple, Benning. And aye, from under these same rose bushes. No, the red ones, over there.

Sun glared. Hatless, he wiped the bitter water gathering in his eyes. The glare only, of course. Never mind how many years he had steered a great ship, dry-eyed, across sun-glazed seas. Never mind how all his losses rolled over him now in one terrible wave that took him, in the end, to his knees.

When Jimmy found him, he was sitting on the ground, doubled over, his head in his hands.

"So there you are. Asleep again, are ye?"

Prentiss met his friend's face hot-eyed and weak with self-loathing. His breathing came harsh, as if dragged out of a throat tight with despair.

"Too late. It's too late. She's gone."

"I know." Fitts nodded, dropped to one knee and clucked over him, searching the bruises. "What'd ye do, climb the damned window again?"

He ignored the puzzled look as he pulled an old but serviceable handkerchief from his jerkin, and stuffed it between Dick's new shirt and the outraged stitches. "What a bloody hero."

"Wait." Dick caught his hand. "What do you mean, you know?"

Jimmy sighed almost maternally. "If you'd waited ten minutes, you'd have had Kate and Davy both to tell you, and we'd be there already. Instead of having to run, as we will now, and with you in such a state."

"Run? Christ, quit fussing! What d'ye mean run. Run where?"

"Didn't I say? She's to be married in—" The eight o'clock bells rang out from St. Paul's and half a dozen churches, and even the little synagogue in Lime Street. "About ten minutes," said Jimmy brightly.

On his feet at last, Prentiss patted sandy earth from his new breeches and felt ravaged nerves shudder into place, his mind suddenly, wonderfully clear.

"She can't. We… We've already been through this."

"There it is, see," said Jimmy as they ducked out the garden gate and broke into a trot up Silver Street. "Everyone thinking we was dead, and all."

"But I told her!"

"Aye, and then she watched you die. She's been a rich young widow for about as long as you've been a corpse."

They ducked into and out of a sunny alley. Half a step back, and Dick stuffed a quick pinch of someone's honey cake into his mouth. "So who turned her head? Not Benning, unless she means to kill him in his sleep."

Jimmy slammed him against an iron-bound door as a chamber pot emptied its noxious contents into the street from an overhanging gable. "Call a warning, eh!" he shouted. "Don't be daft. The good Colonel Rhetford it is, so Kate says."

"Hunh. And he almost deserves her. All right, so where are we going?"

"Church Street, where else? St. Dismas."

If he'd had the breath for it, Prentiss would have sighed. Instead he ducked a string of tumbling baskets, paused to look for alternatives when an ox-cart barred the way, and struck left. Long way round, but faster.

"Catholics," he shouted, just slightly hysterical. "Of course!"

Shadows still clung to the buccaneer city in deep corners and hidden passageways, all familiar as breakfast. Where one door closed, another opened. Twice voices shouted after them, presuming some deviltry. Once a girlish curse floated over them, then shrieked with delight.

"Why it's Jimmy Fitts, is it? They said you was dead!" Jimmy paused long enough to land a cheerful kiss on bright red lips, then Prentiss danced him away.

The town straggled along a sandy spit of no more than fifty acres, all told. It should have taken no more than ten minutes, even in market day crowds, to navigate from one side to the other, but it seemed like forever. From sunlight to shade they ran collecting friends as they went. Owen Jones was gulping tea on a street corner, his fiddle under one arm, when they dashed passed him with a call.

They nearly fell over Matt Christy, just sitting down to a shave in the crisp new light of a barber's corner in Cannon Street Market. Just seeing Prentiss alive was enough to change the big gunner's plans. Without waiting to ask the cause, he joined them, spilling over the barber's chair and a pack of razors as he left the square.

While the barber shouted curses, Jimmy quickly gave the news. Matt shouted and Owen laughed, and together they broke into Church Street, where the wheeze of a portative organ broke from the almost Puritan galleries of St. Dismas, ambiguous against the southern sea wall just now being touched with a shaft of light.

In one tall room of white washed local stone, banked on its long sides with tall frame windows, St. Dismas's church hunkered under a stand of fat palm trees, pretending not to be there. For the first five years of Port Royal's existence, Point Cagway as it used to be, had been the jewel in Cromwell's —well, not his *crown* of course. Say rather, the feather in his sober, Puritan bonnet. Restored to Stuart grandeur, the King had declared for tolerance. Catholics were free again to open their churches, train their children to pray in Latin, if they would, and sell their souls to the Pope if they cared to, so long as they were loyal. Port Royal, as the city fathers renamed her, hardly noticed or cared one way or another. Still, who knew how times might change? There was safety in obscurity.

When liveried soldiers opened the broad doors before her, Molly, acquainted with Europe's ancient cathedrals, expected to step into a cave echoing in medieval darkness, candlelight spilling mystically from a golden altar; rigid saints staring above ranks of honey scented candles exposing livid holy wounds, and veiled women muttering over their beads.

Compared to the morning glare, it was dark certainly. And fat yellow candles on the altar gave off a honeyed air of sanctity. As her eyes grew used to the sunlight falling through the tall windows, she found herself grateful that there was, after all, no mystery. No magic. In its unseemly desire not to offend, the church had a strangely empty feel, like a bungalow lately abandoned. Good. The fewer witnesses, the better, she thought.

For a moment, unexpected and somehow fraught with meaning, the emptiness stopped her. Her hands were cold. She could not feel her feet in the satin pumps with their hard red heels.

And then all at once, she smiled. She knew exactly where he was, she could feel the touch of his mind on hers. He was nearly there. Comfortably, happily, she stepped away from the door to pace sedately up the aisle that was just as suddenly, inexplicably, filled with people she knew.

She recognized a dozen faces: Well naturally, it was Jack Rhetford's wedding, not only hers. Celia Trout was there, of course, simpering more than usual as she fell into place to walk the bride to her new husband. George Alcott, and his diligent mother; Drake Ffoulkes, whose name came to her only when he returned Celia's look. And oh! Sir Henry Morgan, the rogue, a vast curling wig rolling over his shoulders. She threw him a surreptitious wink, which seemed to startle him.

And more and more half-familiar figures stood about, some frowning their disapproval, others smirking behind their fans. They could think what they liked, Molly thought. None of them would recognize the mysterious smile that hung about her lips as the barely controlled urge to laugh.

He was alive! This was all the most outrageous play acting, Pyramus and Thisbe enacted by fools, governed by the Moon.

Here was Lady Morgan. The Modyfords, Lady Vaughn, even—oh my!—the Admiral's widow, who was as near to a grandmother as Molly could claim. Madam had never forgiven Rafe for stealing away her darling girl, and Rafe's daughter qualified only for a bastard's scorn.

Molly caught the old lady's eye and grinned, brazenly, without bothering to watch the reaction. A few others of name were here who Molly had met once, even twice, and forgotten. As she drew closer, still smiling with a happiness they could only misunderstand, a delicate figure stepped away from Morgan's shoulder, the better she supposed to view the bride.

Why, Sir Simon Benning (you rancid handful of, oh dear, *bruised* pond scum), how very nice.

Sure, quite sure, just how thoroughly she had damaged him, she could spare a victorious smile. Her step never so much as faltered as the daggers of his eyes met hers and rebounded away like a spear shaft glancing off plate armor. Oh, surely he had some evil to work, some new conceit, but what matter? Prentiss lived. She was Fortune's child.

She was invulnerable.

She was the queen of the western isles.

Wrapped in certainty, Molly halted politely when someone stopped her at the dim end of her walk. And settling her mind for the first time in weeks, she let Jack Rhetford take her hand. She never noticed the curious frown troubling his long face.

The music ground to a halt, and the Latin drone began.

Outside, Kate and Davy waited impatiently at a sun bleached side door with Hughes the carpenter, and Gil Denham, and old Dan Rhys and half a dozen others rounded up from the Saracen's Head and the Bull and odd corners along the way.

"And about bloody time!" Davy bellowed, and waved as Dick and Jimmy and the others came pelting up, Prentiss clearly in the lead. "Come on, lads, come on!"

As Dick skidded on the pounded earth littered with palm fronds and the silver, long-tongued leaves of gum trees, Kate halted him gravely.

"Catch yer breath, now. You've another minute while the music plays, that's certain. And Cross of Christ, lad, put a comb to your hair! You want to make a good impression."

"Good impression!" A fist curled up in desperate anger, but she never flinched. "Christ Almighty, Kate, get out of my way!"

"I said comb it, boy-o. You've an entrance to make. Bad enough you look like death on a platter."

What an awful morning! Flung from coma and suffering to panic to awful loss all in an hour's time, then racing toward reprieve and reward, to be stopped by yet another nightmare, shaped like a friend!

All right, he had to catch his breath anyway, and surely there was as much time to spare as the organ interlude lurching towards a coda; a few seconds at least. Overhead, the broad palm rattled cheerfully in the morning breeze

No matter how sensible, the wait was insupportable. "If I'm too late, you'll…"

"Ye've time. Trust me."

And somehow, out of the parallel dimension where she kept these things, Kate produced first a fine lace-edged shirt, which he climbed into on her order; then a tortoise shell comb which she dashed across the damp, tangled locks once or twice before he shook her off. "Say what ye like, Pilot, at least now there's some chance she'll know ye."

"Kate!" Earnestly, Dick took her hard-worked hands and brought them down, and kissed each one with grace. "Kate," he said with surpassing gentleness. "She'll know me. May I go in now?"

Her surprise lasted only a moment. Briskly restored to irony, she appraised his look and his manner, now collected and orderly, and gave a sharp nod. She handed him a hat which he agreed to carry if not to wear.

"Aye, Pilot, now you are yerself. You may."

With a flourish of her own, she stepped aside.

The little-used door was grey with dead leaves and cobwebs and, Davy supposed, inclined to stick. The order was swift and wordless, and in Matt's relentless grip, the iron-bound door ripped open with a shriek that challenged the organ's final jarring chord bouncing off the rood screen.

20

Come, My Corinna

Come, my Corinna, come, let's go a-Maying.

IT WAS TRUE. She would know him anywhere. She would have known him in the darkest pit of Hell by the shape of his mind alone. So as the grainy notes of the organ faded and the sonorous Latin began, she also knew that the frivolous screech and the solemn bang behind her on the right betokened a profound readjustment of everyone's expectations.

Still leaning on Jack's arm, she turned toward the noise and the square of light forced upon the white washed stone. It might well be true that every girl on the edge of her first battlefield knows her lover is still alive, but some of them, sometimes, must be right. Today, it was Molly's turn.

A door banged open and for an endless moment, that lithe figure framed in silhouette stood as if it held the tiller against an angry sea.

The quarterdeck voice sang out. "Molly Prentiss!"

Alive! He was alive, and he had come. She could hardly speak, but she wanted to sing. The name burst from her: "Dickon!"

Framed in the doorway while eyes adjusted to the gloom and the flickering golden flames at the altar, he turned unerringly for her voice.

The hall buzzed, perhaps, with shout and conjecture and objection. Soldiers she had failed to notice came suddenly, ridiculously on guard, as if they could stop him. The universe spun on a single point: Prentiss striding like an avenging angel through the hall. A musket opposed him, he wrenched it down and let someone else deal with it. He smacked down half drawn swords with naked, careless hands to reach her. To come to her, as he had promised.

And behind him, though she hardly saw them, the whole troop of his friends ranged behind him calm as fury, like the Capulets marching into the square. Easily, they took up positions that held the rest of the house at bay. The nightmare was over.

Ignoring them, ignoring everything else, Molly hiked up her skirts, kicked off the red-heeled shoes, and ran to meet him. He caught her up by the waist half way to the altar, smothered in silk and joy. Hardly breathing, he laughed, "Molly!" and lifted her off the pavement, swung her about until she shrieked with laughter, still saying his name. Then let her slide down to drown in his kisses.

He was music, he was light, he was her hope of heaven, the world, the father of her children, the world's wide wonder. Enclosed in his arms, nothing else mattered. The hubbub around them was for others, damn their eyes. In this moment alone, kiss on kiss, she was home.

Finally, reluctantly, Dick took a calming breath and held her only slightly away, the better to examine and re-examine the darling face. Yes, he thought. Yes. Exactly as he remembered.

"So it was not a dream," he said at last, numb with wonder.

"No," said Molly. Hungry fingers combed through the tangled hair, traced along the lines of his lost, beloved face, and stopped. "A dream? A damned long dream, you precious bastard! Where the hell have you been!"

Her fingers in his hair, she pressed anxious lips to his mouth again as if her breath depended on his. The world comprised no one and nothing but their laughter. Not light nor dark, no wet or dry, nor heat nor cold could touch them; no voice could intrude though many, had they been able to tell, were trying.

"I'm sorry, Sweet. I've made you worry. But see," he shrugged, "there was a knife."

With sudden comprehension, she realized how badly he had been hurt and how much this had cost him, especially how in spite of all, as if it were nothing, he had swung her about. "Oh my dear!"

The simple words restored him. Defying pain, he closed her in his arms, reveling in the feel of her breasts pressed sweetly to his chest; the dear pressure of her arms closed around his waist; the delicious scent of her hair.

Thought came without words, informed only by color and image, a world to which hue and tint had returned all in a rush. Death could come now, she thought, and welcome.

"My word!"

Of course, the world inevitably is wider than love restored. The strangled, half-broken voice which Simon Benning had recovered since Davy had lifted his boot from the serpent's neck had not lost its virulence.

"I suppose that's the way of things here at the back of beyond. In civilized countries, a lady would think twice about marrying her father's murderer."

Morgan roared, "That's a lie! It's a God-rotted lie!"

"No, Harry!" cried Prentiss over the clamor that erupted. "No! It's true. You know it's true."

Into the abrupt silence Molly, coalescing from universal joy, said, "What?"

"I wasn't there, my dear little whore," Sir Simon sneered. Fists clenched though no one moved. "But everyone knows. I presumed you did as well."

Storm green eyes fluttered from the serpent she despised who might be telling a truth for once, to the man she loved and longed for, who had been hiding one from her; from Davy, who had tried to tell the secret she did not want to hear; to Jimmy, who was frozen in place; and returned at last to Prentiss, trembling under her hands. She took heart from the fact that he was willing to meet her eyes.

"I reckon, my love," she said quietly. "It is time for a story."

He nodded, and told her.

Once upon a time, the *Jealous Mary* had coursed the Caribbean under different hands than she did now. Rafe September, the finest pilot ever to sail these seas—ask anyone—was her master: the golden, laughing man who had won the heart of a high born lady, and who named his bright and boisterous ship for his little girl.

His men would have followed him into hell, and had done so twice already. Twice in three years Rafe had gathered his men at Morgan's call to Portobello and Maracaibo, and at his command, again, they came with *Jealous Mary* to the slender isthmus that divided the vast oceans. Davy York sailed then as Rafe's lieutenant, Keaton his quartermaster, and Dick his sailing master, still young but gifted and second in skill, by Rafe's own reckoning, to the captain himself.

That winter when the green season was past, they banded under English colors to stand in with three dozen other great ships at the broad mouth of the river Chagres, where the fort of San Lorenzo guarded the back door of the golden city of Panama. Five hundred men took up the fight under Rafe's command, while Morgan raided elsewhere up and down the Spanish Main. And of those, a hundred died at the Chagres for a pile of brick that yielded little and would surely, Rafe swore, betray them to the Spaniards.

Morgan, when he arrived, was prepared to leave a token force holding the fort, while the rest pressed on, but Rafe was betting on word arriving at Panama long before they could get there. There's no surprise, he had said, if they know we're coming.

He was right, of course, but who could have known that then? Men trusted him, but they lusted after Morgan's treasure.

No one could know, and no one cared. The wounded and those who feared the jungle with its wild river and its fevers, its hostile inhabitants and plague-filled swamps—places Englishmen were not meant to live—those volunteered to hold San Lorenzo and the mouths of the Chagres. Nearly everyone, including the *Mary's* crew, were eager to go on. After all, they had won the keys to the treasure house. How could they skulk away now, and leave all that gold just lying there in Spanish hands?

The captains quarreled in the forecourt of the captured bastion. Morgan, never at a loss for argument, had laughed at Rafe and called him an old woman. Drake had done it, he said. A hundred years ago! Why couldn't they now, in this modern age? He had almost 2,000 men, how could they lose? The fat city of the Dons, luxurious and corrupt, was ripe for their picking.

Rafe September still said no. Even his own men wondered what had come over him. There was a fortune waiting for each of them, keen to fall into their ready hands. Must be that pretty little wife and the red-headed brat on Barbados were making him careful, chancy, worrisome. Women could do that to a man, they all concluded soberly. As soberly as buccaneers ever concluded anything.

Prentiss and York, for friendship's sake, sought for a middle ground between loyalty and greed. Let this be the one last caper, they said. Take a fortune home to the pretty wife, enough to retire on. Become an idle merchant, and let Prentiss take his ship out for him hereafter. Rafe might, they said, buy a big house when this was done and sit and draw maps and write books like Cabot and Chancellor and Mandeville, if he liked. But for godssake, take this one last chance!

There on the sand, the blazing January sun beating on his broad shoulders and easy temper, the glare off the sea and the rum and the glitter of gold seething through everyone's blood, Rafe stood his ground.

Henry Morgan was famous for his rages. September should never have turned his back. In a sudden fury, sword had rasped past the bronze throat of a scabbard as Morgan rounded on him and, cursing, slashed at his head. Davy leapt forward and turned the blow on his own blade as Prentiss threw the tackle that should have moved Rafe out of harm's way. Instead, it sent his captain spinning towards the deflected blow.

On instinct, Rafe's hand went up and slapped the blade aside so the slashing edge only glanced off his scalp but laid a cut deep across his hand. The head cut was slight but bloody, as such wounds will be. The slash to the hand was worse, but easily dismissed, tied up with a rag. It might have ended there, but the whole thing was awkward, practically farcical. Caught off guard and stupidly wounded, Rafe collapsed—as much from chagrin, Davy said that night, as from anything else.

Morgan, immediately contrite, called for a surgeon and watched beside Rafe all night until he awoke. Both feeling foolish, they had made up, and Rafe conceded to Morgan's—and his own crew's—will.

"So," Molly said into the breathing dark. "So he didn't die there at the Chagres?"

"Oh good lord, no!" sniffed Benning. He had used up his allotment of ill manners. Jimmy's long suppressed anger took immediate shape as a fist in Simon's stomach. No one seemed to mind. Matt caught the man as he fell and dragged him outside to recover under a tree, if he would.

Knowing how much more there was to come, Prentiss led Molly to a hard wooden chair that creaked as she sat her fragile weight upon it. As much as he would have preferred to stand, her witness at the bar, his head was swimming and every joint flared with pain. Davy would have brought him a bench, but he waved it away and sank, instead, to puddle with the satin at her feet.

"Nay, lass, he didn't die there. More's the pity."

"Pity?" She blinked down at him.

If the story had been anyone else's, he might have laughed. "Then it would have been Harry Morgan that killed him, and you'd have known of it long since."

Morgan affected a wounded air and sat down, but said nothing.

They had given Rafe's wounds what care they could. Jimmy Fitts had stitched up the hand and patched the scalp wound, though he was no surgeon, to be sure. And if Rafe seemed a bit dizzy from time to time, it was only to be expected.

"The world knows most of the rest," Davy interjected hastily. "We left the provisions at the fort because someone thought we could eat off the land."

Attention shifted at once to Morgan, but Sir Harry only shrugged. "I was wrong. But we survived it—"

"Most of us."

"And we won!"

"Aye, in the end," said Dick, the bitterness behind him. He had tarried ashore three long years because of this, though he might be the best pilot alive in these waters.

"And came home rich."

"Some of us," Jimmy snapped.

Trouble was, though Rafe's wounds had seemed slight, in the jungle every tiny cut begins to rot. In such places, nothing heals properly, and the infection grew with the hunger and the filthy water, and the daily pestering of little dark men with darts, like feathered insects, that buzzed out of the trees. The fever came swiftly to some, but subtly to others.

Rafe, unused to illness, forbore to mention his own discomforts while his men were starving. But he was bigger than they, and hardier, so his decline was more terrible. He tried to rally them at first, but day by awful day he himself sank further into fever and bitter melancholy.

The barber-surgeon—sober, for once, from the lack of rum but just as bone ignorant as ever—bled him from the arm and thigh before Jimmy could stop him, and then those cuts festered as well. Davy pressed one of their native guides to redress the wounds with whatever magic he had, but nothing helped. The fever claimed his mind. By the time they had at last won to the Pacific side, their captain was raving, seeing enemies in every shadow, and more than anything, blaming Morgan for their misery.

The company had stumbled at last on a herd of milk cows, which they fell upon like the starving men they were, snatching half cooked meat from the green fires and puking themselves stupid afterwards. The first to recover found the energy at least to set about cleaning their weapons, checking their powder, and drinking, carefully, what clean water they had found.

Refusing food, Rafe was ranting like a drunken man through the camp, cutlass waving, when he staggered past Prentiss and Davy on his way to the Captain-General's tent. Muskets freshly charged, they watched in horror as their captain stopped and called for Morgan to show himself.

Henry Morgan, who had brought them somehow through hell, turned unarmed from the short, dark men who were his new allies, and stared uncomprehending at the bent, wasted figure of Rafe September bearing down upon him out of the sun, shouting the madness that lighted in his eyes.

Davy and Prentiss speechless sprang to their feet. One ran to catch him, the other to intersect his path, but there was no time. The sword swung up. In a moment, it would be too late. With a single word from Davy, each stopped, took aim, and fired. And Rafe September, their captain and their pride, halted, caught up, suspended suddenly in the middle of a vulgar word. The sword fell from his hand and, his face filled with surprise, he spun to earth.

By the time they had reached him, he was gone. One bullet had lodged in his heart. "Davy's shot went wild, y'see," Prentiss said. "So—"

Davy objected loudly. "It never did!"

Dick shook his half-combed head sadly. "It's no good, captain mine. I know it was my shot killed 'im."

"You're the worst shot I ever saw, you miserable bastard. I know it was mine!"

She knew what they were doing, but it was more than Molly could bear. Sick at heart, she stomped her stockinged foot till the echoes came.

"Oh do stop it! Christ wounds, anyone else would think you were vying for credit!" They stared, stung out of their habitual bickering by the caustic observation. "I know that each of you wants to spare the other from blame. But my dears, you must stop!"

"Nobody blames 'em," said Morgan abruptly. The uneasy rumble made the others jump. "Neither one. Nor Rafe, for that matter."

"Nor you sir, neither," Prentiss added, fixing the same grave gaze on his old commander. Morgan shifted his weight, admitting perhaps to some discomfort, nothing more. "But you, Sweet. You see why we... Can you look at me now, and not see..."

"Hush!" She leaned forward to lay two lissome fingers on his mouth to stop it, then fumbled for a moment in the pocket under the gorgeous skirts and drew out a small, red ring carved into a rose.

He caught at her hand. "Molly!"

"When I look at you," she said, sliding the ring onto her finger. "What can I see but the man I love above all others. My husband, and—oh! Goodness!"

She turned at last to Jack Rhetford, forgotten entirely as he stood attentive and stricken just a few feet away.

While his life collapsed in front of him he had effectively silenced the priest's stammering objections, and made someone open all the doors to let in the morning breezes and sweep out the clogging fumes of incense and beeswax. He had stilled intrusions and sent away the glittering guests. He had not said a word in all the long tale which, as Benning had said, everybody knew. Everyone but Rafe September's daughter.

"Oh, God! Dear Jack! I am so sorry!"

A slight bow, eyes bright over a tight but gentlemanly smile of resignation. He'd had too much time to consider what he might say, so that now he was nearly speechless. She could see the options formed and rejected, till he settled at last on none of them.

It occurred to Dick, just then, that perhaps he had some issue with the Colonel. He said, "I understand you've been courting my wife, sir."

"Only because I understood she was free."

Prentiss considered this a bit under Molly's solemn eyes.

"He has been my very good friend, Dickon."

"So," her husband said. "I suppose we have no argument? Presuming you return the lady unharmed."

She smacked his arm: "Prentiss, I've already told you!" And cried out to see him cringe. He gasped, but straightened out of pride.

"Wrong shoulder, love," he said stiffly.

With grace, Rhetford nodded. "Entirely unharmed, sir. Even, perhaps, in better condition than I found her."

Dick accepted the rebuke with good will.

"Then I am in your debt, sir. Could I have sent word, I would have done. I would have spared her, and you—all of you—your pains on my account." He gathered his friends with a glance, returning quickly to his pretty young wife, to whom he whispered conspiratorially. "Is that it, then? Can we go?"

Molly laughed lightly and looked about, still lost in his eyes. All their friends were here. The plain serviceable altar was dressed with vanilla orchids and Advent green embroideries, and Father Titchfield, however disgruntled, still waited.

"My dear," she said, the jade eyes sparkling like sun on sea. "You know, there is a perfectly good church here, and a priest."

"Idle bastard. I suppose he wants some employment."

"And a bridal feast waiting afterwards," said Morgan. "If there's a proper bride."

"Seems a pity to waste it," Molly said.

"Besides," said Dick, "the last time was such a rush, Jimmy missed it."

"For Jimmy's sake then?"

"And so everyone can see how much I love you."

Before he could kiss her again and leave them all waiting, Kate produced from somewhere a handsome coat of deep blue brocade. No longer surprised, Prentiss shrugged into it, smoothing the fabric over broad shoulders, and set the hat she returned to him at a jaunty angle.

"And then, of course," Molly added, watching him with gleaming eyes. "We'll have to see about tracking down the Preacher, and getting our treasure back from…"

"Molly!" Davy gurgled, unexpectedly frantic. "Christ!"

"Can we get married first?" said Prentiss.

Then he bent over Molly's graceful wrist and led her, grinning shamelessly, to the altar rail.

THE END

North Hollywood, California
1975–2011

www.ingramcontent.com/pod-product-compliance
Lightning Source LLC
Chambersburg PA
CBHW071153250626
47159CB00001B/69